The Inmost Light

Book One:

The Celestial Clockwork

STEVE SPEER

ISBN: 1467936022
ISBN-13: 9781467936026

DEDICATION

For all the lights that tried and failed…

CONTENTS

CONTENTS

CONTINUED

CONTENTS

CONTINUED

ACKNOWLEDGMENTS

Many thanks to June Abele for all her help with this story and the fight against hydraulic fracturing of the Marcellus Shale...

1 STARS FADE OUT

"Oh man! There is no planet sun or star could hold you, if you but knew what you are."
~ Ralph Waldo Emerson

Like diamonds scattered haphazardly upon black velvet, the stars glittered in the void of black space. These specks of fire hung like lanterns, beckoning in the clear voice of light from across immeasurable spans of space and time.

Adjusting the controls, the man at the telescope guided the girl's sight to a section of sky where two shimmering points of white sparkled in the dark. As she watched this duo blink to each other in secret communications, her one wish was that she might decipher their secret language. When the scope's focus tightened, a tiny spot, darker than the night itself, emerged between the two stars.

A whisper came from her side. "Do you see it?"

"I do," she answered, not moving from the eyepiece.

Suddenly and without warning, the third point erupted. Thick smoke oozed from the lightless pinhole, pouring forth like boiling tar. As the girl gasped at this utter affront to the laws of physics, the man shifted uncomfortably in his chair. The stars themselves seemed to shudder as the stain of darkness crept near.

"What's happening? What is that?"

"I have no idea, Stella." The uneasy voice was that of Doctor Perceval Ray, one of the world's greatest astrophysicists, and the girl at the scope was his daughter. She knew, as did everyone else who had ever read a book on stars or planets, her father knew all there was to know about space. If he didn't know what was happening, then no one did.

The malignant ooze filled the space between the two bright stars, and Stella's eye jerked from the eyepiece, not wanting to view what seemed so certain to occur.

"Watch!" Perceval pleaded. "I need to know you see what I see; that this is not some trick my mind has played on me. Please Stella, tell me what you see!" The tone of his voice was troubling. Whenever in the past he had spoken about the stars or space, it had been with awed enthusiasm. Now, there was only fear.

"I see a spot," she began, trying hard to concentrate on what was happening, "that started out so small I could barely see it, but now is larger, much larger. And it's growing."

"Yes," her father confirmed. "I believe it's an unknown type of black hole, and very aggressive. What else can you see?"

Stella knew what a black hole was. It was a kind of backwards star; instead of giving light it took it. She remembered her father explaining how a black hole could pull things in and never let them go. "I see the two bright stars that were there before the dark star, I mean the black hole, appeared". From where had it appeared? She wanted to ask, but knew she would have to wait until later for that. Now she had to watch and tell, obeying her father's urgent request. "The dark spot is growing, almost as if it were alive." The way the stain crept through space, reminded Stella of a time-lapse film she had seen of mold growing on bread, but this was happening much more quickly. "It's very near the bright stars. What's going to happen when they touch?"

There was only a tense silence as dark tendrils sprouted from the void and reached around the twinkling stars. In next to no time, both were encircled in a tightening noose of thick impenetrable smog.

"The stars are totally surrounded." Stella reported, realizing suddenly that she was breathing in quick short puffs and her heart was beating fast.

"Yes, I see that too," Perceval murmured gravely.

"Wait!" Stella exclaimed," I think the stars have realized they're being attacked. They're getting brighter, and pushing back the dark with their light."

As the captive stars flared, the small ring of space that separated them from the darkness widened, giving Stella hope the battle was not yet decided. She didn't care to see what the darkness might do if it won this struggle.

"What's happening now?" Her father asked as the pulse of blazing light forced the circle of murky smog away.

Stella jumped from the scope and clapped as the darkness retreated. "Yippee! The stars have won!"

"Don't look away yet." Perceval's voice was solemn and not yet ready to join in his daughter's celebration.

Turning back to the eyepiece, Stella watched as the dark hovered beyond the ring of light, like a predatory beast outside the reach of a bonfire. As if the effort taken to shine so bright had fatigued them, the stars flickered momentarily, but as the dark circle slid back, it seemed the conflict was over.

Then, like a viper that had feigned retreat only to deceive its prey into dropping its guard, the darkness struck. In a furious flurry, it viciously throttled the stars until all that remained was a stagnant cloud hanging leadenly in space. Whatever light there had been was gone. The sight filled Stella with dread. Stars could fade out, she knew, but it should take thousands of years. She had just watched it happen in a matter of seconds.

For how long she sat at the scope staring into the murky darkness where once had been two beautiful stars, Stella did not know. When she finally did look away, her father was still next to her, pale and trembling. "Dad? What just happened?"

Looking down at his jittering hands, Professor Perceval Ray shook his head in pained disappointment. "I'm afraid I just don't know."

"Don't know?" Stella had never heard him use those words before. She waited silently as he removed his glasses to nervously wipe the beaded sweat from his brow.

Struggling to maintain his composure, Perceval resolutely shook off his uncertainty, and adjusting his glasses, resumed the professorial demeanor Stella had always known him to exhibit. "There must be a logical reason for what we have seen." he pronounced stiffly. "For every phenomenon, there must be an explanation. If the correct theorems are applied, anything can be understood in scientific terms. It is a simple fact of logic!" As he spoke, he turned the levers that closed the lens caps on the scope. He never left them open, even here in the crisp Arctic where there was very little dust.

High up on the telescope, one of the caps had jammed and Perceval let out a soft grunt as he struggled to force the mechanism to cooperate. After a few moments of exasperation he hesitantly turned to his daughter. "I hate to ask you to do this again, but if the lens would get damaged, our observations might not be accurate. At this juncture, it is essential all our data is correct."

Stella had no problem with the request. Carefully straddling the scope she shimmied her way up to the faulty cap.

"Almost there!" Perceval shouted. "But do hurry! If your mother knew I had you doing this, I'd never hear the end of it!" Stella understood her father's concern, knowing that if Celeste walked in and saw her daughter so high in the air, she would have a fit. Reaching the cap, she turned it to cover the lens.

"Thank you! Now hurry down." Perceval looked nervously to the door.

Getting down was Stella's favorite part of the climb. Loosening her grip, she slid gently down the slick body of the telescope. Being his daughter had done him such a favor, Perceval paid no mind to this slight misuse of his equipment, and when Stella reached the base of the telescope he helped her gently to the floor "We need to get to dinner, or your mother will be as prickly as a pear!" Stella knew her mother never got angry if they were late, but thought it was cute her father used those words. "Besides, we'll need our strength; we have a long night ahead of us. We must find an explanation for what we just witnessed!"

Following her father, Stella walked through the tunnel that connected the observatory to the rest of the dome. At the end of the tunnel she knew she would find her two brothers, Tim and Pace, and her mother, Celeste, the only other people she had seen for the last four months. The only thing that offered any relief from the monotony of these same old faces, was the fact that soon there would be a new one, as Stella's mother, Celeste, was very, very, pregnant.

The base the Rays now called home, was situated at the center of the Arctic Circle, and on all sides was surrounded by deep white snow. It was, the helicopter pilot who had flown them to the dome had said, the most remote place on Earth. Stella had quickly learned what that meant. Shortly after arriving, her father had shown her a picture he said had been taken by a satellite that floated high in the sky above them. Stella had thought the blank white sheet was just another bit of her father's absent mindedness, but when he pointed to a small spot at its center and handed Stella a magnifying glass, she saw details that told her there was something more to that small gray dot. Then, in the way it happens when all of a sudden you realize that what you had thought was not actually how things were, Stella realized that the dot was the dome where she lived. Putting the magnifying glass down to survey the paper at arm's length, she couldn't help but notice the vast expanse of white surrounding the tiny dot, and imagined that she was just like that; isolated and lonely.

Dome C, as this observation base was known, was also the place where Stella's father worked, and his job was the reason they had moved from sunny Florida to live in the frosty Arctic. Professor Perceval Q. Ray, which was how his name was printed on the thick books he had written, was an astronomer. "The atmosphere here," he had explained when they had first arrived, "is very clear and offers near perfect viewing conditions. But the real reason for our residence at the North Pole is that there is less of the problematic wobble caused by the planet's spinning! From here we will have a more pristine view of the stars."

Stella had nodded her head, understanding that to her father the most important thing was to be able to see the stars clearly, and to unlock the secrets that lay so far away in space. She had written in her notebook, equations her father had given her, that described the revolution of the Earth and its wobble. Later in her room, Stella huddled at her computer, snuggling in the warmth of the red down parka she had been given when they left Florida, and ran a simulation that showed how at the Earth's axis, the rotation of the planet was not as severe. It was immediately apparent that what her father had said was true; the view of space was far better in the Arctic than anywhere else on Earth.

With little else to do in the months since they had arrived, Stella soon became an assistant in her father's experiments. After doing her schoolwork and emailing it off to a teacher she had never seen, she would put on her parka and climb the stairs to the observatory. There in the chilly air that filled the dome she would find her father engrossed in his research, wearing only his thin white lab coat, its pockets brimming with pens and pencils. Then, until her mother called her to bed, Stella would help him with the endless calculations he hoped would unveil the mysteries of the stars. Solving such problems, Stella had learned early on, was the greatest pleasure in her father's life.

While Perceval was great with numbers, her mother was good at lots of things, but most especially at helping things grow. In Florida she had worked in large greenhouses and Stella had many pleasant memories of the flowers and plants her mother had cultivated there. Since they'd moved to the Arctic and into Dome C, Celeste hadn't had much of a chance to do any real gardening. Outside it was too cold and inside there wasn't enough room to grow many plants, so she had to make due with just a few small herbs planted in containers that hung from a shelf in the kitchen. When they had first arrived these small plants had begun to wither away, but Celeste, and it had amazed Stella to watch, had nursed the dying plants back to health and now the kitchen was filled with the smells of fresh mint, rosemary and chives.

Her uncanny ability with plants was one of the things Stella loved about her mother. She had always been Stella's best friend, and they had always known that they were the two girls in the house, and had to stick together against the three boys. It was their private joke; that two girls equaled three boys.

That was another reason Stella felt so lonely, as Tim and Pace were no longer the babies she had helped her mother with. As they grew, Celeste had her hands filled with the two rambunctious boys, who seemed to always be getting into mischief. Since they had moved, the boys cooped up and exploding with energy, were monopolizing Celeste's time, and Stella not wanting to make matters worse, had begun to fill her day working with her father.

Stella hoped the new baby would be a reason to spend more time with her mother, if only just to help. But at the moment she was very happy just to sit at the kitchen counter and watch Celeste's belly sway as she stirred a bowl of icing, whistling cheerfully as fluffy dollops spun on her whisk. Sirius lay nearby, happily dreaming, while down the hall her brothers played a noisy game of *Smash'em up*, the point of which, as far as Stella could tell, was to destroy as many toy cars as possible.

There was a time when Stella would play with her brothers, but as she grew older, their games lost interest for her. So on most days while Tim and Pace raced wildly through the halls, Stella, if she wasn't with her father, sat in her room working on long strings of equations, with Sirius dozing at her feet. Only occasionally would Stella look through her small window to the stars and try to understand how all the numbers on her desk could ever describe those bright shining lights.

But with the boys busy at the moment, being alone with her mother felt wonderful. Inhaling the sweet smells that wafted through the kitchen, Stella knew her mother was baking a special cake, one for her thirteenth birthday. It had been a months since Stella had been so happy.

Abruptly she was broken from the peaceful lull, noticing the raucous sounds from the hall had stopped. Where seconds before had been shouts and screams, now there was silence. Stella looked anxiously to her mother. Dropping her whisk and balancing the large bowl of icing on the stacks of pans that covered the counter, Celeste headed out the door. "Let me see what's going on out there. I'll be right back!" Stella wondered how her mother could be so calm; knowing just how much trouble the boys could stir up. "Tim! Pace! Where have you gone off to?" Her voice receded down the hall, leaving Stella alone with the sleeping Sirius in the all too quiet kitchen.

Stella knew from experience that such silence meant trouble, as the boys were never this quiet unless some serious mischief was involved. Stella had taken the brunt of her brothers' antics too many times and this type of quiet made her, she hated to admit, nervous. Hurrying to follow her mother she stepped from the stool, stirring the dog from his sleep. "It's okay Sirius, I'm just going to go find mom." But, as Stella moved towards the door, her dog stood to follow.

A loud crash shattered the calm of the kitchen and Sirius was off like a shot. An even louder racket ensued as the startled mutt raced through the kitchen chased by a series of pots and pans tied to his tail. The poor animal jumped wildly about yelping excitedly, and terrified of the metallic monsters pursuing him.

"Stop running, Sirius!" Stella shouted, chasing the dog around the room while trying to remove the clanging cookware. "Stop moving, so I can help you!"

Then Stella heard a sound that set her blood boiling. From behind the kitchen door came a volley of snickers. Turning to the mocking giggles she shouted angrily at the two boys, whose faces were gleeful with devilish delight. "TIM! PACE! How could you?" But before Stella could get her hands on her brothers, Sirius, darted frantically between, mercilessly pursued by the clanging pots and pans. Taking the opportunity for escape, the boys slipped behind the kitchen counter.

Celeste's voice shouted from the hall. "Stella? Tim! Pace? What's going on in there?"

Twin heads popped from the other side of the counter, tongues out to mock their sister. Infuriated, Stella stretched through the clutter of pots and pans and tried to snatch one of the twin's tongues, but Sirius, in his wild panic, had somehow gotten under the girl's feet. Knocked off balance Stella struggled for some hold. The clutter on the counter scattered as she grabbed wildly at the stack of pans, and then, in that slow motion kind of way where time seems to slow down, the bowl of icing lifted from the counter and flew through the air. It tumbled in space, once, twice, and on the third spin landed with a loud plopping noise right on Stella's head.

Time returned to its normal speed as Stella fell to the floor, crowned with a dripping mess of goo. The kitchen door flew open. Celeste rushed in. Sirius ran out, clattering loudly down the hall. Behind him went the boys, sneaking out as Celeste bent to help her daughter.

After washing the sticky goo from Stella's hair, Celeste turned wearily to the mess of the kitchen. Batter covered the counter and floor, and pots and pans were scattered everywhere. Stella watched as her mother began to mop the floor, her large round belly looking suddenly like so much extra weight to carry. "Mom? Why don't you sit down and rest? I can do that!"

Celeste looked up from her chore. Her hair hung in her face and her apron was covered with the dark brown stains of chocolate. Through the mess, she managed a tired smile for her daughter. "It's your birthday, Stella; I'm not going to let you mop the floor! Besides, you should find Sirius; he's probably scared out of his wits. Why don't you go and make sure he's alright?"

Stella got the feeling that beneath the forced smile, her mother wasn't pleased. She knew that when Celeste finished cleaning, she would have a talk with the boys, something that had become increasingly common. Since they had moved to the isolated confines of the Arctic, the twins' behavior had taken a turn for the worse. "Do you think Tim and Pace will ever grow up?" Stella asked.

Celeste's smile warmed as she replied. "Everyone grows up, Stella, in their own time. Just look at you. It seems like just yesterday you were my baby girl, and tomorrow, you'll be a teenager!" Then, noticing the wrecked kitchen, her smile faded. "But go find Sirius before the boys do. I can't deal with any more trouble today. We'll talk later, okay?"

Stella, not knowing what to do to make things better, walked glumly away. Celeste must have noticed the moping gait, because just as her daughter reached the door she called. "Stella, wait a second." Taking a sealed jar from a high shelf she popped the lid and pulled out a fistful of biscuits. "These might make Sirius feel a little better."

Stella quickly counted the biscuits and handed two back to her mother. "This should be enough. Let's save some for later. I know there won't be another shipment for while."

"Well, this is a first! I remember when I had to hide this jar to keep you from spoiling that dog!" Celeste chuckled. "I can't argue with your trying not to waste anything, but I must admit that I'm surprised by this new responsible Stella."

Stella forced herself to smile back, "I'm a year older! I guess I'm growing up."

Celeste looked deep into her daughter's green eyes. "So I've noticed! And guess what? If you can wait a few more hours your father and I have a special birthday surprise for you!"

Stella loved surprises, but right now with the prospect of her brothers waiting outside, she couldn't get too excited. "Sure mom..." she said, shoving the biscuits into her pocket and heading cautiously out to find her pet.

When Stella did find Sirius, he was collapsed in a quivering pile behind her bedroom door. Offering him a biscuit the jittery dog only tentatively sniffed the treat. "It's okay, the twins won't bother you anymore." Stella assured him, wondering if that was a promise she could keep. Sirius must have believed her as he took the biscuit and began to quietly gnaw. Untying the pots and pans from the dog's tail, Stella looked to the clock whose hands formed an arrow pointing straight up. "It's only noon", she murmured to her pet, though out her window the sky was dark as night. "And already this is my worst birthday ever. Nothing's had gone right, from those disappearing stars to what the boys did to you." Slinking down next to Sirius, Stella fell asleep against his warm fur.

From a crack in the door came a whisper. "Stella? Can I come in?"

Stella felt bad hearing her mother speak in such an apologetic tone, but after what had happened in the kitchen was glad of the attention. "Hi, mom", she glumly answered.

Celeste entered the room and sat next to her daughter. "I'm sorry about what happened. It's just the boys… Sometimes, they're quite a handful."

Stella fidgeted, "It's okay, Mom, I understand."

Coming nearer, Celeste put her arm around her daughter's shoulder. "I know. But it seems like every time we have a chance to talk, something happens. And that's in a place where nothing ever happens." With a giggle, she waved her hand at the walls. "I know being here, away from your friends, hasn't been easy for you. And the boys, they seem to take up more and more of my time. It's been much harder to school them than it ever was with you." She squeezed her daughter gently.

"I'll be okay, mom. I'm really learning a lot about astronomy from dad. You should have seen what we saw today, it was something strange, something he'd never seen before." Stella wondered if maybe she shouldn't talk about the scary black cloud that had blotted out two stars; it might only make her mother nervous. "But we're going to figure it out. Dad thinks we can explain it with his equations."

"More equations? Sometimes I wonder if you're getting too deep into all those numbers! You'll forget what it's like to just be young. Wait," Celeste held up a finger, "I have an equation for you. One plus one equals three."

"That's not right", Stella replied quickly realizing her mother was up to something. "That's totally illogical. One plus one always equals two."

"Are you sure?" Celeste seemed amused with herself. "Maybe there are other ways to see things. Maybe sometimes one and one do equal three. Or maybe one plus one can equal five!"

Stella decided she could play this game too. "So I guess you're trying to say that I should believe that one plus one can equal three AND one plus one can equal five AND at the same time one plus one can equal the same old plain two that I've always known."

"That's right! I did forget about one and one equaling two. And yes, all three of those 'equations' are correct!" The woman chuckled at the idea.

"All correct at the same time, huh?" Stella scoffed; trying to show as best she could her disbelief, while resisting laughing with her mother at the absurdity of it all.

"Right! Now you're getting it!" Celeste cheered. "Can you solve that equation?"

Stella knew she couldn't. That was not how numbers behaved. Her father always called numbers his "faithful little soldiers", meaning they always acted the same way and always would, leaving no doubt that they would always do their duty. Stella could picture in her mind the regiment of numerals, the one "soldiers" separated by the plus sign "soldier", and following behind, after the double dash of the equal sign "soldier", the numeral two "soldier". If she tried to place a numeral three "soldier" into the spot where the two stood it would refuse, as even under her direct order the numeral three would not defy the laws of logic. No number would break the laws that had been in place for as long as there had been human minds.

"There is no way to solve that. One plus one can never equal three," Stella stated bluntly.

"You're sure of that?"

"Very! It just can't be!"

"Maybe, my darling daughter, you should try to see things in ways that are not so absolute. But if your father ever heard me say that, he'd go ballistic!" Celeste looked to the door in mock horror before gleefully continuing. "Now, do you want me to tell how one plus one can equal three, and at the same time equal five, and also the same old two?"

Of course Stella wanted to know. While her mother may have only been joking, her brain was hurting as it tried to figure how numerals could break ranks and do things they had never done before. "Yes," She answered, trying hard not to sound like she was surrendering, "I'd like to hear how that can be done."

Celeste pointed up to a photo of the Ray family on the wall. "How many people are in this picture?"

Stella knew but her mind couldn't help doing a quick mental count. Perceval, one, Celeste, two, Stella herself, three, Tim, four and Pace made five. "I see five," she stated, cautious her mother might have some trick up her sleeve. If Celeste could say that one plus one equaled five, she would probably be willing to twist anything around.

"That's right." Fishing into her pocket Celeste pulled out another photo, one of her and Perceval standing together, looking quite a bit younger. "And how many people are in this picture?"

"Just dad and you: Two."

Celeste held her hand over the half of the picture, leaving only the younger Perceval to be seen. "Now how many?"

"One." Stella said.

"And now?" Celeste moved her hand to reveal her own younger self and cover the smiling face of her partner.

"One."

"One and one," Celeste said, moving her hand back and forth to reveal first herself and then her husband. "When I first met your father, I was just one person, and so was he. Then the two of us," Celeste took her hand away to reveal the couple in the photo together again, "were one. And now, that one plus one is five." She pointed to the picture of the whole Ray family.

Stella could only sit and stare. It went against all logic, but it was true, her mother and father were one and one and when those two got together they were one also. And eventually that one became five.

"And now," Celeste said, rubbing her belly with mischievous triumph in her voice, "our family will add a new one, making our one, six."

Celeste must have noticed how confused her daughter had become, because she suddenly stopped sounding like she was having fun, and more like a mother concerned for her daughter. "I'm sorry Stella, I shouldn't play these games with you. It's just that lately I've noticed you've fallen under the spell of your father's obsessions. There's a place for all that logic, but I'm hoping you're not leaving your childhood behind too quickly," she sighed. "I think tonight you should have a night off, with no working for your father, okay?"

Stella nodded, "I am a bit tired. Maybe I'll just read a while."

Celeste paused for a moment in thought, and then confessed, "Sometimes I wonder if we're doing the right thing by keeping you kids up here, so isolated and away from other kids."

"It's okay mom, really. I'm fine here. I just wish it could be like it used to be, when...when…" Stella hesitated for a moment, and looked to her mother to see if she could finish the thought.

"Like when the boys were younger? Sometimes I find myself wishing for the same thing, but you can't stop time, can you?" Celeste moved nearer, asking, "We'll always be best friends though, right?"

Stella held her mother tight, still unsure if she liked hugging her mother this way, with her big tight watermelon of a belly, or if she liked it better the way it was before. "That's right, mom; Always!"

When Celeste had gone, Stella found she couldn't focus on her book. Her attention was drawn to the snowy landscape outside her window, and following the white expanse to the horizon, she looked up to where the full moon hung amidst the innumerable pinpoints of light. Sometimes, when there was only a crescent moon, Stella would tilt her head and imagine the curve of light was a grinning smile, but now the moon was a luminous hole in the dark sky, presenting a welcoming gateway from the cold endless night of the arctic into the warmth of some other world. Turning off the lamp near her bed, Stella sat wondering why there was needed to be any darkness at all.

It was later, while tucked under the covers with Sirius curled snugly at her feet, when Stella woke to familiar footsteps coming down the hall. As the doorknob turned, Sirius stirred from his sleep, his pointed ears erect, as the door opened to reveal Perceval. He held rather awkwardly, a long box, and from the hall a shadow gestured, coaxing him to enter. Stella knew just how nervous he must be, as this was to be an official father to daughter chat, one orchestrated by the head of the household, Celeste.

Stella sat up in bed as Perceval approached, a sheepish smile frozen on his face. Behind him, a hand reached into the room to take hold of the doorknob, and as the door was slowly pulled closed, father and daughter were left alone. Though Stella had been spending a lot of time in the observatory with only her father, this was different. Here there was no chance to hide behind the notebooks and instruments.

Sitting timidly on the edge of the mattress with the box across his lap, Perceval fumbled with the package, exhibiting just how uncomfortable he found the situation. "Umm, uh, your mother tells me that you're… uh…umm, feeling a bit blue today."

Stella knew he would much rather be in his lab, solving some equation. "I'm okay, dad, It's just, well, sometimes I wish I had my friends nearby." Sirius must've understood her words, because his ears drooped as he gave Stella a sad look.

"A friend?" Perceval seemed surprised. "I thought you knew, Stella, the sky is full of friends." Walking to the window he pointed upwards towards a gleaming point of light. "Look there. You know that star, don't you? I discovered it the day you were born."

"Astraea," Stella whispered, instantly entranced by the twinkling point of light.

"Yes, that is the name I gave her, as I named you Stella. Astraea, my first important discovery! A new class of star, a wandering star and one that moves so slowly across the sky, its movements are barely noticeable to human eyes," Perceval explained. "How can you ever want for a friend when in the sky is a companion who will never falter, never fail? Whenever you might feel lonely, you need only look to the sky for Astraea."

Stella knew the star well. How many times she had wished upon it, she could not count. Stella quickly corrected herself. That jewel in the night, that lovely point of light, was not an "it" but a she and the name of that elegant lady was Astraea.

"I can remember when I was just your age, Stella, lying in fields and gazing out at the heavens. From those far cosmic regions, I felt the irresistible pull of the stars and came to be enthralled by the unfathomable mysteries of space. Longing to travel to those bright lights, to voyage to the vast spaces beyond Earth, I dreamed of being an astronaut, but finding I could never withstand the rigors of space travel, committed myself to study astronomy. I memorized every star and constellation, learning all I could about those worlds beyond ours. To prove my ardent admiration of those denizens of space I studied at the university, striving all the time to get just a bit closer to the heavens through my studies."

Stella had heard her father talk this passionately only once before, when her mother had brought her to a university class he had been teaching. She remembered how proud his speech had made her.

"Even now", Perceval stared transfixed into space, "when I turn my eyes to those myriad lights, so palely beautiful, shining with undying flame in the gulfs of night, I hear them speak to me…" His thoughts lost in the stars, he cocked his ear as if to listen before speaking again. "From this Arctic base my vision is clearer, and, with no harsh glare from cities to cloak its secrets, the cosmos more glorious. We have come to this cold and barren place to penetrate mysteries beyond the comprehension of man." Returning from his reverie Perceval sighed deeply before softly asking his daughter. "You do understand that, don't you? And what it is I'm trying to accomplish? I know it must be hard for you; a girl your age should not be alone."

Stella stopped him, "I understand, dad. I know how important it is for us to be here, but I'm not really alone. Besides Astraea, I have Sirius to keep me company, and mom, and you, and", She paused, trying not to let her true feelings show, "the twins."

Perceval frowned. "Your mother told me about the incident that occurred today at," He fumbled in his pocket and fished out a slip of paper to read," Eleven thirty seven. I wish the boys would behave better, but I fear that they have cabin fever. I dislike seeing them treat you poorly, and on your birthday!"

He smiled proudly at Stella. "It's your thirteenth, isn't it? That's four thousand seven hundred and forty five days, or one hundred and thirteen thousand eight hundred and eighty hours, or", Perceval squinted his eyes, "six million eight hundred and thirty two thousand and eight hundred minutes! Four hundred and nine million nine hundred and sixty eight thousand seconds! Astounding!" Retrieving his package from the bed he offered it to the girl, "Your mother and I agree that you could use this. Would you care to open it?"

In seconds Stella ripped the box open to find, nestled in crinkly tissue paper, a telescope. She picked it up, feeling the coolness of the gleaming chrome.

"Now you can watch the stars from your window and make your own discoveries! Remember, when an eye is armed with a telescope, it sees well beyond what mundane vision allows." Perceval paused, perhaps remembering his first telescope received on a birthday morning years ago. "Would you, like me to set it up?"

Before Perceval could move Stella had her arms around him, hugging tightly. For a heartbeat he stood stiffly and then awkwardly put his arms around his daughter, wedging the scope tightly between them. His eyes went moist and he quickly wiped away the tears with a deft flick of his handkerchief. "Can I tell you a secret?" he asked guardedly.

Stella looked up at her father. "Of course you can."

"I think things are going to change for our family very soon."

"I know, Dad, but I'm going to help take care of the baby. Things won't change that much." Stella offered, thinking her father had just experienced another episode of absent-mindedness. Celeste had been pregnant for over nearly nine months and now Perceval was acting like it was breaking news.

"That's not what I meant," Perceval corrected, freeing himself from his daughter's embrace before continuing. "The observations we made this morning were so spectacular that I imagine we won't be here much longer. I've radioed to have a colleague sent here by helicopter right away. Once we obtain some further data, I'll need to get back to use the university's computers. We'll head home and you'll be back with your friends."

Stella's head spun. She might be going home soon! That was a better birthday present than even the telescope.

"I believe what we have observed is something unheard of in the history of science! As soon as my calculations are verified I will make my findings known to the world." Perceval stopped, to collect himself. "But, we can talk about all that tomorrow! It's almost time for bed, and we need to calibrate your telescope."

Perceval reached for the box on the bed and extracted a tripod. Taking the telescope from Stella's hands he skillfully fitted it to its base, then placed its legs on the floor and pointed the scope skywards. Bending, he put his eye to the lens and adjusted the knobs on the scope with an "hmm" and an "ahhhh". "There's an unusually fine view of the moon tonight. But please, don't stay up too late. We'll need our sleep, tomorrow looks to be a busy day." He spun and walked briskly to the door, but turned as his daughter cried out.

"Dad?" she started, "I…I…"

Perceval interrupted, pushing his glasses up his nose, "I know Stella, and I feel the same about you." Then spinning quickly on his heels he retreated.

Alone, Stella put her eye to the telescope and found the moon fully in view. Sirius came from the corner where he was lying and pushed his muzzle into her hand. She gently scratched his neck while gazing upwards; reaching with her free hand to her parka that hung on the bedpost. Pulling a biscuit from its pocket she slipped it into the dog's waiting mouth, her eye never leaving the lens.

Time seemed to slow as she viewed the silvery orb hanging palely in the sky. The shades of gray of the moon's surface were colorless rainbows leading into unfathomable depths. Stella wondered what secrets each deep crater might hold, and as she contemplated the mysterious sphere, the impression of a face emerged from the random patches of crater and ridge. Two deep hollows hinted of eyes, while a line of ridges suggested a jagged mouth. Having always found optical illusions fun, Stella kept her eyes glued on the strange face. As she did, the features became clearer, until the jagged ends of the crater mouth bent up in a smile and the left eye winked. Stella was dumbfounded.

A hand on her shoulder gently pulled her back from the astral plane. "Stella?" Her mother whispered in her ear, giggling, "Earth to Stella!" As Stella pulled her eye from the telescope her mother's face took the place of the Moon's, just as large and just as bright.

"Are there two people in our family that I'll have to make sure keep their feet on the ground? The way you were staring through that scope, why, that's something I'd expect from your father," she said smiling. "You're beginning to remind me an awful lot of him." Stella smiled too, happy for her mother's visit. "I just came to say goodnight; it's bedtime. You'll have plenty of time tomorrow to watch the skies. Did your father mention the guest we'll be having?"

"He did. Who is it? Is it someone I know?"

"No one we know, I imagine. It'll be a scientist, sent here to check on your father's work." Celeste looked genuinely disappointed, and Stella realized her mother was as lonely as she was. "I'm sure you know how important this is for your father. But, enough of that! Come on, it's time for bed, I'll tuck you in."

"Mom! I'm going to be thirteen," Stella laughed, jumping into bed. "I'm old enough to put myself to bed!"

"I guess you're right Stel, You're not my little girl anymore, but..." Celeste bent in to kiss her daughter's forehead. "Let me tuck you in this one last time."

2 NIGHT VISITOR

Stella woke to the sound of gentle rapping. Rubbing her knuckles in her eyes, she glanced sleepily around the room searching for her clock. Midnight; when the clock's two hands, joined to form a single rocket ready to fly. Reaching down for the lump of dog that was always at her feet, she grasped empty space and groggily wondered where was Sirius?

Tap. Tap. Tap. The tapping had the familiar ping of a tree branch against glass, but here in the Arctic Stella remembered, there were no trees. She rolled in her bed to find Sirius standing frozen at the window, one eye glued to the telescope's eyepiece. The only movement was the dog's ears, which jerked tensely upwards, then relaxed before twitching again.

"Sirius, what are you doing?" Stella asked, pushing the covers off and standing in the silver light that flooded through the window.

Tap. Tap. Tap. Stella examined the window for what could be making the sound. There was nothing outside but the moon, the bright stars, and soft white snow glowing in the lunar light.

Tap. Tap. Tap. Her senses weren't playing tricks; the sound was definitely coming from near the window. She put her ear close to the window frame and tried to locate the tapping.

Tap. Tap. Tap. Now it was behind her! But there was nothing behind her…except… The telescope! She moved her ear toward the shiny tube.

Tap. Tap. Tap. The sound was coming from the scope! Reaching both hands around Sirius Stella tried to move him from the viewfinder, but even pulling with all her weight he would not budge. Clapping her hands lightly Stella pleaded, “Come on, Sirius! Come on!!” But to no avail, the dog would not be distracted from whatever he saw in the scope.

Tap. Tap. Tap again, and this time Stella was certain it came from within the metal tube of the telescope. Taking a chair to the window she stood on it and peered through the upper lens of the telescope. There was nothing but the dog’s blinking eye staring up through the empty tube. Sirius let out a frightened whine, and then his eye was gone.

The dog darted across the room and cowered in the corner. It took a second for Stella to figure out what was the matter, but then knelt to calm the trembling dog. “You’re such a scaredy cat! It was only my eye, there’s nothing to be afraid of! Sometimes I’m not sure how…” *Tap!* … Stella turned back to the window… *Tap! Tap!* … And with Sirius slinking cautiously behind, she walked towards the scope, curious to see what had held the dog’s attention so intently.

Stella let out an astonished gasp as she put her eye to the viewfinder. For visible in the lens of the scope was the shape of a man, manically waving his arms. Jolting back, Stella rubbed her eyes in disbelief and then took another look through the lens, half expecting whatever she had seen to be gone. The figure was still there, only now even more agitated.

Now thoroughly confused, Stella examined the window for some clue. The panes of glass were clean, and still outside, were nothing but the sky, the stars, the snow, and the bright full moon. There was no man. Removing the scope from the tripod, she checked its lenses for dirt or scratches. They were clean.

Stella put the scope back on its stand and looking through the eyepiece, realigned it to the moon. When a bright blurry circle filled her view she carefully focused the lens. A mournful whine from Sirius caused her concentration to slip.

“What’s the matter now?” She asked. “All of your whimpering is making me jumpy. It was just my magnified eye that scared you, and what I saw was just a bug on the lens.”

Just a bug, Stella tried to convince herself of that, knowing all the while that no insects lived in the cold arctic frost. The last bug she had seen was in Florida. And she hated to think it, but what she had seen pressed against the telescope's lens, was not like that of any insect she knew. The dog slinked away and slid his face under the bed. "Okay, scaredy cat, have it your way." Stella twiddled with the scope's knobs until the blurry disc came into sharp focus. When it did, her fingers dropped limply in shock.

Formed from the cratered surface of the moon was a broadly smiling face. Pale blue eyes floated in a pair of craters that sat on either side of a mountain range, which was oddly, also a nose. Beneath those, a deep craggy canyon stretched, resembling a crooked mouth. The ridges bordering it shifted in a way Stella had never before seen mountains move. They closed, sealing the crevice and then opened again. Stella suddenly realized the rocky lips were repeatedly forming shapes, and those shapes were forming words. In another moment she knew what the mountains of the moon were saying. Three words repeated over and over, and when she looked into the pale pools that were the moon's blue eyes, the same entreaty was echoed there. Stella mouthed the words, matching the movement of the moon's lips.

"Come with me?"

The face fell back to reveal the surrounding stars and as it did, Stella could see that the moon face was attached to a body, one that seemed a bit too small to support such a large round head. Stranger still, the body was dressed in a dapper, tidy suit. As he receded into space, the moon man's hands gestured wildly for Stella to follow. She knew somehow that this offer would not come again, and understanding that if she did not answer quickly, the chance would be lost forever, she grabbed her parka off the post of her bed and slipped it on. Taking a deep breath, she peered back through the telescope, nodded her head, and whispered "yes".

At the word, the man reached out with an open hand, which shot forward on an arm that elongated like an elastic band. Stella glanced away to where, outside, the moon was just the moon, and then looked back through the scope to find the hand had grown much larger. When it seemed like it could go no further without being stopped by the glass of the lens, the hand passed right through, ballooning from the viewfinder of the telescope and quickly grasping Stella's wrist. She heard Sirius growl then bark, and before she knew what was happening, she felt an odd sensation and realized she was shrinking, or the telescope viewfinder was getting larger. With no warning and a loud Pop! Stella found herself pulled through the viewfinder and up into the telescope.

Pulled along, Stella slid through the telescope's tube, not feeling particularly cramped or uncomfortable but only surprised at her current situation. Through the top lens she could see the moon man laughing as he reeled in his arm. Then, with another Pop! Stella was out of the telescope and flying through the sky. Looking behind, she saw she was already far above her home, the dome now only a dark spot surrounded by the white of snow, and growing smaller by the second. Passing through clouds Stella lost sight of her home and realized she was soaring through the atmosphere into outer space.

The hand grasping her wrist pulled upwards, reeling the girl ever nearer to the moon man. "We're so glad you said yes! We've been hoping you would!" he said, his craggy toothed mouth turned up in a large smile.

Stella, now floating little more than arm's length from this being, could think of nothing to say but, "Who are you?"

"Me?" The strange man poked his chest with a crooked thumb. "That's very funny. You've been looking at me for so long, and now you pretend not to know who I am!" He let out a shrill, cackling laugh, and put out his hand in introduction. "I know those that live on Earth call me the Moon, but everyone out here calls me Loony." Stella took it politely. "So," he said, cocking a rocky eyebrow and showing the deep blue pool that hid beneath. "Are you going to tell me your name?"

"Stella, my name is Stella Ray." Looking around, she couldn't believe she was actually floating in space. Hoping to wake up from the dream, she pinched her arm, but nothing changed. Stars that glittered like diamonds in the night still surrounded her.

"Pleasure to meet you Stella Ray; I'm glad you accepted my invitation. They've been waiting to talk with you."

"You've been waiting to talk with me?" She pinched herself again, this time harder, and again nothing changed.

"They", Loony corrected, "I said 'they've' been waiting to talk with you." The brows turned down, the blue pools deepening. "I'm not included in their group."

"Loony?" Stella asked.

"That's my name, don't wear it out!"

"Can you do me a favor and pinch me?" She pulled the sleeve of her parka up and held her arm out.

"If that's what you want, why not? Where? Here?" The moon man pointed to the patch of skin near Stella's wrist. At her nod he quickly pinched her, his rocky fingers biting into her skin.

"Owww! Not that hard!!"

"Hey," the moon man huffed, his face darkening, "You asked for it, didn't you?"

The pinch, even one so hard, hadn't jolted Stella from what she had thought was a dream. She was still floating in space and talking to a creature stranger than any she could ever imagine. "Did you say 'they'?"

"You heard right," the moon man replied sharply. "I said 'they', as in the big nine, the Planets. They're going to be glad when I bring you to them."

"Bring me to them? The Planets? Where are they waiting? Aren't they in orbit?" Stella blurted in a breathless rush.

"You sure are funny." Loony laughed. "They're waiting in Heliopolis, where they always are. What were you thinking? Are all humans as dumb as you?"

Deciding since she had no idea where she was or how to get back home, that she had better not respond nastily to the Moon's accusation; Stella looked around for a way back to Earth, and saw nothing but deep, endless space. "Well," she replied, trying her best to sound informed, "I've studied the planets and their orbits. Only on rare occasions do they come near each other, but even that will happen with at most, three planets." Stella remembered her father calling these instances "conjunctions", and as the word sounded impressive, she decided to use it. "Those conjunctions don't happen often, *and never*," she emphasized, "Are all the planets near each other at once."

The moon man let out a hooting laugh, "I guess you're not as smart as they hoped! I can't believe you think that just because things look a certain way, that's the way they are. When you look up at the stars, you could tell yourself they're only tiny lights stuck on a flat black sheet, right? But they're really far away from each other, and in different levels of space. You could also pretend that the stars that look larger are actually bigger than the ones that seem smaller, but seeing alone, can't show what something is. There's always more to the picture than meets the eye!" He spoke authoritatively, but Stella wasn't sure if what he said made any sense. "Understand?"

Staring speechlessly at this little man with the moon for his head, Stella had no idea how to respond.

"But enough talk, we have to hurry to Heliopolis. They're waiting for us; or to be exact, they're waiting for you. And they don't like to wait." The moon casually folded his arms and gazed vacantly into space. "Yes, We'd better hurry, they can be very difficult if they're kept waiting."

Stella wondered why they hadn't left, if they needed to be on time. "They'll be angry if we're late?"

"Very!" as his eyes wandered aimlessly the moon man smiled a gnomic smile.

"Loony?" Stella asked, breaking a silence she felt had lasted hours. As if his name was the last thing he expected to hear, Loony's head snapped with a startled jolt. "What are we waiting for? And why, if we're in a hurry, are we just standing around?"

"Waiting for?" Loony asked dreamily. Stella nodded in response but the moon man only resumed staring into space, as if her words had no meaning.

"Well?" She asked impatiently, growing ever more frustrated.

"Well?" Loony echoed still spacey.

Stella, through clenched teeth, asked the question once more. "If we are going to be late, just *WHAT* are we waiting for?" Seeing that Loony's eyes were locked on a point out in space, she followed his line of sight and saw a smoldering comet heading straight towards them.

Stella lurched back in fright as Loony came suddenly alive, shouting, "What are we waiting for?" As the comet hurtled by he grasped the girl tightly around the waist and with a swift leap landed nimbly on the speeding rock. "This!" A rush of wind blew back Stella's hair as she crouched against the rocky surface. Finding some cracks she held tight, her knuckles white with terror. The moon man stood with his feet firmly planted surfing the giant boulder. "Now this is the way to travel! An express straight to Heliopolis!" he hooted over the piercing whistle of the comet cutting through space. "We should be, right on time!"

As they plummeted, Stella peered cautiously over the comet's edge. Zooming into view below was a gigantic tower of amorphous stardust, its base lost in the depths of space. Though she couldn't be certain, it seemed Loony was steering the comet towards the mountainous form.

"Don't hold too tight! You'll hurt your fingers!"

Hurt my fingers? We're going to crash!" Indeed they were, as they were rapidly approaching the mountain.

"Ready?" The lunatic cackled as the distance swiftly closed.

"NO!" Stella screamed. Pulling the hood of her parka over her head, she shielded for impact.

The whistling suddenly ceased and from within the tight ball she had curled into, Stella heard Loony proudly proclaimed, "Welcome to Heliopolis!" At first too frightened to look; Stella opened her eyes to see Loony spreading his arms, as if to encompass all that surrounded him.

Stella jumped up but found it hard to stand, her sense of balance so off, it felt like she had just been rolled down a hill. Looking down, she saw she was standing on a surface of translucent billowing dust, while far below, the comet they had ridden continued its speedy flight, unbelievably, through the gaseous mountain. She did a quick check if her body was still intact, then satisfied she had not been smashed to bits, felt her stomach slide back down her throat.

"I guess you've never traveled by comet before!" Loony snickered at the shock on the girl's face, and then marched briskly away. Stella dipped a pointed toe into the dense fog, testing the surface on which she now stood. It gave way to her prodding, but her foot did not penetrate deeply into the mist.

"Well, come on, don't dawdle! You'll make us late!" Loony shouted, already far ahead and rapidly climbing a fluffy hill. Stella took a cautious step, and her foot sprung off the surface like she was walking on a firm mattress. She began to trot after her guide, bouncing lightly with each step and joined him at the top of the hill.

"What on Earth…" Stella exclaimed as she stepped over the crest. Far ahead, nestled within a shallow valley, studded, stood a gleaming city surmounted by a tower that loomed high overhead, disappearing into a cloud of bright light. Hundreds of questions came to mind as she wondered how this city could be here, and no astronomer, not even her father, had ever discovered it.

"It's nothing from Earth! Loony scoffed, "This is *Heliopolis*, the city of the Planets!"

Stella followed the moon man into the valley, and found herself in a strange forest of columns that spread out in every direction, creating endless alignments that shifted with every step. Each column was lit by the soft glow from thousands of small flecks of light, and as she walked, Stella ran her fingers over their surfaces. The tiny flecks responded to her touch, by glowing brighter and shifting as if they were floating in a thick gel. Engrossed by the shimmering particles, Stella stopped, put both hands to the column and spread her fingers out, raking across the surface. For a moment the ten long streaks of light held, before fading away.

"Ahem!" A voice growled. " Do you think perhaps you can tear yourself away from your games?" The little man grabbed Stella's hand and began dragging her along. "If you make us late, I'm the one who'll be held responsible!"

Stella dug in her heels and pulled her hand free. "Wait a second! If you want my help, you'd better be nicer to me! You can't just pull me around and treat me like your prisoner."

As the edges of his jagged mouth turned down, Loony began to blubber. "I didn't mean to pull you, but I don't want to be yelled at by you or the Planets!" He swung a hand towards the city. "If I don't get you there quick, I'll be in big trouble!" He stepped behind a column and stood sobbing, his big round head bowed against the mound, forming a shimmering circle in the glowing gel.

Stella couldn't believe the moon was behaving this way. It was exactly what her brothers would do; cry and sob and make her feel guilty, when it really wasn't her fault. Though he was barely Pace's height, Loony surely wasn't a child, the moon was millions of years old. "Come on, stop crying. You don't want to be late, right?" Stella pretended to care as she put her hand on Loony's heaving shoulder.

Responding to her touch, he only sobbed more heavily and snorted a big sniffle. Stella hated that even more. Her brother Tim also sniffled; big snorting sniffles, which always grossed her out. Then, to make it worse, he would rub his nose with the back of his hand and she couldn't bear to look at what he would wipe away. She hoped Loony wouldn't do that now.

"Okay, okay!" Stella blurted. "I'll keep up with you…"

Loony turned glumly and choked out the words, "And you won't yell at me anymore?"

Stella understood how this worked; she had done this many times. "I won't yell at you anymore," she whispered in defeat.

The wretched moon looked up. "You promise?"

"I promise." Stella stated weakly.

"Okay," he heaved between softening sobs.

In his eyes was the same look she would always see in her brothers' after similar episodes, the look of triumph. Satisfied he had won; Loony immediately ceased his outburst, and without another word raced ahead towards the towering structure at the center of the city. Stella trotted grudgingly after; fearful she might lose the odd moon man and be lost amongst the endless avenues of the strange stardust columns.

Suddenly Stella realized there was something alive on these streets. Blurs of motion flashed through every row. There was one, vanishing behind a post before she could make out what it was. And there! Something moved at the end of a street and just as quickly disappeared.

"Loony? Is there something…."? The moon man was already too far ahead to hear the question. …"Something following us? "She finished, knowing that there would be no answer if she did not find it out herself. Bolting off down a crossing aisle, Stella ran quickly through its columns, the blurs of movement hiding as she came near. As soon as she thought she was out of sight of whatever haunted these streets, she ducked behind a post.

Peeking down the avenue, Stella waited holding her breath, until slowly and with obvious trepidation, little heads popped out from anything that could be hidden behind, and tiny eyes began to search for the missing object of their curiosity. One of the things; and it must have been very brave one, because it was more than a few moments until another followed, moved into the street. Stella almost laughed out loud at the sight.

It was cute, she thought, in the way you could have a pet so homely, that it was kind of cute too. At first glance, it resembled a small ugly snowman made from clumps of dirty snow. Its misshapen head resembled a lump of gray clay that had been thrown to the floor too many times. It had a face, but set on the surface of the uneven blob, the features weren't quite in the right place. Its two eyes weren't even, or the same size, the smallest pointed up at a strange angle, while the larger stared straight out, pop-eyed. The glob that hung close to the area where a nose might be was like a shard of broken pottery, stuck haphazardly into the face. There was a mouth beneath all this, a small round hole that seemed frozen in a perpetual "o" shape, as if someone had pushed a pencil eraser into the clay ball. This uneven mass of head sat on another gray globule that was larger but just as ill formed, with neither arms nor legs. From the creature's back, sprouted two rudimentary wings, gray, leathery and not at all looking that they could sustain any prolonged flight.

Stella watched as the little creature, barely higher than her knee, began to make its way across the avenue to her hiding place, bouncing like a deflated basketball. She ducked further behind the column as it neared to investigate, and as it approached, others, many others of these tiny creatures revealed themselves. Each was unique, with no two quite the same in shape or size or features of their faces. An army of them now filled the street like bouncing balls of nervous energy. With quizzical looks on their squashed faces, they watched as their bravest approached the column Stella hid behind, gesturing with a series of emotive hops and jumps for them to come nearer.

Stella wasn't sure why she did it, but as the little creature was about to discover her, hidden behind the post, she grabbed it. In a silent flurry, all the others vanished from the street. She held the creature up by its stubby wings and lifted it to where she could see its face. Its larger eye stared unblinking, like a scared animal's, while the other eye drifted off unconcerned, into space. Its mouth moved dumbly, unable to articulate speech.

"That's an asteroid." Loony offered, as the moon man slumped against the column next to the one Stella hid behind. "We only call them meteors after they bite."

Stella's arm jerked out stiff and straight, holding her captive at full arm's length. "After, they bite?" She squealed, turning the little creature slightly to look in its mouth for teeth. Its maw was lined with pebbles; some quite sharp looking, and Stella decided that even though the creature was small, its mouth was big enough to give a painful bite.

"Well?" She asked Loony, who continued to loiter casually nearby. "What should I do with it?" Suddenly agitated, the asteroid struggled to break free and strained to reach it captor with its teeth. It began to jerk violently about, making it extremely difficult for Stella to hold the restless asteroid away from her body.

"Do with it?" Loony retorted. "I'd imagine you knew what you wanted to do with it, or else you would have left it alone!"

If Stella's hands were free she would have throttled the moon man. The asteroid mouth snapped hungrily as her tired arm dropped. Its teeth had grown larger, or so it seemed. "Loony! Tell me what to do with this thing! Now!"

"Well, I don't know why you even picked it up, it wasn't bothering you..." was his snarky reply.

Stella knew that if she shouted, Loony would only do what her brothers had always done, which would be nothing at all. There was only one way she knew to get her brothers to help with anything, and that was to bribe them. "If you tell me how to get rid of this thing, I'll give you a bar of chocolate, okay?

"What's 'chocolate'?" Loony asked curiously, and something in his voice gave Stella cause for hope.

"It's probably the best thing on Earth!" Stella enthused cheerily, though her arm ached horribly under the asteroid's weight.

"Best thing on Earth? What do you do with this...chocolate?" Intrigued, Loony moved closer.

"You eat it. It's so good! Everyone on Earth loves chocolate!" With her free hand she reached into the pocket of her parka, pulled out an open bar and took a bite. "Hmm! This is so good!" Having done this many times with her brothers she knew exactly what to say next. "If you've never tasted chocolate, you don't know what you're missing. It's so good I'll probably eat it all right now." she took one more bite, making sure that the moon man saw that the chocolate was indeed disappearing. Loony's eyes widened. "If you'd tell me what to do with this asteroid, I'll let you have the rest, even though," she used her saddest voice for this, "I'd hate to give it away."

"Okay!" the moon man said, "I'll tell you what to do, just give me the chocolate."

"Do you promise to tell, and not to even take a bite until you do?" Stella asked, not certain how much to trust him.

"Yes, I will," said the moon with a greedy look in his eye," Just throw it!"

She threw the half eaten bar. The moon man snatched it out of the air and immediately began gobbling the chocolate.

"Loony! You promised to tell me first!"

"I did tell you!"

"You did not!" The snapping teeth were dangerously close as Stella's fatigued arm sagged.

"I did too!" retorted Loony, his rocky lips covered with brown goo.

"Well," Stella squealed. "Tell me again!"

"Throw it!" he shouted, "Throw it as far as you can!"

Then Stella understood, and stepping from behind the column, she began to twirl, once, then twice around, and on the third spin, let go and flung the little monster as far away as she could. It landed halfway across the street and tumbled violently before rolling to a stop. As it righted itself to stand, the lumpy snowman face that Stella once thought cute, contorted into a horrible mask. The mouthful of rocks opened wide in a scream, and other asteroids hopped back into view, spilling into the street as if a truckload of basketballs had been overturned.

"What're they doing?" Stella asked, as the weird pack of blob headed creatures bounced closer.

"Meteor shower" Loony muttered while greedily devouring his chocolate.

"What should we do?"

"Run, I guess!" He cackled, stuffing the last of the candy into his mouth. In a flash he was down the lane. Stella took one look at the kinetic crazy chaos flooding towards her, and followed as fast as her legs would carry her.

While only rarely slowing to check over their shoulders, that they had eluded the meteors, in no time the duo reached the city. Stopping, Loony adjusted his clothing, smoothing his jacket and fixing the collar on his pale silvery shirt. Stella pointed to his behind. "Ahem," she cleared her throat.

Loony twisted his head and looked down. "Oh." He tucked the back of his shirt, which had hung below his jacket, into his pants' waist. He stuck a bony finger into his mouth, and Stella looked away as he pried a pebble from between his crooked teeth. Then he stood up straight and tall, and shrugged his shoulders back. "I'd watch yourself in there," Loony advised, pushing the gate open, "and be careful what you say about Terra." A bell pealed out as they stepped through the gate.

3 THE PARLIAMENT OF THE PLANETS

The first thing Stella noticed upon entering Heliopolis was the startling spectacle overhead. The star dotted sky was abruptly gone. In its place, hung an enormous vaulted ceiling, covering the whole of the city and decorated with the most amazing depiction of the sky. The constellations, wonderfully represented with vivid lifelike illustrations, gamboled about in their eternal interplay. The hunter, Orion, was in his place nearing Taurus the bull, and Hydra the snake, coiled hissing at Cancer the crab. Cygnus, the swan, taunted Vulpecula the fox, and Cassiopeia preened. Stella had been to many planetariums, and had seen constellations projected upon their domed ceilings in many clever ways, but this was extraordinary.

At the center of this sheltering sky, was the brightest and largest star in the tableau, and from this dazzling luminary descended a slender tower, incandescent with light. All the constellations revolved around this brilliant axis, and it took only a moment for Stella to realize that this central star was her own sun. A second bell rang out, and Stella though fascinated by the unusual ceiling, was jarred from her reverie. She looked for Loony, and saw him already far ahead and approaching the base of the dazzling central tower. Loony chided her as she reached his side. "Don't dawdle! They're assembling! Follow me!"

Stella snarled back. "Maybe someone should teach you the difference between following and chasing. If you wouldn't run so fast, I'd be able to keep up. She reluctantly trailed the moon man through the ring of structures that circled the central tower. There were some large buildings and numerous others, surrounding those which were vaguely reminiscent of doghouses. "What are those?" she whispered, amazed to see buildings here in outer space.

"Those are the houses of the Planets!" Loony snapped, "Don't you know anything?"

They passed between two. The one on the left was so lovely Stella could only compare it to a fairy palace, while on the right stood a cozy dwelling not unlike a woodland cabin on a pleasant spring day. The cottage was so inviting, that Stella wished she could rest inside for just a moment, but Loony was already waiting in the courtyard that surrounded the central tower.

Nothing on Earth could have prepared Stella for what she saw next. As she stepped to the moon man's side, a third bell rang out, and at its sound, the doors of the houses swung open, and out walked eight beings so strange they made Loony almost seem normal. Each possessed the body of a human, but on their shoulders rested weighty globes. From within the smaller dwellings, trooped retinues of beings who looked as if they could be the siblings of Loony, and these other moons produced nine large chairs that they arranged in a semi circle about the girl. The first to sit upon one of the thrones was a Planet whose red face lay embedded upon a ruddy globe. This odd character returned Stella's glance with an angry scowl. She looked away quickly, not knowing what she had done to garner so sour a reception.

The largest of the Planets, wearing a tunic that hung from massive shoulders, stepped to the middle seat. The orb of his head was covered by swirls of colored mist, whose bands of greens and blues intermingled with curls of red. A great red spot within the clouds rotated slowly out of sight, and then reappeared as the globe spun slowly on the shoulders. At moments when the swirling clouds thinned, the features of a noble face with penetrating eyes and a kind smile could be seen. Jupiter nodded to the girl in recognition.

To the left of the colossal Jupiter sat another giant even stranger in appearance. Around this planet's head, spun a wide flat ring banded with color and tilted jauntily forward. Though a variety of warm hues colored his face, his demeanor was somber. He studied the girl with pensive eyes, until dropping his gaze to the floor which was etched in a complex network of inscriptions and diagrams, all glowing slightly and shifting slowly in the milky stardust.

Stella knew this being well. The banded head matched exactly what she had studied so often through her father's telescope. This was Saturn, the sixth planet, with its surrounding rings of ice and water.

Stella quickly recognized all the other Planets who faced her. The farthest to the right, was hardly larger than Loony, and with a face so dark and cold, was no doubt, Pluto. Next to him was Neptune; watery and blue, his moist eyes gazing from mysterious depths. Mercury, a small grinning figure, fidgeted incessantly in his seat, and then there was Uranus, whose cool blue green surface was smooth and impenetrable.

But it was the loveliness of Venus that brought Stella's survey to a pause, her gaze lingering to admire the beauty of the feminine planet. The pale gold orb of her head sat gracefully on a shapely torso draped in a diaphanous gown. She was as beautiful as a Greek statue, if that Greek statue had a perfect sphere for a head. The shimmering pools of liquid gold that were Venus' eyes, met Stella's and then darted to her side. Stella's sight breezed past a vacant chair to meet the smoldering glare of an angry Mars. Stella quickly diverted her glance back to the empty chair, and then suddenly realized that Earth should be in that seat. Why, Stella wondered, was her home planet absent? If all the other Planets were here to greet her, why wouldn't Earth also be present? A booming voice pulled her thoughts from that puzzle.

"We welcome you to our Parliament." Jupiter spoke, and it was obvious from his demeanor that something serious was afoot. "We are only sorry to greet you under such grave circumstances." There were quite a few of his moons nearby and they looked up to their host planet with rapt admiration.

In a soft voice, Venus continued, the fine features of her face veiled in wisps of ethereal mists that curled elegantly around the globe of her head. "We see you are small, but believe there is greatness within you. We, Sol's planets, have gathered here in hopes of soliciting your assistance." A grunt of protest erupted from Pluto, but the lovely Planet paid him little mind. "Although some of us fear there is little hope at all."

An irate snarl from Mars shattered the calm Venus had instilled on the Parliament, "If a solution to this crisis is not found, the Terra's foolhardy experiment will be over, wiped away. For while we Planets are in deadly peril, you humans…" the hate in Mars voice was apparent as he spat the words, "face the same annihilation."

At the far end of the dais, a small Planet jumped from his seat and began pacing rapidly before the assembly. Stella almost laughed at this comedic character that seemed unable to keep still and gestured wildly as he spoke. "We must act quickly, for there is little time. Why even now, there are portents of impending doom. The signs in the stars, I have seen them myself!" The Planet's hand jerked up, stabbing towards the ceiling. The place on the dome he pointed to was only a dark stain in space, but Stella knew it was where two stars once had been, for she had watched their demise. As despair twisted his anguished face, the little Planet darted forward. "The extinguished lights; they are harbingers of our demise!"

"That is enough Mercury!" A voice, bubbling as if from oceanic depths, gushed. "We need not discuss our problems in front of this human if it is beyond her abilities to aid us." Mercury skittered back to his chair as Neptune bellowed, "Loony!"

"Ye…Ye…Yes Sir?" the startled moon responded.

"Explain yourself! Why have you brought this…this… creature before us?" Neptune motioned towards the girl, his voice dripping with disdain. "What is it you think she can accomplish?" Stella cringed at Neptune's tone and wondered what these Planets had against humans. If they disliked them so much, why were they bothering with her?

Intimidated, Loony stammered unintelligibly before stopping in embarrassment at his inability to speak. His bulbous head nodded down to his feet, which shuffled nervously.

Saturn addressed the assembly in a voice, dreamy and distant. "I will speak for the Moon of Terra. Loony has been watching the human for some time now, observing her study of the heavens."

"Watching me?" Stella found it hard to believe that she was of any interest to these planetary beings.

"Yes, watching you," Saturn acknowledged. "He believes, along with others of our Parliament," he gestured towards Venus, who graciously nodded back," that with the wisdom accumulated through your diligent studies, you may be able to help us. For one so small, your knowledge must be very great."

Stella couldn't help but notice that not all present shared the same thoughts. Some Planets were clearly holding her in judgment, while others such as Mars, had obviously already condemned her. Only the warm smile of Venus gave her comfort that she might have friends here.

Jupiter continued, "She has been watching the stars and has studied them in ways we cannot. We have seen her eye in the scope searching the heavens. If there is to be hope for us, who else might it be? We need to find a way to aid Sol. Who else here has a plan?" he asked, scanning the Parliament for a response. Whatever was being discussed here, it seemed to be very serious, for the uneasiness amongst them was obvious.

Pluto broke the silence, his icy attitude chilling the discussion. "So then it has fallen upon Terra's Moon, one who is little more than the creature he brings before us, to formulate a plan? By what right does one of his stature dare to fashion our fate?"

With his face darkening and his fist raised in rage, Loony started towards the smallest of the Planets to refute his insult. Then suddenly his hand relaxed and his face brightened, as if a light from somewhere not seen was cast on his face. As his erupting temper evaporated, his rocky lips bent in a crooked grin as he spoke, "By what right, you ask?" With no hint of intimidation he looked from Planet to Planet, catching the gaze of each, before stopping to match the arrogant stare of Uranus. "I am, as are each of you, a member of this system. Though I am only a Moon, I too bask in the light of Him around whom we all orbit. None here have the right to judge me, as only judgment may come from our father, Sol." At the mention of the Sun there was a hush of reverence. "And in his light, I am your equal." Loony pointed towards Stella. "And this 'creature' as you call her, may be greater than any in our system, though you are unwilling to believe it."

Uranus, his face dappled with dark mist, stirred noisily. "Here now! That is ridiculous. This creature is greater than we? Why, it lives only by benevolence of our sister, Terra, who has allowed herself, and only Sol knows why, to be host to numberless hordes of such vermin. You have seen how they treat her and the damage they have done. It is beyond all reason why Terra allows such activity to continue."

Mars sneered. "She never listens. I have begged Terra to purge herself of these parasites who are bent on ruining her!"

"And, I have also!" Mercury cried feverishly. "She will listen to no one! She loves these creatures that cause her nothing but pain, and practice nothing but destruction! It is by her own foolish choice that she endures the human stain."

The Planets began to squabble amongst themselves, the mere mention of Earth having unnerved them. What Stella couldn't understand, was no one mentioned why Terra was absent. How did her mother put it? It was like the elephant in the room, everyone knew it was there, but no one would talk about it.

"We know all about Terra's stubborn resolve in regard to these pests, but, Mercury, you are the closest to her, surely there is something that you can do. Her harboring of these 'humans' …" Pluto snarled, and again Stella felt the icy sting in his words "is dangerous to us all."

Jupiter pointed towards Stella and responded in her defense. "This human, though small, possesses abilities beyond ours. We planets are stuck in our course, tethered to our father, Sol. If the threat we face is to be averted, there is the need for someone to travel beyond our solar system. Who will do that? Will you, Mars?" The angry red Planet did not answer the query, but slunk down in his seat. "Or you Mercury?" Jupiter cast a condemning gaze around the room. "No I thought not. Or perhaps you would, Saturn?"

Saturn glowered from beneath his banded rings. "You know that is impossible, Jupiter. None here have the ability to leave this solar system. We are eternally confined to our orbits."

"That is not true", Venus replied. "There is one here with the freedom to move by her volition." She gently pulled Stella forward." This human has the ability to define her own fate, an ability we Planets do not possess. If fortune were to smile on her, she could accomplish what needs to be done."

"That is what the moon of Terra would have us believe," said Neptune, "but how can we know if that is true, or just some folly that occurred to him, in one of his darker phases?"

Loony muttered something nasty under his breath, and Stella hoped he would maintain his composure, as she was not eager to witness what might happen if he made the watery Planet angry.

"Is the human not able to speak for itself?" Saturn turned his weighty gaze on the girl. "Tell us, do you have the ability of which we are being told? Can you travel beyond Sol's embrace?"

Under the curious eyes of the Planets, whose impatient gaze demanded an answer to a question she had never even pondered, Stella had no good answer to give. "I'm not sure you have the right person," she finally responded. "If you were hoping to find the person whose eye you've seen in the telescope, that wouldn't be me. That's my father, Perceval. He's been an astronomer for years and always has his eye to the scope". She looked around at the beings surrounding her, trying to determine if she was being believed.

Saturn spoke slowly as he studied the girl. "Are you saying that you are not the eye in the telescope? But, Loony pulled you through, and it was your eye that was at the scope when he did."

Stella tried to explain. "That's probably because this is the first night I've had my own telescope. It wasn't my eye you'd seen before, because it was my father who would usually be looking through the scope. Loony should have pulled him up instead of me. If your problem has anything to do with space or the stars, my father would know how to solve it."

Loony moved nearer to Stella and peered into her eyes. "Are you sure about that? The eye I saw was green, same as yours. We need the help of the eye that has watched, and the eye that has studied."

"My eyes are the same color as my father's, and I have the same hair color as my mother's. It's called genetics. It's a thing we humans have that decides what we look like. That's how we 'humans' work." When she said the word humans she looked right at Uranus and tried to say it with as much pride as she could muster.

The crooked mouth of the moon man fell in the small "o" of surprise. "You mean I've grabbed the wrong human?" He whispered.

Stella nodded affirmatively.

Mercury leaned forward in his chair "What did you say, Loony?"

In the blue pools of the moon's eyes, Stella could see shock, and watched as shock turned to shame. Loony answered Mercury, stammering nervously. "Uh, um, I, uh, didn't, uh, say, umm, anything." "Is something wrong, Moon of Terra?" Pluto inquired icily.

"Um, uh, uh, um." The ball headed imp sputtered.

Stella felt horrible for the moon man. If he was being held responsible for pulling up the wrong human and it seemed that this was the case, it looked like he was going to be in deep trouble. Trying to take the attention off him, she spoke up. "I think maybe there was some misunderstanding when Loony pulled me through the scope. He wanted to pull up my father. Maybe, if I went back to Earth, I could talk to him…"

Loony turned irately to Stella. "You're not helping! It's all, your fault! If you hadn't been looking in the scope, if you hadn't taken my hand, if you…." The moon man's face darkened, his eyes narrowing into angry rocky slits. "If you're not the right human, you're going to get me in a lot of trouble!"

Venus appeared at Loony's side and reached out to put a gentle hand on his shoulder. "Loony," the lovely planet's voice was as soothing as a cool breeze on a hot day. "No one is in trouble. You've done well to bring Stella here."

Pluto bolted from his chair. "This is a disaster. Why are we wasting what little time we have with these two? Loony has failed, and we dare not present this human to Sol, he will be angry at our incompetence. Let us dispose of her before he becomes aware of our blunder, if he does not already know." He looked up towards the central star on the ceiling and cowered.

"We have failed Sol!" Mars whined hysterically. "I fear his wrath!"

At this panicked cry, Saturn began to moan dolefully. "We are doomed! Doomed! The darkness is coming and all is lost."

Though the Planets were fretting and quibbling, when Venus spoke her voice calmed the commotion. "Every action has its reasons, as there are no mistakes under the Sun. Perhaps our choice of this girl's father, which we intended to make, was not the right choice at all. Maybe chance has sent us this child as a gift."

Pluto snarled angrily, "And we are supposed to *chance* everything on a human? It is useless if she does not possess the gift of astral travel. If she cannot pass beyond our influence she surely will not be able to find her way to Sol." The icy planet looked anxiously to the luminous central tower. Stella wondered what waited up there and why he seemed to fear it so much. The Sun must be very severe, she decided. "And what if Sol finds that we have put our hopes into one that will not suffice? I, for one, dare not risk his anger."

Uranus spoke. "That is a point that we all must consider. This human, whether brought to us by chance, or choice, must have her abilities tested before we present her to Sol."

Pluto's frosty glare made Stella shudder. "If it is the one Sol seeks, it will need to travel beyond the borders of our solar system. Whoever wishes to leave our system must pass Orthrus, who guards the gate between this solar system and the outer realms of interstellar space." The other planets nodded in agreement.

"We know of your creature, Pluto," said Jupiter. "What are you proposing?"

Pluto stated his case. "We planetary bodies cannot travel outside our orbits, that much is known, but why should we believe that a human can do what we cannot? I propose that before we place our fate in this human's hands, we first test its abilities."

"I really wish you would stop calling me 'it'." Stella interjected angrily, "I think maybe I should just go home. You can find someone else to take your test."

Loony pulled on Stella's sleeve, and as she bent to him, whispered. "But you were the eye in the scope, and you were the one that came through." Then in a last ditch effort to salvage his efforts he turned to address the Planets. "She was able to come here though the scope. That alone is proof that she is capable of moving between the realms of space."

Abruptly, Uranus stood and stomped over. Looming over Loony, who was not half the height of the planet, he scowled down and clucked his tongue. "You tell us this human can offer us aid, but why we should believe you? We are well aware of the phases you go through. What you say today will be different from what you will tell us tomorrow. We know your dark side, though our sister Terra refuses to acknowledge it. Do not pretend your advice should go unquestioned."

Loony glowered like an angry child confronting a parent in a tantrum. Stella watched his face redden, just like the moon she would sometimes see from Earth on autumn days. That dark auburn moon conjured up images of Halloween, and witches and ghosts. "My advice would be to be careful what you say, Uranus." He gestured towards Stella, as if to indicate that it was she who had been insulted and not himself, but no one viewing this exchange could mistake that it was Loony who took offense at Uranus' words. "She is here to do a job for Sol that you can't. Maybe just once you should try to see past your own narrow orbit." Loony was on the tips of his toes as he spit his words at Uranus. Stella could see the mounting anger in the Planet's eyes, but Loony had no intention of backing down.

Uranus bellowed. "Be careful what you say, Moon of Terra! I will not suffer your insults lightly!" It looked as if Uranus was preparing to crush Loony. He towered over the moon in a fury, fists up, ready to strike.

Stella felt suddenly protective of Loony, in the same way she could never bear to see her brothers being hurt. Even in spite of his brash behavior, she had always loved the moon, its changing shape in the sky, and the nights where it lit the landscape with cool pale light. Stella didn't want to see the moon, her moon, hurt by this giant.

The irate imp, blind to the repercussions, continued his tirade. "What are you going to do, Uranus? Or should I say, *YOUR AYN…*"

Cutting Loony off before he could finish his offensive slur, Stella shouted the only thing she could think that would end the confrontation, "I'll take the test

4 A FERRY RIDE

Following Pluto from the courtyard, Stella considered if she shouldn't have offered to take the test before knowing what it was. She was more than a little nervous about where she was being lead, as although Pluto was the smallest of the Planets, he was also, Stella felt, the creepiest. Mars was angry, Uranus enjoyed making people nervous, Saturn was more like a tired old man than anything else, but Pluto was plain weird, reminding Stella of the odd gnomes she had read about in fairy tales. Shuffling along with dragging steps, Pluto headed for one of the houses circling the courtyard, the most remote and desolate dwelling of all.

Gloomy and glacial, Pluto's house resembled a haunted mansion after an ice storm. Skewed steeples dripping with icicles studded the structure's ice covered roof, and from behind the cracked windows, issued a blast of hail more vicious than any ever to afflict the Arctic. In the front yard, the three dwellings of his moons jutted from the barren ground like ghastly tombstones in a wintry graveyard.

As they approached the door, it swung open with an eerie creak and frigid winds gushed from within. Before entering, Stella looked back nervously. Standing just outside the yard, was the entire assembly of Planets and Moons, all watching her every step. At their front stood Loony, who gestured impatiently for her to proceed, but it was the warm smiles of Jupiter and Venus that gave Stella the strength to enter.

Once inside, Stella pulled her parka tight to ward off the chill. She heard the crinkle of cracking ice as the door slammed shut, leaving only the dimmest of light by which to see. As her eyes adjusted to the gloom, she began to make out the furnishings of the dismal residence. All the furniture was shrouded in pale sheets, giving the pieces the appearance of wraiths. Stella couldn't be sure if some of these ghostlike forms moved as she passed, or if it was just the winds whistling hollowly through the room that lifted the sheets with their gusts.

Stella was glad to see that Pluto went straight through the house to the back door. Opening it to reveal a long corridor of purple stardust, she quickly followed him through, for as far as she was concerned she couldn't leave the eerie domicile soon enough. There was a sound in the tunnel, like one you would hear when putting a seashell to your ear; and with each step it grew louder, until it began to roar like waves crashing on a beach. Stella could barely hear Pluto over the noise. "Hurry along, we're almost there." The smallest Planet pulled at Stella's parka impatiently as they continued towards a cold black square that lay at the end of the glowing stardust tunnel.

Stella stepped from the tunnel to join Pluto on a clump of stardust that stood encircled by churning waves. Above, the stars were calmly alight, but below, turbulent swells of energy seethed, smashing against the tiny outcropping upon which the duo perched. Pluto shouted over the din. "You're ride will be here in a moment." He pointed out into the vast ocean of waves to where a small globe of light moved across the sea.

As the light came nearer, Stella could see that it was of all things, a lantern, swung on the bow of a very old boat, rowed by a very old man, whose face was hidden beneath long plaits of graying hair. The tiny craft bobbed and rocked so violently on the perilous sea, that she wondered how he could control it. Pluto tugged at the girl again, and then pointed at the boat and yelled. Stella couldn't hear him through the noise, so she bent and cupped her ear while Pluto screamed up at her, his icy breath chilling her face. "That is Charon." The planet shouted, pointing to the mass of matted hair that manned the oars. "Get in his boat."

Since the ocean seemed incredibly wide and dangerous, and the boat ridiculously small, the whole situation struck Stella as unreasonably risky. "Is this the test; to take a ride? For how long do I need to stay in the boat?"

"This is your ride to the test," Pluto sneered, his mean little face set in a cracked ball of ice. "Charon will ferry you across this ocean to the edge of our Solar System. There you will encounter Orthrus, the guardian of the passage between this system and the outer spaces. If you can prove your ability to find a way past him, we the Planets, will allow you to meet Sol, and he will decide if you are the one to take up his mission. Personally, I do not think you are the one, nor do I think you will complete this challenge, so I will say farewell to you now. Goodbye, foolish human."

Pluto's nastiness made Stella want to shove him off the cliff and into the crashing waves, but she reminded herself that a temper had never made anything better, and usually just made situations worse. With all the warmth of an icicle, the planet pointed to the boat, "Now get in."

Stella understood this was a command, not a request. She looked to the ferryman, who sat motionless at his oars and did nothing to invite her aboard. Studying her surroundings, the sea and the stars, her eyes came to rest on Astraea, who winked warmly. "At least some things are friendly up here", Stella thought as she fell onto her butt, slid off the ledge and stepped unsteadily aboard the rickety boat.

Stella edged closer to Charon. He was dressed in ragged robes, and his wrinkled arms were taut with muscle. His face was covered by thick dirty hair that spread into a long unkempt beard. These clumps of matted hair were much the same thing as what would appear on Sirius, if Stella forgot to brush him. Once upon noticing the dog's wild scratching, she had found a large plait of hair behind his leg. Just that one itchy mass had driven the poor dog crazy. The shaggy ferryman had dozens of such clumps, and Stella was certain whatever face lie beneath the tangled mass of hair, must be grimacing in discomfort.

The ferryman's wrinkled hands pulled on the oars, and Stella grasped the edge of her seat tightly as the boat pulled out onto the sea of waves.

As Charon skillfully steered the craft, the figure of Pluto receded into the distance.

The boat seemed far more ancient than even the ferryman, and that must be very, very, old. It was narrow where Stella sat, and wide in the back. At its center, a short mast stood and the ragged bit of sail that hung there was so torn and shredded, it didn't seem to be of any use in propelling the vessel. Stella wondered to where she was being paddled; knowing it had to do with the edge of the solar system and something that waited there. But as her father had always told her, to understand any problem, you needed to know enough of the variables. She hoped Charon might supply them.

"Hello?" Stella greeted her chaperone. "Where are we going?" Stella could just make out a pair of eyes peering from deep within the mess of hair, but they paid no notice to her and only stared towards the horizon as his arms strained to propel the boat along.

The violence of the waves lessened as the boat went further from shore, and soon the roar of their crashing, was only a soft humming buzz The sound was relaxing and the stars above were bright, and Stella thought that if she could just forget for a moment the challenge that waited at the end of this trip, she might actually enjoy the ride. With one hand gripping her seat she peered over the edge of the boat.

What the boat traveled upon, was an ocean comprised of translucent strings that pulsed and undulated, like a cord when wiggled at both ends. As Stella watched, groups of these strings would oscillate causing the sea to hum with quivering energy. The overall impression was that of a loosely woven fabric, but one with rippling threads, made of something entirely different, something cosmic.

"Cosmic waves; or is it string theory?" She deliberated having heard her father say those words, but never really understanding what he had meant until now. She felt a small pang of loneliness, missing him and all she had left behind on Earth, but she was certain her father would want her to see as much of outer space while she was able. Besides that, before she could get back to Earth, she'd have to pass the test proposed by the Planets. They said that when she did, she would be allowed to meet the Sun. She hoped that when she could explain that she'd been pulled up by mistake, the Sun would send her home. She wondered if the Sun would be like the planets, with the ability to walk and talk. Some of the Planets had been friendly, and she hoped the Sun would be too, but from what she had heard in Heliopolis, he sounded more than a bit frightening. On Earth, the Sun had always been warm and friendly, and Stella couldn't see why he wouldn't be that way in person.

It struck her then as the boat sailed along, that Astraea was a Star too, and if the Sun incredibly could be a being named Sol, then Astraea could also be a person. More than anything else, Stella wished to meet her lucky star, who would surely be friendly.

That thought so cheered Stella that she began to sing a song she had sung with her mother, when they would put the twins to sleep. She could barely remember the words; they were buried under all the numbers and equations that had occupied her mind in the last few months. But once she called that rhyme from deep within, it came beckoning to her quickly, happy to be retrieved.

"Twinkle, twinkle, little star

How I wonder what you are
Up above the world so high
Like a diamond in the sky
Twinkle, twinkle, little star
How I wonder what you are"

As Stella sang, the humming waves rose in accompaniment, following the singsong rhythm. It appeared that the light of Astraea glowed brighter, so the girl repeated the verse, a little louder this time. The star blazed even more brilliantly, pulsing with the highs and lows of the song, and Stella stopped to listen in hopes that it would answer her call. Then Stella sang louder, and again the humming of the waves rejoined, but now a third element joined the tune. A plaintive whistle fell between the low hum of the waves and the higher pitch of the girl's voice. For a moment Stella could not place where the sound came from, until turning in her seat, she faced the surprising source of the sound. It was Charon, whistling along to the tune.

As the ferryman's rowing slowed, Stella realized he was no longer focused on the horizon, but looked only at her. Beneath the thick veil of hair, were eyes dark and mournful that glistened with the welling of tears. From within the matted beard came a voice as forlorn as a cry from the bottom of a dry well, rasping as if it had never tasted a cool drink.

"I remember that song." The voice croaked as Charon pulled his oars across his knees, and laid his hairy face upon them. Weeping sounded from the downcast head as the boat drifted on the waves, and the stars began to spin in spirals above. Stella was still for a moment and then carefully moved across to where the ferryman sat. Seating herself on the bench besides him, she cautiously touched his shoulder.

"Are you okay?" She asked softly. "I didn't mean to upset you."

The unkempt mess of Charon's head shifted, and one moist eye looked up. "No, you did nothing wrong, it's just been so long since I've heard that song." He heaved with a sob. "It reminded me that once I was young, like you. I hadn't thought of that for so long."

Stella took a close look at the eye peering from beneath the knotted hair, and saw it was quite different from any of the others she had seen up here in space. It was unquestionably human. "You're a man?" she blurted out, and then clamped her hand across her mouth embarrassed at her outburst.

The head turned up, the body straightened, and Charon parted his matted locks to reveal a pale wrinkled face. "I was once, but I'm not sure if I am anymore. It's been so long since I've felt any emotion, I'm not sure you'd still call me human."

"You seem human to me." Stella carefully pushed back more of the hair to uncover a face that was cracked and weathered. "That's the most human face I've seen since I left Earth. After so many strange beings, I'm very happy to see it."

Stella reached into the pockets of her parka and fished around through the assortment of stuff that somehow always managed to accumulate there. Within a few seconds she pulled out a hair band. "This should do the trick." She said, holding Charon's long hair back and quickly circling the elastic around it. It took just another moment to adjust the stretchy, so the plastic daisy was visible. Stepping back to admire her work, Stella smiled, "That's better, isn't it?"

Charon's mouth turned up at the corners and his cheeks buckled into a mass of cracks. Stella could see it was an attempt to smile, by a face that had not done so for a long time. "Your song brought back memories of my mother, but I'm not sure I can even remember her face," he lamented.

Stella wasn't sure how to respond to such a sad assertion. "But you remember her song. That means a lot."

Charon looked up with a surprised expression on his face, and then the smile was back, but this time it was bigger and Stella knew it would not fade so quickly. "Yes, I do remember her song, thanks to you." There was a light in his eyes, a warm glow that had not been there before. "And I think I can remember one more! …" Holding one oar he reached behind Stella to grab the other and began to paddle again.

"Row, Row, Row your boat

Gently down the stream

Merrily, Merrily, Merrily, Merrily

Life is but a dream!"

The boat lurched away and Stella fell back abruptly into the crook of Charon's arm. He eased her back onto her seat and they both laughed out loud as the boat smoothly glided forward. Cheerfully drifting along, they sang together, enjoying each other's company. When the ferryman rowed with just one oar, causing the boat to spin in a tight circle, Stella clapped and let out a cry of glee.

"Charon?" Stella asked at a moment when they had paused in their singing. "I haven't introduced myself." She held out her hand and Charon took it in his. Stella had never felt anything more rough and blistered. "My name is Stella Ray. I'm very happy to have met you."

Charon's smile widened. "And it is a pleasure meeting you, Stella Ray." He squeezed the girl's hand with such ardor, that for a second she was afraid it would be crushed, but when the ferryman let go there was no harm at all. He grasped the oars again as if he felt more comfortable holding them, and leisurely rowed as he spoke. "I've been ferrying this boat for quite a long time, but you are the first passenger whose name I've learned. I've never spoken to anyone I have ferried; they all seem so sad and afraid, that I'm certain the reasons they need my services, are not happy ones. But you are quite different, quite cheerful, so I'm going to ask you, why has Pluto sent you to the end of the Solar System? You do realize what awaits you there?"

The questions brought Stella's anxiety flooding back. "The Planets want to see if I can get outside the solar system. I'm not exactly sure how to do that, Pluto didn't say much; But to tell the truth." She tapped her foot nervously against the boat's side, "I'm sort of nervous."

His concern was evident as the ferryman spoke. "If I take you to the end of the Solar System, as I have been commanded, you will be at the mercy of the beast guarding the gate that leads beyond. Only Pluto can control the brute, and without his consent no one may pass. Those who have tried have met a terrible end. Let me ferry you elsewhere," he implored, "perhaps to some other shore."

Stella tapped her foot faster. "Well, there must be a way to get past, or else they wouldn't bother giving me the test, right? If I don't do this I think the Planets won't return me to Earth. I need complete this challenge if I want to get home."

"But it is a terrible beast," the ferryman offered, "...and vicious. It has large sharp teeth and feeds on those who dare try to pass. Listen!" He hushed and the sound of howling could be heard over the soft hum of the ocean. The eerie sound gave Stella the shivers. "That is Orthrus", Charon cautioned, "He knows you're coming".

For the rest of the trip, Charon couldn't persuade Stella to turn back, though he tried desperately to convince her that she had no chance against the beast. As they neared their destination, he became quiet, paddling silently, resigned to the fact that the girl could not be dissuaded. Dark cliffs appeared, and Charon navigated towards a pier that stretched from them. The ferry bumped lightly against the large posts that supported the pier over the churning waves, and the stardust glowed slightly as contact was made. A cold wind blew from the cliffs.

"I'll wait for you here." Charon said glumly as he helped Stella onto the dock. As a loud growl roared from the darkness, the ferryman offered the girl his boat's lantern. "Take this light, you might need it."

Stella thanked her ancient friend, and then turned into the wind that gusted down the long dock. Zipping her parka tight to her neck, she moved forward into the bleak shadowy haze. The light that filtered from the lantern offered little illumination, so Stella made sure to stay in the middle of the walkway and not risk falling into the turbulent ocean below. When she was nearly halfway to the cliffs, she could make out just beyond her small circle of dim light, something piled next to one of the pier's posts. Approaching cautiously, she held the lamp high over the heap and was surprised to find the bundle was a child, squatting with his arms wrapped tightly around his shins, and his face hidden between his knees.

"Hello?" Stella asked, and the ashen face of a young boy barely older than her brothers looked up. Finding it hard to believe a boy was here alone at the end of the Solar System, so far from Earth, Stella rubbed her eyes. "Are you okay?"

The boy's pale countenance brightened under the lantern's glow, "Are you my guide?"

"Your guide? I don't think so."

"But you have a light, and only guides carry lights...I think…" He seemed confused, as if just awakening from a long sleep.

"What are you doing here?" a stunned Stella asked.

"I'm waiting for my guide," he answered, still huddled against the post. "Are you sure you're not one?"

"Yes, I'm sure I'm not a guide. But how did you get here? Where did you come from?"

"I'm not really sure. I had a bad fever, and my parents took me to the hospital. I remember just going to sleep and when I woke up, I was on that ferry, and the man paddling… Chiroc? Cheeran?"

"*Charon.*" Stella corrected gently, holding the lantern closer to get a good look at the boy's face. To her surprise, he cast no shadow, and the light from the lamp passed through him unimpeded.

Managing a weak smile, the boy pointed down the pier. "Right, that's it. The guy in that boat, *Charon…*" As his arm lifted, Stella could see stars through the ghostly limb. Quickly, she checked her own hand, relieved to find that her flesh still had substance. "He left us here."

Stella almost dropped the lantern upon understanding the boy was not aware of his own state, one she had just chillingly realized.

"Our guide took everyone through that gate, but I was afraid, so I stayed back here and hid. Now I can't go anywhere. I can't go back and I definitely can't go forward. There's something behind that door, something really scary."

Stella didn't need to hear how frightening whatever lay ahead of her might be. She was frightened enough speaking to the spirit before her, though she felt ashamed of being spooked by such a helpless boy. "You said *we*. Where have the others gone?"

"They went through the gate. And I don't know how I know this, but when you go through that gate, you don't come back. I don't want to go. I want to go home!"

Stella didn't like the way that sounded.

The boy looked puzzled. "If you're not a guide, then where is yours?"

"I don't have one, I guess. But I have to get through that gate anyway." Stella held her hand out. "Do you want to come with me?"

The boy shook his head. "No way. We can't get past the monster; it's impossible without a guide. Another guide has to come by eventually. I'll just wait here," The boy whispered forlornly, "alone..."

Stella continued walking down the pier, now without the lantern. Not willing to leave the boy alone in the dark, she had lent him Charon's lantern. If she could get past the gate and whatever it was that waited on the other side, she would come back for him, and help him on his journey. She knew now, though the knowledge was unsettling, what that journey was, and why the boy could never return to the Earth. "I just hope I don't end up the same way." she murmured worriedly

5 ORTHRUS

Without the lantern, Stella proceeded cautiously down the dock towards the high cliffs that loomed ahead. Set within the craggy stardust wall was a massive door, unfathomably old and so weathered and cracked, that it had been fitted with many large braces to hold it together. The door was set into the cliffs between two massive pillars capped with an enormous slab of rough-hewn stardust, and held there by many large makeshift hinges on one side, but only one small latch on the other.

"If I walked through this gate would I really step beyond the Solar System?" Stella wondered, thinking the challenge couldn't be that easy. Standing on the tips of her toes she reached to unhook the latch, but as her fingers brushed the door, a ferocious bark erupted from within. Jumping back, she cautioned herself, "Maybe I should find out what's on the other side before I open this door."

Searching her pockets for her penlight, she fumbled among a clutter of objects; an old key, a domino (number seven, a three and a four, her two favorite numbers), a broken toy car. She dug deeper, certain the light was in there. Something wet and slimy met her touch. "Yuck!!" Stella squealed as she pulled the gooey clump from her pocket, examining it between two fingers. It was one of Sirius' dog treats, half eaten and soggy with slobber. "Gross!"

Stella was about to flick the sloppy tidbit into the ocean of cosmic waves, but remembering how they were in very short supply at the Dome, decided to save it for Sirius. She'd give it to him, she thought hopefully, when she got back home. "Ugh!" she sputtered, holding open the pocket on the front of her parka and gingerly sliding the sticky biscuit in. Reaching back into her hip pocket and hoping there would be no more surprises, Stella touched a set of keys, a small plastic lizard, and another dog biscuit (thankfully fresh and dry) and felt two pencil nubs, and an old cassette tape. "How did this get in there?" Stella asked herself. The fading ink on the tape's label reminded Stella that the tape was a lecture of her father's, titled "Does time reverse in a black hole?" It was the lecture that had made him famous, sort of, so putting it back in her pocket, she kept fumbling until she found the penlight.

Checking for a gap wide enough to see through, Stella moved along the edge of the door. She discovered a crack right above her head, that when standing on her toes, she could just see through. Aiming the penlight through the narrow fissure, Stella whispered. "Hello? Is anyone there?"

A snarling response surged through the crack on a blast of stinking, steaming air. Stella retreated from the odious fumes. "Pee U!!" She gasped, "Someone needs mouthwash!" Holding her breath, she peered once again into the crack, and the light of her penlight reflected off an enormous red eyeball.

Over a low simmering growl, Stella fearfully implored the eye. "I hope I'm not bothering you, but if you don't mind, I need to open this gate for a moment. I don't want to disturb you, but the Planets want to see if I can leave the Solar System, which is sort of a challenge they set for me..." The response to her plea was another blast of stinking breath, the stench of which made Stella queasy. The overwhelming smell was like that of Sirius' breath, after he had eaten the kind dog food labeled "fish flavor". Holding her breath, Stella quickly moved from the door to ponder her dilemma.

Charon had said Orthrus was some type of beast. Jupiter had called Orthrus, Pluto's pet. The breath of whatever was behind the door, smelled just like the breath of her dog. All clues pointed to the fact, that what lurked over the threshold might be some kind of dog, but Stella found it hard to believe there could be such an animal out here. In space there was only one "dog" she knew of, and that was the constellation Sirius, after whom she named her own pet.

From out of the blue an idea came to Stella. The creature's bark and smelly breath made her pretty sure that Orthrus was some kind of dog, and if it were, she'd bet it'd liked treats as much as her dog. Searching her pockets again, she found two full biscuits and the broken half of another. To test her idea, she held the broken biscuit to the crack.

"Hey boy! Want a biscuit? Come on, boy! Come on, Orthrus!!" Stella tried to sound cheery, as if she were playing with Sirius back home, though she was more than a bit frightened, certain that whatever was behind the gate was something that shouldn't be played with. A loud sniff came from the crack, and in an instant ferocious clawing could be heard from within the gate.

"Want the biscuit, boy?" Stella shouted as the commotion on the other side of the gate intensified, while trying to convince her own self that Orthrus was even listening. "If I give you the biscuit you'll be my friend, right?" She slid the broken biscuit through the crack beneath the door, and the scratching stopped, to be immediately replaced by a burst of vicious chomping ,

"Good Orthrus! If you're a good boy, I have another biscuit for you. Just let me pass and I'll give you other treats, okay?" Slobbering was the only response. "So, it's okay for me to open this gate and give you another biscuit?" Cautiously, Stella reached for the latch, continuing to cajole the creature. "We're friends, right?"

As her fingers touched the latch, crazed barking exploded from within the gate, and Stella bolted back in dismay. "Oh please Orthrus, please! Let me pass! I won't stop for even a second! I'll just run right by you."

Completing this challenge, Stella realized, was going to be trickier then she had thought. Taking her father's cassette from her pocket, and spooling out the tape, she tied it to the latch, tugging lightly to feel the bolt shift in the lock. If she pulled any harder the latch would open. As Orthrus barked, Stella unrolled a long length of tape, and slid the cassette back into her pocket.

Overhead, where it joined the stardust cliff, the top of the doorframe formed a narrow shelf. Though it would be a bit of a climb, it was not much higher than the top of her father's telescope, and Stella had always climbed that, easily. So with one end of the tape still tied to the latch, she wedged a foot into a gouge in the door and began to climb. As she grabbed the crack in the doorframe, hot breath warmed her fingers. Then finding a small hold a couple feet overhead, she pulled herself further up. Though on the other side of the door Orthrus was going wild, Stella concentrated on the climb, and soon made her way to the top of the door. Pulling herself up onto the narrow ledge of stardust, she breathed a sigh of relief that there was enough room to stand.

Once on the slim shelf, Stella examined her surroundings. Below lay the dock at whose end, she could just make out Charon's boat bobbing on the cosmic waves. The spectral boy, barely visible in the lantern's dim light, hadn't moved at all and still huddled against the post. Stella checked that the cassette was still in her pocket and the long piece of tape still stretched to the latch. A gentle tug showed the knot still held tight. Now that all the pieces of her plan were in place, it was time to put it into effect. If it didn't work, Stella anxiously reminded herself, she could be trapped on the ledge for a long, long time.

From her perch Stella pulled on the tape and the bolt slid from the latch. What had secured the gate and what waited behind it, was now gone. "Come on boy! Come get your biscuit!" Stella shouted, and as if on command, the beast burst through the gateway. It was not so much a dog, as an enormous wolf that appeared, raving and drooling and hungry for a meal. It took only a bewildered second for the monster to find where Stella was, and when it did, it jumped wildly to reach her. Its jaws came within mere feet of the girl's feet, and looking down past the sharp snapping teeth, she could see within the beast, a fiery furnace. Just one misstep would send her plunging into the beast's maw, it being so wide her body could pass without being chewed.

"Without being chewed? Stop thinking like that!" Stella admonished herself. Examining one of the biscuits, she wondered if she had miscalculated. The beast appeared ravenously hungry, but the biscuit was merely a crumb to such a giant. However, it was her only chance, and holding the biscuit over the beast's mouth she hoped it would notice. Just as if tempting Sirius with a treat, she boldly taunted, "Orthrus want a biscuit?" At its sight, the creature went wild and leaped high into the air, reaching almost where Stella stood. She quickly pulled the biscuit away, further enraging the brute. Whenever she had done this with Sirius, it had been a game of harmless teasing. Her pet would never bite, but if this beast could reach, it would eagerly chomp off her arm.

At least, Stella thought, the first part of the plan had worked, but now that Orthrus was going crazy, she had to make sure the monster saw what she would do next. She remembered how sometimes Sirius had gotten so wound up, that he didn't even notice when she threw the biscuit, and would just stare at her empty hands, wondering where the treat had gone. It was important that Orthrus saw the throw. Stella had only two biscuits and that meant two chances. If she didn't accomplish her plan with those, she would be trapped on the ledge indefinitely.

"Okay", Stella shouted, trying to get Orthrus as excited as possible before she flung the biscuit. "Here you go, boy! Chase the biscuit!!" The monster bounded after the airborne morsel. Stella watched the biscuit's flight, hoping it would reach its target, but her heart sank when the biscuit fell short, landing on the dock a few feet from the ocean. The monster pounced on the biscuit, gobbled it down in a gulp and in a flash was back at the door, frantically jumping to get to Stella.

She waited for the wind to abate before she made her second throw. This was her last biscuit, and her last chance. When the wind died down, she threw the biscuit with all her might, almost falling from the ledge in the process. Her hope rose as the biscuit hit only inches from the dock's edge, but just as it was about to bounce into the ocean Orthrus snatched it from the air in his slathering jaws.

With both biscuits gone Stella's plan had failed. Disappointed and shivering in her parka, she slunk against the wall and wondered how long she could last on the ledge. Below, Orthrus frantically clawed at the gateway, desperate to reach his next meal. His hungry howling was nerve shattering and Stella tucked her head deep into the fluff of her parka to muffle the sound. With her face hunched into her chest, she sat wishing for just one more chance.

It seemed her mind was playing a cruel trick on her, as the smell of dog biscuits reeked through her sniffles. Lifting her head to test the air, the scent disappeared, with no hint on the breeze of what she'd smelt just seconds before. Putting her face back into the cavity between her chest and knees she sniffed around, taking deep whiffs until she located the source of the smell, curiously, at her chest pocket. Pulling out the half eaten biscuit she had saved for Sirius, Stella jumped up so fast; she nearly lost her footing on the ledge.

This was the chance she had wished for, and determined to use it well, she decided to put all her strength into this next throw and not let worries about falling hold her back. This would be her absolute last chance and if this attempt failed, she would fall soon enough. Dangling the tiny morsel over the edge, her hope was renewed as the creature went wild. "Want another biscuit, Orthrus? Gonna fetch the biscuit?" she shouted, knowing the crazed barking meant yes.

Stella threw the biscuit as hard as she could towards the crashing cosmic waves and held her breath as Orthrus gave chase. His hungry eyes never left the morsel that flew spinning through space, over his head. Stella's spirit surged as Orthrus lunged at the treat that fell towards the waves. He leapt from the dock and clamped his jaws down on the biscuit. Then, with an enormous splash, the creature that guarded the gate at the end of the Solar System, crashed into the turbulent sea, and was lost amidst the crashing waves.

Stella sighed in relief and then gasped as Orthrus explosively reemerged, his enormous paws paddling furiously towards the dock. The seething ocean smashed the beast but he struggled so mightily, that for a moment it looked as if he might save himself. But each time the wild-eyed creature surged forward, it was beaten back by the waves of cosmic energy, until finally the frenzied beast succumbed. With one last haunting howl, Orthrus sunk in the pulsing ocean and disappeared.

Stella stared at the spot where Orthrus had vanished, until she was certain he was gone for good. Remembering the holds used when going up, she carefully climbed down from her perch. Going cautiously to the edge of the dock, she peered once more into the roiling ocean, until assured her plan had indeed worked, then turned to face the gateway.

The battered door was flung open wide and a soft glow radiated from within. All that was left to do was to walk through, and the challenge would be won. Stella held herself tall and proud as she strolled through the open gateway, "When all the Planets hear about this, I bet they won't ever call me a stupid human again!"

"Wait! Wait for me!" A small voice cried, and Stella turned to see a light moving through the haze. "Take me with you! Please!" Out of the mists came the pale boy holding Charon's lamp, and where there had been the pride of victory, Stella now felt the sharp sting of shame, realizing what she had forgotten in all the excitement. "You weren't going to leave me here, were you?" The boy's asked dejectedly.

Deciding a little lie wouldn't be too wrong given the circumstances, Stella answered, "of course not," and then taking the lamp from the boy, she continued. "I was only going to make sure nothing dangerous was on the other side of the gate, and then I was coming back for you."

"Even if there is something bad on the other side", he beamed, "I'm sure you'll find a way around it. I saw how you beat that monster! You must be the bravest person I've ever met!"

Stella smiled, "Thanks, now stay here a second while I make sure there are no more 'monsters' on the other side. Okay?"

The boy nodded his head enthusiastically. Stella walked to doorway, stuck her head through and glanced around. "It's safe, we can go through." The boy, tentative of his next few steps, reached for her hand. She took it gently, and felt as if her grasp could almost pass through his fingers, so ghostly had his body become.

Reaching the threshold, the boy hesitated. Then peeking through the gate, he smiled broadly. "I can't believe I was afraid of this!" Excitedly pulling Stella along with every step, he became more wraithlike. Soon all that remained of him was a mere wisp and his hand passed through Stella's. She watched him, now nothing more than an ethereal mist, drift away into the vastness of outer space, but before he disappeared completely, a final question was asked. "What's your name anyway?"

She shouted out. "Stella Ray!"

From the depths came an echo, barely above a whisper. "Thank you, Stella Ray!"

With the Planets' challenge completed, Stella savoring her success, stood at the gateway and looked around. Out here on the perimeter there was nothing but stars, vivid and alive in a whole new way. Skimming past the constellations of Lupus and Libra, and looking above the crescent of stars known as the Corona Borealis, Stella found Astraea. As if she had been waiting for Stella's eyes to land upon her, the star blazed brilliantly alight.

A ray of Astraea's light flared through space, and following it, Stella's attention was drawn to a cluster of stars arranged in the shape of a hook. Well familiar with the constellations, she knew this group was named Scorpio, and it was easy to see how it could be mistaken for its sharp tailed, pincer's namesake. Each of its glowering lights pulsed hypnotically, and it was impossible for Stella to dismiss the feeling that these stars were subtly different from all the rest in the sky, that they were somehow abnormal, somehow profane. Mesmerized with an enchantment she found difficult to dispel, Stella watched as the stars of this arachnid constellation dislodged from their places in the heavens, and began to move through space. Out of nowhere, a mantle of seething smoke, blacker than night, appeared to cloak the creeping skeleton of stars.

As the shroud of shadow enveloped the constellation's starry frame, the dark shape of a scorpion was formed. Two claws snapping menacingly, emerged from the smoke, and a tail, the end of which was capped with a curved, deadly looking spike, began to whip across the heavens. On six spidery legs the giant insect scurried towards its prey. Struck with revulsion, Stella moved to escape but found herself paralyzed by something other than fear. A weight fell upon her heart, heaviness on her limbs, and she could not look away from the approaching horror, no matter how she tried.

The shadowy scorpion was almost upon her, its body blocking out the light of all other stars. The clattering of its claws was loud in Stella's ears as she stared into beady eyes devoid of all warmth, the eyes of a predator, of a killer. From the twitching mandibles that lay beneath those insect eyes, came a hissing voice. "Foolish human, did you really think you could challenge Moros?? Your fate is sealed, and your journey done. Now fall to the sting of Scorpio!!" Whipping back, the scorpion's tail poised to strike.

There was a flash from above, as a shard of brilliance blocked the assault. The dark creature recoiled with a shriek, as the radiant figure of a woman wielding a luminous sword, let forth a flurry of swift and sure blows. As its claws stabbed and snapped, the woman skillfully fended off the scorpion's attacks with her dazzling blade, and forced the poisonous insect away from the girl it had threatened. Though dwarfed by the monstrous scorpion she drove the creature back, and with each strike it retreated further.

As the woman's sword clashed against the jabbing pincers, the scorpion's deadly stinger readied to strike. Stella screamed in warning as the barbed tail lashed out and the woman of light, alerted by the cry, twisted clear of the stinger and in one swift slash, severed it from the scorpion's body. The barb exploded in a noxious mist as it fell through space.

Stella's protector dashed in for a finishing blow, but before she could strike, the wounded scorpion fled back into the darkness, leaving only a smoldering stain against the night. It seemed to Stella the battle was done, but before she could thank her rescuer, an angry bellow roared through space. Both turned to where another group of stars was ripping from their place in the firmament. They quickly assumed the form of an enormous bull, composed of the same dark smoke as the scorpion. In a mad gallop, it charged towards the luminous woman who raised her blade to ready for the onslaught. She turned briefly to confirm the girl's safety, and in that instant,

Stella saw her face was both as beautiful as the morning and terrible as an army with banners.

"Escape!" The woman shouted before rushing to meet her horned opponent.

Fleeing back through the gateway, Stella raced down the pier to the ferry, where Charon greeted her so happily; his smiling face appeared on the verge of cracking in pieces. After helping the girl to her seat, he pulled at his oars, and the boat swung swiftly off across the sea of cosmic waves.

Trying to make sense of what happened wasn't easy. Stella wasn't sure why the Scorpion had attacked her or what it meant when it had spoken of "Moros". She hoped the woman who saved her was okay, but as she watched the dock fade from view, she mostly felt anxiety about what might be planned for her next. She had beaten Orthrus and made her way out of the solar system. Now, from the way the Planets had spoken, they would send her to the Sun.

Charon was humming his ditties as he happily rowed along, and hearing his tune Stella couldn't help to think of her family back home. She wondered if they had noticed she was gone, and if her mother was okay, and if the boys were behaving. She imagined her father was probably even now in his observatory, working on equations to explain the strange phenomena of the disappearing stars they had observed. Lost amidst all these thoughts, Stella stared out across the oscillating ocean.

Beneath the waves something flitted past, breaking Stella from her reverie. The boat's bobbing made it hard to track whatever it was, but certain something was out there, Stella peered over the edge of the boat. Suddenly, there it was again, a dark shape, no, two, darting through the waves. As they broke the surface of the sea Stella saw they were two large fish, black as night, and following the boat. "Charon?" she asked, interrupting the ferryman's song. "What are those?"

Slowing his rowing the ferryman exclaimed. "Those fish? Why, I've never seen them before! I haven't seen fish since I was back on Earth. Did you by any chance bring them along with you?" Unworried and carefree, he went back to rowing while happily humming his newly remembered tunes.

The uncomfortable feeling of being spied on crept over Stella. Whenever the shadowy fish approached the boat, and she tried for a better look, they would quickly drop back. But if she looked away for just a moment, they were back close, studying her with dark disc eyes. It was so unnerving that she moved from the back of the boat and sat next to the ferryman, concentrating on the sound of his happy humming, and trying to not think about what was trailing them.

Somewhere along the way, the fish must have gotten bored with their chase, because when the ferry finished its passage, they were nowhere to be seen. Now Stella's concern turned to Pluto, who stood on the cliff with a frown frozen on his icy face, as if not pleased she had made it back. When Charon helped her up onto the cliff, she saw that Pluto was more shocked than angry and even more so to see Charon, no longer brooding, but now with a bright smile on his face. The plastic daisy in the ferryman's hair glittered; as he turned the boat quickly out onto the cosmic sea.

"Good bye and Good luck Stella Ray! I hope to sing with you again someday!" He shouted, as he rowed off and Stella couldn't help but smile as she heard above the crashing waves, the whistling of the song she had helped him remember.

6 A GIFT FROM EARTH

As they walked back through the tunnel, Pluto questioned Stella as to what had happened. "Well, Orthrus won't be scaring anyone any more." She announced proudly, not saying more, but savoring that Pluto could scarcely believe she had completed his challenge.

"And what do you mean by that?" The Planet asked sourly.

"Just what I said," Stella retorted, in a dismissive tone that had her mother heard it, would have gotten her in big trouble. Trouble that probably wasn't worth it, as what she said didn't feel as good as she thought being so snotty would feel.

Continuing to walk in uneasy silence, Stella trailed her hand along the wall of the tunnel and watched the flecks of light swirl. She still wasn't sure of what this wall and the rest of the things she had seen here in space were composed. It wasn't dirt or rock or the kinds of things you might find on Earth, but something entirely different. How would Stella describe dirt to Pluto, if she cared to try? Dirt would probably seem as alien to him, as the strange substance she now walked on was to her. This stuff was most likely the same to the Planets as dirt was to people on Earth, stuff that had been around for so long that no one questioned it anymore.

"What is this stuff?" She asked kicking a little clump of translucent flecks into the air, and watching it dissipate before it could touch down again.

"It's star dust." The icy planet grumbled, approaching the door to his house.

"What's that?" Stella asked inquisitively.

"It's just what I said." Pluto said, with a vengeful smile on his face as he stepped into the frigid rooms of his mansion. Trying not to dwell on the nastiness of his answer, but instead on exactly what he meant, she remembered the theory that everything originally came from a "Big Bang" that formed the universe. All matter came from one giant star that had exploded and started everything. That one star had shattered into dust, and all that *star dust* had come together in different combinations to make everything that existed. It sort of made sense, though sometimes thinking about how that could happen, baffled Stella.

Thinking of something else, made passing through Pluto's house less unpleasant and when Stella stepped outside, Loony was waiting. Pluto brushed past Loony, and the moon man stuck out his tongue, put his thumbs in his ears and wiggled his fingers behind the icy planet's back. Stella found herself laughing at his antics, thinking perhaps he was the closest thing to a friend she might have up here.

"So you won the challenge and made it out of the Solar System! What was it like? What did you see?" Loony was so excited, he grabbed Stella's hand and pulled her along. Stella was so glad to be back, that she didn't even mind. "You'll have to tell me quick. The Planets are gathering. You should see their faces; I've never seen them so surprised. You sure threw them out of their orbits, if you know what I mean!"

As they waited for the Planets to assemble, Stella told Loony as fast as she could, about her adventure. Loony almost tripped over his feet when she explained how Orthrus had crashed into the waves, never to be seen again. Stella felt proud to see how impressed he was, but she ended her story there, not certain she should tell Loony about the scorpion or the dazzling woman who had saved her. Something inside told her maybe she shouldn't talk about that just yet, and should wait to hear what the Planets had to say.

"Well", Loony said, seeing that the parliament had taken their seats. "They're ready."

As Stella walked into the circle of Planets, every eye was fixed on her, and for a moment she didn't know what to do. She felt on display and didn't like it. She looked to Loony, but he was hiding behind her, the craggy hollows of his eyes peeking nervously from her side. And Stella had thought he was her friend!

Stella decided that she wasn't going to be bullied by any of the Planets any longer. After all, she had done their challenge, hadn't she? She had done something none of the planets themselves had ever done. That was something to be proud of, wasn't it? So, head held high, she stepped before the Parliament of Planets.

Pluto watched silently with icy eyes, while Saturn sat with the weighty globe of his head, resting on his fist and studying every move the girl made. Neptune, the features of his face veiled by watery mists, passed a hand over his eyes, and in the momentary clearing, Stella saw his stark eyes unblinking like a fish's, staring at her.

Noticing Earth was still not in attendance; Stella's puzzlement was dismissed by the sound of soft clapping. Venus, with a loving smile on her face, brought her two small hands together. Jupiter joined in, the sounds of his massive hands filling the chamber. Then Neptune began to clap, and for a moment the air was filled with the sound of applause.

Loony was suddenly back by Stella's side. "I guess this means we did good!"

"*We*!" Stella seethed. There was no, *we,* when she climbed the gateway, and there was no, *we* when she had tricked Orthrus into jumping into the crashing waves. One minute, Loony was abandoning her, the next; he was her best friend. Stella decided she needed to tell the moon man how a real friend behaved, but this wasn't the place or the time.

Venus went to Stella and bent to whisper. "Terra wants me to tell you how very proud she is of you." Then leading Stella forward, Venus silenced the applause. "She has completed the challenge," she announced, "and accomplished what none have ever done before. She has passed into the outer darkness and returned. For that alone she should be honored."

Jupiter gestured, "Métis, Io…" and two of the moons that had been hovering about the giant Planet's throne, ran forward. "Bring a chair for our brave young friend." The moons ran off, reappearing seconds later.

Venus nodded and Stella took it as a signal to sit. Though the chair wasn't big enough for two, as she sat, Loony quickly squeezed in next to her. His elbow was in her side, jabbing her ribs as he jostled for more room on the seat. Not wanting to make a scene in front of the Planets, she suppressed a grimace of pain and turned angrily towards Loony. The oblivious moon man only flashed a grin, showing crooked rows of rocky teeth.

Venus continued. "We had decided that if this human completed the task we would submit her to our Sun, Sol, for consideration as our champion." At this sentiment, a grumble arose from members of the dais, as Mercury, Saturn and Pluto shifted with obvious irritability upon their thrones. "Is there any disagreement that she has indeed completed the challenge set before her?"

Mercury and Uranus feigned uneasy ignorance, as if not understanding the question posed. Pluto looked at these planets and seeing they were going to be of no help in answering, exploded. "The human didn't fight Orthrus. She tricked him and is doing the same to us. She won the challenge through trickery!"

Venus gently responded to the outburst. "What was the challenge that we presented to her? Do you remember what it was, Pluto?"

"She was to make her way out of our Solar System, and into the spaces beyond." Pluto said, with a suspicious look on his face. He seemed to know, Venus was going to use his own words to prove his accusations false.

"And did the she complete that challenge?" she asked soothingly.

"Yes, she completed the challenge," Pluto admitted begrudgingly. "But Orthrus was my pet and she killed him!" Pluto was more upset than Stella had realized. She hadn't known he was so attached to the beast.

"Then," Venus offered, "She did not *trick* anyone, but merely did what she needed to do, to accomplish the mission."

With the way the icy planet was glaring at her, Stella appreciated that Venus was trying to smooth things over with him. She didn't want another enemy among the Planets, already knowing that at least one planet, Mars, blamed her for whatever ailed Earth.

Jupiter stood to address the Parliament. "She has succeeded, and if there are no more objections, I propose she be sent to Sol. He will assess whether she will be his champion."

Stella groaned. Things were getting further and further out of hand. Completing the challenge hadn't succeeded in getting her out of this strange situation, instead it had only dug her in deeper. "When will I be sent back to Earth?" she wondered aloud.

At the mention of Earth, the Planets shifted nervously. Understanding that there was something she was not being told, Stella decided that now was the time to find out what that was. Trying to sound as naive as possible, she asked, "By the way, where is Earth?" The Planets all straightened stiffly in their chairs and though aware of their discomfort, Stella continued, feigning ignorance of their unease. "I would really like to meet her."

Before any Planet could respond, Loony was tapping Stella's shoulder. His rocky lower lip trembled and if the moon had water, which Stella knew it didn't, she imagined the moon man's eyes would be full of tears. Sobbing pitifully he explained. "I guess you should know that Terra is awfully sick. I'm the closest to her, but she won't even speak to me. There's something happening to her that I know isn't good."

How scared Loony looked made Stella very nervous. "How sick is she?"

Venus answered. "That Terra is not well is true, but she is safe. Her fate however, may hang in your hands alone, human child."

"And perhaps the fate of us all…" The somber interruption drew the chamber's attention to Saturn. From his throne he slowly poked the floor, and with that touch, the inscriptions he had written there began to move. Stella couldn't really tell what he had written from her chair, but what she could see looked like equations, the kind her father wrote when hard at work on his whiteboard, only Saturn's equations moved. As the ringed Planet passed his hand over the writing, the numbers and letters rearranged and recombined into new permutations, and the diagrams spun and shifted to form intricate geometrical designs. As the formulations slid around the floor, some of the numbers and letters drifted away, moving beyond Saturn's reach. From behind his throne, a number of moons fanned out to retrieve the renegade text that they gently corralled back in front of the melancholy Planet. Saturn studied these as if for portents, and all eyes in the chamber anxiously watched these conjurations, waiting for some further pronouncement.

"The Stars are of a magnitude of majesty above us, and as such, beyond our understanding. However, I have learned that Terra has been attacked by an evil that seeks to challenge the dominion of the Stars themselves."

Everyone listened intently, as there was something about Saturn, though sullen and mysterious, that commanded respect.

"Though she is bearing the brunt of this battle, Terra is not alone in her sorrows." As if what he was about to admit pained him, the heavily robed planet sighed, "and recently, in the course of my studies, I discovered a way to move through time. Determined to know the future I cast myself forward, only to be halted by a wall of darkness not far ahead. Perhaps it was foolishness but desiring to learn what lay within that void, I endeavored to enter. I had only put my toe in when I recoiled in horror and pain." The ringed planet lifted his heavy robes to display a foot absent of toes. The Planets let out a collective gasp of horror. "This was the reward for my curiosity. From that brief contact with what awaits, I learned of a fate so terrible as to defy description. Something, I know not what, intends to plunge the universe into darkness. All that now exists will perish."

The gloomy figure wearily raised his ringed head, and Stella looked into somber eyes that had seen much more, than their ability to understand. Collapsing on his throne, Saturn thrust one finger at the dome above, pointing to the place where light had been and that was now only a patch of empty space. "Just as those Stars, no longer exist…"

An anxious hush hung over the Parliament. Stella hadn't realized it, but as the ringed Planet had spoken, Loony had sidled up to her and pressed tight against her side. She reached down to put her arm around the moon man's trembling shoulders.

After what seemed an eternity of dreadful silence, Jupiter stood. "Uh, yes," he began, making an obvious effort to suppress any tone of distress. "It seems things are more serious than we had previously supposed. I thank our brother Saturn for his valuable efforts and sympathize with him for his injury." The ringed Planet did not acknowledge the accolade but only stared grimly at the ever-changing array of equations at his feet.

Uranus jumped from his seat. Moving to where Stella sat, the watery planet eyed the girl suspiciously. "How do we know that it was not she who extinguished those stars?" he snarled accusingly.

"I didn't destroy those stars." Stella countered fiercely.

"Who else was there?" Uranus spurted, abruptly returning to his seat.

Jupiter spoke, ignoring the watery Planet's outburst. "This human has successfully accomplished the task we had set before her. Now we must keep our part of the bargain and allow her an audience with Old Sol."

Mars jumped from his seat. "I am against it! We cannot allow a human to meet him whom none of us have ever met…" His ruddy face flushed a livid red as he abruptly ceased his tirade suddenly embarrassed.

"Silence, Mars! We will not discuss that in front of the human!" Uranus shouted.

"You will not discuss what?" Stella insisted. "What have none of you ever done? If there's something you want from me, you'd better tell me what you're hiding." Glancing from Planet to Planet, each avoided her gaze until she reached the end of the dais, and Pluto.

"Yes, yes…" the tiny Planet's voice dripped with icy malaise, "tell the human of our shame. Inform her how none of us have ever met Sol." Every Planet shot angry looks at Pluto, obviously irate at his disclosure.

"What did you say?" Stella asked.

After glancing in annoyance at Pluto, Venus softly answered. "It is true, Stella. None of us have ever met our Sun. We cannot ascend to his realm and he has never deigned to descend to ours. We know him only through his gracious light which keeps us alive. Light is the lifeblood of the universe."

"None of you have met the Sun? Then why did you act like I wasn't worthy?"

Jupiter spoke, giving the closest thing to an apology Stella would receive from the Planets, for their deceit." It was believed that you would never complete the challenge and we would not have to reveal our shame. But you have earned a right, none of us have ever been granted. You will ascend to the Sun's chamber."

"The human will be rejected." Mars snarled. "Just as none of us have been granted audience with Sol, so shall it be with her."

"But that is not for us to decide. It will be Sol himself who will choose whether to meet with Stella." Venus whispered reverently, looking up, to the vibrant representation of the Sun that hung at the center of the great starred dome. "But before that, I believe our guest should rest. It would be best if she were refreshed before she meets our Sun."

"Could I?" Stella asked, stifling a yawn and realizing just how tired she was. It had been a long day, or night, or however it was that time worked up here. There were lots of things she didn't understand, but sleep was too good an idea to pass up; rather than try to figure it all out now. Maybe, Stella thought, all this craziness would make sense when she awoke.

Venus nodded kindly and taking the girl's hand, led her from the Parliament. Passing the abode of Mars, whose fortified walls spotted with weapon ready turrets that hardly seemed inviting, they moved on in the direction of Venus' palace. Not stopping at that lovely structure, they continued to the pleasant cottage beyond.

"I'm sure my sister wouldn't mind your resting here." Walking through the lovely garden that surrounded the cottage, Stella was thrilled to smell the scents of Earth. The aroma of flowers and plants intermingled with the refreshing whiffs of a warm spring breeze. Inside, the cottage had all the charm of a rustic cabin. A bed sat in the corner of the room, covered with soft downy quilts, patched in every color. Stella flopped on top of it, and even though she would like to explore this wonderful house, she could barely keep her eyes open.

"I hope you find this suitable." Venus whispered.

Exhausted, Stella curled on the soft bed and murmured drowsily. "It's wonderful!"

"I will leave you to sleep, but first…" the beautiful planet knelt beside the bed…"This is a gift from someone who loves you very much." Stella was surprised to be receiving a gift, not able to think of anyone she and Venus would have in common.

Venus placed in Stella's palm, a small ball hung on a thin chain. It took just second to see that the intricately carved trinket was an exquisitely detailed miniature of Earth, so finely detailed, that Stella could feel beneath her fingers, the bumpiness of the mountain ranges and the smoothness of the waters. A thin chain, comprised of every metal from Earth, was attached to the globe at the North Pole, fitted to a very tiny, but perfectly sculpted, model of the observatory dome. All the oceans were crafted from inlaid gems, and each continent, from different woods.

A thin crack ran around the wonderful bauble at the equator. Lifting a small clasp Stella opened the case. Inside, beneath a clear glass bubble, a filigree arrow slowly spun. She spun the globe slowly and watched the needle spin freely. "I've never seen anything like this before," she commented drowsily, "It's like a compass but with added directions of up and down."

"A compass? No." Venus corrected, "What you're holding is a *Compyxx*, made by someone who thinks you are very special. Terra has crafted this for you and wants you to know that wherever you go, a part of her will be with you, just as you will always be part of her. Wherever you might travel, this *Compyxx* will lead you home."

Before Stella could ask just where she was going, Venus stopped her. "It's time to sleep, you need your rest." The lovely Planet backed quietly to the door and before she had left Earth's cozy cottage, Stella was asleep.

"Wake up! Wake up!" With a poke in the ribs and a voice at her ear, Stella was stirred. "Come on, time to get up. The Sun has risen!"

"Just a few more moments, I'll get up in just a couple minutes," Stella murmured. She pulled her parka snugly over her shoulders, tucked her knees to her chest and tried to find her way back to the dream she had been having.

She slipped quickly back beyond the wall of sleep. Curled upon the bed, she held the dangling globe by its thin chain to her eye and saw the little ball was no longer just a finely crafted trinket, but was now a whole world teeming with life. All of humanity in their tireless travels and endless transits, hung by the slender thread in her hand. Stella trembled realizing the awesome responsibility with which she had been entrusted.

As the ball spun slowly on its chain, she felt herself drawn towards the surface of this diminutive Earth. With so much going on, so many people, so many stories being played out before her, the astounding amount of activity was overwhelming. Her vision raced in dizzying flight across the lively landscape, before heading north, to where the chain from which the Compyxx spun was attached. Ensconced in the tiny arctic observatory, was another Stella who began to climb link by link, the chain from which the world was suspended, unaware that the efforts she exerted would only lead back to Earth. Stella wanted to shout and tell the girl of the futility of her climb but held her tongue; somehow knowing her voice could never be heard, except as some distant thunder in the sky.

After scaling the links to a distance high above the crafted globe, Stella looked down. Instead of the Earth, populated with the toiling legions of mankind, the globe below was now densely speckled with a host of sparkling lights, bright against a blue ball. Looking above to where the stars should be, in the sphere that comprised the vault of heaven, she could see that for each light that had hung, there was now a human being. All this reminded Stella that she was in a dream, where logic scarcely applied.

At that realization, a conjuration sounded, "Everything will merge into the night until the great and the small are joined in the light." When the words had ceased, Stella noticed the chain to which she had clung was no longer there. Suppressing the urge to scream, she plunged through space. It was precisely halfway through this harrowing descent between the Earth above and the Stars below, that the moon appeared, silver and shining. Reaching out and grabbing the girl by the shoulders, he stopped her fall. "Get up!" Loony's voice reverberated, as Stella flew up from the well of dreams. "Get up now!"

Surprised at not waking in her bed, she pushed Loony away, who even as he landed with a thud on the floor demanded, "The Sun is up, and you must rise to meet the Sun!"

"Okay! Relax! Just give me a second!" Rubbing the sleep from her eyes, Stella rolled from under the soft stardust quilts and sat on the edge of the bed.

"We need to go now, before the Planets stop you." Loony blurted impatiently.

"Why would they stop me? Didn't I pass their test? Don't they want me to meet the Sun?" Stella asked, pulling on her parka.

"Some do and some don't, but those who don't, have been scheming to find a way to stop you." The moon man looked around, the tiny eyes in the rocky sockets shifting from left to right as he peered about the cozy room. When certain they were alone, he whispered secretively. "Mars and Pluto are saying that you're responsible for those Stars going out. They say you'll probably try to extinguish Sol, if you're given the chance to meet him."

This was all too much for Stella. One minute the Planets wanted her to go on their mission, and the next moment, they wanted to stop her.

"But the Sun wants to meet you, right now. He doesn't want any interference from the Planets. He told me he has a plan and that you're a big part of it."

"You've talked to him?" Stella exclaimed, with surprise. "I thought he was someone no one talked to. Isn't it supposed to be impossible to meet with him?"

Loony became even more furtive, and skulked over to a window near the bed. He slyly pulled aside the curtain and peeked out, then did the same at each window in the room, while Stella looked on with puzzlement at his paranoid pantomime. Quietly sliding back to Stella's side, he moved his large head close to her face. "I talk to Old Sol all the time." He whispered conspiratorially. His voice, though low and guarded, beamed with pride. "And he wants to see you, right away."

Stella would have liked to stay in Earth's house a bit longer, it was warm and comfortable, but not being caught by angry Planets sounded like a good reason to hurry. The moon man nervously peered out the door and then together they stealthily made their way towards the tower at the center of the courtyard. Cautiously, Loony snuck along on the tips of his toes, and the spectacle of his round head bobbing up and down as he proceeded desperate not too make a sound, looked so ridiculous, that if Stella were not scared half out of her wits, she might almost laugh out loud.

Even so, an amused giggle could be heard, and Stella turned to find Venus walking beside her. "Out of all the moons in our Solar system, Luna is surely the most unique." The planet smiled down at Stella while matching her every step.

Hearing his name, Loony turned back. A hostile grimace formed on his rocky face as he realized their escape had been discovered. "Don't laugh at me, Venus, and don't try to stop us."

The loveliest of Planets replied in a pleasant voice. "Have no fear, moon of my sister; I would not delay the progress of one with determination such as yours. You are free to do what you like. Your choices are your own, and I have faith that in the end, every choice will be proven the correct one. I only want a word with our young friend before you spirit her away."

Under Loony's harsh glare, Venus led Stella away to where they would not be overheard, and then gathering her long flowing gown, knelt next to the girl. Stella found herself engrossed in the soft swirls of warm tans and browns that moved like summer clouds across the Planet's face. As she studied the topology of the globe, her eyes came to rest on the soft features that rose from its surface. Though Venus was not human, but a being strange beyond comprehension, her face was beautiful nonetheless. Stella followed Venus' serene glance to where Loony paced nervously at a distance.

"What a handful Loony can be. But despite being oft times troublesome for Terra, she cares for him deeply." Venus sighed as she cast a melancholic look towards the irritated moon man. "I, myself, have no moons."

Stella nodded, knowing that fact from her time studying the planets. While at the Parliament, attendant moons had surrounded the other planets, only Mercury and Venus had no such retinue. Stella thought they had both seemed a bit lonely.

. "For all the trouble that Luna can be, I would gladly have him in my orbit, if it were so fated." Venus looked towards Loony, who, catching her glance, stuck out a tongue the color and texture of gravel. She turned back to Stella with lovely pitiful eyes. "Saturn has told me that in his visions, he has seen a companion with you on your quest. He believes that companion will be Terra's moon."

Stella wondered why he would ever want to accompany her. What Venus said next was in a whisper so low, that Stella moved closer to make out the words. "You'll need to be careful if he goes with you. The further you travel from Terra, the less her influence will be over him. Loony's dark side is usually kept in balance by the light of Old Sol and the influence of Terra. Now, with her not well, and his contact with her scant, he has been behaving more erratic than ever before."

"I can only hope he will realize the seriousness of your mission, and do nothing to hinder you. The fate of your mission might hang on the ability of Loony to remain in light, and not surrender to his darker tendencies. I only wanted to warn you of the possibility." The Planet concluded with a seriousness that made Stella warily scrutinize the irate imp.

Loony, who had been waiting impatiently, noticed the girl's attention and grumbled. "If you're done with your chat, maybe we can get going. I don't want to keep the big guy waiting."

"*The big guy*?" Venus chuckled. "Is that how you refer to Old Sol? Surely dear Loony, even you could be a little more respectful."

The moon man flashed a nasty grin. "Perhaps Venus, you should not be so quick to give advice on things you know little about." And with that, took Stella's hand and escorted her towards the tower stairs

7 MERRY OLD SOL

As Loony led the way up the stairs that ran around the giant column, Stella felt a little afraid but even more excited. She hadn't seen the Sun since she had moved to the North Pole, and in all that time there had been only the dark of night. Now she was not only going to see the Sun but also meet him. The Sun, from what she could understand, was a person in the same inexplicable way, that the Moons and Planets were people.

Looking up, she had to turn from the light overhead. So brilliant that her eyes could not stand to look at it, she knew without a doubt it was sunlight that blinded her. This light was brighter than all the other stars displayed on the canopy that covered Heliopolis. This made sense, because the Sun was the star closest to the Planets, and appeared brightest to them. Though it was just one of millions in the sky, it was special to Stella nonetheless, as its light had warmed her since birth. Now with the strangeness of all that had befallen her, nearly overwhelming her, she prepared to meet the life-giving Sun.

Loony was unflagging in his rush upwards, his little legs never faltering, taking every step in rapid succession. Though the ceiling of stars hadn't looked so distant from the courtyard, the lofty perspective the duo had achieved, told Stella they had climbed very high and there was further to go. As they ascended, the city of Heliopolis, its courtyard and outlying avenues, were all displayed below. "Is that the whole Solar system?" she asked between breathless huffing.

Loony didn't break his stride as he effortlessly replied. "Yep, that's it, that's the whole ball of wax."

Heliopolis looked so small from this vantage point, like a town fit for dolls. Stella chuckled to herself, remembering how impressed she had first been. "I'm glad I have gotten it all in proper perspective now," she thought. "The Planets act just like anyone you might meet on Earth. Their grandeur hardly makes any difference; some of them behave very poorly." Now she would see what the Sun was really like, if she could find the strength to continue the climb, "Are we almost there?" she asked, wondering if her legs would hold up.

"Be patient!" Loony replied impatiently.

As they climbed higher, the light gradually enveloped the duo. Soon it was so bright that, Stella, blinded by its brilliance, shut her eyes tight. For just a second, she let go of the railing. Quickly reaching back to find it gone she groped for some guidance until Loony's hand met hers and pulled her onward. She followed his tug gratefully. "How do you know where you're going? I can't see a thing." Stella whimpered.

"If you can't see why don't you open your eyes?" Loony responded. His pull stopped and Stella felt his small hand leave hers.

"Yes, please," A voice, other than Loony's chuckled heartily. "Why, if you want to see, would you close your eyes?"

The lids of the girl's eyes reluctantly unclenched. As the dazzling glare abated Stella who thought she could be surprised no more, was astonished. For where she had been led, up through the very heart of the Solar System and through the blinding storm of light, was to a small and simple room. Its furnishings though made of glistening stardust, were nothing more than a few roughhewn chairs and table. The one distinguishing element to the room was that it was not square, but circular. Its curved walls were lined on the bottom half with numerous drawers and cabinets, while the upper half was set with windows open to the vastness of space. Stella looked to see where she had come from, but behind her was only a mass of dazzling incandescent light. The light flooded the room and spilled out through the windows all around, its bright shafts piercing the darkness of space beyond.

Stella recognized it as very much like a place she had been in once before, when her family had vacationed on the coast. "A lighthouse," Stella chuckled,

"I'm in a lighthouse." She had climbed with her mother to the top while her father waited far below with Tim and Pace. They stood with their back to the lighthouse lantern and stared out into the sea around them. The place where she had now arrived was just like that, and it felt strange to be in a place that had so much in common with that lighthouse room on Earth.

"Welcome!" A voice boomed, and within the blazing beacon appeared the figure of a man. As he stepped forward, it was immediately apparent to Stella that although no larger in size than Jupiter, somehow, and she couldn't put her finger on exactly how this was so, this being was undeniably grander.

"So, this is our heroine?" A hand like glowing gold reached out. "It is a pleasure to meet a daughter of Terra." Stella could not bring herself to take the extended hand, fearing she would be terribly scorched. The puzzlement on Stella's face prompted him to ask. "Don't you know me? I am the Sun of your Solar System! I am Old Sol!" The words came from a mouth as fiery as a furnace, surrounded by a beard that blazed in an irrepressible conflagration. He placed the seemingly hazardous hand on Stella's shoulder, which to her surprise did not burn, but warmed her in the most delightful way.

Her eyes squinting while shifting her head, the familiarity of this being suddenly struck Stella. He was indeed the Sun she had seen in the Earth's sky, in the same impossible way that Loony was the Moon she saw at night. But as the facts in her head clashed with the reality of what her heart told her, the absurdity of it all struck home. Stella managed only a few words through her bewilderment. "How can you be the Sun?"

"Perhaps I have some explaining to do that will make it easier for you to believe." Old Sol chuckled, and the roiling swirls of hot gas that formed curls of hair around his head shook as he did." I imagine the humans who live on Terra's surface have some very strange beliefs about what goes on out here in space."

"I'd say!" Loony, who was now stalking the perimeter of the lighthouse room, sneered as he peeked into a slightly opened drawer. "She thought I was a chunk of rock! Are humans that dumb?"

Old Sol laughed off the moon man's jibe, though Stella didn't find it funny. "Let me explain another way of how things might work. I think you'll find it interesting." Walking to the table, he politely pulled out a chair. Accepting the invitation, Stella sat, noting the chair would be just like any of the millions of chairs on Earth if it weren't made of glittering stardust.

"Somewhere along the way," the Sun began, "a bit of confusion has arisen amongst humans about the nature of things. For example, they think of me as a large burning ball without thoughts and feelings, which rises every morning in their sky. But I am aware, that I am much more than a fiery ball, much in the same way that humans are conscious of being more than just lumps of Earth's clay."

"But being in our bodies sometimes makes it difficult to observe things from any other perspective. This inability affects the way we view ourselves, and we think of only what lies within the confines of our body, and forget all we really are. From another higher perspective, we would see that we are something quite more than fire and clay. For there is something wonderful that manifests through us; in quite the same way that light can be focused through a lens to become fire. Humans, from what I've noticed, form the most perfect of lenses to focus the light, even more so than Planets and Stars."

"Each and every human has a tiny part of them that is capable of remembering how important they are to everything else, and how perfectly they fit into the grand scheme of things. But sometimes that small but most important bit can get lost and confused in the hubbub surrounding it." Old Sol pulled a glowing wisp from the flames that were his hair, and held it out. "But when that small part remembers itself, you have a thing that humans call *consciousness*, and what I would call, *the inmost light*." He blew gently on the wick and it burst into brilliant flame.

Studying the light for a moment, Stella felt herself drawn to it as if it were something she had lost, and now wanted to reclaim. "Venus told me that light is the lifeblood of the universe," she mentioned.

"Yes, I imagine she sees it that way. My Planets are prone to seeing only part of the whole picture."

"What's the rest then?" Stella asked.

Old Sol stared deep into the girl's eyes as if weighing that interior quality of being, of which he had just spoken. The sign he sought, must have been evident, as he whispered, "the Planets are unaware of the pulse of the universe."

"*Pulse of the universe?*"

"Yes," He said softly. "For if the lifeblood of the universe is light; then the pulse of the universe is time. Time allows light to flow through the universe. If there were no time there would be no movement, no life, and no light. And although I have been alight much longer than you, both Stars and humans live in the flow of time. And why I have had you brought here is nothing less than a matter of time."

Noticing the girl's confusion, Sol explained. "In the course of my existence, I have witnessed the birth of Planets and the death of Stars; but the rise of your kind, was a rare moment, unique in this galaxy and possibly the Universe. "The passion in Sol's speech reminded Stella of her father's, when he became excited by some discovery. "That is the reason why at this desperate time, I have turned to the humans of Earth. It is your kind, and if I am not mistaken, you in particular, who can save us from the terrible dilemma with which we are faced."

Stella sat up in her chair. "Me? How can I be involved with whatever is threatening to the Universe?"

Old Sol smiled. "I know it's hard to understand, but I believe your kind holds potential greater than any in the universe, though nothing is easier for humans to do, than err in their notions of the distinctions between the great and the small. Let me show you something."

Reaching into the fiery mass of his head, he pulled from it a fleck of flame barely the size of a marble, and stretching as far as he could, placed it in space. With just a gentle tap, it began to orbit his head slowly. Then, from his flaming whiskers he pulled out three more clumps of flame and began to juggle them, quickly shaping them into balls of varying sizes. Placing one a little closer than the first, he tapped it quickly to set it spinning around his head, all the while juggling the two remaining balls with one hand. With his free hand he pulled more balls from the flames atop his head, and Stella clapped with glee as one by one he flipped them skillfully into orbit. To finish his performance, Old Sol threw the two juggled balls deftly into their orbits, and took a slight bow as the nine spheres circled his head forming a perfect model of the Solar System.

Pointing to the miniature planets revolving around his head, he continued. "My planets, all nine of them are tied to me inextricably, and though you can't see them, they are right now revolving around me as they always have. They have no other choice. They continually follow and do not veer from their appointed paths. It's just that here now in my lighthouse, you perceive me in a different, and I hope, not unpleasant way."

"Now watch this!" Sol exclaimed. The chairs, the walls and the whole of the lighthouse room suddenly vanished, and Old Sol began to grow or Stella to shrink or perhaps both were happening at the same time. Old Sol's smile was lost in a haze of nuclear heat as he swelled into a massive flaming orb, and Stella screamed as she felt herself shrink into a mere speck.

What had a moment ago, been Old Sol, was now a far away and unbelievably huge Sun. Planets slowly orbited the fiery globe; and with a pang of anxiety Stella noticed that the Earth was missing. It was only the edge of a small blue ball appearing from behind the Sun that calmed her. Before she could get a good look at Earth, Stella suddenly felt like a balloon being filled with air in one quick gust. She was getting larger while the Sun was getting smaller. Features became distinct, as glowing eyes and a bright smile formed from the curls of flame that erupted from the blazing surface of the Sun, and in the wink of an eye Stella was facing Old Sol once more.

"How did you do that?" Stella gasped, as she fell back into her chair.

"I really didn't do anything", Sol answered nonchalantly, though the smile on his face showed he was pleased with his performance." I only wanted you to see that big and small are only a matter of perspective, while greatness is another matter altogether," he said, his eyes brightening and his smile blazing. "Now I suppose you have another question you'd like to ask me, am I correct?"

Stella did have a question, one she didn't have a clue as to what the answer might be. She didn't think this was the question that Sol expected her to ask, but it was the one she really wanted answered. "Why me?"

From nearby, Loony who had been peeking into the cabinets and closets that lined the lighthouse walls, answered absentmindedly, "Because she was the one who was looking through the scope!" Stella could tell the moon man was not really sure, even though he acted very confident when he had spoken to the Planets.

"That's part of it," Old Sol responded," but there's something more, something special about our friend here."

Stella had to ask, "Special? What's so special about me? Why do you need me so badly?" "I don't!" Loony retorted. "I wasn't asking you!" Stella shot back.

"Sounded like you did!" And before Old Sol could reprimand him, the moon man skipped off.

Exasperated, Stella fumed, "He's crazy, isn't he?"

"I've heard he has a dark side," Old Sol confided, "But to be honest, I've never seen it. I imagine it hasn't been easy for him, what with Terra's absence." There was sorrow in the Sun's eyes as he watched Loony's bulbous head bobbing away.

"But why you? After studying the beings that live on Terra's surface, I've come to the conclusion that there's a spark in them unlike anything else. That spark is definitely not from within our universe. It comes from somewhere beyond. I'm hoping that spark can lead a human back to where stars and planets are unable to go. The planets orbit around me by no choice of their own and are unable to veer from their endless circumnavigations, just as I am fated to hold my course through the galaxy."

Using his finger on the tabletop Old Sol traced a series of circles, one inside the other. "Try, for the moment, to think of the universe as a series of nested balls, or shells, one inside the other. The boundary of the universe is the outmost shell and inside that would be shells of galaxies, and stars and planets, each growing smaller and all encompassing the final shell…" Drawing the smallest circle he took his thumb and pressed it into the center. "…*Earth.*"

He moved his finger outside the largest circle. "The spark that makes humans so special comes from a place out here, past the bounds of the universe. When a human is born they blaze a trail as they fall through the spheres of stars and planets. The path they travel while speeding to Earth, is one defined by the alignment of the planets and stars at that particular moment. The time of their birth is marked by that unique configuration of the stars and planets." He traced with his finger a line through the shells to the thumbprint marking Earth.

"Then the cosmos shifts again, the planets turn, the galaxies whirl and the trail is lost." Sol blew lightly on the tabletop and the wheels within wheels of his sketch began to turn at various speeds, clockwise and counterclockwise.

As they turned, each took in its rotation the little bit of sketched line that marked the passage, and in no time the path was scrambled.

"Lost!" Stella echoed forlornly, feeling more distressed by the demonstration than she would have expected.

"Watch though," Old Sol whispered as the wheels spun, "as how sometimes on that person's birth date, the cosmos turns back to the positions that had been in place when the human was first born, and the path that the human had entered upon is realigned and the way back is unlocked." And the wheels did turn and Stella watched as the line that had been broken became whole again.

"If the spark within has not been extinguished, it might be possible for the human to retrace the course back up," Old Sol uttered softly, "and find the way back out of the universe. We were hoping," he lifted a bright finger through the air, leaving a wispy trail of flame in its wake and pointed at Stella, "that the human who could do that, might be you."

"But why me?" She asked again.

"That is always the question, isn't it?" Old Sol queried. "It is your birthday, is it not?"

Stella nodded her head and a smile bloomed on Sol's beaming face.

"Now, how the universe works is not quite as simple as my explanation, but I hope you get the idea. Humans, and no other beings in the whole of our vast universe, are the possessors of this freedom to travel. It's why we need you so badly to take up this mission."

There was another question, one that Stella was not sure she wanted answered. "What is this big problem that everyone up here has been talking?"

The smile left Old Sol's face and Stella had an inkling that he was going to tell her something she probably didn't want to hear. "The problem," he stated gravely, "is that the *Celestial Clockwork* is winding down."

"*The celestial clockwork*?" she repeated, unsure of what that meant.

"Yeah," Loony snorted from nearby, "*The Celestial Clockwork*. Which word didn't you understand?"

Old Sol sighed in resignation. "*The Celestial Clockwork*", he offered, when certain there would be no further interruptions "is that which animates the whole of the universe, bringing light and life to both Star and human alike. It is the source of all time and what you might call the heart of our universe. But now it has become apparent that someone is tampering with the clockwork. Someone…"

Loony's head popped up next to the table… "Not just someone! It's Moros! You know that!"…And disappeared just as quickly beneath.

"*SOMEONE*!" The Sun countered, "Is trying to stop the clockwork. If that happens, everything will stop dead. If the Celestial Clockwork falters and time ends, all will be entombed in darkness. In this there is no distinction between humans, stars, or planets. We all face the same extinction."

Beneath the table Loony squirmed, bumping and crushing Stella's feet, making it very difficult for her to concentrate. She remembered her father had told her, the universe could be seen as a machine where each part worked in sync with all the other parts, but she couldn't remember him mentioning any Celestial Clockwork; no matter how hard she tried.

"How could time end? Isn't time something that will always happen?" She felt the sharp jab of a stony elbow in her shin and kicked with her foot, aiming to push Loony away.

"Time is what allows things to take place. If the clockwork stopped, there would be no time in which anything could happen. Even rays of light would be frozen, unable to shine. Without time there would be only darkness."

"So who is this Moros, and why would he want to stop light?" Stella asked.

Old Sol moved to one of the windows circling the room; Stella followed glad to leave the table and the annoyance underneath. From there the planets were visible moving slowly through space, orbiting the lighthouse of the Sun. "There are those who play a part that might seem disagreeable to most, but are necessary nevertheless. Although it might be hard to comprehend from the small space we occupy, every part, the great and the small, the good and bad, are essential to the working of the grand design. Each tick of the clockwork, each movement of the cosmos, is hinged upon the total performance of all, though most do not realize in the slightest, the essential part they play, just as you, Stella, do not yet understand yours."

"What part is that?" she asked.

"The clockwork can only be wound from outside the universe. The power to reanimate the clockwork and time, issues from the same place as does the spark of humanity. Time will run down soon, unless you," Sol's eyes settled on the girl, "can travel to the Celestial Clockwork and wind it."

Now that Loony was no longer underfoot there was a chance to think with no distractions. "I guess I understand. Winding the clockwork from inside the universe would be like me trying to start my own heart, if it were stopped!" Then realizing the analogy she was making was not quite right, Stella corrected herself. "But wait, I'm part of the universe, aren't I? How would I be able to wind what I'm part of? It would still be like I was winding myself. It gets very tricky knowing where inside and outside begin and end!" She exclaimed.

Sol smiled at the girl's bewilderment and stroked his bearded chin. "It is not an easy thing to understand, in fact, I'm not sure that it is the kind of thing that you can ever understand with just your head. It's sometimes better to let your heart make things clear. A human's heart, I believe, could contain the whole universe, if their heads didn't take up so much space." He counseled.

"Perhaps it would be better not to force some ideas into the tight confines of knowing, and best if these wonderfully confounding thoughts, were left free to play unfettered in your mind. Otherwise it would be like locking a playful pet in a tight cage and how much fun would that be?"

Stella could feel all sorts of dark thoughts roaming around in her head, and to tell the truth it wasn't enjoyable. Thinking about the Stars she had seen extinguished, the horrible monster Orthrus, and the scorpion that had attacked her, were nearly too much to deal with.

From across the room Loony shouted. "Fun? Nobody better have any fun without me! A trip sounds like a lot of fun! You'd better be taking me along!"

Stella whispered to Old Sol, low enough she hoped, that Loony couldn't hear. "I keep trying to tell everyone, you don't want me for this mission. You want my father. He's so smart, he'd know exactly what to do."

"I really feel, Stella, that you're the one. And besides," The Sun chuckled merrily, "Loony would feel horrible if he thought he had brought up the wrong human."

The Sun was so warm, Stella smiled back. "Well, even though he's a bit unpredictable, I like Loony, he's the closest to a real person I've met here." Suddenly feeling embarrassed by what she had said Stella quickly backtracked. "I mean, I like you a lot, Old Sol. You're really nice, but, uh, um…"

"I understand completely, Stella. I'm not as *human* as Loony. It would be hard not to see how different he is from other celestial beings. Terra and her children have affected him tremendously. He's the closest to Terra, and has had quite a bit of exposure to humans. He has become, let's just say, a little odd due to that close proximity. All my Planets have noticed it."

"Why do some of the Planets talk about humans as if we're bad?"

The whiskers of flame around Sol's mouth sulked. "I'm sorry about that. But I guess that some of the planets in my solar system are angry about what they believe humans have done to Terra."

"What have I ever done to hurt the Earth?" Stella asked, but as she did, her voice was drowned out by a loud screeching noise that abruptly filled the air.

"Stand behind me", Old Sol commanded over the din, and not knowing what was happening, Stella quickly did as she was told. The lighthouse room suddenly darkened as the screeching intensified to what sounded like a thousand cats hissing, mixed with the roar of an army of bulldozers rumbling. It was the most horrible sound Stella had ever heard. Holding her ears she peeked around the bulk of the sun.

A vortex, the color of lead, was forming in front of Old Sol, ripping through space. From within the growing rift, a pair of dark eyes leered, holding the young girl lasciviously in their steely gaze. She wanted to turn away, but couldn't.

"Keep close behind me and don't say anything," Old Sol whispered, his light flaring brighter. Stella could feel enormous power swelling within him, who was also the Sun that had warmed her since birth.

The eyes, black diamonds within the blistering void, bloomed into flowers of obsidian shards, and from within each blossom, sprang serpents whose tails were anchored to the vortex that had been the pupil of each. Unfolding like sheets of origami being cruelly mutilated, the serpents spindled out. The crumpled snakes strained to mimic clawed fingers surrounding palms, from which unblinking, un-lidded eyes resembling black oily pearls stared. While the darkening storm swelled, these haphazard pairs of hands joined in obscene grasps to perform a ghastly display of shadow puppetry, aping ravens struggling for flight from the horror in which they were ensnared. Razor'd talons closed on the necks of the struggling birds and strangled them in a flurry of unbridled rage. From the ensuing turmoil, glared ravens' eyes, each a shining trapezoid of frozen blood, an asymmetrical ruby, whose jagged facets endlessly reflected the tortured avian heads. Stella gasped at the utter wrongness of the spectacle as the last of the birds was violently dragged into the maelstrom of black angled shards, which were rapidly reconfiguring in a series of clattering shuddering jerks.

What had appeared before the girl and the Sun was a seething tempest of shadow and smoke, a dark storm-cloud laced with spiking bolts of night, which penetrated space like the fractures in a breaking egg. From behind a rush of hot air buffeted Stella, as if any warmth was being ripped from the surroundings, and dragged into this jagged void to be extinguished.

The shadow spoke, crackling like a radio that could not be properly tuned and as it moved forward, a nearby chair of stardust shuddered at its passing, turned dark and exploded into splinters of black ice. "So this is your champion, Sol? This human?" Moros howled in a screeching whine of feedback. "Have you sunk to such low spaces that you consort with the vermin that infest the Earth? You would waste your dwindling time parlaying with this fledgling? They are but mice in the cathedral of space."

Sol whispered to Stella. "Stay behind me, no harm will come to you if you are near me."

From the shadow, a command spiked out on forked tongues. "Listen to me, human! Time grows short. With every tick the clock winds down. Can you hear it?"

It jolted Stella to realize that she did hear, as clearly as if it had always been there, a ticking that seemed to permeate… everything. It was a bewildering sound, one which, what to make of it, she wasn't quite sure. It wasn't that the ticking was loud, because the sound of the shadowy being's cackling was of greater volume. But it couldn't be called soft, because each tick seemed to overpower everything else. As Stella listened, she could somehow sense the effort the clockwork took to tick just once more. The interval between ticks felt as if it could never be filled, an eternity of fretful waiting in hopes of the continuation of…everything, and in that anxious moment, the whole of reality seemed to dim as a gloom snuck in. Stella gasped in relief, as a tock filled the void and the suspense was broken and the light of the universe flared back to full strength.

"With every tick the clockwork weakens and my strength grows! Soon nothing will be able to withstand my power, and darkness will reign over all!"

Sol countered the darkness, with a power in his voice Stella had not detected before. "Agent of darkness, you are not welcome here! I compel you to return to the void from which you came."

Shrieking with diabolical malice, the shadow spewed jagged tentacles that crackled around Sol. "You would command me, Sol? I think not! Your weak glow cannot dispel me! I go where I desire. The light of this universe will soon fail, then only darkness will hold dominion!" A shriek of static screeched, as the crackling intensity of the form stabbed towards Sol who lurched back, almost knocking Stella to the floor.

"Do you hear me, creature of dirt and mud?" Knowing Moros was addressing her, Stella crouched more tightly behind Sol." Do you dare presume you can change what has been fated? You who are not, even of the Stars?" As the shadow cackled with demented laughter, bolts of dark matter viciously slashed Old Sol who momentarily reeled. Icy fingers reached around him, groping for the girl.

As Stella cringed, an incandescent heat rose to meet the frigid dark. A sphere of warmth surged from the Sun, forcing back the assault of night. Spirals of flame billowed from Sol, and each dark shard Moros flung was met with one of these swirling coils of light. A thousand conflicts raged in the space, as black lightning clashed against sun drenched clouds. Bright and dark, angle and curve, their clash seemed bent on shattering space itself.

Over the roar of the battle Moros crowed. "I've amused myself with you and your filthy pet enough for now, Sol. Though I'd like to stay and play some more, I have more important business which to attend. But I leave you with a reminder of what lies ahead."

There was a split second of total darkness, and then in an instant, the shadowy shards retracted into the void of Moros' body, folding inwards in ways that confused Stella's eyes. With the ragged sound of a zipper zipping, the ragged rift in space closed and Moros was gone.

What had been chaos now was quiet and still. The Sun turned to where Stella was crouched on the lighthouse floor. His voice was strained. "That was unfortunate for you to have endured, but he's gone and no harm done."

The change the girl saw on her friend's face was shocking. A dimness began to take more definitive form, as stormy clouds cast dire shadows across the bright yellow surface of the Sun. Muddy blotches formed where had been brilliant flames, and darkness where there was once light. Looking at the stains on the Sun, Stella was dismayed. "What was that?" She asked with a quivering voice.

A crash sounded across the room and the girl nearly jumped out of her skin, fearing it signaled the return of Moros. From beneath a jumble of collapsed chairs blown through the room in the battle, out popped, Loony. "Yeah," the cratered head asked, "What was that?"

"That", Old Sol answered grimly, "was Moros, the adversary responsible for the grave dilemma with which we are faced. He and his minions believe that when the Celestial Clockwork runs down, only darkness and death will prevail. They will do anything to stop the clockwork from being wound and restored to its full power."

Stella had never been more frightened. "His minions? You mean there are more like him? And they want to destroy light? Can they do that?"

Old Sol was somber, as the flames about his face smoldered. "When the Celestial Clockwork is in need of winding, there is the chance to upset the balance of light and darkness. For those who harbor such diabolical ambitions, this window of opportunity comes but once in millennia. Only the oldest of Stars have any memory of a similar occasion. We who bask in light have grown complacent over the eons, and ignorant of the threat that has been growing in our very midst. We have been blind to the enemy's preparations; woefully unaware to what extent his plans have been laid."

"Plans?" Stella gulped.

"The clockwork relies on the balance of light and darkness within the universe to run smoothly. Moros plans to upset that balance by extinguishing as many sources of light as he can. The dark forces have already begun their villainous attack. A pair of Stars whose light had long warmed a deep part of space, Stars whom I counted as friends have disappeared without a trace."

"I…I…" Stella was unable to speak of what she had seen with her father, the terrible darkness that had swallowed the two brilliant points of light.

"Spit it out, Stella!" Loony snorted, as he sidled up to Old Sol to study his blemished face.

Noting the girl's distress Old Sol queried gently. "What is it Stella?"

Remembering what she had seen plunged Stella into despair. "I… I saw those Stars destroyed. I watched through my father's telescope as the darkness swallowed them and left nothing but empty space. It was horrible!"

"The darkness you saw was Moros. That attack, those murders, "Old Sol said sadly," will be only the first. He will not stop until he has turned all light, to cold dead darkness. And now as the Celestial Clockwork winds down, he sees the opportunity to accomplish his goal. The clockwork needs to be wound to its full power before Moros can cause any greater harm."

Stella thought of the dark Arctic sky and how the bright lights of the stars, seemed so small in that vast black space. How could those lights survive with so much darkness striving to snuff them out? She shivered as she looked at the dark sunspots on Old Sol's face that his encounter with Moros had left. "There's so much more empty space than Stars." The concern was evident in her voice. "If all that dark space turned against the Stars, how could they survive?"

"Yeah, how can they survive?" Loony repeated, all the while scrutinizing the damage to the Sun.

Small curlicues of flame turned in tiny whirlpools about the round orb, but what both Loony and Stella's eyes were locked on, were the dark patches of sunspots that Moros had left on Old Sol's face.

"Oh! I see," said the Sun, noticing their anxiety. "Is it these spots that are upsetting you? Why they're nothing! You shouldn't let them bother you. Watch…"

Lifting his hands, Old Sol pressed them against the flaming curve of his forehead. He pulled his hands down across his face, and as he did, the dark spots were wiped away leaving only brilliant yellow fire. Holding out his hands, the Sun spread his fingers which were now covered with a film of dirty oil.

"See," He laughed, flicking his fingers as one would with wet hands to shake off any final drops, but what flew from Old Sol's hands was dark and dingy. "There was no harm done!"

"Though the quantity of light might seem small compared to the great vastness of the darkness, there is no reason to despair. The strength of light is perfectly balanced against the threat of darkness. That balance is somehow the very universe itself. Moros is attempting to tip the scales into chaos, and disrupt the working of the clockwork. He has declared war, but it is for us to stand and endure." Sol pronounced confidently.

"That's right!" Loony cheered, though Stella wished he would just be quiet. "We have to stand and endure!"

The Sun smiled at the moon man's enthusiasm. "That we must, Loony, if we wish to remain in light." He continued, cautioning, "Although before, when the clockwork slowed, it had only to be wound to set things aright. What is different this time is the troubling appearance of Moros, who is set on exploiting the weakness of the clockwork to accomplish his aim of extinguishing light. He will do anything to stop the clockwork from being wound. That puts the winder in serious jeopardy." His tone changed to one much more serious. "And Moros knows just who the winder is now."

Moros knew about her! The thought turned Stella's blood to stone. She wished she could shake the horrible feeling of dread concerning the perilous duty that had been thrust upon her, but its weighty responsibility was heavy on her heart. Closing her eyes against the obligation, she shut out the Sun. Behind the shade of her eyelids a spectre waited to lure the girl deeper into darkness with a promise of cold comfort, and she followed, allowing herself to sink further into the solace of solitude.

A black pool opened at her feet. It had no bottom. As Stella was plunged into it the darkness she heard Old Sol, his voice distant as if in a dream, asking if she were all right. Terrified, she tried to scream "NO!" but the words froze in her throat and no voice sounded. As she struggled the liquid night turned to tar. Suddenly, her hands felt like two lead balloons and leaden worms invaded her mouth and nostrils. They slithered through her skull, coiling around her brain, constricting, anxious to snuff whatever ember still smoldered in her panicked mind. The dark bonds tightened, entombing the girl's soul in shadows until there was no more difference, no outside or inside, she was the darkness and the darkness was Stella and there was nothing else. There she lay immobilized, suspended in a hole where she could distinguish nothing.

Then somewhere in the infinite night, a spark struck. Like a sputtering match dropped into a midnight canyon, it was small but blazed undeniably in the grim darkness. From some place far, far away, beyond the silent stone stillness came the slightest whisper. Aloft on a soft breeze the call came, in a tongue alien to this wasteland of the dead and dismal.

"The light," The words found the girl's ear, a drop of sweetness into the bitter well, "Go towards the light!"

And Stella did, and the spark grew stronger, and as she rushed towards it, its flame flared to the size of a candle, then a torch, a bonfire, and finally an immense fireball, to whose embrace she rushed, away from the darkness, away from death. Diving into the blaze of glorious light, feeling its warmth, its vitality, its life, Stella was free.

"Stella, Stella!!" Warm hands shook her, as she was yanked back from the abyss. "Are you alright?" Brilliant sunlight greeted her eyes.

"It was so dark, so cold," were all the words she could manage as she focused on the fiery face hovering worriedly overhead. "It was like nothing could move, as if everything was made of frozen stone. Thanks for calling me back."

The look of concern on Old Sol's face turned to confusion. "I couldn't pull you back, though I tried. You were lost to us."

"It was a voice, so warm and friendly. It called to me, told me to go towards the light. That wasn't you?"

Pursing his lips, the Sun thought for a moment. "No, it was not. I was powerless to help you. You seemed, for a moment, what you humans would call dead."

"DEAD?" Stella exclaimed. "You thought I was dead?"

"Dead as a doornail!" Loony interjected, with manic glee.

Sol shushed the moon man away with a flick of his fiery hand, "It seemed that way. You did not respond to any stimulus. I feared you were beyond any power of mine to revive."

"I was dead?" Panic struck Stella as she came to grips with what she was being told. "Dead as in, never waking up? Dead, as in, never seeing my family and friends again? That sort of dead?" she squeaked.

Stella looked around at where she was. Far away from home, and she suspected from further, than anyone had ever returned. She was alone with a talking moon and a juggling Sun, and they wanted her to travel beyond the edge of the universe to where she was supposed to wind a clock! And now, something, no, someone… no, Moros! Had pulled her into somewhere dark and terrifying where she seemed to be dead!

The panic held her in its unyielding grasp and Stella forgot the light, and saw only her doom. "No," she cried, "I can't go on this mission and I won't be able to do what you want me to do. I'm sorry, but I want to go home. Now!"

Old Sol could not help but recognize the absolute terror in the girl's eyes. "No one can make you do this, Stella. It needs to be your choice. If you're sure you'd like to go home, I'll have Loony send you back immediately."

Stella couldn't think of anything but getting back to her father and mother and yes, even the twins. "I'm not the one you're looking for. I'm here by mistake. It was only luck that I made it past Orthrus, and if it wasn't for the dog biscuits I don't know what I would have done. When I get back to Earth, I'll talk to my father and ask him to help you."

Smiling with understanding, Old Sol declined her offer, "I believe, you Stella, are the one to divert the catastrophe with which we are faced. But if you choose to go home, if you feel you cannot find the strength within yourself to attempt the task, go knowing, there is always hope. We will find some other way to defeat Moros, if we must." He shouted sharply, "Loony!"

In a wink of an eye the little moon man appeared before the Sun, standing straight and exhibiting a respect that Stella had not seen from him before. She could see that unlike his attitude towards the Planets, Loony held the Sun in the highest regard. It was as if the moon man was torn between the anger at his treatment from the other moons and planets, and his desire to try to do the right thing. "Yes Sol? Is there something I can do for you?" The moon asked meekly.

"Our human friend here wants to get back to her family. Do you think you could help her find her way?"

Loony seemed surprised. "She's going back to Terra? Can I go with her?"

"I'm sorry Loony." Sol answered kindly "You know that wouldn't be the right thing to do. You're place is here in space. Only Stella can go back."

The moon man sulked just a moment and then arched a moonscaped brow. "I thought she was the one who was going on that trip for you? Didn't she pass the Planet's test? I'm sure I pulled up the right one for the job!"

Old Sol's warm glow covered the lunar orb with a shimmering silver patina. "It's okay Loony. I too believe you made the right choice by pulling up Stella, but other circumstances have arisen and now she must go home."

Thankful that Old Sol hadn't made it seem like she was afraid or anything that would get the moon man angry with her, Stella wished she could help him but was certain she wasn't the one to do this job. When she got back to Earth she would find someone better for the job, if not her father then maybe an astronaut or someone like that.

Loony curiously studied Stella. "Okay, but I'm sure she's the right one."

"It's alright, Loony, just help her down to her home. I'm sure, somehow, we'll find another way to accomplish our mission, though I fear there is no other human as well suited as our young friend here." Old Sol's eyes met Stella's for a moment. "Well, then, this is goodbye, my young human friend. Remember to say hello when you see me in the sky of Terra!"

Stella wasn't sure what to say. "I'm sorry," she sputtered, "Goodbye." Old Sol turned and walked away, into the dazzling beacon of light from which he had come.

"I'm not sure why you needed to apologize." The moon man said. "It's not like you chickened out or anything, right?" Walking to the lighthouse wall, he slid open a window, then a door below. Stella looked down below where the deep purple of space was speckled with light. "If you go down this way you won't have to pass the Planets. I'm not sure how they'd treat you after all that's happened."

"Ready!" Loony shouted, as a globe green and blue with soft white clouds caressing its surface swung in its wide orbit towards the duo.

Stella squealed excitedly, "It's the Earth, Loony! There she is!"

Reaching into his vest pocket, Loony pulled out a silver handkerchief gingerly holding it by a corner. "Set!"

Drifting nearer, the Earth was crystal clear. "She's beautiful!" Stella exclaimed as she reached to touch the approaching planet.

"Go!" Loony shouted, and with a swift kick of his foot, booted Stella from the lighthouse. The girl shrieked as she fell through space while above Loony laughed, "Don't be a scaredy-cat! Enjoy the ride!"

The handkerchief billowed out in a series of shimmering silver curves that flowed to Earth. Stella felt the coolness of the silver light beneath, as she softly landed in the moonbeam slung through the sky. Down she slid with the stars above gleaming like lamps against the inky black space, while the Earth waited below inviting Stella from cold space to her warm atmosphere. Gliding on through the puffy clouds so quickly she could barely catch her breath, Stella saw below the vast white spaces of the Arctic and then the small dot that was her home. Whizzing towards her window in the dome, Stella hit the lens of her scope and with a loud pop, was back in her room. The light of the moonbeam held for a moment, its glow spraying like silver icing across the bedroom and then drew back into the eyepiece.

Sirius was on Stella before she could get off the floor, licking her face and wagging his tail. "Shhh! Down boy, down!" the girl hushed. The clock on the wall's softly glowing numbers said 6:54, but the inky black of arctic darkness outside the window did not disclose whether it was morning or night.

Three knocks sounded on the door as a voice summoned from outside. "Stella! Its time to get up! Rise and shine!"

Pushing Sirius away, Stella jumped into bed and pulled the blankets up to her neck. She pretended to be sleeping while wondering how if it was morning, all that had transpired in the spaces above could have happened, in less than seven hours. Through squinted eyes, she watched the door slowly open and Celeste's head peek in.

"Stella?" Celeste asked, with sudden concern. "Do you feel okay?"

Surprised by her mother's tone, Stella barely managed to maintain her imitation of sleepy grogginess. "I'm fine, why?"

"You're looking awfully flushed", her mother stated in worried surprise. "It almost looks like sunburn! But we haven't seen the sun in months."

Stella's eyes widened as she murmured unconvincingly. "It, uhh, must be the light."

"Hmm, I guess. I just hope you're not getting sick. We have guests coming and there's a lot to do to get ready. Your father's been up all night in his lab working on his equations. Do you feel well enough to help me make breakfast? "

Sitting up, Stella stifled a fake yawn. "Sure Mom, I'll be there in a minute." Once the door closed, she jumped from bed and rushed to her telescope. No evidence of her night's adventure was apparent.

Then the only reasonable answer to the question of how so much could happen in the short span of seven hours, struck Stella. Sleep, was the answer to the fantastic events that had transpired. There had been no Planets, no Loony, No Old Sol and no Moros. It had all been a vivid dream, brought on by the unsettling disappearance of the two stars. And the rosy red glow she noticed when she passed the mirror on her wall? Stella decided she'd find an explanation for that after breakfast.

Entering the kitchen, Stella was relieved to see nothing was amiss. Whatever the Sun had said of the darkness and its plans, none of it had affected the kitchen of the Ray home. Tim and Pace were racing toy cars across the floor and challenging each other to imitate the roar of an engine the loudest. They were playing *Smash'em up*, their favorite game and one that consisted solely ,of rolling cars across the floor and crashing them together as hard as possible. "VROOM!!" shouted Tim as he thrust his car at his sister. "VROOM! VROOM!" Pace moved to the other side of Stella, rolling his car menacingly. Avoiding the opportunity of being a target, Stella hurried to where her mother was laboring over a counter strewn with pots and pans.

"Uh, Mom?" said Stella, trying to get her mother's attention. "Want to hear about the weird dream I had last night?"

"Okay, Stell" Celeste answered, balancing a large bowl of batter on a stack of dirty plates. "But can you get me some eggs first? I'm trying to get these muffins in the oven before your father comes down. He's been in his lab all night. It seems he's made a major discovery."

Stella couldn't help but notice how large her mother's belly was, big and round and looking like it might burst at any moment. Perhaps, she thought, she shouldn't bother her by telling her about the strange, vivid dream. She put the eggs quietly on the counter and grabbing a sponge from the sink, wiped some splotches of batter from the floor.

"Mom?" she asked, "What are these?" Where the sponge had stopped its passage across the floor, Stella pointed out tiny specks of white.

Bending towards the floor, Celeste clucked and shook her head. "Why, they look just like little tracks. Strange, they told me there were no mice here in the Arctic, but I've wondered what had been getting in my flour. I'd order some traps, but I guess it's too late for this month's shipment. That delivery is already on its way." She moved back to the stove and began cracking the eggs into a pan. "So what was it you wanted to talk about?"

"Oh," Stella remarked, trying to sound casual, "It was nothing."

"It didn't sound like *nothing* just a minute ago. If something's bothering you, I wish you'd tell me."

Stella didn't like keeping secrets from her mother, but realized it was probably not the best time to talk about darkness and death. Maybe after the baby came, she'd mention the weird dream. Changing course from those unsettling thoughts, she asked, "Are you sure it'll be okay delivering the baby here? Shouldn't you be in a hospital?"

Stella had often heard her father and mother discuss their options in delivering the baby. Celeste was perfectly comfortable with giving birth at Dome C, and had sounded pleased, with having a child born at the North Pole.

"I'll be fine, Stella. This is my fourth child; giving birth has almost become a routine. Besides, they'll helicopter in a midwife any day now. I just wish you wouldn't worry." She smiled wryly. "It'll give you bad dreams."

There was a ruckus at the door, as Perceval with a look of combined exhaustion and terror on his face raced into the kitchen. Trying to maintain his balance, he skated across the floor on the wheels of a toy car before landed fortuitously in a kitchen chair. Everybody in the kitchen, including the twins, was silenced by his dramatic appearance. Celeste pulled a tray from the oven, and briskly handing it to Stella, moved to her husband. "Perceval, what's the matter?"

Sobbing, he buried his face in his wife's shoulder. "Celeste, if I am right; and I regret to say that I have never been wrong, this may be the end!"

"Come on, Percy, relax. Nothing can be that bad." Celeste rubbed her husband's neck.

"It can be!" he whined pathetically. "I was rechecking my calculations on the fading stars in hopes I might be wrong, and while doing so I happened to look to the sky where I saw the most horrific sight of my life."

"And what was that?" Celeste asked with gentle patience.

Perceval hesitated, apparently unable to speak the words, but then they came rushing from his mouth in a torrent of alarm. "Another star, Shaula of the Scorpio constellation, has vanished from the sky!" Stella dropped the pan and eggs splattered the floor as she ran from the kitchen.

Perceval found his daughter in the observatory, sitting on the small set of aluminum steps that led to the telescope, wrapped in her parka and with her head down. "Are you okay?" he asked with a shaky voice.

Looking up and seeing her father's face so ashen and trembling, Stella knew she couldn't tell him her dream about the invading darkness. Already he seemed so unhinged, she feared that if she detailed her imaginary adventures it would send him over the edge.

"What's the matter?" he asked. But Stella knew her emotional state was not what occupied her father's troubled mind.

"I'm okay, dad. It just freaked me out to see how scared you were, but I'm better now." Stella said, trying to sound confident. "There must be a reason those stars disappeared. I'm sure you'll figure out why."

"It's true, I've found a reason, but it's one I hope I've come to in error." Walking to his desk, Perceval took a thick stack of paper from the piles heaped high on top. "These are my calculations," he sighed, dropping the papers back onto the desk and picking up a small notepad nearby. "And these are my results." He put the pad on the step next to Stella.

On it there were lines of equations and as Stella followed them down, each grew simpler and shorter than the line above, forming a downward arrow inked on the paper. The last line was very short; only a couple of symbols followed by an equal sign. On seeing what was scribbled below, Stella understood why her father had given up hope.

"What does this zero mean?" Stella asked, though somehow she knew it meant darkness, and death.

"*Entropy.*"

Sometimes when Perceval talked Stella wished she had a dictionary. "What's entropy?" she asked.

Taking a deep breath, Perceval began to speak in his professorial voice. "Entropy is the degradation of the matter and energy in the universe to an ultimate state of inert uniformity. Entropy is the process of running down, or the trend to disorder." Stella still wished she had a dictionary. Walking to the large whiteboard he began to scribble the equations that had been on the page. Beneath that he wrote the zero again, and then an equal sign, followed by the words, *absolute cold.*

Stella needed to learn more. "Could you say that entropy is like the wearing out of a machine? Or like a clock that winds down?"

Perceval momentarily managed a weak smile at the brightness of his daughter. "Yes, I suppose you could say it that way."

"And there's no way to wind that clock back up?"

Perceval frowned. "No way that I know of. When entropy takes hold, there's no way to reverse it. It's like falling into a black hole."

A chill crossed the room, and Stella fearing it might signal an appearance by Moros, moved nearer to her father. "When is this *entropy* supposed to happen?" Stella asked, her arms stretching around him and holding tight.

Perceval returned the hug. "I guess that's the thing I'm really worried about. By my calculations, it all stops soon."

"Soon?" Stella gasped.

"That's why our guests are so important. They're making a special trip here to check my calculations. I'm hoping they'll find some mistake in my findings, as this is one time I would be glad to be found wrong. But I've gone over my work time and again and can find no incorrect calculation."

"Who's coming?" Maybe, Stella hoped, it would be someone who could make sense of all that's been happening.

"They're sending, Professor Paul Duncan, you might remember him from the university, along with an obstetrician to help your mother." Stella's spirits lifted. She had always liked Professor Duncan, a smart, friendly man. She was sure he would be able to settle things down.

8 VERENA MALDEK

The clock on the wall said noon. Stella with her father scanned the dark and stormy sky to the south for a sign of the helicopter. They waited bundled in their parkas on the landing pad, ready to clear any windblown snow from the lights that would show the pilot where to stop. Before they had stepped out of the dome, Stella's father had gone over the precautions they needed to take outdoors, the same warnings her mother had told her inside. Stella didn't mind hearing it all once again, as this was the first time she would be outside when the helicopter came, now that Celeste, was too pregnant to help with the deliveries. Stella knew that the copter could only hover; the snow on the landing pad was too deep. When she had first flown here with her family, there had been only a frost and the helicopter had landed to let them off. Now that same platform was covered in deep shifting snowdrifts.

While they waited, Stella pondered what she had learned from her father and how that all related to her dream of the winding down clockwork. Only once when she started to ask a question did her father speak. "Please Stella", was all he had said over the howling wind," I'm trying to think." He went back to scanning the stormy skies; pad and pencil in hand and at unpredictable intervals, would look away from the turbulent horizon and scribble onto the rustling paper.

Alone with her thoughts, Stella struggled to come to terms with how what her father had learned, was nearly the same as what she had been told in her dream. Entropy meant the running down of everything, planets stopping in their orbits, stars fading out, and Earth becoming a dark frozen ball. That was just what Old Sol had said would happen, if the Celestial Clockwork ran down. Her father called it entropy, but Stella had no problem putting the face of Moros on that word.

In the stormy sky, a lone star flared through the clouds. Seeing the light, Stella shut her eyes and whispered, "Star light, Star bright, brightest star I see tonight, I wish I may, I wish I might, have the wish I wish tonight." Stella crossed her fingers tightly and wished the frightening situation she found herself in, would be explained away. She kept her eyes closed an extra second, thinking this might make the wish even stronger, then opened them looking up see that the star had grown much brighter. Tugging on her father's parka she pointed out the star. Perceval took a pair of binoculars from his pocket, and aimed them towards the light.

"It's the copter. We'll go inside while they approach," Perceval suggested over the growing thrum of the helicopter's blades. They stepped behind the frosted glass of the elevator that ran to the storage area. Perceval's breath formed a circle of white where it hit the glass, and reaching up he scrawled a string of numbers in the frost, then abruptly stopped with an equal sign which seemed to plead for a number to complete the equation. Perceval furrowed his brow for just a moment, and then wiped the line away in frustration.

The blades of the hovering helicopter kicked up large clouds of snow as the crew dropped boxes of supplies silently into the soft drifts. When the last had fallen, a ladder unfolded and a hooded figure in a dark jumpsuit nimbly climbed down into the high snow. They waited a moment for a second passenger to disembark, but no one did. Her father rushed outside to help the passenger. He paused only briefly amidst the gusting winds to signal goodbye, and then with his guest, hurried back inside to watch the chopper fly swiftly away.

When the helicopter had gone, they hurried to bring the boxes of supplies indoors before they were covered in the drifting snow. There was no need to speak as they packed the supplies into the elevator that would lower them into the dome's storerooms. Perceval handed a box to his daughter who struggling with its weight, made her way back to the doorway, to see the new arrival standing there making no move to help. Stella pushed past and looked up to see her face darkly reflected in the glass of the guest's goggles. Quickly depositing the box in the elevator, she trudged back to where her father was extricating a large package from the snow, and together they carried it inside.

Between huffing breaths, Perceval shouted over the howling winds. "I'll get the last. Wait here," then made his way once again through the squall, leaving his daughter alone with the mysterious guest. That this person was not Professor Duncan was the only thing of which Stella could be certain.

Perceval reappeared with the last box and pushed into the elevator. When there had been just two, there was plenty of room, but now with an added body and the boxes of supplies, the elevator was tight and uncomfortable. Stella found her face pressed against the new arrival's back, and when the elevator door opened the person blocking her stood for a moment. Then Stella heard something that caused her to forget her discomfort. Shedding a heavy parka and thick thermal pants the figure stepped from the lift and surveyed the premises. It was a stern female voice that mocked, "So *this* is Dome C."

"Who are you?" Perceval asked, "Where is Professor Duncan?"

"Professor Duncan is indisposed. I am Doctor Verena Maldek." The woman was tall, thin and dressed impeccably in the darkest of hues. Tight black leggings rose to a short black skirt and a black turtleneck clung to her body. Her eyes were heavily lined with mascara and her lips were glossed with a purple lipstick that stood on a field of flesh, whiter than snow. Straight black hair fell to her sharp shoulders and around her neck hung a large pendant of onyx, intricately carved.

"I am here to test," the words slithered from her mouth, "your findings. Where is your laboratory?" At the sudden command, Perceval said not a word, but sheepishly pointed to the stairs that led to the observatory.

Verena Maldek turned in the direction of Perceval's finger. "Very good. You will follow me." On shiny black boots, she clicked swiftly to the stairs and Stella watched as her father obeyed, enthralled.

Stella wasn't sure she had been invited, or by the way her father had responded, commanded to go to the observatory, but she followed anyway. Something told her it wasn't a good idea to leave her father alone with this new arrival. As she made her way up the stairs, she felt Sirius at her side. "Good boy", Stella whispered, running her fingers through the dog's hair. Though now they were three, Stella was uncertain that this made the sides equal.

They had only been in the observatory a moment when there was a soft knock on the door, and nimble even with a large swollen belly, Celeste spun into the room. "Professor dear!" She cooed, sporting a wry smile, knowing that these public endearments flustered her husband. "I brought some hot cocoa." She must have known her daughter was in the observatory, as there were three steaming mugs on the tray she carried.

"This is Doctor Maldek." Perceval sputtered by way of introduction.

Celeste offered a mug to their guest. "Pleased to meet you, Doctor. You've had a long trip and must be chilled."

Taking the steaming drink, Verena's polished nails clicked on the white ceramic. "Yes," she hissed, pausing to light a cigarette. Heavy lidded eyes of deep purple glared unflinchingly at the pregnant woman, as dual plumes of smoke jetted from her nostrils. "I am very cold."

The room went silent as the women's eyes locked. On Celeste's face, lines of strain deepened as she matched Verena's glare. Tensions mounted until even Perceval felt the clash of energies and looked up blankly from his papers. When her mother winced, Stella jumped between the two women, shattering the spell. Taking the remaining cup of cocoa from the tray she blurted, "Thanks mom!"

Celeste answered her daughter with a look of haggard relief. "You're welcome." Dazed, she walked away and then stopped at the laboratory door. "*BE CAREFUL*, Stella," the young girl took her mother's words, rich with inflection, as a warning, "that you don't disturb your father or his guest in their work."

The door swung shut, sealing the observatory with an ominous thud. The steaming cup in Stella's hand felt like the only warmth in the room as she glanced at Verena, who responded with a wicked smile of victory. It was only then, Stella noticed that the cocoa in the cup held in the pale woman's hands was frozen solid, a block of muddy ice. "Now show me what you have discovered."

Under Verena's scrutiny, a flustered Perceval set to work. Scribbling equations on the whiteboard, he would nervously shake his head and obliterate the spidery script with a swipe. He lurched from the board to the telescope, fumbled with its controls, jotted notes on his pad and with sweat streaming down his face, raced back to the board to scrawl another lengthy equation. Moaning audibly he once again attacked the board with his shirtsleeve, erasing his work. Doctor Maldek did nothing, but watched with an amused smile as Stella's father labored through his furious dance from scope to board and then back again.

Realizing the futility of his attempts at mathematical clarification, the humiliated Professor Ray attempted to explain in simpler terms, the phenomena he and his daughter had witnessed. Like a nervous child addressing a harsh mistress, he stammered out his case. "I have seen with my own eyes, stars extinguished in a matter of moments. These stars have been destroyed by some phenomena for which science offers no explanation."

"No explanation? I see. With all your mathematics and all your science, you find no cause." The eyes of Verena cruelly mocked the anguished man.

Perceval desperately tried to validate his apprehension to the imperious woman. "If this continues, it is only a matter of time; we will eventually suffer its impact here on Earth."

"Eventually?" Verena purred with a relaxed casualness, dismissing Perceval's words as if they were the musings of a child. "Perhaps you are not yet aware of more recent developments." The tip of her cigarette smoldered, and a thick stream of smoke issued from her mouth to form a ghostly veil upon her face, as Verena paused to savor the news she was about to deliver. "Just hours ago, as the Sun rose over the eastern part of the United States, a number of new sunspots were noticed, darker and larger than any previously recorded." Stepping behind the desk she pecked at the computer keyboard and pushed the screen around to Perceval, who edged nervously closer. "The footage of the occurrence has already been posted online." Stella moved to where she could see over her father's shoulder. A video of the sun appeared on the screen, filmed with some kind of filter that allowed the camera to take pictures of the blinding orb. It showed nothing unusual. "It will happen," Verena exhaled with enthusiasm, "Now!"

The sun on the screen suddenly convulsed. Long plumes erupted from its surface as ruddy patches welled everywhere on the solar globe. These blots swelled and coalesced into large dark spots that stained the sun.

"Simply wonderful," Verena hissed as she jabbed the mouse at the pause button. The haunting image of the sun froze on the screen. "There has never been another time where the sun has been so… What is the word?" Her wicked eyes locked on Perceval's, pulling him deeper into the dual dark voids. "Afflicted!"

Stella drew in a sharp gasp of air. The Sunspots on the monitor, matched exactly those that had blemished the face of Old Sol after the attack by Moros. What she had tried to convince herself was a dream or a nightmare, was neither, for what she had seen was real, the proof, flickering before her eyes on the computer screen.

The façade Stella had constructed collapsed like a ton of bricks, as she was struck by a disconcerting revelation. If the spots on the Sun were real, then Moros was real, and if Moros was real, the threat to the universe was real too. What was happening was no dream, and it dawned on Stella that she was inextricably involved in something very dangerous, the extent of which was far beyond her understanding.

Stella watched mutely as Professor Maldek slinked behind the desk and took the seat where her father always sat. Perceval stood meekly before her, like a guilty schoolboy waiting for punishment to be pronounced. Verena held a notebook up between two fingers as if it were a dead rat. "This is a log of your observations?" Perceval nodded nervously. Dropping the notebook to the desk she began to rifle through it, her long polished nails, painted the same dark purple as her lips, clawing at the sheets. Scanning them brusquely as she flipped from page to page, Verena resembled a crow, head jerking from left to right, as if preying for something to snatch from the page and devour. "You note a corroborator in your observances?" Verena did not lift her head as she spoke.

Perceval sputtered out his reply. "Yuh… yuh… yuh ...YES!"

"And who is this observer? Are they qualified to observe and evaluate the data you describe in your notes?"

"Em, eh, em, ehem, "Perceval stuttered again.

"Speak up! Who is this other witness?" Verena demanded.

Perceval blurted out, "It's my daughter. She's seen the phenomena too. She is as qualified as anyone to …"

"Your daughter?" Verena interrupted with an air of disdain, "Well, I see. Your findings were formed in collaboration with a child? That is very interesting. Very interesting indeed!" She slammed the notebook shut. "This is how you dare to waste my time? I have come so far to deal with what a child and her father fantasize, while playing with their telescopes? Your research is worthless! "

Stella had enough of Verena treating her father like some sort of fool. She was going to tell this lady that she shouldn't talk to her father in his own laboratory this way, and that guests should not be so rude to their hosts. But before she could speak, she was stopped by the piercing voice of Professor Maldek. "So this is the special child who would ask the world to take notice of her fanciful theories." It was not a question and as Stella met Verena's pitiless gaze, she was unable to answer her father's tormentor.

Verena toyed with the pendant at her neck, her fingers slowly twisting the chain on which it hung. It glittered, blinking and fading, blinking and fading. "Step forward, special one," she ordered. "I would like to see more closely, the child who would advise adults in such important matters." Stella found herself stepping forward, drawn to the play of light and darkness from the medallion. "Stop there. Yes, now I can see you better."

As all her attentions were focused on the flashing flickering stone, Stella heard the words as just an echo from some distant place. She could see the pendant more clearly now, as she was just a few feet from it across the desk, and a word hung on the tip of her tongue to describe it. *Talisman.* As it flickered against the black of Verena's sweater Stella could make out symbols inscribed on it. Each in its own sector, the designs lined the perimeter of the circle and it was certain they had something to do with stars, even though there were no stars on the medallion. It was somehow unquestionable that Verena would never wear a star and that she might even hate stars.

As the flashing pendant flipped, Stella watched each symbol appear and then return to darkness. A second symbol appeared and was quickly consigned to an even darker place. Then a third and it was as if, a lightless pit had opened. The fourth, and when the blackness came, it felt to Stella like she could never return from an abyss so deep. Five and Stella almost screamed in terror when the chasm opened wider, and threatened to engulf her.

At the twelfth, there was nothing but the panicked certainty that there would be no escape from the darkness that had so completely ensnared her mind. Then a voice rang through the darkness and Stella clung to it, like a drowning man to a lifeline.

"I will spare you, human," the voice assured, "if you will tell me all you know." A face drifted through the shadows of the pit. Smiling, Professor Maldek leaned across the desk; her face only inches from the girl. "Tell me who wounded Scorpio."

Stella fought to remain silent. "Do not resist me!" Verena hissed. "Tell me about the plans of that damned star, Sol." In a flash, Stella understood what was happening. The darkness had agents here on Earth. "Or I will send you back into the darkness."

A voice in her head implored, do it, tell her, and then you can go back to just being Stella Ray. "Okay!" Stella cried.

"Good," Verena whispered, and the words dripped with a sickly sweetness, like candied poison. "Now tell me how the Stars plan to thwart Moros."

"Moros." Just hearing the name was reminder enough for Stella to know she could do nothing to aid that dastardly monster, no matter what she would be put through. The defiant look on Stella's face told Verena that the girl would not comply with her desires. Rage flared in Verena's eyes, as Stella felt herself plunged back into darkness. Trying to scream, the breath was not there and as blackness closed in around her, Stella knew her life was about to be snuffed out.

As Stella collapsed, a blur shot across the room and flung itself at Verena Maldek, knocking her to the ground. Jarred from her trance, Stella gasped for breath, while from behind the desk a battle raged with Verena shrieking and…Sirius, barking!

Amidst the mayhem the door to the laboratory burst open. "What is going on here?" Quickly sizing up the situation, Celeste ran to pull the dog off the heap of black that thrashed wildly on the floor.

"Get that filthy creature off me!" Verena screamed.

Helping Verena up, Celeste began to brush the dog hair from her now less than perfect clothes. "I'm so sorry, Doctor. Sirius has never behaved like this before." Shooting daggers at her husband she exclaimed. "Honestly, Percy! She is our guest; you shouldn't allow her to be treated this way."

Perceval, as if in the midst of a dream, nodded his head slightly. Celeste shook her head in disgust and turned towards Stella. "How could you let

Sirius do this? What were you thinking?" Dazed and confused and barely aware of what had happened, Stella pulled herself from the floor.

Celeste grabbed Sirius by the collar and pulled him towards the door. "Come on, Sirius! And Stella…" She glowered at her daughter. "I think it's time you leave the observatory. Your father has his work to do. I'm sure he doesn't need any more interruptions."

Certain her father would be unable to resist Doctor Maldek alone, Stella yelped, "But Mom! I can help with…"

Celeste cut her short. "That's right Stella; you can help with getting dinner ready."

Stella knew her mother had spoken her final word. She followed, and looking back from the laboratory door saw the blank stare on her father's face that signaled he had already fallen deep under Verena's spell.

The woman in black offered Stella a predatory grin. "Yes, little one, go help your mother. We will talk later."

The door closed before Stella could respond, leaving her alone in the hall with an angry Celeste. "Stella! How could you do that? She's our guest!"

"Mom," Stella sputtered "There's something not right with that woman. You should see the way she treats dad!"

Celeste countered sharply. "Stella, please. You're letting your imagination run away with you. I know the woman is strange and more than a bit rude, but you've been around enough scientists to know they aren't quite normal. No matter how eccentric she might be, she has a lot to contribute to your father's work. He needs time with *Doctor…*" Celeste emphasized *Doctor…* and Stella knew it was her way of saying Doctors deserved respect, "Maldek, to find out what is going on."

Stella looked at her mother in silent desperation, wanting badly to tell her about Moros, and what she had learned while away through the scope, but she couldn't. Seeing Celeste's swollen belly, Stella knew she could not do anything that might upset her mother or put the baby at risk. Sirius began to pull back toward the laboratory door.

"Stella, can you please take your pet?" Celeste asked, eyeing the canine with a look that would wilt flowers. "Until the Doctor leaves, you'll keep him in your room. If I find him out, we'll have to put him downstairs in the storage rooms. What he did to that woman was totally unacceptable." Celeste passed the dog's leash, as Sirius whimpered and slunk next to Stella. "Put him in your room, and then help me fix dinner, alright?"

As soon as Celeste turned the corner of the corridor, Sirius jerked towards the laboratory door. For a few steps Stella went along, but then dug her feet into the carpet that covered the floor. "Hold on, Sirius! Wait a second!" The girl knelt next to the pooch to explain. "If we go in there, and I fall under Verena's spell again, I bet this time she'll find a way to hypnotize you too. If you hadn't stopped her before, I don't know what might have happened." The dog licked at Stella's face, appreciating the praise. "If we both go in to help dad, and she manages to put us under her spell, then it'll be over for us all. Moros will win and everyone else will lose." The dog whimpered at the prospect.

"So I know what I have to do, Sirius." The dog shook its head, as if to say "No, don't", but Stella was committed; seeing no other course to take. "I have to do what Old Sol wants. I'll find the way to the end of the universe, wind the Celestial Clockwork, and then we'll deal with Verena together." Stella promised all this in a whisper, wishing there could be some other way. "But first I have to find a way to get back up," she glanced towards the ceiling and what lay beyond, "*there.*"

She rubbed her cheek on her dog's fur. "I need you to stay here and make sure that nothing bad happens while I'm gone. Not to dad or Tim and Pace and especially not to mom…" Stella felt a lump form in her throat, choking off the words, "or the baby. Do you think you can do that?" Sirius stood up, straight and tall, and Stella could see in her dog's eyes that he wouldn't let her down, not if his life depended on it.

"Now, there're some things I have to find out." Stella hurried off to her room stepping carefully through the parking lot of toy cars that Tim and Pace had arranged in long lines down the hallway, and past where they had built a wall of Lego's across the doorway of her bedroom. Turning on her computer, she used the few seconds that the machine would need to boot up, to peer through the scope at her window for some sign of the moon. Not certain if it hadn't risen yet or perhaps its absence signaled something dire, she could only hope it wasn't too late.

Clicking the icon that opened a search engine, she paused to decide where to begin in this whole complicated mess, and then started to type. First, she entered "celestial clockwork" and clicked on one of the resulting links. It showed an odd clock, the dial of which was on a globe that sat on the shoulders of a silver statue of a man. That was Atlas, and though she wondered if he might be real like the planets and Old Sol, no one had mentioned him as being involved with the problem.

The next link was for a music group called "The Celestial Clockwork" and showed a picture of three men and two women, each wearing colorful clothing and smiling widely. Stella imagined they played a very happy type of music and was tempted to click on the link to hear what a song might sound like, but knew she didn't have time to waste.

Clicking again brought up a movie called "Celestial Clockwork". Reading the review, it didn't seem to have anything to do with space or planets or the running down of the universe, so Stella clicked the back button.

Deleting the word "celestial" to leave just "clockwork", she clicked search. There was "clockwork" software, "clockwork" accounting and just about "clockwork" everything else. There was lots of information on gears and watch making but nothing about space or planets. Passing over an interesting word she copied it, and then opening up an online dictionary pasted the word, then clicked enter.

Main Entry: ho·rol·o·gy
Pronunciation: -jE
Function: *noun*
Etymology: Greek *hOra* + English *-logy*
Date: 1819
1 : the science of measuring time
2 : the art of making instruments for indicating time

Stella studied the definition, knowing that clocks would of course be concerned with time, but there was something else. "Horology", Stella said aloud and as she did another word came to mind. "Horoscope" she whispered breathlessly, knowing, through that inexplicable feeling of things coming together, that an important connection had been made.

Stella knew that horoscopes were supposed to predict the future. Everyone had a horoscope sign, and that sign supposedly determined what type of person you might be. Excitedly, she typed, *horoscope.*

There were many, many results and scanning the daunting list Stella wondered how to narrow the search. Stars, she guessed, what was happening had to do with stars. And time. She typed in, *stars horoscope time*, hit search and scrolled down to find thousands of results.

Stella read a few.

Mistress Selma reads the stars, tells your future, and charts your horoscope in record time!

Unlucky in love? The stars say it's time to find your perfect mate. Matchmaker horoscopes can help, for the low price of…

Jupiter also squares Pluto early in the month and at the same time, Saturn forms a tense angle to Uranus, so ... Click to go to our weekly horoscope page. ...

Stella hadn't realized that planets had something to do with the horoscope, having thought it was only about the stars. She clicked the link, and the browser loaded the page. Stella skipped to a link at the bottom labeled, *A Brief History of Astrology*. Astrology was a word very close to astronomy, which is what her father did, but even though both words had something to do with stars, Stella knew they were two very different things.

Stella's eyes widened as the page loaded. Its central image was a match of the medallion that Verena Maldek wore, the same symbol, a circle divided into twelve sectors, each sector with a unique symbol. *The Zodiac,* the picture's label read. Clicking to the online dictionary Stella entered the word.

Zodiac: An imaginary band in the heavens centered on the ecliptic, that encompasses the paths of the planets and is divided into 12 constellations or signs, each taken for astrological purposes to extend 30 degrees of longitude.

Signs? Searching for, *Signs of the Zodiac,* a list appeared. *Aries, Leo, Sagittarius, Gemini, Libra, Aquarius, Cancer, Scorpio, Taurus, Virgo, Capricorn, Pisces.* Stella studied the names and the symbols next to them. Scorpio; she had been attacked by a scorpion after passing beyond the solar system. The next sign was Taurus, and hadn't a bull attacked the starry eyed woman who had saved her from the scorpion?

It was no coincidence, Verena's medallion and the Zodiac and the creatures that had attacked her, it wasn't just chance. Stella concluded; all these things were somehow tied up with Moros' plan. She had always thought her father knew everything about stars, but now realized this was not quite true. While he viewed stars as phenomena brought about by gravity and pressure, others thought differently, believing that stars, especially those of the Zodiac, were the powers that controlled fate. Now Stella had discovered her own way of seeing things, finding that the planets, the sun, and even the moon, were all just like people, people in an enormous amount of trouble.

9 CLIMBING LOONY'S LADDER

Stella sat in her chair, not sleeping but waiting and watching until a curve of light broke the horizon. Training her telescope on the silver orb that rose in the sky pale against black velvet space, she couldn't help but notice a small crescent of darkness shadowing its side. "Loony?" Stella whispered to the waning moon. "I want to help. Please, take me back up." There was no sign of Loony's face on the silent silver satellite in the sky

Stella needed Loony's help to get off the Earth and out into space. She had no idea how to do that otherwise. Squinting through her window, she tried to see beyond the stars to where the Celestial Clock was supposed to be. Old Sol had said it was somewhere beyond space, the idea of which, was confusing. Space was what was, so what could be beyond space? How could there even be a, *there,* there?

"Please Loony! I have to do something. Professor Maldek is working for Moros!" Stella pleaded for a response. "Don't be mad at me! I believe it all now!"

Stella peered into the scope and a tiny spot on the moon's surface caught her attention. She fumbled with the scope's knobs to further sharpen the view and saw then that the spot had grown. Only slightly, it was true, but enough to convince Stella that something was emerging from the moon's surface.

It unfolded in a series of long thin segments ratcheting into space, and as the line extended further, Stella clapped happily. It was a ladder and it was angling straight towards Earth. In only a moment it was right outside. Stella jumped back as the ladder unfolded effortlessly through the window, passing through the glass and setting two legs firmly on her bedroom floor. Snatching her parka from the bedpost, Stella stepped on the first rung. A plaintive whine from behind stopped her rush. "Don't cry, Sirius!" Stella jumped from the ladder and put her arms around the animal's neck. "You remember your promise? You'll take care of things while I'm gone and not let Doctor Maldek hurt Mom and Dad or the twins?"

Sirius let out a low bark of affirmation. Stella gave her pet one last squeeze, mounted the ladder and began to climb. Reaching for the rung that waited on the other side of the window, her hand slid right through and Stella felt a tingling feeling as she passed through the glass and entered the cold outside air.

Climbing above the compound in which she lived, a tiny haven amongst the snowy white landscape of the arctic, Stella whispered good-bye to all she was leaving below her. "I won't be gone long, I promise. I'll be back as soon as I can." Ascending rapidly, when she next glanced down her home was lost from sight, and all that could be seen was a vast expanse of white surrounded by darker patches of ocean.

Above stretched the luminous river called the Milky Way, which Stella knew was the rim of her galaxy. The Milky Way galaxy was shaped like a fried egg, sunnyside up, with Earth located towards the center but still in the thin egg white part. Looking in the direction of the Galaxy's rim, there were so many stars spread through that vast distance that they collectively formed a soft glowing band which stretched across the sky. If you looked away from the Milky Way you'd see fewer stars, each distinct against the darkness of space, and that was because there was much less distance from the Earth to the edge of the galaxy, and with less distance, less stars.

It was simple when you thought about it, but Stella imagined that someone had once spent a lot of time figuring out that the galaxy was shaped like a fried egg, and why there were so many more stars in one direction than in any other. That was how scientists like her father worked, discovering things by making sense of the mysterious.

Looking up the ladder toward the moon, Stella saw it was going to be a long climb. Looking for a way to make the time go faster, she decided to count every rung until she reached her destination and discover just how many steps it took to get to the moon.

The sky was shot with stars, diamonds, and rubies and emeralds. Captivated by the beauty of these dazzling points of light, Stella almost lost count after a mere fifty rungs. Remembering her promise, she caught herself just in time and then admonishing herself for the lapse of attention, resumed her tally. Reaching the five hundredth rung, Stella congratulated herself on the accomplishment and confidently continued her ascend to the moon, counting rung after rung.

Meeting a thin layer of clouds that hovered around the ladder, she climbed through, her nose tickling as she passed. Upon exiting, Stella realized she had left Earth's atmosphere and was now in outer space. Stopping to look back, the soft curve of the horizon glowed with warmth. Stella knew that the Sun was just behind there and that somewhere on Earth it was morning. She couldn't help but think of how many people below were waking up to the Sun's light without appreciating just how special it was.

Without the atmosphere to block their light, the stars blazed vividly. Stella wondered if each had its own personality, like Old Sol. He was the only Star she met, and had liked him a lot. She supposed there were probably nice Stars and not so nice Stars, just like people. She thought about Moros and why he would ever want to destroy the stars, it didn't make sense, wanting to put out their lights. From this height the Earth was so small, that if Stella moved her foot, it was blocked from sight. Could the Earth be blotted out with such ease? If Stella could do it with just her foot, perhaps Moros did have a plan to cause the Earth to disappear forever, and everybody and everything with it.

With a sinking feeling, Stella's thoughts left the problem of Moros and shifted to the task she had assigned herself. She couldn't for the life of her, remember where she had lost count. It had seemed such a simple thing to do and she couldn't even accomplish that. The disheartened girl huffed, "And I'm supposed to save the universe?"

Although certain she could be of no help to Sol, Stella decided she still needed to tell him about Verena Maldek and her appearance at the Arctic base. She hurried up the ladder to where it ran alongside a bright hole cut into the purple of space. The rays of light that streamed through left no doubt in Stella's mind that Old Sol was nearby, so she jumped off the ladder through the portal and right into the garden of Earth's cottage in Heliopolis. Waiting for her there, was the little man with the round rocky head.

"Loony! Why didn't you pull me up?" Stella asked, puffing from the exertion of the ascent.

Loony pointed to a dark crescent that shaded the side of his head. "You know how tides rise, right? They rise because I pull them, but there are times when I can barely make them move at all. When I pulled you up before, I was full and had all my strength, but that won't happen again for another month or so. The way you were talking down there I figured you didn't want to wait". He pulled the ladder up; folding it up in the way an old fashioned wooden ruler might fold, with each section disappearing swiftly into the small slat which the moon man held. "I just hope you're not too tired, we still have to get to Old Sol's place."

"Where did you get that ladder?" Stella asked between puffs of air, hoping to catch her breath before the moon man insisted on moving.

"This?" Loony nodded his bobbling head towards the packet, which though it already had many ladder sections folded into it, had not grown. The moon men kept folding, clack, clack, clack, as he explained. "Well there was, and this is years before you humans had rockets, a man who wanted to visit the moon, so he made this ladder and climbed it all the way up to me." Loony laughed. The final section folded into the rest, leaving Stella no clue as to where the bulk of the ladder had gone. "You humans called him the man in the moon."

"I hate to say it, but he itched so much when he walked around, I had to scare him away," Loony cackled evilly, making Stella realize, she didn't want to know just how he did that. "He rushed back down that ladder lickety split and didn't pull it down, so I pulled it up before anyone else could climb it. I don't like the idea of humans crawling around on me, but don't get me wrong; I'm not one of those who think Terra has gotten out of hand with her affections for humans. I kind of like them. I just don't want them crawling on me. So when I couldn't pull you up, I got the idea of getting the ladder so you could climb here. Pretty neat, huh?" The moon man gloated. "I bet Old Sol would say I was pretty smart to think of that." Taking the neat little packet, which somehow contained the whole long ladder, he held it out to Stella. "Hey, why don't you keep this? You might need it sometime."

It was as small as a deck of cards and fit easily in her pocket. "Thanks Loony." Ready to move again, Stella asked, "When can I see old Sol? Something terrible has happened that I think he needs to know about."

"Something terrible, huh?" Loony snickered, not taking the girl serious at all, "We'll see him soon, if we're lucky. But first we need to get past the Planets, and that might not be so easy."

"Do they know I'm back?"

The moon man looked around nervously. "I hope not, that'd be big trouble." Grabbing the girl's hand, he began to pull her along with him, out of Terra's garden and towards the Sun's tower at the center of the courtyard. "Let's get going, it won't be good if anyone saw you."

"What do you mean by that?"

"Maybe you don't want to know," Loony sneered, "Maybe it'd be best if we got out of here before anyone catches you."

"Catches me? What are you talking about? I'm here to help, why should anyone be angry with me?" Stella exclaimed.

"I'll tell you why." Loony spat, "The planets are convinced you caused those spots on Old Sol. And they blame me for bringing you up in the first place." He looked around anxiously. "Now, can we get out of here?"

He shot off, and no longer resisting his tug, Stella followed. Now she also watched as nervously as he did, while they snuck towards the tower. "I didn't do anything to Sol!" she whispered, defensively. "It was Moros!"

"Well if they catch you, you can tell them that, not that I'm sure they would even listen. Mars is on the warpath, and Pluto is so angry he's freezing over."

Loony lead Stella past Mercury's abode, a small dwelling built into the side of a fuming volcano. "Are Jupiter and Venus angry too?" Stella asked. "They must know I would never do anything to hurt Sol." Loony said nothing as they stealthily made their way to the staircase that would take them to the sun.

"Hold it right there!" Mercury raced from his house screaming in alarm. "The human is here! Stop her!" There was the patter of tiny feet, as from the houses of Saturn and Uranus rushed troops of moons, who surrounded the duo and blocked their way to the tower. Unfettered rage seethed across Mercury's face, "You're a disgrace to Terra, Loony. How can you help this traitorous human?"

"Do not judge me, Mercury," Loony snarled back defiantly. "You know nothing about what is involved here."

Appearing at the door of his stately mansion, Saturn barked, "Mimas! Fetch the other Planets!" and a cratered moon quickly scurried away. Marching triumphantly forward, the ringed planet looked down on the trapped duo. "Where did you think you were going? Did you think we would allow you to harm our Sun again?"

"I never did anything. It was Moros! And he's planning to do something much worse!" Stella pleaded. "You have to let me go so I can to tell Old Sol!"

"We have to do nothing of the kind." There was a blur of blood red as Mars rushed into the courtyard and raced towards the captives. "You will pay for your treachery!"

The courtyard was abuzz with angry tension as Venus and Jupiter entered. Stella hoped they would offer some assistance, but the two planets only stood back from the angry crowd. It was unbelievable to Stella, that even they thought she could hurt Old Sol, but they seemed bewildered and uncertain as to just what course to take.

Left with no other option, Stella considered running at the moons, knocking them down like bowling pins and trying to reach the spiral staircase. She was searching the crowd for the path of least resistance when inexplicably the noisy mob hushed. Stella followed their startled glances upwards and saw a pencil thin beam of light, like the sun cast though the crack of a window shade, shining from above. Angry grimaces changed to reverent awe as the beam fell like a small circle of gold on Stella's forehead. As she reached to touch this small coin of light, it widened, bathing her and Loony in its warm glow. The circle expanded until it reached the surrounding moons, which fell back from its advance.

From the center of this flood of light, a hand emerged. Stella hesitated, unsure of what was happening, "Loony, What do you think we should do?"

The moon man grasped Stella's hand. "It's our only chance, so don't think about it, just..." he shouted, clutching the hand reaching from the light, "Take it!"

Light spread from the luminous hand to cover Loony's arm and then his body. The glowing sheath surged over the moon man until it reached Stella's hand, quickly enveloped her arm, her chest, and as it covered her eyes she felt as if she were slipping into a warm bath. She blinked and when she opened her eyes… she was no longer in Heliopolis.

As the veil of light fell from her body, Stella rubbed the dazzle from her eyes. Before her stood a woman, tall, lithe and dressed in a billowing gown that glistened with the light of diamonds. From the top of her head shone rays of starlight nestled amongst a luxurious cloud of hair, and crowned features whose loveliness transcended the power of words. Though ephemeral as a spring breeze, there was no hint of weakness from the fair female form, but instead an overwhelming aura of strength. A long sword hung from the lady's hip, further enhancing the sense of untamable energy.

"Aren't you, weren't you …" Stella stammered, as she recognized this dazzling being as the beautiful warrior who had defended her at the end of the solar system, "… didn't you save me from the scorpion?"

"Why, yes I did!" Her voice was as pleasant as the tinkling of chimes in the breeze. "But we have not been properly introduced. I am Astraea, a friend of Old Sol and all who love the light!"

As the woman spoke the name of the Star she had always considered her own, Stella's head spun. "You're Astraea?"

"Yes, I am!" she chirped, "And you are Stella Ray, and this is Luna, the brave moon who has been such a help to Old Sol in these troubling times." Every word left her lips like a song.

In some strange way Stella had no doubt that this marvelous lady was indeed Astraea, the Star that had always lifted her spirits when glimpsed in the night sky. Bewildered by being in the company of a lifelong friend she had never met, Stella struggled to be polite. "It's very nice to meet you, Astraea. Thanks so much for saving me from Scorpio."

The Star woman's face turned serious. "It seems that the minions of Moros are already aware of your importance, though I know not, how they have been alerted. I fear there are some who masquerade in light, but are allies of the darkness. I must guard you carefully, if the hope we have placed in you is to come to fruition."

"Guard me?" Stella was confused.

"Yes, Stella, Sol has asked me to be your guardian and to assist you in your journey." Astraea placed her hand on the pommel of her sword, showing the girl her willingness to fight. To know that she might not be traveling alone, that she had someone so strange but so familiar going along with her, was beyond anything Stella could have hoped for.

"Why should we trust you?" Loony rudely snapped, "How can we be sure you're not working for Moros?"

Stella rushed to Astraea's defense. "Loony, be nice! She saved me! If she hadn't stopped Scorpio's attack, I wouldn't be here."

The moon man snorted irritably. "Okay, but if she's not working for Moros, what's she done with Old Sol?"

Astraea answered sweetly, unfazed by the lunatic's attitude. "I've done nothing with Old Sol. He will be here shortly and you will see."

"Old Sol is committed to protect Terra and her children from the adversary. There have always been those who believe the fate of the universe is entwined with the humans of Earth. That puts Terra in great peril, from those who have openly declared war on all that is good and others who wait in the shadows for their chance to betray the light."

"Verena Maldek!" Stella thought, "She's one of those, I just know it."

"Even those closest to us may fall to the temptations and false promises of Moros. His lies are persuasive and his power to corrupt, enormous. It is why Old Sol must remain vigilant in his guarding of Terra …" Astraea hesitated a moment, studying the two before her as if to measure if they could accept what she had to tell them, "and will be unable to accompany you on your quest."

Stella stuttered, "So it'll be just you and me? You'll come with me all the way to the end of the universe?"

A reassuring voice answered. "I was born a wandering Star with no planets in my orbit; hence I am able to travel where most Stars dare not. I will escort you to the end of the starry realms, but because I am not human" Stella was awed by the tone of respect used when the Star said the word, "I doubt I have the qualities needed to accompany you further."

"What 'qualities'?" Stella had to ask. "What could I possibly do that you couldn't?"

"I'm sure it's just as hard for you to understand a Star's life, as it is for us to understand humans. Even though Sol has spent quite a bit of time observing Terra's children, I doubt seriously he'll ever truly understand them, humans are so strange, so different from others who dwell in space." Loony studied Stella suspiciously; eyes her as though she was some exotic animal. "But!" Astaea continued, noticing the trepidation with which the Moon regarded the girl, "Both Sol and I are certain that they are perhaps the most special beings in this universe. So be patient with our human friend, Loony, as she is perhaps our only chance to thwart Moros' plot."

"The only chance?" Loony asked.

"What qualities?" Stella still wanted to know.

"Stars are alight in accordance to their size, age and location. In the realm of the Planets, orbits define their range of freedom. At each level of the cosmos there are properties different from those above and below, and those properties define the existence of the beings that live there. Humans however, can steer their own course if they choose. It would be untrue to claim the rules for humans, are the same as those for Planets or Stars."

"Or Moons!" Loony interjected.

Astraea continued, ignoring the outburst. "It is peculiar that only humans, some of the smallest of beings in the universe, are capable of traversing across the realms of space, of moving beyond their place of origin."

Stella wasn't sure she understood all Astraea was saying, but there was one thing she needed to know. "You'll come with me as far as you can?"

The Star smiled and looked deep into the girl's eyes. "Yes, for as far as I am able. But wherever we may go, I vow upon my inmost light to protect you."

"So! I guess you two have it all figured out, huh?" Loony snarled, brusquely jumping between the Star and the girl, "You're both heading off to the end of the universe to save everything, right? Just the two of you, the big heroes, right?" The moon man was glowering red. "And I guess you're just going to leave me here, right? Just take off and say, 'Goodbye Loony, maybe we'll see you later!' and not even look back."

Stella recoiled from the invectives. "What's the matter, Loony? Can you please tell me why you're so angry?"

The features on the moon's face twisted from rage to sadness. "Well, the Planets think I've been helping the person who hurt Sol, so I can't go back to the solar system." he blubbered. "I'm not sure what they'd do to me. Terra isn't even around to protect me. I'll be all alone."

"And?" Stella asked, not exactly sure what to say.

"And…" The moon man blurted, "You won't take me with you!"

Stella was stunned. "You want to come on the mission with us?"

The moon man looked up with hurt eyes. "I don't really have any other choice, do I?"

Before Stella could respond, a blinding flash filled the room.

"Sol," Stella cheered as her radiant friend appeared. "Where have you …"

Hastily placing a finger to his lips, Old Sol put a halt to the girl's question and began rushing around at a frantic pace. Poking into a crack in the wall here, and looking in a crevice there, he carefully inspected his dwelling, as Stella, Astraea and Loony silently watched. After a few moments he whispered nervously, "You're sure no one has been here? There's been no chance of spies listening?"

"Neither Moros nor his minions have intruded into your space while I have been here." Astraea answered confidently.

"I should not even be here at the moment, but I wanted wish you luck on your journey." The Sun addressed Stella in a hushed voice. "I'm so glad you'll help. I'm certain you're the one who'll be able to …" his eyes darted suspiciously around the room, "Stop Moros."

"Where," Stella continued asking, "Have you been?"

Looking warily about his room, Old Sol whispered, "I've been with Terra."

"With Terra! Where is she?" Loony shouted excitedly.

In a flash Old Sol had his hand clamped over the Loony's craggy mouth. "Speak softly! We have no idea who might be listening!"

Stella had to know more. Risking Old Sol's anger, but willing to endure it if it meant some word of Earth, she whispered, "Where is she?"

Holding the squirming moon man, the Sun moved closer to Stella. Muffled complaints murmured from beneath the his fiery hand as he responded, "For now she is safe under my protection, though Moros aims to harm her even more so, now that he is aware of your willingness to aid us. He knows the only chance to wind the clock is by some human agent, therefore he will focus his wrath on Terra, hoping to wipe her clean of life and end the only threat to his plan."

"Wipe her clean of life?" Stella cringed at the thought.

"At present I still have the power to hold off the assault, though as the Celestial Clockwork winds down, the darkness grows stronger and the power of light weaker. If the clock is not wound soon, I fear the time will come when I will not able to withstand the attacks of Moros."

Loony squirmed from Old Sol's hand, which had steadfastly maintained its silencing grip on the struggling moon man's mouth. Pulling away, he whispered, "Why, if Terra is so important, are some of the planets so angry with her?" Loony's anxiety was evident, and Stella was touched by his concern.

"Mars and Saturn are annoyed that Terra has allowed her humans to flourish so freely, that now they are capable of leaving her surface to pester them. I suppose other planets may be jealous of the attention I have paid Terra", Old Sol said sadly, "but that is beyond my control. She must be protected. If she should fall to Moros and the humans perish, there will be no hope at all."

"The Planets", Astraea interjected passionately," need to understand that everything in our universe plays a necessary part in the whole. Time is fastened to the movement of the cosmos, and the movement of the cosmos is the coordinated action of all. The winding down of the clockwork, though troubling, is natural; there are legends of times like these in distant eons. But Moros' interference is unprecedented. He seeks with false promises and lies, to spread dissent and create imbalance in the working of the clockwork. If he would have his way, he would arrest the flow of time itself and turn light into darkness"

Stella thought of how Verena Maldek had lied to her father; she hadn't come to the North Pole to help at all. "What sort of lies is Moros telling?"

Astraea sighed, "Moros believes that when time stops, when it ceases to move forward, all will be one. Past, present, eternity, will coexist and *nothing* will happen, as there would be *no time* in which it may happen. He promises that when all is the same, and there is no more difference between one thing and the next, there will be no more pain and no more strife."

"What's wrong with that?" Loony whispered, "No more being hurt? I think that would be great. I'm tired of being picked on."

Old Sol looked sadly down at the doleful moon. His voice was sympathetic but concerned. "The doctrine that Moros preaches, Loony, is just another word for death."

Yes, Stella thought; darkness and death. She had seen both when Moros attacked her, and knew it meant an eternity locked in a lightless, lifeless tomb. Stella couldn't let that happen to anyone. "Okay, I'm ready to start," she announced to the Stars before her. "Which way is the Clockwork?" The radiant faces went blank. "What's the matter? Shouldn't we get started? Just point the way, I'm ready." Neither Star responded. "Why don't you tell me?" The Stars exchanged embarrassed looks.

"Don't tell me you don't know the way out of the universe!" Stella exclaimed. "How do you expect me to find the Celestial Clockwork, when you don't even know where it is? You must know the way, you're Stars!"

"I find the admiration you hold for Stars quite remarkable, Stella. But you must try to understand", Astraea suggested, "that though you might think we are greater than you, we are incapable of much. The way to the Celestial Clockwork is beyond the Stars and can only be uncovered by a human."

"Well", Stella answered, "I have no idea how I'm supposed to leave the universe. I have no clue as to which direction to go…" Remembering the Compyxx, Venus had given her; she asked "Loony, do you have something for me?"

"Like what?" the moon cagily replied.

Quickly reaching into Loony's breast pocket, Stella responded, "Like this!" Opening the Compyxx, she held it out for the Stars to see. "This is supposed to help me on my journey and get me back home afterwards." The Stars stared blankly at the bauble. Stella held it up to see that its needle spun idly beneath the glass dome, showing no inclination to point in any direction.

"Uh…yes… of course", Old Sol skeptically assured after registering the girl's disappointment.

Stuffing the trinket into her pocket, Stella sighed, "but I'm not at all sure it works."

The Stars, the Moon, and the young human girl, stood together pondering which step to take next. Looking out the window past Loony, Stella thought she could see what looked like a dark cloud forming far off in space. She blinked and it was gone, but it reminded her just how close they all were to disaster. "I suppose I'll need a map then. Whenever we'd take a trip on Earth, we would always bring a map. Do you have a map of the universe?"

"A map? What exactly is a map?" Old Sol looked to Astraea who only mirrored his puzzled look. He called to Loony. "Moon of the Earth, do you perhaps know what a map is?"

Loony shook his gray globe, causing Old Sol to turn back to the girl in bewilderment, "What, if I may ask, is a map?"

From her pocket Stella produced a sheet of paper covered with equations, and then a small nib of a pencil. Turning the paper over to find it blank, she began to draw. "A map," she said, sketching an irregular shaped outline that vaguely resembled the state of Florida, "shows you where something is, in comparison to, something somewhere else." She drew at the top of the page another shape, one she imagined, that looked like the Arctic. "So if I wanted to go from here," she put her pencil on the Florida shape and ran it across the paper to her little Arctic," to here, I would know which way I'm supposed to go. Maps help you not get lost."

"Truly amazing!" Old Sol said. "If you are going to travel to the Celestial Clockwork, it certainly does seem as if you will need a map."

"Let me see!" Loony popped up from nowhere and snatched the paper from the girl's hands. Before she could do a thing he was out of reach, gleefully running off with his prize.

Doing his best to ignore the moon man's disruption, Old Sol asked. "Perhaps your father has such a map? Surely, if he is such a wise man as you have told us, he would." Both Old Sol and Astraea looked to the young girl, eagerly awaiting her answer.

Stella felt cheated, as neither seemed to care when she had spoken about her father before, and now, they were hoping he knew about the one thing he wouldn't even believe in. "I'm sure he doesn't have a map of the universe. My father is only just discovering the structure of the galaxy."

"Maybe if she looked in *the Astrophelarium*?" Astraea muttered to herself in a halfhearted whisper.

"What was that, Astraea?" Old Sol asked.

"The Astrophelarium," the Star woman offered, "Maybe she could find a map there?"

"Why, Astraea!" Old Sol's face lit up, every whisker glowing brighter with flame. "That's a brilliant idea! Why hadn't I thought of that? Of course! The Astrophelarium! They must have a map there!"

Stella thought it must be a good idea if Old Sol was so enthusiastic, but looking around, there was nothing nearby that looked like a laboratory, outside the lighthouse there were only the planets and nebulous sheets of stardust that shimmered and shifted. It was all very beautiful, but there was no "Astrophelarium".

"What is this *Astrophelarium,* you are talking about?" Stella asked.

"The laboratory of the telescopes!" Astraea smiled widely, as if she expected Stella to know what she was talking about and be equally as happy.

Old Sol clapped his hands together. "Yes! I'm sure one of the Earthlings there will have what we need."

"Earthlings?" Stella was surprised. "You know other people from Earth?"

"No, Stella," Astraea explained. "As Stars we are permitted little contact with the people of Terra. We can only reach them with our rays. You're the first human I've ever met. The men in the Astrophelarium are those who have attracted the special attention of Old Sol."

Old Sol interjected, "I've tried to study all I could about Terra's children. I learned a bit, but not as much as I'd like." He walked to a cabinet in the wall of the room, a trail of steaming vapor formed in his wake. Pulling out a drawer and peeking in, the Sun shook his head in frustration. Opening others, he continued his search. "I wish I knew more, your kind is a continual source of amazement to me. I so enjoy watching humans go about their random ways! But you are all so tiny, so far away; I can barely keep track of your activities." Having been through most of the drawers in the cabinet, he was still empty handed. "I also, if you have not noticed, have trouble keeping track of my *Terrascope.* Where could I have mislaid it?"

Stella looked to Astraea, who giggled softly with amusement. Loony, who had been suspiciously quiet while watching the Sun's travails, stepped to a nearby cabinet, opened it, and from within pulled a small cylinder of glittering stardust. Stella reached to take it but Loony sidestepped her deftly. "Is this what you're looking for, Sol? The *small make large*?" The moon man asked in his nicest voice, but it was obvious to Stella that he was only kissing up to the Sun.

Old Sol bent and took the device. "Why thank you Loony! You've found my Terrascope! I was beginning to think I'd never find it. You are such a help." Loony beamed at the praise, his surface glowing bright with the warmth from the Sun.

Opening the Terrascope Old Sol asked, "What did you call it, Loony? A *small make large*? That is a very apt name, for it indeed makes the small seem large and allows me a closer view of Terra's surface."

Pointing the device out a window he whispered to Stella. "I hate to say it, but humans are much more diverse than the Planets orbiting me. They go about their business willy-nilly, but somehow it all works together. Fascinating!" He handed the scope to Stella who eagerly searched for some sign of her home. She could see Earth and people racing about on it, like a hive of ants, but the Arctic was out of sight. Small wonder, as the rays of the sun did not reach that land of endless night. Disappointed, she handed the Terrascope back.

"I can't tell you how excited I was when Terra first showed signs of life on her surface. Keenly observing every development, I couldn't believe some of the things I saw. Why, you Humans have actually left the Earth's surface, which has led Mars to complain that he's had some unwelcome visitors of late. Mars is a bit of a hothead, isn't he?" Old Sol laughed heartily but Stella shuffled nervously, understanding all too well what he meant.

He continued, "But I have to let the planets be, and hope they can work out their differences. Not too long ago something happened on Mars, quite similar to what has occurred on Terra. I remember it quite vividly. Deep blue canals ran across Mars' red face, and for a time, even life! Creatures seemed ready to appear, when somehow inexplicably, all traces of life disappeared. All that potential, wasted! So now, out of all my planets, only Terra has flowered and is home to wonderful human life." Hearing the Sun's compliments Stella couldn't help but be proud.

"All your planets are wonderful, Sol. You know how your doting over Terra has not always been in her best interest" Astraea offered diplomatically.

"So perhaps some of my Planets are a bit jealous of the attention I have paid to Terra, but look what she has given the universe!" Old Sol exclaimed with a sweep of his hand. Turning to see what he was speaking about Stella blushed, as nothing was there and the Sun's eyes were focused solely on her. She hadn't ever thought humans were important to anyone but themselves.

"The Astrophelarium, Sol," Astraea prodded, "Weren't you telling Stella bout the laboratory?"

"Right! Let me do that, if I may." Old Sol said apologetically, "As I watched the beings that came to cover Terra's surface, I realized gradually that they were also observing *me*. From the earliest days when man first appeared, there have been those humans who have expressed an unwavering interest in things that lay beyond their world."

"Astronomers!" Stella shouted, "Just like my father!"

"Astronomers. Yes," Old Sol repeated the word solemnly. "I became aware that some men, some astronomers, more than anything else, loved to gaze out into the universe and study the mysteries of space. Imagine my surprise when I peered through my Terrascope to see what new tricks you humans had learned, only to find them studying me in return. I was quite impressed."

"Impressed is an understatement," Astraea laughingly chided. "Tell Stella what you did!"

"Well…" Old Sol hesitated.

"Tell me!" Stella cajoled, joining in on Astraea's game.

"Well, uh…" Flustered Sol pointed the scope to a different part of space and gestured for Stella to look. Stepping up to the scope, all Stella could see was a large chunk of space rock floating in space.

Astraea burst out laughing, "So he kept them as pets!"

Old Sol looked hurt by the words used, and with a quick gesture collapsed the Terrascope into a compact tube. "Don't say that! They aren't pets at all! They're free to do whatever they like; I have no control over their actions."

Astraea chuckled lightheartedly at Sol's dismay. "Maybe you should explain what it is you've done. Go ahead; tell Stella what the Astrophelarium is."

Old Sol reluctantly complied. "It's a laboratory to which I send those humans who have selflessly dedicated their lives to learning about space. If their lot was called before they had completed their studies, I found I couldn't allow them to perish with their labors unfinished. It took a bit of doing but I found a way to give them some extra time." Stella listened attentively as Old Sol was talking about people who were just like her father. "I moved them to a place where time behaves more like it does for Stars, thereby extending their lives for just a bit. I'm sure you realize that a millennium for Humans on Earth is more like a year for the planets, and mere days for us Stars."

Stella considered if maybe Old Sol moving these people into a place where time was slower wasn't sort of what Moros was doing, messing with time. But then she realized that changing from a faster time to a slower time was not stopping time. Because no matter how fast or slow time went, it meant there was still movement, still life, and Moros wanted neither.

"It was only after much searching that I found a suitable locale, where men could live, but where the passage of time is a less rapid than on Terra's surface." Once again Old Sol pointed his Terrascope in the direction of the strange planetoid, and only then did Stella realize that the planetoid far below was where Old Sol had sent the astronomers. Somewhere on its rocky surface must be the Astrophelarium.

"They have been there for many of your human years, working to complete their life's work", Old Sol pronounced proudly. "I'm sure they've amassed quite a sum of knowledge, in that industrious way humans do."

"So why don't you go talk to them?" Stella asked, "Wouldn't they be willing to help fight Moros? I'm sure if you asked they'd do anything to help."

"I would go if I could, but Stars may not descend to the realm of humans. The effects would be disastrous. Though I believe the heart of a human might hold the entire universe within its confines, it would be impossible for the Earth to contain the power of a Star." Sol paused before offering, "but you could go."

"Me?" Stella exclaimed, suddenly wondering if perhaps the Stars were only using her to do jobs they didn't want to do. "Go to the Astrophelarium?"

"I think it would be helpful to visit the laboratory and see if the scientists there have discovered anything that might aid you on your journey. The men I have gathered there are the most brilliant humans from all the eras of Earth. I imagine they must have a map of the universe."

"So how would I get there? If," Stella asked suspiciously… "I was willing to go?"

"I, uh, we," Old Sol answered apologetically, "have never been there, so we would not have a way to get down, would we?"

"Soooooo," Stella dragged the words out, trying hard not to get impatient, "How do you expect me to get down there?" There was an uncomfortable pause, as they exchanged dubious glances.

"Maybe use the ladder?" The answer came as Loony crawled into the lighthouse through one of its many windows, casually ignoring the stares of the Stars and the girl.

"Where have you been, Loony?" Astraea asked.

"Nowhere," the moon snapped defensively, "just waiting for you three to form a plan."

It was obvious he was hiding something, but Old Sol seemed not to notice at all. "Very well then!" he exclaimed, "Now what was your suggestion, my little silver friend?"

"I bet the ladder I gave Stella would be long enough to reach the Astrophelarium. That is, if she still wants to help."

"Why," Old Sol said, displaying only a hint of amusement at the moon man's belligerence, "I'm sure Stella wants to help, as do all who love the light."

"Well, if she really wanted to help, maybe she would've remembered the ladder. That should've been obvious to her." The moon man retorted.

At this point, Stella wasn't at all surprised by Loony's behavior. He had so many moods she couldn't predict what he would do, except to do the unexpected. First he helped her back up, and now he was all but accusing her of lying to Old Sol. Loony, Stella realized, had the ability to be a severe pest. "I forgot about the ladder!" She confessed. "It had never occurred to me that I could use it to get to the Astrophelarium."

"A likely story!" Loony snorted.

Gently, Old Sol admonished the moon man for his rudeness. "Now Loony! Stella is new here. I'm sure all that has happened has left her slightly confused. If she had known the ladder might help, I'm positive she would have mentioned it. Wouldn't you, Stella?" Stella shook her head vigorously. "Well then…perhaps we can see this ladder."

Though Stella knew she had put the ladder in a safe place, she could not remember where. Digging through her pockets, she fumbled through their contents in an effort to find the small packet. Loony snickered loudly at how clueless Stella appeared and Astraea gently put her hand on the moon man's shoulder to silence him. The imp glared at the Star woman with a particularly nasty face, as if offended by the touch.

"I know it's here somewhere," Stella griped.

"I hope you didn't lose it. That'd be the last thing I give to you." Loony taunted. Stella really wished he would just shut up for a moment. She hadn't lost the ladder; she was just a little flustered.

"Maybe you should check the pocket inside your coat." Loony suggested impatiently. Stella touched her breast pocket and immediately her fingers recognized the small square of the folded up ladder. She pulled it out, her sense of relief matched only by her annoyance at Loony.

"You knew where it was all along, didn't you?" Loony snorted. Stella moved towards the little moon man but Old Sol reached an arm out to gently block her way.

"It's alright." Old Sol whispered. "Let Loony have his little joke. We can't expect him to behave all the time, can we? Now, may I see this ladder?" Stella handed the small box to the Sun who examined it, along with Astraea.

"You climbed from the Earth on this?" the Star woman asked in astonishment.

Before Stella could turn to answer, Loony butted in. "I was the one who lowered it to her. Sending her the ladder was my idea."

"And I climbed all the way up," Stella added, not allowing Loony to so easily dismiss the work she had done. "And it was a tough climb, if I say so myself."

Astraea studied the packet closely. "If it reached Stella at the Earth's pole I suppose it would reach to the laboratory, if Stella would be open to the attempt." Behind her Loony had his thumbs in his ears and was flapping his hands. She decided that going down would be better than staying another moment with Loony, now that he was in one of his nasty phases.

"Sure, I'll give it a try." Stella said bravely.

"And I'm going too", Loony shouted.

"No you're not!" Stella blurted. Whatever else, she just wanted to get away from him for a while.

"If you leave me here, I'll, I'll…" He brayed.

"What will you do?" Astraea's voice rang out firmly, the moon man's antics having stretched her patience a bit too far.

Sensing the tension, Old Sol patiently explained to the upset imp, why he could not go. "You know you cannot descend into the realm of men. If you were to go there, it would only aid Moros' plan. There is an order to the universe Loony, and that order dictates that your place is up here." Putting a hand on Loony's shoulder, Sol chuckled. "Besides, I'm afraid that if you went down to the laboratory, the men there would be unable to tell you anything, so stunned would they be to see the handsome likes of you!"

The compliment calmed Loony. "Okay," he pouted, "But when she comes back, I'm going with her on the rest of the trip." No one, not Stella or Astraea or even Old Sol, dared to dispute his claim.

The Sun turned to Stella. "Please, when you get to the laboratory, don't mention that you've met us. I've come to feel from my studying of Earthlings, that unless it's an absolute necessity as it was in your case, men don't need to know how Stars act."

Stella was confused. "Why is that?"

"It would be cruel to have those who have always looked to the Stars as beacons of hope and perfection," Old Sol chuckled, "to find out that we're not much different from them in our behavior, with all the same frailties and foibles."

Stella remembered how the Planets held the Sun in such reverence. "The planets seemed to think you were perfect. All their fuss made me nervous to meet you."

Old Sol broke a bright beaming smile. "And I wouldn't want them to think any less. Why, if they ever saw me doing this…" He pointed his finger in the air and began turning it in tight small circles. Brightly colored rays of light shot from the finger and with a quick flip of his wrist, Old Sol flipped the beams into his other waiting hand. With an end of the beam in each hand he bent the rays, forming a large arc whose ends rested in each of his palms. Stella squealed with delight as Old Sol put the rainbow around her neck and tied it like a luminous scarf.

"What would they think? If my Planets ever saw me do that, I don't think they'd be too inclined to stay in my orbit!" Old Sol exclaimed, and Stella having met the pompous planets, knew it was probably true. "So please don't tell anyone about me. It's best they discover that for themselves."

"I can't tell the scientists in the Astrophelarium about you either? What am I supposed to say when I get down there?"

"Well, they're explorers and inventors." Old Sol said.

"And?" Stella countered.

"And," Sol continued, "As explorers if they knew the answers, then they wouldn't have to explore anymore, would they?" As the argument seemed reasonable, Stella nodded in agreement. "So if you told them what you've learned about the stars and the planets or how the universe works, maybe they'd think that their explorations weren't needed."

Astraea spoke up. "Humans need mysteries in their lives. It's the way they are. It's what keeps them alive."

Stella thought about how her father would spend so much time studying the stars, searching for the next piece in the puzzle, and how happy he would be when he made even the smallest discovery. "I understand. I know someone like that."

"Thank you, Stella. So you'll promise not to mention me or Astraea or any of the Planets?"

Stella nodded her head. "I promise."

"Or about your mission?"

Stella nodded again. "Then what should I tell them? I'm not a very good liar." She had never been good at telling stories, not half as good as were Tim and Pace.

"Just ask for their help." Astraea answered, "Ask for a map of the universe."

Stella thought, if she only asked for a map and avoided any mention of the Sun or the Stars or the Planets, she wouldn't have to tell any lies. "I can do that," she exclaimed.

The Sun beamed happily. "Great! Now let me see if I can get this ladder down to the laboratory." He went to a window and unfolding the ladder, dropped it over the edge.

Astraea went to him and together they worked on positioning the ladder. Old Sol would check the ladder's bearing through the Terrascope and the Star woman shifted the ladder according to his recommendations. "Just a hair left. A little more.... now to the right..."

Stella sat nearby; saving her energy for what she imagined would be another long climb. Next to her, Loony was digging a finger into his ear. Stella could hear rock rumbling inside as he probed deeper. "Can't you just slide me down to the lab?" she asked.

"That's an easy one." Loony responded, pulling his finger from his ear with a pop, "No." He chuckled, seeming pleased to deliver the negative response. "The further it gets from your birthday, the harder it gets to move you through the spheres. Now, well maybe they won't tell you", he jerked a rocky thumb towards the couple at the window, "but the mission is going to be a lot harder than you think."

"But then why were you so angry when Old Sol said you couldn't come with me? Why would you even want to come along? I'm the one who's unlucky enough to have been picked for this."

"You don't know how lucky you are."

"Why is that?" Stella asked, not believing how nutty Loony could be. The Earth, no, the whole universe was in danger, an agent of darkness was threatening her family and she was being sent to find a way to the end of the universe, which seemed a near impossible task. Stella wouldn't call that luck.

"Cause you're human."

Stella was surprised that the Moon could be jealous of a young girl. "Lucky because I'm human? You're the Moon; I can't imagine being anything better than that." Actually, Stella could, imagining that being the Sun or one of the Planets might be better than being the Moon, but she didn't dare say that.

"Oh yeah?" Loony pouted, "Well you know what? Old Sol only sees humans through his scope, but I've watched them up close. A lot of times when I see what they're doing, I wish I was a human. You get to do such cool stuff, whatever you choose! I don't get a choice of what I want to do. I have to orbit Terra, because I'm her Moon. But if I were a human like you, there's so much stuff I would do. If I could be a human, just for a day, I'd lay in that green stuff... What do you call it?"

"Grass?" Stella supposed.

"Yeah! I'd lie in that grass and look up at a blue sky, instead of just seeing the same old dark space. Then maybe I'd drink some of that wet stuff I always see you human's drink. There are so many fun things humans get to do. I wish I had just one chance to know what that's like and not have to be stuck in the same old orbit."

It was obvious that Loony wasn't happy, but Stella couldn't tell if it was because he missed Earth, felt abandoned by her, or really wished he were free of her orbit. The many moods of the madcap moon were difficult to gauge, harder than even Tim and Pace, who Stella had always thought behaved in the least understandable ways. "But", she asked, "You love Terra, don't you?"

The moon man looked from beneath rocky brows, and in them Stella saw a flash of uncertainty and doubt. "Of course I love her! But am I supposed to stay in her orbit forever? Lately, she doesn't even seem to care how I'm doing. I haven't heard from her for so long! There's got to be a better way." The tiny eyes smoldered in their rocky sockets as they shifted towards Astraea. "Sometimes I think the Stars like making us Moons and Planets do exactly what they want, no matter how we feel about it. Sometimes, I wonder why I just can't do whatever I want."

Stella tried to reason with the Moon. "Old Sol told you why you just can't do whatever you want; it's not how things work. Don't be so rebellious; you know that only helps Moros. We all have to work together, and do our part if we want to keep Terra," She eyed the maniacal moon to see if he was grasping her logic, "and the universe, safe."

"Well," Loony snapped, "I still don't see why you get to have all the fun!"

"It's ready Stella!!" Old Sol called out, and relieved to end the futile exchange, Stella walked quickly to the window. Peering down, the ladder disappeared into the depths.

"I think we have the ladder correctly aligned. It should bring you to the laboratory." Old Sol handed her the Terrascope and looking through it, Stella tried to figure out how far it was to the bottom. It was impossible to tell.

The look of dismay on Stella's face let Astraea know the girl was not pleased about what she had seen. "It's urgent you find a map. How else will we know where we are to travel?"

Old Sol was at her side. "Please hurry, Stella. There is little time left to thwart Moros' plans. It is vital that the Celestial Clockwork is wound before it stops. Listen, do you hear it?" He tilted his head, and pulling back some of his fiery locks cupped his hand to his ear. "It is slowing with every tick."

Stella concentrated and could hear it too then. The sound was so familiar she felt as if she had heard it many times before, and even though it was not loud, she realized it must have been there all along, only she had never noticed. What resounded through her mind was a low thud that permeated everything and then fell silent, leaving emptiness, like the gap between breaths. And with that Stella could somehow see, in that moment in-between the ticks and tocks, a hint of dimming as if light for a moment had lost its hold on the universe. Then all space was filled once again with the sound of the mysterious ticking, and the disturbing suggestion of a challenge to light vanished.

"That's the ticking of the clockwork." Old Sol whispered urgently. "It's far slower and weaker than I have ever heard before. The clockwork must be wound, or I fear what the consequences might be."

"*Consequences*." Loony repeated, but in a questioning tone that suggested he was unfamiliar with the meaning of the word.

"Please come back quickly." Astraea pleaded and that appeal prompted Stella to action. As she lifted a leg over the shimmering sill of the lighthouse window, Old Sol helped her by gently steadying her shoulders. Finding her footing, Stella took a last look at her strange new friends and began her descent

10 THE ASTROPHELARIUM

As Stella climbed out of sight, Astraea called for her to be careful and promised they would see each other soon. That reunion could not come soon enough, for soon as her descent grew tiresome, Stella wished that the Star woman or Old Sol could have come with her, if only for the company. Going down was supposed to be easier but that was not the truth, and soon Stella's hands and legs hurt so much that she couldn't wait to let go of the ladder and just sit for a while. Perhaps, she considered as her every muscle ached, offering to retrieve a map from the Astrophelarium had been a mistake.

But going back up could only be worse, even though she was not yet able to see her destination. The ladder below her faded into the mists of space, while above the sun seemed uncomfortably distant. It was these in between moments where the safety of the past was gone and the unknowable future laid ahead that concerned Stella most.

After climbing for longer than she cared to think about, Stella was stopped by a *chirp* that broke the sterile silence. On a rung below her feet, a bird perched singing. Its bright vermilion breast and glistening opal eyes, reminded Stella who had not seen a bird in all her months in the Arctic, just how beautiful these creatures could be. Catching her breath she let the bird's gentle cooing caress her ears, and moving closer almost fell from the ladder when she heard between pauses of the beautiful birdsong, the surprising whir of gears. As the bird flew off, Stella caught sight where its wings met its body, the glint of metal. "Now that was strange!" she commented before continuing her arduous descent.

With muscles aching at the touch of every rung, eventually but not soon enough for the sore climber, a large chunk of rock came into sight below. Studying her destination, Stella was glad to see in one of the deep crevices scarring the craggy planetoid, the dim glow of light. She was even more pleased, the ladder pointed in just that direction. Soon the rim of the crevice was overhead and as the girl moved further into the canyon the light grew brighter. Nestled deep in the rocky crack was a large structure, its windows glowing with light, and the nearer Stella came to it, the more familiar the building seemed. There had been a building just like it Stella remembered, constructed of equally austere blocks of stone, on the campus where her father taught. That was the College Library, whose grim granite façade belied the storehouse of novelties within.

Looking down to where the ladder ended, Stella saw a large skylight cut in the building's roof and through the skylight a cluttered room. Dim shapes of men moved about a large telescope that stood directly beneath the window. She could glimpse other men off to the sides, standing at workbenches or sitting at desks covered with stacks of books and papers. Golden letters inlaid in the floor and encircling the base of the telescope spelled the words "Wisdom begins in wonder."

Stella was glad to see the men below; with all the strange beings she had recently met, it would be nice to be with some real humans for a while, and astronomers at that. Now she only needed to find a map to the Celestial Clockwork, and when that was done, Stella groaned at the thought, climb back up. "Hopefully they have what I need. At least then there'd be a reason for this climb." Now close enough to catch her reflection in the skylight's glass, Stella imagined that when she reached it, she would be able to pass right through, just as she had at her bedroom window.

With her hands becoming blistered and the soles of her feet growing sore, Stella couldn't wait to get off the ladder. Encouraged by the prospect of getting off the ladder and onto solid ground, she raced downwards taking each rung, sometimes two, in hurried bounds. Rushing towards the skylight she bounded, her feet reaching for rung after rung until they found… nothing.

With her feet meeting only air, Stella's hands instinctively tightened their grip on the rungs. For one terrifying moment she struggled to hold her weight as she dangled in the air. With the last of her strength she pulled her self back up onto the ladder, tired arms aching as she did. Her heart pounding as she clung to the ladder, she looked down to see that its last rung was some fifteen feet short of the skylight window.

Relief that she had saved herself, was Stella's first emotion, anger her second, unable to believe Old Sol and Astraea would let her climb all the way down, only to be left hanging exhausted in space. If the ladder didn't reach all the way to the laboratory, they shouldn't have sent her at all. She'd have a talk with them when she got back, she was sure of that, but now she wondered, what was she expected to do?

Below, the large crystalline lens mounted atop the telescope, stared from beneath the skylight like an enormous unblinking eye. Around the telescope's hefty base, a strange group of men were convened. One wore what looked to be a sheet wrapped around his body, while another sporting a bushy beard, was in long robes more likely seen at graduation ceremonies. Shifting on the ladder to get a better look into the room, Stella saw that each of the men within was wearing a different type of costume; some familiar from movies and books, others in styles she had never seen. It appeared an argument was occurring, as everyone was wildly gesticulating while they meandered about the telescope.

Knowing she couldn't hang on the ladder forever, Stella searched her pockets for anything that might help her get safely into the lab. She fished out three pennies and two dimes from their hiding place deep in her parka's hip pocket. The first penny hit the window with a sharp, *plink*. While engrossed in arguments so vehement, no one heard the sound. Stella wondered if she should wait until the discussion subsided before trying again, but being so exhausted she knew she couldn't risk waiting.

She didn't drop the second penny, but threw it. It met the glass with a louder, *PLINK*! Again no one noticed. Stella thought it odd that not one of the men below had yet to look into the telescope, even when it was obviously the cause of their disagreement. If they did, they couldn't help but see her.

Then, one, two, three... Aiming right for the center of the window, she flung the last three coins. Each hit with a distinct, *thwack*. The heated discussion continued unabated as if there was nothing that could break the men from their debate. Feeling dispirited and abandoned, Stella clung to her perch with aching arms and wondered how long it would be before she lost her grip and plummeted through the skylight glass.

Then from the corner of her eye, she noticed that one of the men who had been working at a cluttered desk near the telescope had gotten up and was timidly making his way beneath the window. He was a short dapper man with brown hair and moustache, and although his clothes looked like antiques, they were more modern than most of the other costumes in the room. He kept his distance from the group of arguing men, circling cautiously around them, but it was immediately obvious to Stella that he was trying to get a better look through the skylight.

Looking directly at her, the curious man shielded his eyes, scratched his head and stared a moment. Then he briskly walked away. Stella screamed after him, "No, don't go! I need your help!"

The man returned to his desk, again avoiding the disgruntled men who argued, oblivious to all else. Back at his desk, he pulled a pad from beneath stacks of books and scribbled something with a pen. He made his way back beneath the window and held up the pad. Seeing the words, *HELLO, MY NAME IS PERCEVAL*, printed in large script, the flowery kind, as if someone had diligently practiced their penmanship, Stella smiled. That was her father's name! The dapper man smiled back.

Holding a finger up as if to say he'd be back in a moment, Perceval shuffled over toward the group arguing around the telescope, to a man somewhat older and wearing what looked like wizard's robes. Perceval paused anxiously, as if to consider the consequences of his action, and then reluctantly tugged at the wizard's sleeve. The wizard was not pleased with the intrusion, though Stella thought that any relief from the intense debate would be welcomed. Before Perceval had a chance to speak, the wizard angrily scolded him for interrupting, so loudly even Stella high above, could hear a muffled roar. Through with his outburst, the wizard abruptly turned back to the argument, seemingly with renewed vigor.

Perceval shrugged his shoulders as if to say he was aware of what was coming but had no choice in the matter, and pulled on the sleeve once again. Feeling the tug, the wizard threw his palms up to the group with whom he fought, immediately halting the heated debate. Dramatically he turned and glaring at Perceval, began to unleash an unrelenting stream of verbal abuse. The volume of this volley forced even those with whom the wizard had been arguing, to take a step back. Perceval though stood his ground, and Stella was sorry that he, who was only trying to help her, had to suffer such an assault.

When the wizard had fully vented his rage and paused to catch his breath; Perceval who had patiently endured the abuse, seized the opportunity of having the attention of all and pointed to the skylight. Only the wizard chose to ignore the motion, but the others followed his finger out into the sky. All eyes widened upon seeing a girl hanging precariously on a ladder from the sky. Stella, arms locked to the ladder, nodded in greeting. The wizard, finally deigning to take notice of Perceval's gesture, turned to look. The anger on his face swiftly melted into amazement.

Feeling her grip beginning to slip Stella shouted, "Can you help me? There's not enough of this ladder to make it down. I need help!"

Only Perceval responded, scampering off to a device comprised of gears and pulleys and turning the crank on its side. The skylight opened, its two windows of paned glass parting in the center and sliding into recesses in the roof.

Through the opening, Stella begged for assistance. "Can you find a way to get me down? I can't hold on much longer!"

From the surrounding desks and workbenches, a curious crowd had assembled beneath the skylight to gaze in astonishment at the girl. The wizard pushed to the center of the mob in a swirl of robes. Gesturing for silence with a flourish of his hands, he addressed Stella in a pious and pompous voice, "Oh heavenly messenger, what news do you bring us from the stars?"

"Can you help me down?" Stella implored. "Please! I'm slipping!"

The man who looked like a wizard didn't hear what she was saying, or if he did, he didn't care. "Oh brilliant messenger of the stars!" he beseeched dramatically. "Do you come to end our imprisonment?"

"Please help!!" Stella cried as her legs gave out and her feet slipped from the rungs. Sliding off the ladder she caught the final rung and dangled there, high above the laboratory floor.

Within the commotion below Perceval sprang into action. Yanking the wrapping off the toga wearing man, he shouted instructions, and upon his orders the men nearby hurriedly grabbed an edge of the piece of cloth. Slipping from the ladder, all Stella saw was a large white square being pulled taut amidst the crowd below. Plunging from above she hit the square, bounced lightly back into the air, and then fell gently into the soft white cloth. The faces of the men who held the sheet looked down to where Stella had landed, safely. One wizened and half naked bleated pathetically, "Can I have my clothes back now?"

Perceval extended his hand as the men lowered Stella to the ground. She felt the sheet pulled from beneath her feet and stumbled off, as an old man cold and shriveled, hastily retrieved his toga.

"Easy, Aristotle! Let her off first!" Perceval laughed.

Aristotle grumbled crossly while he dressed. Throwing a corner of sheet over his shoulder and tucking it into the belt of fabric around his waist the ancient Greek retreated in embarrassment to the back of the crowd, furious at being humiliated but too curious about the new arrival to leave.

The wizard pushed forward to snatch Stella's hand from the resourceful Perceval's and in a flowery voice began his oration. "We welcome you, oh emissary of the Stars, to our humble laboratory." He took off his cap and bowed low. "We beseech thee to teach us the ways of the heavens."

Prying her hand from the wizard's grip, Stella replied. "I'm sorry to say that I'm not a Star or an angel, but only a human, just like you."

Hearing Stella's reply, an agitated Aristotle shouted from the rear of the crowd. "You are a being from the sky, but not of the stars? Girls are of the Earth, and stars of the heavens. If it falls from the sky, it must be of the Stars. That is irrefutable!"

A man in a powdered wig, who had been observing quietly, walked up to Stella. He took a strand of her hair in his hand and pulling a small monocular from his chest pocket, examined its length.

"I conclude this girl is quite human. Of this there is no doubt." The dandy pronounced in an eloquent voice. "So logic dictates that humans, through some development of which we are not yet aware, now inhabit the heavens!"

Stella started to correct the man's mistake, but before she could, another stated abruptly. "You are incorrect! She fell from above so she must be an example of what a star would drop! I am afraid for us, my colleagues! She is only the first of many, I fear. Soon the droppings of the stars shall cover us all!"

This rather odd theory concerning the origins of their new arrival, prompted many bellicose responses with no one listening to what anyone else had to say. As the volume of the argument grew, some men sheepishly abandoned the dispute and slunk off to their desks. Though central to the raging debate, Stella was all but forgotten in the violence of the argument, and stepping cautiously away from the fray she studied her surroundings.

She stood at the center of a cavernous room that might once have been orderly but now was in complete disarray. Everywhere stacks of devices and equipment, mostly unrecognizable, were abandoned in unruly heaps. Shattered telescopes and astrolabes lay in piles, and clocks of every type, some with large dials painted with astronomical designs, others with any number of hours but twelve, some with four, six, ten hands, tottered in the debris.

Whoever wasn't laboring at a workbench on some strange device was hunched over a desk engrossed in studying or transcribing some crumbling old scroll or dusty leather volume. The floor was littered with papers, and those close enough to read, were scrawled with many languages. Some were covered with long equations and others showed sketches of planets and star systems. Some were blueprints of machines and mechanisms, some impeccably drafted, some scribbled in hasty scrawls. Teetering towers of books were stacked everywhere amongst the clutter. Overall, the Astrophelarium was a shambles.

The one object that stood out amongst the mess was the gigantic device beneath the skylight. It looked to be a telescope, but was the weirdest Stella had ever seen; so festooned with piping and dials and knobs, that there was not an empty inch left on its casing. Capping its upper end was a lens of polished glass nearly five feet across. Stella, knowing that the larger the lens the more chance there would be defects in the glass, wondered what could be seen through it. Even stranger, not one of the scientists who stood perpetually arguing at the scope's base exhibited any inclination to gaze through its lens.

As the others argued about what exactly Stella might be; star or girl, star dropping or reject; the wizard looking man turned to the girl. "If you are not from the Stars, where are you from?" He scowled angrily. "Casual visitors are not welcome here. We do not need our experiments disrupted. If you are not a messenger from the stars, and do not come bearing that which will complete our opus, then you will need to leave, now!" Taking Stella by the hand, he began to drag her across the debris strewn floor.

"Nick!" A shout from behind stopped him in his tracks.

The Wizard turned to glare at Perceval. "My name is not 'Nick'. I demand you address me as Copernicus."

"Let her go, she's just a girl. You remember them, don't you? That's something you should remember no matter how long you've been trapped here. If you don't want her, maybe you should let me take care of her." Perceval winked at Stella and gently took her hand from the angry wizard. "Besides, Mister Copernicus, you know that no one can get off this rock. Now young lady, perhaps you would like a tour of our.... home."

Perceval led the girl quickly away. Careful not to look back, Stella could feel Copernicus's angry glare burning a hole in her back, and only when they had turned a corner and were hidden from his sight did she breath a sigh of relief. Peeking back from behind a jumbled stack of books to make sure they had not been followed, Perceval chuckled. "He can be so angry. I often wonder if his time trapped here has made him that way, or was he so irritable even back on Earth."

With his easy smile and twinkling eyes, Perceval's friendly demeanor made Stella feel at ease. As she looked around the laboratory, a crop of questions about this strange place popped into her head. There were so many odd projects going on, each being intensely worked on by different men, and strangest of all, the men themselves seemed to be from far-flung periods of earth's history.

"Why is everyone dressed so differently?" was the first question Stella asked her guide.

There was an immediate look of surprise on Perceval's face. "Do you not know where you are?" Stella shook her head. She only knew what Old Sol had told her and that wasn't a lot.

Perceval closing his eyes placed a finger to the side of his nose as he deliberated on how to answer the girl. "I'm worried about how to explain this all to you. It is exceedingly strange, this situation we find ourselves in, and I do not wish to shock you."

"I'm not sure anything could shock me," Stella thought, careful not to say it aloud, "after meeting the moon, planets and Sun."

In an uncharacteristically bold flourish, the proper gentleman flung his arms out as if to encompass the entire hall. "We call this place the

Astrophelarium. It is where scholars from all ages have mysteriously found themselves; and all here combined, can't figure out why."

"You're telling me these men have been brought here from different times? You expect me to believe that man was really Copernicus?" Stella's eyes widened as she remembered her history, "He was born in 1473!"

"You know of Copernicus? You are very knowledgeable for one so young." Perceval studied the girl with admiration, and Stella felt herself blushing under his gaze. "Yes, he was born in the fifteenth century. I myself come from a later period, the 1890s. You are American, am I correct?" He peeked through his glasses at Stella, who nodded. "Ah yes, very good! So am I! Most of the others working here, such as Copernicus, or Koepler, and even Abul Warif the Arab astronomer and alchemist, are familiar to me through their writings and through history. But most of them here have never heard of me at all, which is perhaps why I receive so little respect. "Perhaps you have heard of me?" He whispered hopefully. "My name is Perceval Lowell."

Stella's jaw dropped; of course she knew of Perceval Lowell!! He was one of the most famous American astronomers. If it were not for him, astronomy would not be what it was today. "I know this might sound strange, but you're my father's hero," she confessed.

His eyebrows arched, "Really? His hero?" Professor Lowell seemed pleasantly surprised. "And who is your father, if I may ask?"

"His name is Perceval Ray. He was named after you."

"Named after me? I'm deeply honored. And what might your father's profession be? Is he a studier of the stars? An astronomer, perhaps?"

Stella took a deep breath and tried to calm down, so excited was she to be talking to the real Professor Perceval Lowell! At school she was the only person who knew who Perceval Lowell was. When all the other girls would talk about the latest pop idols, she would try to bring Perceval Lowell into the conversation and talk about how cool he was. She would tell how he had made his own telescope and built his own observatory in Arizona when hardly anyone else lived there, and how he had spent all his time studying Mars. She would try to explain to her classmates just how hard it had been for him, being out in the mountains alone, trying to discover what no one else knew. He had been a real explorer, exploring a place faraway from Earth.

Most of the other girls though, would just stare at Stella and giggle and then someone would inevitably say something mean. It was usually Brittany who did this; Brittany who thought she was the coolest girl in the class. She would start talking about how there was nothing cool about anything from a long time ago, because there was no TV then, no Internet and no MP3s. Then Brittany would laugh at Stella, and some of the other girls would join in, but not all of them. Some of them, Stella always felt, sort of understood what she meant about how living their dreams was the coolest thing someone could do; how if someone would do that, even if they weren't big stars on TV or the radio, or even if what they were doing was something that not many people knew or cared about, that it was still cool. Sometimes people did things simply because they believed in them, and that, Stella had decided was the coolest thing anyone could do. And Perceval Lowell had done precisely that.

"Yes, my father is an astronomer, and he's made a discovery, a big discovery. But it's not a good thing he's discovered, it's a terrible thing and I found out that it …" Stella stopped, realizing she was already saying too much. Though she wanted badly to tell Professor Lowell all about her mission, she had given her word not to tell.

"What's the matter, young lady?" The Professor asked, concerned. "Is there something wrong?"

"No…" Stella replied unconvincingly, "nothing's wrong." But in her head another voice roared, reverberating against the bony walls of her skull, *everything is wrong! Moros! And Verena Maldek! And a darkness, that's trying to extinguish all the light!* She winced and fought the voice down, trying to act as if in fact everything was fine.

"Hmm…" Professor Lowell responded, as he inquisitively eyed the young girl. "Well, if there is anything wrong, anything at all, I'd hope you'd feel safe confiding in me, Miss…." Perceval's face flushed red in embarrassment. "Oh please forgive me! I have been such a bad host, why we haven't yet been properly introduced!" Bending at the waist the genteel scholar spoke. "I am Professor Perceval Lowell, of Flagstaff, Arizona. Would you do me the honor of telling me your name, young lady?"

Charmed, the girl responded. "It's so nice to meet you. My name is Stella Ray. I'm from Florida."

"Wonderful!" The Professor exclaimed, "A simply marvelous name! And now, Miss Ray, of what service may I be to you?"

"Service?" Stella asked.

"Assistance? Aid? You mentioned you had arrived here seeking help?" Professor Lowell asked.

"Yes, that's true." Wondering how to phrase her request without sounding totally ridiculous or spilling the beans about Old Sol and Astraea, Stella simply spit it out. "I need a map of the universe, as quickly as possible."

She waited, wondering when Professor Lowell would laugh and call her crazy. He did neither, but only stroked his mustache, contemplating the request. "A map of the universe? What need would such a lovely lady have for that?"

Staring at her feet which were nervously tapping the wooden floor, Stella answered. "I'd rather not say, but I'd really appreciate any help you can offer."

Perceval arched his eyebrows, uncertain how to respond. "Well I'm sure that some of what we've discovered about the universe might interest you, if learning about it is why you are here. But since the universe extends endlessly, no map would be able to chart its confines, as they are boundless," he sighed.

Leaving Stella no time to respond, Perceval quickly led the way down a crooked aisle. "But before you ask any more questions, I'd like to introduce you to other inmates of this grand prison in which we find ourselves trapped."

As she followed, Stella looked about for any sign of bars or locks. "Inmates?"

"Do not let your eyes deceive you; this is beyond doubt a prison. Just as we have no clue how we were brought here, we are equally certain that there is no way out. Those who have been brought to the Astrophelarium seem destined to remain here. We have lost all hope of escape."

"I'll find a way", Stella promised herself. She had found a way in, and when she found a map, she would find a way out to continue on with her mission. "There's always hope, there has to be hope." She whispered.

Not wishing to dishearten her, Perceval merely answered softly, "Yes, you are right. There is always hope." And then changing subjects from one so dreary, he took Stella by the hand and led her away. "I'll introduce you to one of our companions, one who has never lost hope. Perhaps he'll have some idea as to how to help you."

As they made their way down the aisles, Stella couldn't help but wonder if Old Sol had really imprisoned these scientists. He seemed so kind and thoughtful; it was hard to believe he was capable of holding anyone against their will. True, he had saved them from death, but now they were stuck here by no choice of their own. Following Perceval down the rows of desks, it was hard for Stella to understand just what Old Sol had been thinking when he filled the lab with these men.

Walking past a discussion held by a group of men, Stella stopped. "Who is that?" she whispered.

"That," Perceval Lowell whispered back, his voice tinted with a hint of trepidation, "is Tycho Brahe..." He shrugged a shoulder towards a stout man wearing a fancy set of velvet clothes with a large ruffle encircling his neck. Stella didn't like to stare, but she couldn't take her eyes off the man's nose. It seemed to be made of nothing less then shiny silver.

Perceval pulled her away nervously, "Tycho lost his nose, and I believe it was in a duel with swords." A shudder shook his body, "If stared at, he can be very cross."

Stella quickly looked away from the nose and her gaze passed to a man that seemed old beyond belief. "And who's that?"

"Irarum," Perceval answered, "the oldest inhabitant of the Astrophelarium and the first to arrive here. He is a Chaldean, the earliest people to study the stars."

Stella once read about Chaldeans in a book on the history of Astronomy. The very first page mentioned the original astronomers and there had been drawings of a person dressed just like this man, Irarum, who wore rough leather sandals, a tunic that had the texture of a burlap bag, and a leather cap sewn with a thick piece of cord. Both looked very primitive, almost stone age.

Continuing, they made their way around a high pile of books that had collapsed in a landslide from a nearby desk. Perceval intrepidly climbed over the stack, papers sliding beneath his feet and when he had reached the other side, Stella followed. Scrambling across, she found the scientist staring upwards, petrified as the lights of the laboratory dimmed. As the candles within the elaborate chandeliers flickered and shrank, the air in the room became thick with gloom. The bustling racket of the scientist's labors quieted as a gust of unknown origin blew across the desks, eerily lifting papers from their piles, to deposit them haphazardly amongst the clutter littering the floor.

Stella felt Perceval's hand grip her shoulder as the darkness deepened and an icy chill permeated the room. "Be brave, it will pass..." Stella couldn't be sure if the professor was addressing her, or himself.

For a few long moments no one moved and a disquieting apprehension hung in the air. Stella shivered and pulled her parka tight around her body. Then as unexpectedly as the lamps had dimmed, they brightened and the frigid breeze ceased. The room stirred slowly back to life as the morbid darkness dissipated. Loosening his hold on the girl's shoulder, Perceval wheezed in relief. "I'm glad that's over."

Stella didn't need to ask what had just happened; she'd seen it all before, only couldn't be sure if it was a symptom of the clockwork winding down, or due to some malign influence of Moros or a combination of the two. "What just happened?" She asked, purposefully widening her eyes in surprise.

Perceval shrugged off the chill before answering. "To be honest, we do not know. That phenomenon had not been observed until recently, but now occurs with increasing regularity and strength. We are concerned that soon the lights might not revive, and this inescapable prison will be plunged forever into darkness." He cast a wary glance toward the ceiling and Stella could see just how deeply the intrusion of darkness had upset him. "I think it would be best to introduce you to the wisest of our band. If anyone here has the ability to answer your questions, I truly believe it would be him."

Stella was led to a small shanty, constructed using bookcases as walls. It was one of many dotting the laboratory, obviously built as a reprieve from the endless hubbub. Walking into the cubicle was like stepping into the past, as its walls were covered in weathered tapestries. Stella had seen such artworks before in museums on Earth, but these were much more curious examples. One of the richly embroidered landscapes was populated with all types of fantastic beings, engaged in a fierce battle. On the right side of the tableaux were creatures bright and shining, while the left was seething with a horde of darker monsters. Both groups clashed in the center, where Stella was surprised to find meticulously depicted in the most skilled needlework, a mechanism ready to burst from its bulging overflow of gears.

"Doctor?" Perceval whispered, careful to avoid startling the bearded old man who sat deeply involved in calculations of some sort. Noticing a set of copper instruments upon the desk, Stella recognized a compass and ruler, but others were unfamiliar. At the sound, the doctor laid down an odd device that he had been using to measure out divisions on a thick piece of parchment.

"Yes! Well hello!" The doctor happily greeted his guests. "Perceval! How grand it is to see you! And who is your young friend? Perhaps, she is a new arrival to the workshop?"

"This is Stella Ray, and she has just fallen, literally, into our midst." Perceval said in way of an introduction, "I am endeavoring to make her comfortable while here, for however long that might be."

Maybe it was the austere style of the room or the august bearing of the elder man, that made Stella bend her knees in a tiny curtsy. She surprised herself with the action, one she had never performed before, but had seen in old movies. It seemed like the right thing to do, and she did it without thought.

"Pleased to meet you Doctor…" She hesitated, realizing she had not picked up his name.

"Doctor Dee, fair child!" With his long white beard flowing around him, the old man bounded around the desk in a youthful movement, oddly mismatched to someone of his obvious age. "Your name is Stella Ray? Why, you so remind me very much of a child I met once long ago. Her name was Madimi, and a most astounding child she was."

With deep blue eyes the doctor studied the young girl, and Stella felt as if he were searching her soul. "And may I say," He continued, "that I can also see that you are not an ordinary child, though it is true that none who come to the Astrophelarium are of common stuff."

"And she has come to us through the oddest of circumstances." Perceval added.

"Yes?" The doctor asked, with evident interest. "What would those consist of?"

"I fell from a ladder in the sky!" Stella blurted, hoping to avoid any other questions of how she had arrived.

"A ladder in the sky? That is a most peculiar way to arrive." The doctor studied the girl with even greater scrutiny. "From where did that ladder descend?"

Even though this old man appeared kind and wise, Stella couldn't tell him about Old Sol and his lighthouse. "I don't remember!" she squealed, it was all she could think of to stop the questioning from veering towards things she had promised not to discuss.

"You don't remember where you've come from?" The old man asked suspiciously, though the smile on his face never faded. "Then how will you know where you are to go?"

This was a question Stella wished she could answer. "I wish I knew!" It felt good to say something honestly and mean it. She hated to deceive the good doctor or her new friend, Perceval.

"Then perhaps I can help you. By reading the cipher of the Stars I may see what fate holds in store for you. What do you remember of how you got here?"

Stella thought for a moment, not sure exactly what to say. "I remember going to bed at my home, and then waking up on the ladder." She thought that was as good an answer as any, as it left out any mention of meeting Sol or the Planets.

"I see. That explains why you can remember your name." Doctor Dee said agreeably, "Might you also remember your birth date?"

Stella wondered why the old man would ask that question, but it didn't seem as if he would try to trick her. This made her feel worse, because she was trying to trick him. "My birth date? Yes, I remember it. Why would you like to know?"

"It might aid in discovering where you have come from and more importantly, help in understanding where you might go."

That was what Stella was waiting to hear, "Could you really do that? Could you tell me where I'm supposed to go?"

The bearded man chuckled. "The oracle of the horoscope will reveal where you are destined to go. But whether you go where you are fated is a choice for you alone to decide. Destiny is only the end which fate seeks to impose. But we as Humans have the ability, or rather the blessing, to foil the harsh designs fate seeks to imprint on us. Through my labors I may be able to provide you some insight as, how to avoid a less desirable destiny and achieve one of your own choosing, one more harmonious with the workings of the universe." Suddenly becoming very serious, the old man reached for a nearby book, flung it open to a marked page and jabbed a finger into its depths.

"These figures represent the figures of the zodiac. They enclose our world in their harsh band…" Stella stood on tip toes to make out what the old man was pointing to, and saw animals and strange beings arranged in a circle. The Zodiac; Stella was reluctant to even say the word. Doctor Dee's finger brushed the image of Scorpio and the girl felt a wave of dread cross her heart. "The drawing of a horoscope is based on understanding the influences and powers which these twelve living figures seek to exert on unsuspecting humans."

Stella couldn't help but ask, "I've heard about horoscopes, people use them to tell their future, right?"

The old man looked up, his long white beard flowing, and pushed the book aside. "Forecasting the future is a corruption of the sacred science of Astrology. Some use the horoscope to predict the future and tie themselves to the lot that it foretells. By slavishly accepting the fate that has been so assigned, many fail to venture from that predetermined path." Using his compass he drew a circle on the paper before him. "And the path that fate prescribes is always one of sorrow and perpetual return."

The doctor skillfully sketched a series of symbols around the perimeter of the circle. "Astrology, which is ancient and venerable, was originally contrived to inform people on how they might be able to break free of the fate assigned for them at their birth. At the time a child is born, the Zodiac lays chains upon it, constraining its freedoms, restricting its movements through life, seeking to control that person's destiny."

He drew lines across the circle, from symbol to symbol, complications on the simple circle that had originally graced the page. It began to resemble a web, in which one could be trapped inextricably. "If the child would grow to be truly free, it must learn to defeat the tyranny of fate and live according to true essence of his self, which lies unassailable beyond the Zodiac's influence."

Stella looked from Doctor Dee's sketch, to the book he had open on his desk and the picture of the twelve figures arranged about a circle. Enclosed within that parade of constellations was a small central circle that she thought could be Earth, or any person on Earth, trapped by the Zodiac. Or the imprisoning circle might be Dome C, and the little trapped circle might be Stella herself, isolated within.

"So the Zodiac is bad?"

"They are merely constellations composed of Stars," The old man stated, "And as such, they have little choice in their actions, so they cannot be accurately described as bad. They are merely performing their predestined part in this universe. Only humans have the mysterious potential and…" he reached across the table to take Stella's hand and gently pressed her flesh," the *obligation…*" he stressed this word, "to create their own destiny."

"But isn't the Zodiac too powerful? How could anyone ever overcome them?"

"Powerful yes, but undefeatable? Not at all. There is no fate but that which we make for ourselves, would you not agree?"

Stella felt that this man understood her plight and was prodding her towards saying some word, and if she said that secret word, it would prove she understood and was ready to continue and learn more. Then he would be free to tell her all that she needed to know. Looking into the pools of his eyes, she searched for what it was she needed to say, for the simple breath that would rise from within, form the word and blow away the dust that veiled the secret. But only a lump rose in her throat as she realized she had no way to respond to this stately ancient, not possessing the word to unlock his secrets.

The moment of opportunity passed. As Dr. Dee spoke with an air of resignation, Stella realized she had failed his test. "I see. Well, I suppose I must chart your horoscope. It might foretell some trap fate has set for you."

"I'd like that, but I really don't know much about this sort of thing."

"All you'd need to tell me is the date of your birth, if you can remember that." The man's thin lips formed a conspiratorial smile, a web of deep wrinkles crinkling at their sides.

"Yes I can!" Stella said, "March fourth. As a matter of fact, yesterday was my birthday!"

"Why, congratulations, my young friend!" He smiled slyly, and with a twinkle in his eye, as if he had known that information before she told him. He wrote it down on a slip of parchment in small tight script as he spoke.

"Very good." Putting down the feathered quill with which he had recorded this information, he reached for a book on a nearby shelf. A plume of dust bloomed as he pulled it from its space. It was bound with cracking old leather and inscribed with symbols inlaid with dull gold. Stella remembered seeing some of those symbols before, at Saturn's feet back at the parliament of the Planets. She moved forward to take a closer look but the doctor slid the tome out of the girl's sight. "This will take some time, perhaps you would like to continue your tour of our laboratory? I will call for you when I complete your chart."

Perceval, who had been standing quietly at Stella's side, took the doctor's cue. "Why yes, there is so much more to see. We thank you very much for your kindness, Doctor, and look forward to seeing you again."

Nodding his head in acknowledgement, the old man bent to his work and Perceval gently guided his charge out of the cubby. As they walked through the cluttered rows between desks and worktables, Stella stopped to view a beautifully detailed sculpture of the solar system standing on a desk laden with tools. A golden globe occupied the sculpture's center, and from that miniature sun ran thin wires on which perfectly painted models of the planets were suspended. The whole arrangement, built upon an ornate box of intricately carved wood, formed a perfect model of the solar system.

The man at the desk had a magnifying monocle clasped in his eye and was involved in some delicate operation. With a tiny file he was carefully cleaning the teeth of a gear, so small, Stella had to squint to see it. His fuzzy sideburns and feathered felt cap reminded Stella of craftsmen she had read about in fairytales, those who never tired in their work of making something beautiful.

With the gear precisely honed, the man opened the box on which the model stood, revealing an intricate assemblage of mechanisms. Using tweezers he carefully placed the new gear into the complicated arrangement. "Vonderbar!" He exclaimed, dropping the monocle and looking up from his work. Pale blue eyes situated beneath fuzzy eyebrows calmly examined Stella. "Such a pretty girl! To what do I owe the pleasure of such a visitor?"

Stella smiled, and responded with equal warmth. "I'm looking for a map to the end of the universe."

"The universe! Such a grand plan for one so young! And where is this map? Have you found it?" He winked to Perceval, as if they shared a private joke.

"No, I haven't, would you know where it is?"

"Well, I am not too familiar with the rest of the universe, the solar system is all I seek to model", he offered pointing to his machine.

"It's very lovely", Stella said, "I've never seen a more beautiful sculpture."

"A sculpture! Oh no! Much more than that! Would you like to see?"

Stella was led around to the back of the desk where protruding from the base on which the sculpture stood, jutted a delicate hand crank.

"Would you like to do the honors?" The man stood back and allowed Stella to grasp the handle. "Just a few turns and gently please," he advised.

She turned the crank once, twice, and then a third time. A whirring noise buzzed from the sculpture's case and to Stella's delight, the mechanism came alive. Each planet glided on its orbit and every moon revolved slowly around its host planet. The moon of Earth even went through its phases as a small dark shell slid over its surface. Waxing from crescent to half to gibbous, the silvery orb of the moon soon turned full again.

"What an astounding device!" Perceval exclaimed. "I had no idea that you had come so far in your work." Moving forward he took the carpenter's hand and shook it vigorously. "With such ingenuity here in our midst, it is quite puzzling that we cannot find the solution to our dilemma." Perceval quickly shook off the wistful look that had crossed his face. "But we have a guest and it would be impolite to get bogged down in discussions of our shortcomings." Turning back to Stella, he asked. "It is a marvelous invention, is it not?"

Stella nodded earnestly in agreement. "What's it called?"

"It is an orrery." The craftsman explained.

"It's wonderful." Stella remarked, "Like wheels within wheels, the planets rotate around the sun, the moons rotate around the planet. It all runs like clockwork." She waited to see if the word, *clockwork,* might have any special meaning to this clever man.

"Yes, the solar system is very much like clockwork running precisely and smoothly. It is a miracle in its simplicity." The craftsman answered.

"Will it ever run down?" Stella questioned.

"My mechanism? Of course it will. Watch!" And as he spoke, the whirring sound stopped and the planets came to a halt.

"I was asking about the universe." Stella responded somberly. "You can wind that box up when it winds down and the little planets will turn, but what would happen if the real Solar System ran down, who could wind it up then? Or would we all just stop, dead?"

Perceval looked askance at the young girl. "That is a dreadful thought. A young lady as bright and lively as you should not have such notions of despair forefront in her mind."

With a paternal nod, the whiskered man tried to quell the girl's fears. "I'm certain the planets are in no danger of running down for a very, very, long time. It is only our manmade machines that run that risk." Turning the crank on the orrery, the planets began to swing through their orbits once more as he spoke with a voice of weary resignation. "And as you can see, this solar system may always be wound up again."

Stella looked at the man's skillful hand on the crank of his device. "But only from the outside," she whispered.

Saying their goodbyes, the girl in the bright red parka and the man in his neat brown suit continued their tour of the cavernous laboratory. It was fascinating to see so many experiments ranging from the sublime to the ridiculous being performed by men from all the ages of Earth, but Stella knew she had little time to waste. "There are so many smart people here," she remarked, "doesn't anyone have a map of the universe?"

11 INVENTIONS AND DISCOVERIES

Entering a cluttered workspace surrounded by tall cabinets, Perceval called out in a low voice. "Jacques? Are you here? I've brought a guest who I'd like to see your inventions, if you have a moment to spare." Stella stood nearby, her attention immediately drawn to a duck that sat on a desk, perfectly lifelike but motionless and returned her stare with beady eyes.

"Perceval? Is that you?" A hand reached from beneath and groped along the desk's clutter until it came to a clump of white hair. Grabbing that, it disappeared back below and in just another second a plump little man popped up, pulling the white powdered wig onto his head. Quickly brushing off his rumpled velvet suit, he approached with an outstretched hand. "Perceval! It is you! It's so nice of you to stop by and visit!" He shook Perceval's hand with vigor, his round red face standing out vividly from the white wig framing it.

"And hello to you too, my friend." Perceval said warmly. "This is Stella Ray, a visitor to our Lab."

Stella reached out her hand and to her surprise the squat man kissed it. "Jacques De Vaucanson, Mademoiselle, at your service!" And with that he clicked the heels of his velvet shoes together and executed a graceful bow.

At the sound of the click, the duck that had been sitting silently on the desk, stood up and began to waddle around the desk, flapping its wings and quacking loudly. Seeing Professor Lowell, the duck began to squawk louder. Jacques face reddened to a deep beet red. "Stop that right now! These are my guests!"

From nearby desks came shouts of protest as the din of the honks became unbearable. The Frenchman pursued the raucous duck as it waddled across the desk. Perceval moved to help but the unruly fowl skillfully evaded their grasps. Jacques quickly shifted to the opposite end of the desk to trap the bird between him and his friend. Cornered, the fowl made a desperate attempt to escape. It jumped at Stella, its impact knocking her to the floor, but as she fell she grabbed the squawking duck and with both arms tight around it, she could feel within its struggling body the turning of gears and the whirring of springs.

In seconds Jacques came to Stella's aid, grabbing the rambunctious creature by the neck and pulling it from the young girl. With a deft movement, he lifted the bird's head and poked a finger firmly between its eyes. It fell limp immediately. Stella thought only the worst. "Is it dead?" She asked, horrified that perhaps they had killed the poor animal. Both men only smiled.

"Dead?" Jacques answered jovially, holding the duck up for the dismayed girl to see. "It was never alive!"

"Is it a robot? " Stella asked, offering a possible explanation.

"Robot?" Jacques corrected, "I call it an automaton." He lifted a wing of the bird and to show the mechanisms that crowded the duck's body.

The memory of the bird Stella found perched on the ladder rushed to mind. "You made that?"

"I did." Jacques answered; sounding a bit dejected as he took the duck and placed it, now lifeless, on the desk. "But this example is far from perfect. I still have not figured out how to make it behave. That is a recurring problem."

Perceval cut in. "Jacques is the greatest clockmaker here in the laboratory. His inventions are legendary." Stella knew that he was not speaking for her benefit, but for the Frenchman's, in an attempt to cheer him up.

"That is amazing," Stella said, realizing what Perceval was attempting to do. "I saw a small red bird as I was climbing down here. I only had a quick look before it flew away, but it was marvelous!"

"My robin! I wondered where it had gone. Is it still functioning?"

"It sang beautifully." Stella remembered.

"Did you think so? I'm so glad you liked it. My birds are perhaps my favorite inventions, as they remind me of Earth."

"Ah yes!" Perceval grinned, "Your aviary! I forgot the trouble into which you had gotten."

"Trouble? How were you were in trouble?" Stella asked the clockmaker.

Jacques walked to a series of tall cabinets at the back of his cubicle. "I hoped that my songbirds would bring some joy to this staid environment. Though I love the song of birds, others here have expressed dissatisfaction, complaining the songs interfered with their concentration." One after another he began to open the doors of the cabinets, revealing hundreds of immobile birds neatly arranged on shelves. "So now I must keep my creations silent, so as not to disturb my fellow inmates."

Stella examined the wonderful collection of simulations. The brilliant blue, red and green feathers formed a magnificent rainbow of plumage. "You made all of these?" She asked in amazement.

"I have been here quite a long time", Jacques said forlornly as he carefully groomed the display, turning a head slightly here, lifting a wing a bit there. "Every species of bird on Earth is present here, though their songs have been silenced."

Perceval consoled the grieving Frenchman. "It did get a bit noisy in here, Jacques, with all of the chirping."

Professor Lowell bent to his confused young friend, and explained while Jacques busied himself arranging his creations. "He had let all his birds loose in the laboratory. It was quite a scene. As they flew around unchecked, their collective song grew to be, quite honestly, deafening. Some of the fellows in our laboratory were quite angry at the distraction; violence was only narrowly averted, when all sides came to an agreement. It took quite a while to capture them all, though I do believe the robin you saw was the only one that escaped."

"What was the agreement?" Stella asked.

Perceval spoke softly. "That when we depart from this place, he would be allowed to release all his birds, and his creations will be free to sing their songs forever."

"These birds," Jacques said as he delicately adjusted the head of a bluebird, positioning it as if cocked to listen, "are no less caged than we who inhabit this lab."

It was heartbreaking to watch the Frenchman lavish attention on his creations, all the while pining for them to be free. "They are so beautiful, you should be proud of them all." Stella remarked.

After fluffing a small finch's feathers with a light puff from his lips, Jacques dramatically shut the cabinet's door. "Thank you for your kind words, Madame. Que sera sera," he sighed. "Perhaps you would care for some tea?" At the touch of a button, a panel on the desk slid open and a pair of wooden arms held out a tray on which a porcelain tea set was arranged. A third arm reached from the panel opening, and lifted the teapot. Jacques took a cup from the tray and held it out as the arm poured.

"Thank you." Stella said, accepting the steaming cup from the Frenchman.

When all had been served, the pair of hands pulled the tray back into the opening and the third closed the wooden panel, leaving nothing unusual to be seen about the desk. Jacque's mechanical marvels caused Stella's eyes to widen.

"I think perhaps our guest would like to see any other automatons you might be willing to demonstrate." Perceval mentioned before sipping his tea.

A dull thump emanated from a rather shabby looking cabinet at the rear of the workspace, but Jacques completely ignored the sound. "Well, you have seen my duck, and my birds…."

Though sealed with an ornate lock, the door of the ramshackle cabinet shuddered, as another thud sounded. Jacques cast an irritated glance towards the disturbance and then hastily shuffled his guests to the corner of his space furthest from the noisy cabinet. He gestured towards a display of elaborate timepieces, "These are my clocks."

"Are they set to different time zones?" Stella asked, as no set of clock hands matched. Jacques' face flushed pink at the question. Stella wasn't sure what she had said to cause the embarrassment and moved to a clock whose golden hands indicated two o'clock. "Is this the time in France?"

There was no reply as the clockmaker turned a deeper shade of red. Pointing to another clock whose hands were set at eight o'clock, Stella remembered that Florida was a six-hour time difference from France. "And maybe this is Eastern Standard Time?"

Another thud issued from the mysterious cabinet. Jacques' face turned from embarrassment to anger as he glared at the box. "No," He hissed angrily, "They are not set to time zones."

Perceval attempted to distract Jacques' attention from the clamorous cabinet. "I'm sure that a knowledgeable horologist such as Jacques has some scheme that we cannot begin to understand." Though he mentioned this casually to his guest, it was immediately apparent the words were for the Frenchman's benefit. "Perhaps, he might enlighten us as to his reasons for setting each of these clocks at a different time."

"There is no apparent reason why these clocks are not synchronized. I only know it is not a fault of my craftsmanship!" Jacques said, turning from the cabinet to his clocks. "The mechanisms are perfect, but after each time I have set them, they inevitably fall out of order. Since the bouts of darkness have begun, time itself seems affected. I do not understand why." Stella shuddered, knowing just what was affecting the Frenchman's clocks. It was the winding down of the Celestial Clockwork that was causing the disarray.

Another thud, the loudest so far, was all Jacques could stand. In a rage he ran to the cabinet shrieking in French, and although Stella did not understand the language, she knew that what he was shouting was foul. Jacques undid the lock and flung open the cabinet door.

As the thing housed in the cabinet spilled from its cramped confines, Stella cautiously moved forward to see what it was. She supposed that it might best be described as a cross between a grandfather clock and a man. It had been constructed with obvious skill, being fashioned from well-polished wood, with brass fittings at the joints and corners. But it was what crowned the small bit of face, consisting only of a small wooden nose and a hinged puppet-like jaw, which was most intriguing. Sprouting on snakelike cables from the cranium of the boxy creature were too many viewing devices to count. The lenses of the devices glinted in the candlelight and formed a shabby nimbus around the creature's head.

Jacques wasted no time in berating the ramshackle creature, furiously admonishing it for interrupting. "I have guests! You have been most rude with your disruptions. If you cannot behave, I will let you wind down completely and not wind you up again!"

Trying to extract its shambling form from the tight confines, the pathetic creature crawled weakly from the cabinet. Feebly gripping the edges of the cabinet with trembling wooden hands, it began to slowly pull itself out. Showing no mercy, Jacques brusquely shoved the creature back inside and then leaned into the box to command the mechanical man to stay put. Stella and Perceval watched, puzzled by the Frenchman's fury towards such a wretched being.

Jacques sighed apologetically. "I am sorry for the disturbance. This was to be my greatest achievement, but has turned into my deepest disappointment."

One of the eyes that sprouted from the mechanical man's head, if the optical devices that festooned his head could be called eyes, snaked from the cabinet to peer up to Stella. The silent eye pleaded for some understanding with the same pitiful look that Sirius would display when he was just a puppy and had been caught doing something wrong. Jacques began to shut the cabinet and the sad eye pulled back on its stalk to avoid being caught in the closing door.

Stella couldn't bear to see the creature, whatever it was, imprisoned again. "What was that?" she asked.

Jacques stopped before he had fully secured the cabinet's lock. "It is only my failed attempt to construct an anthropomorphic observer, a clockwork watcher. This miserable reject is hardly worth the notice of one so young and fair."

"Please?" She asked, in the same plaintive voice she would use if she wanted some favor from her father, "Can I see it, just for a moment?"

Jacques fell for the girlish trick and slightly bowing said, "If that is what you desire," Stella nodded her head eagerly in affirmation, "then I will oblige you in your whim. It has never functioned correctly, but I will demonstrate it nonetheless." Reluctantly, he opened the cabinet once again and roughly pulled the contraption out. It fell flaccidly to the floor. Jacques found the sculpted dial on its chest and began to turn. "I will wind it fully so you may examine it in action, though I fear its defects will leave you unimpressed."

There was the clicking of gears turning and the soft whir of springs uncurling as the mechanism began to shudder on the floor, and then suddenly as if jolted on a string from above, it stood straight up. Taking a few wobbly steps toward Stella, and its head alive with writhing cables all ending in a variety of ocular devices, it peered down at the girl. With a series of rotations and flips, the assemblage of eyepieces reconfigured, calibrating and focusing. Two of the snake like appendages, one ending in a small loop resembling a monocle, the other the lens of a microscope, hovered over Stella and she saw herself reflected in their glass. Struck by the uncanny feeling of being examined by some alien intelligence, she took half a step back.

Jacques rapped his knuckles sharply against the mechanical man's casing. With a whir of gears the figure jerked erect. Reprimanding his creation, the Frenchman shouted. "That will be enough! She is a guest and is not to be stared at like some unidentified specimen!"

As it moved away from the girl, the mechanical man's eyes sprang to life, desperate to view everything they could. Straining as they fanned out on their cables, the unblinking eyepieces scanned the laboratory. With so many different devices, the creature's head resembled the eye of an insect, with each facet being a unique optical instrument. As the creature struggled to take in all there was to see, Stella wondered how long it had been locked in the closet and what it might actually perceive with so many different types of eyes.

Jacques apologized. "I do hope you will pardon my machine's rudeness. It has never seen a young lady before. It was not built for graciousness, but solely to observe."

Perceval sipped his tea. "What do you call it, Jacques? "

"It is a clock-work-watcher. I built it with the sole purpose of watching the skies. Although we have many astronomers here," and he swept his arm out toward the room in a broad gesture, the frills of his cuff floating through the air, "even they must rest sometimes. And during those few moments of repose, I hated to think some marvelous phenomena might be missed in that time, perhaps even some clue to how we might escape. So I constructed this watcher to be ever vigilante and to watch the skies."

"That's a great idea," enthused Stella, "But why is it a failure?"

"If my watcher is to maintain its vigil, it must be able to be left unattended for days, perhaps even weeks."

Perceval now took a greater interest in the mechanism. "Are you saying I would no longer need to have my eye glued to my scope? I would be able to leave this mechanism, as a kind of watch dog that would alert me when an unusual or interesting event happens in the skies?"

"That was the hope and the impetus behind the enormous labor I have poured into this creation," said Jacques, who grimaced crossly at the mechanical man. "But alas, a flaw in my design has rendered the whole endeavor fruitless. Although my clockwork watcher has the ability to observe just as I had planned, it does not have the stamina or endurance to make it through, even one night." Jacques sighed in deep disappointment, "After only a few hours of operation, my creation runs down and ceases to function if there is no one on hand to wind it."

Stella thought carefully about what she had just heard. It sounded like this machine, this mechanical man, faced the same dilemma as the universe. If no one were there to wind them, both would die. She couldn't help but gape in dismay at the ill fated creature.

Jacques pointed toward the key that protruded from the machine's chest. "It is a simple matter, a few turns will reanimate him and he is back on his feet, eager to observe. But if one forgets or is unable to wind him, his observations are useless."

"Is there no way to remedy it?" Professor Lowell asked.

Stella paid close attention. If there were a way to fix the mechanical man, maybe it would give her an idea as to how to fix the Celestial Clockwork when she reached it.

"I have tried, though my tinkering with it has come to no avail." Jacques answered despondently. "It is a matter of physics. The power needed to animate a mechanism such as this for any length of time, simply cannot be contained in its casing. The energy must be supplied from outside. Without constant attention to its needs, this machine winds down and fails in its observations. It is, in a word, useless."

And at that, as if on command, the mechanical man slumped into a lifeless heap. With some struggle, the Frenchman wrestled the dead weight of the clockwork watcher back into its cupboard, crammed it into the tight space and forced the door shut. "Such a disappointment! So much work for what?" Jacques huffed in abject despair. With eyes downcast he slunk to his desk. Falling into a chair, he picked up a mechanical device and scooping a jeweler's loop from his desk, he peered through its magnifying lens. Within an instant he was lost in the tiny world of gears and cogs which he held cupped in his hand.

"We will leave you to your work." Perceval said, but Stella could see it was merely a courtesy. The Frenchman's attention had moved on and was now deep into the workings of his device. He grunted softly in response to Perceval's farewell, not looking up.

Perceval put his hand to Stella's shoulder and led her quietly away. "My desk is nearby. I have quite a variety of maps and charts that I have been compiling from those in our lab. I'm sure there was a map I've seen, that was exceedingly strange and simply incomprehensible. It had advertised itself as a map of the universe, though such a thing is patently impossible. Perhaps you should see it, as it will show you some of the preposterous ideas men have had about the nature of the universe."

Following Professor Lowell, Stella wondered just how he could be so certain that such a map would be impossible. With so many books in the Astrophelarium, one of them must hold a map that would show the way out of the universe. Stella could only hope there was. Perceval walked to his desk and began to search through the piles of books covering his desk. A chalky white globe that lay among the volumes attracted Stella's attention and picking it up, she began examining the thin pencil lines that were drawn in spider web fashion upon its surface.

Perceval gently took the ball from the girl's hands and placed it on a small pedestal near a few other similar items. "That will be of little interest to you, it is only my attempt to illustrate the surface of the planet Mars. My observations are disputed by many here, though I am certain that these," He gestured towards the series of spheres, each embellished with webs of pencil lines, "depict evidence of water on Mars."

Stella started to speak, then shut her mouth tight. She wished she could tell Perceval she had actually met Mars, had seen him up close enough, but that was something she promised not to do. "That is a very interesting theory," was all Stella could respond. She stepped back as Perceval continued his search.

Shuffling books from stack to stack, Perceval was apologetic. "I do recall seeing that dubious map, now if I can only remember where I put it."

A short swarthy man passing by stopped to playfully chide the professor. "Ah! Perceval", he chortled, "It seems you need to practice the art of memory with more diligence. Then perhaps you would not have such need of what you have forgotten."

Perceval smiled at the suggestion. "Miss Ray, please allow me to introduce my good friend, Giordano! While I search for what I have misplaced, perhaps he can answer some of your questions. You may find him a bit fiery in his opinions but he is the most scrupulous of scholars."

"I will answer what I can, and with what truth I know," said the Italian man with the broad smile and thick moustache. "Now what would you inquire of the Nolan?"

In a stream of words that left her breathless, Stella asked why the inhabitants of the workshop thought they were prisoners and how they were planning to escape and where they would go if they did. She inquired as to what he knew about the Astrophelarium and what they remembered of how they had been brought there. Mostly of all, though she didn't ask it, because she didn't want Giordano to know she had been sent by the Sun, she wanted to find out if Old Sol was telling the truth about why he had brought all these men here.

Giordy arched his eyebrows (Stella thought it was almost one eyebrow as it was a stripe of hair growing straight across his forehead, mirroring above his eyes, the moustache below) and joked to Perceval. "Your little friend here has a palace full of questions crammed between her ears, and they seem to be leaking from her mouth!" Smiling through his frustration, Perceval nodded in agreement and bent once again to his desk to ruffle through the clutter.

"Let me start by giving you any such information I might have on the Astrophelarium, as we have come to call it." He smiled a wide grin, his straight teeth white against crooked lips. "In actuality, we know very little about this laboratory of the telescopes. Exactly what and where this workshop is, we have only the shadow of ideas. All we have is conjecture and a number of mutually agreed upon observations, though all here seem to have their own theories as to what those observations might signify. As I am a philosopher and less inclined to be trapped in the web of mere fact, perhaps it is right that you should hear my theories first and form your own conclusions."

Stella agreed, charmed by this man's matter of fact, though convoluted demeanor.

"We believe, or a large part of those who populate this place believe that we have been cursed, though some might say, *gifted,* with our admittance to these premises. How we arrived here, no one can recall. We remember our previous lives, our families, our homes, our researches, but nothing of the circumstances that brought us here. Look around!" His hand waved, and following its arc Stella saw the whole panorama of the laboratory displayed. There were dozens, possibly hundreds of men all deeply immersed in their work.

"There is a common bond that runs through all these diverse labors. Each of us, we have come to realize, is a disciple of the stars. All of us share that passion; all our lives have been devoted to solving the secrets of space or the wonders of the stars or the mysteries of time. We, who compose this band of explorers, agree that this must be the reason we have been imprisoned here, though we know not for what reason. Some have been here for a very long time," he gestured towards Ptolemy, "others are newer arrivals, such as our friend Perceval here." The professor nodded at the mention of his name, and resumed his search.

"An explanation for our entrapment has been offered by some in our group. They propose that celestial agents have brought us here, as an honor or privilege for our diligence in service of the Stars. I agree with this theory that we have been sent here through some mysterious labor of the Sun. Such musings on the intentions and rationale of the Sun have prompted me to come to a new understanding of the nature of the Stars. I have come to believe that just as humans are upon the earth, so are the stars in heaven, thinking, feeling, and subject to whims and moods."

Stella was impressed how close Giordy had come to guessing how he had arrived here, and surprised that he could reach this astounding conclusion with so few facts. Giordy waved off her look of astonishment. "That theory is plausible but the evidence of its truth has been lost in the sands of time. So now, perhaps not in accordance to the fate planned by those who have brought us here, our research has reached an unexpected conclusion, one which has altered our course and set us in pursuit of a new goal."

"What conclusion was that?" Stella asked.

"There has been little accord within our group through the ages, very little. But we have come through much study, to agree", Giordy pronounced dramatically," that the universe is endless."

"The universe is endless?" Stella repeated, unsure what exactly that meant or why all these scientists and astronomers would care. If the universe were endless, it would mean that they could explore forever and always find new things. Stella thought scientists would like that. Scientists, like her father, needed to explore.

"We have decided to fight against this fate, though we are certain there is little hope in our struggle. You have seen the scope?" Stella nodded her head yes. Of course she had seen the scope; it was the largest thing in the room. Even now she could see over Giordy's shoulder, a group of men poking and prodding at it. One of them, the aged Aristotle, was in heated discussion with a bearded man dressed in robes and a tight skullcap. Ptolemy! Stella thought, recognizing him from a woodprint in an old book.

Giordy continued. "We have been constructing that device for what seems like ages. We have placed all our hopes in its virtues and abilities, but there is some essential component that we have not been able to manufacture, some element which eludes our understanding."

Before Giordy could complete his explanation, Perceval jumped from behind his desk. "I've found it!! I've found it!!"

The blood drained from Giordy's face. "You, you?? You've found it???" Without a breath he began to shout, his voice booming through the lab. "He's found it!! Perceval Lowell has found it!!!"

A flurry of papers and tools filled the air as men jumped from their desks and stampeded towards Perceval's desk. "He's found it? Lowell has found the missing piece?" The crowd grew until Stella and Giordy were crushed in the press. "Where is it? What is it?" voices from the mob asked.

"What it is…" Perceval retorted testily, "Is a mistake of our over zealous philosopher. I have simply found this map I'd been searching for." He thrust an aged piece of parchment up for all to see. A disappointed groan rose from the crowd and hostile glares caused Giordy to slink away.

Perceval shrugged as the crowd dispersed. "Poor Giordano, he has never learned how to keep his mouth shut. I fear that it will someday get him into hot water, if that is the phrase." He cracked a mischievous smile. "But now, let me show you what I have found."

Perceval swept an area of his desk clear and laid his find down. "This," he announced, "is by far the oldest and oddest map in the Astrophelarium."

It was a map of sorts, but not exactly what Stella had been hoping for. "It says here" Perceval pointed to a line of text on the ancient parchment, "that it is a map of our galaxy or as it is commonly known, the Milky Way galaxy, though obviously it is no such thing." And it was true, for written in bold lettering along the map's border were the words, *The Milky Way*.

Stella saw immediately that it was not a map of the Milky Way or any other galaxy, but simply a chart of an island. An ocean drawn with wavy lines and curlicue waves surrounded a landmass from which thin peninsulas spiraled. On the island's mainland, thin straight lines were drawn to show plains. On those plains were hundreds, maybe thousands of tiny stick figures and five little dashes joined at the center to represent people. Whoever had drawn the map had gone to great effort to detail the dense mountain range at the island's center. The convoluted peaks were so amorphous that it was hard to focus on any single one. In the middle of this delirious mass of mountains was a small circle of blue ink, placed exactly in the center of the page and marked by a red *X*.

Perceval interrupted the girl's perusal of the parchment. "It is strange, is it not? You may have it if you like, though I'm sure it is of no use."

"Why would anyone label this, *The Milky Way*? It doesn't look like our galaxy at all", Stella grumbled. Studying the drawing, she turned it over to check the other side for some clue. She found a fading spidery script and tracing the scrawl, spoke out each letter. "*E... M... P... Y...*" She paused, stumped.

"I think that's an, *R*, Stella", Perceval suggested.

Stella saw it then. Funny she thought, how that happens, not seeing something obvious until someone shows you and then not being able to see it any other way. "*R*", she repeated, then continued her finger's tracing, "*I… A… N… I… A… Empyriania*!" She exclaimed. "But what's Empyriania?"

"I have no idea," Perceval answered sheepishly.

"This must be the island of *Empyriania*, wherever that is. And an island is not a galaxy. Someone must have mislabeled it as, *The Milky Way*." She stated flatly.

Someone signaled from across the lab. "It seems your horoscope is ready, Stella," Perceval said, relieved to end the map business. "Let us go see what Doctor Dee has to tell of your circumstance."

Stella followed as Perceval stepped away, and then turning back she took the map and placed it in the pocket of her parka. "I'll find out where Empyriania is when I get back home", she promised herself.

Professor Lowell led the girl through the maze of desks and workbenches to Doctor Dee's cubby. Inside they found the Doctor in deep contemplation, staring pensively into what looked like a hand mirror whose glass had gone dark. Lost in the smoky luster, it took a moment for the elderly man to realize his company had arrived, and when he did, his attention shifted to the young girl. "If you don't mind I'd like to talk with Stella alone."

Perceval excused himself. "I'll be back in a bit, Stella. Use your time with the doctor well, he is the wisest of us all."

With Perceval gone the doctor began to speak. "I have gained insight through my divinations that indicate a great responsibility has fallen on your shoulders. So great, that I am afraid it may be too much for a girl so young to bear." He leaned forward and took Stella's hand in his. His skin was cool and dry and Stella could feel that the bones within were like a bird's, thin and brittle and ready for flight. "Your horoscope predicts great turmoil ahead. And though friends and allies will aid you in your quest, the horoscope predicts that in the end you will stand alone."

"Alone", Stella repeated the dreadful word.

"Now that you know the fate the zodiac foretells, perhaps you would care to learn the futures that lie beyond the harsh mathematics of the horoscope. I have seen them too."

"In that mirror?" Stella pointed to the polished disc on the desk.

"It is a mirror of sorts. Cut from obsidian crystal, in this stone's reflection I am granted sight that transcends the limits of the mundane, and shows the potential futures that gestate in the vast fullness of time. Though the vision was faint, I could see that many, but not all of your futures were beleaguered by darkness." He held up the mirror. "In this smoky glass time is presented as it really is, not as a singular series of events leading to some fixed destiny, but as infinite possibilities from which to choose."

"Would you like to see? Perhaps you can glimpse some destiny to your liking" The ancient handed the mirror to the girl.

Stella gazed into the shiny surface but no image appeared. "I can't see anything."

The old man moved to a place behind Stella and peered over her shoulder. "I think you are mistaken, the mirror is full."

Suddenly the dark glass was not empty, but full of a seething mist that welled up from its depths. Startled by the manifestation Stella almost dropped the mirror, but the doctor gently reached around and held her hand up. He spoke calmly. "The darkness is one possible future but it need not be yours. You must look beyond the confusion to choose your own destiny. It is within your power to do so." The doctor's hand was still around hers, holding the mirror up to her face. "Try to find a way through the darkness. Believe there are other futures and they will be yours to choose. Do not succumb to the tyranny of fate!"

Stella locked her eyes on the mirror's surface and hoped for anything other than a future of darkness. To her surprise a speck of light appeared on the obsidian surface and held within the gloom.

"Very good," the doctor said from behind. "Now go towards the light."

At the doctor's urging, the small speck instantly expanded and through this portal Stella glimpsed beyond the obsidian wall, light and darkness merging in a furious swirling maelstrom. A bounty of images flickered from the mirror's periphery only to be swallowed in the seething kaleidoscopic depths. "It's all changing so fast. I can't make out anything."

"Yes, I see. Try to move towards to the future you desire."

Stella knew what that was. She wanted to get home. As soon as that choice was made, the confusion in the mirror began to flow past her and she began to make out scenes from her past. Familiar faces flitted by, mostly friends from her old school.

"Do not stop there; those are choices from the past. Look forward to where you would like to be. Work past what has been forced upon you, and from those chances, glean a choice of your own."

Each new image blossomed with more possibilities. Her father's face floated at the mirror's periphery, his eyes lifeless and glazed. Realizing this had to be a recent occurrence Stella moved her attention closer, hoping to learn something about what was happening to her family on Earth. Without warning, her thoughts raced out of control and images began to rapidly flood from the mirror. Her father's face triggered a view through his telescope and that led to a sight of the stars at night, and then without warning, in quick succession, Loony's face of appeared. The faces of the planets rushed forward, followed by Old Sol's and then Astraea's. The Star woman's visage set the obsidian disc afire and Stella quickly jerked the mirror down to hide it from the astonished doctor.

"Who were those beings?" Doctor Dee exclaimed. He lifted the mirror and to Stella's relief the images had vanished. "Were they angels or demons? I have gazed long hours into that mirror, but have never seen such beings. And you on your first try bring forth a multitude?" He eyed Stella carefully. "From your chart I saw you were a special child, but I was not aware how special. Have you had contact with such beings before?"

Stella remembered the promise she had made to Sol, and though she wished she could tell the doctor everything, a promise was a promise. She said nothing.

"*Ahhh*," the doctor said, "I see that there are things you are not at liberty to discuss. I only hope you take care of, with whom you traffic. Some of those seemed to be angels, but others though I had only the quickest glance, seemed more likened to demons. I beg you to beware."

Stella held her tongue. The doctor looked at the girl quizzically, and then broke the silence. "If you do not wish to discuss it, I will not pry. Perhaps we should return to the business of your horoscope."

Stella breathed a sigh of relief. "Yes, I would like that, thank you."

"This is the horoscope I have cast for you." He produced a sheet of paper that was covered with numbers and diagrams. Stella examined the page.

Scribbled across the page were numbers and letters of every type; some recognizable, others indecipherable. "What do all these letters and numbers mean?"

A look of concern crossed the Doctor's face. "They mean nothing in themselves. I have given them meaning." He reached for the girl's hand and squeezed it emphatically, "Text and number are just base matter. It is only through the lens of a human's mind that they are transmuted to gold!"

Stella thought that perhaps Doctor Dee might be more than just eccentric, but when her glance met his eyes, she saw that they were not those of a madman, but of one who had seen things no other eyes had seen, wonderful things that lie beyond the understanding of most men. "This chart I have drawn for you, is not mathematics, it is magic. It offers a way to avoid the fate that sinister forces plan for you, and might well lead you through the Stars."

Stella looked again at the diagram beautifully drawn on the aged parchment. Within its inner circle were a series of jagged lines, each in another color of ink, all converging around a center point. "How do I read it?"

The old man stroked his long white beard. "It is not to be read as you might read a book. It is not enough to let this chart serve as a reminder to you, of who you are; if you are to be free, it must be understood as a true memory of where you have come from. Viewed correctly, this chart will show you how to safely maneuver past the hazards of the Zodiac and will lead you closer to the source of your humanity. It is there where you will be free to do what not even Stars aspire to."

Stella's eyes narrowed in suspicion, "What do you know about the Stars?"

"I know that while you have been molested by darkness, you have also been caressed by light."

Stella had to think for a moment. If Doctor Dee knew about the Stars, then there wasn't a secret anymore and she could talk to him. She phrased her next question carefully, not sure just what the doctor knew. "Do you know what my real mission is?"

The doctor shook his head, "The answer to that lies deeper than my vision can penetrate. I feel only that it of great consequence. I know you came here to find a way to the end of the universe, but those trapped here have sought diligently for such an escape and have failed."

"There must be a way out and I'm going to find it." Stella said without doubt.

"My companions believe that there are no bounds to this universe and that it spreads endlessly, an infinite prison. If there is no end, there can be no escape. They have come to the conclusion that the only option is to go inwards, to where they will find the inmost light and some finality to their studies."

She wondered if she should tell him what she knew about the Celestial Clockwork, and how it lay beyond the bounds of the universe. But Stella thought, perhaps these men weren't capable of going outside the universe. If what she had been told about her being special was true, maybe only she could make her way outside.

"Then why haven't you gone already?"

"All good things in all good time." The doctor smiled broadly at Stella. "Perhaps our departure has been forestalled for some good reason that is not readily apparent." Gesturing to the scope that stood in the center of the room he explained. "It is in that device we place our hopes for escape, but it is still incomplete. A crucial element has yet to be acquired, though I feel the time is ripe for that discovery." His eyes glinted as if there were more to say, but he only handed the horoscope to Stella. "I wish I could help you more, but please take this. In desperate times it may cast light on how to proceed."

Stella, disappointed that neither was what she had come here for, put the chart in her pocket along with the map Perceval had found. For all her trouble, she was still no closer to finding the way out of the universe. Her mission it seemed was a disaster. Looking to the skylight, she couldn't even see the ladder. Freedom seemed a distant concept. "Proceed? I'm stuck here just like you."

"I'm sure you will find a way to become unstuck, "Doctor Dee responded warmly. "Now, I feel I should bid you farewell. There is still much to be done before our mutual departures."

"Departure?" Stella asked. "But I'm not going anywhere…"

The good doctor stood, and taking Stella by the arm led her to the doorway of his cubby. "Of course you are. You're going to find you're friend Perceval. And as everyone knows, every great journey begins with its first step. Good bye Stella Ray; may the inmost light always be your guide."

"Goodbye Doctor Dee." Stella exited the cubby with the two maps in her pocket. Once outside, she looked for Professor Lowell. He was off in a corner of the large room near the largest and hairiest man Stella had ever seen. His long red hair looked like it hadn't been washed in years and his beard was separated into three thick unruly braids. Bent over his large wooden bench he was singing in a deep voice while running a file over a thick piece of glass.

"That is Svenn. Don't let his size put you off", Perceval informed Stella as she reached his side, "He is, contrary to appearance, one of the most gentle of our group."

"What is he doing with that glass?" Stella asked.

"Svenn is our lens maker, or at least…" Perceval continued softly, "We so allow him to believe. His lenses however, have never been quite adequate for our needs, but he is very industrious. We try to keep him happy by encouraging him." He addressed the Viking. "That seems like a very fine lens, Svenn. Perhaps it will be the one we require for our endeavor." Svenn grunted happily and held up the piece of glass on which he was working. Stella could see the waves in the glass and the distortion on its surface. "We'll leave you alone now. I know how delicate your work is."

Svenn grunted again, twice. As they walked away Perceval whispered to Stella. "We'd better not disturb him further. If Svenn loses his concentration things could get very ugly."

"What happens when he loses his concentration?" Stella peeked back and the Viking looked up from his grinding to return her glance. His beefy hands were still on the file, inadvertently applying pressure to the glass. Stella started to yell a warning, but before she could open her mouth a loud, *CHINK!* sounded.

Holding the two shards of glass in front of him, Svenn's face turned beet red. Stella looked to Perceval to see if maybe they had better both run, but the dapper Professor only shook his head glumly and pointed back. Stella turned back to Svenn, expecting to see him turn his worktable over and angrily trash his surroundings; instead she saw that the cheeks of his bearded face were covered with tears.

Bawling like a baby, Svenn collapsed to his bench and covered his face with his hands. From beneath them flowed rivers of tears. Stella felt so bad for this blubbering Viking; she went and put her arm around his enormous shoulder as his body heaved with each sob.

Perceval came over to Stella. “It is very kind of you to try to comfort Svenn, but we are used to this.” He pointed over to the corner where hundreds of broken lenses were thrown in a heap. “Perhaps it would be best if we continue our tour.”

Leaving Svenn to collect himself, Stella and the Professor wandered on through the Astrophelarium, until they found themselves next to the mysterious telescope underneath the large window. Having gone to many different observatories with her father, Stella had seen a lot of different telescopes but this was the most unusual by far. Its casing was covered with dials and levers, none of which seemed to serve any explainable purpose. She wondered if perhaps she could get a peek through it to see just what it was focused on, but the eyepiece was so low to the ground, that even if she stooped she wasn’t sure she’d be able to get her head between it and the floor.

“How is anyone supposed to look through this?” She asked, pausing in her investigation.

“It’s not supposed to be looked through, Stella.”

“What good is a telescope that you can’t look through?”

“It’s not a telescope.” Perceval responded cryptically.

“Not a telescope?” Stella eyed Perceval skeptically.

“To be frank, it was once the most powerful telescope in the Astrophelarium, our pride and joy. But since we no longer intend to study the Stars, we have been modifying it, altering it to achieve other purposes. We’re still working on it, but there has been much debate over just how to finish it.”

“Other purposes?” Stella asked.

“When’s it’s complete it will serve as our portal to the inner worlds. We’ll use it to launch us upon our journey to freedom.”

“And leave me here alone,” Stella sighed. Stepping back, she followed the line of the scope up and out through the window to where her ladder hung unreachable in the void. Somewhere out there her family was trapped with Verena Maldek while Moros plotted to kill everything. An immense responsibility had been heaped on her shoulders, but no one seemed able to help her. Even more disheartening was the awareness that as the darkness grew stronger, all her efforts to stop it, were amounting to nothing. A knot of anguish tightened in her chest and a sob rose in her throat as Stella felt her eyes well up. Unable to contain her distress any longer, she burst into tears.

12 THE TELEPORTASCOPE

Stella felt herself being held by Professor Lowell, in the same awkward way her father had always held her. "There, there, whatever is the matter? I'm sure whatever upsets you so, there must be a reasonable way to resolve it."

Sniffling and looking for something to blow her nose with, Stella noticed that a number of inhabitants of this crazy lab had rushed over and were watching her curiously. She felt embarrassed to be causing such a stir.

"She's crying? This young woman is crying!" A man who wore shoes which curved up into points and a turban with a shiny jewel at the forehead, exclaimed.

"Is that a tear?" Another man asked with such breathlessness, it became obvious to Stella that there was something more here than just concern for her well being. She raised a hand to wipe her eyes but someone gently stopped it.

"Please, allow me…" A young man with cropped blond hair produced a small crystal vial and very softly held it to Stella's cheek to catch the drop. An excited murmur rose from the crowd as he held out the vial for the others to examine its contents. Stella looked to Perceval to question what was happening, but he held his finger solemnly to his pursed lips.

The vial was passed to the turbaned man, who accepted it with a bow. Followed by the crowd, he went to a table where overflowing beakers sat below dripping glass tubes, and small burners heated flasks brimming with bubbling liquids. Words in a language Stella did not understand were chanted, as he very carefully set the vial on a small silver stand. Opening a nearby jar, he poured a small mound of its red powder onto a thin marble slab, and from a simmering beaker, splashed a number of drops onto the red powder. Then with a small golden tool he mixed the two into a thick paste, and as the compound fumed with blue smoke, whisked it beneath the silver stand that supported the vial. The mixture burst into green flames that licked the base of the vial and the tear within flashed brightly. As quickly as the flame had ignited, the Arab dowsed it, covering it with a small copper bowl.

All eyes watched as the turbaned chemist took a small thread of gold and twisted it into a tiny loop. Carefully he reached within the vial and caught the tear in the golden loop. The crowd held their breath as the chemist pulled the captured tear out from the vial and held it up for all to see. The globule of liquid hung glistening within the golden loop.

Doctor Dee had joined the observers, excited as all the rest and asked in a reverent tone. "Is it suitable, Abul Wefa? Will it serve?"

"To know that there is but the need to speak the word." The turbaned man responded. "I will leave that honor to you, Sir." He held the captured tear down before the Doctor's lips.

Stella felt Perceval's grip tense on her shoulder, where it had lain gently while both had watched the preparations. Closing his eyes, the Doctor crossed himself and spoke, the breath of the word enveloping the tear.

Stella was certain she had heard the word the Doctor had spoken, but she was not sure she could ever repeat it. However, whatever was said seemed to have the effect for which it was intended. Even from where she stood, Stella could see the tear sparkle brightly as it solidified into a small lens of perfect clarity.

The group of scientists huddled closer to the small glass disc and examined the miniscule object. Ptolemy was ecstatic as he examined the crystallized tear. "By Zeus!" he enthused, "It is precisely what we have been seeking. Our Teleportascope can now be completed!"

Stella tugged on Perceval's sleeve, trying to get the attention of her friend who was craning his neck to get a glimpse of the piece of glass, as it was carried to the large device beneath the skylight.

"Oh dear, have I been ignoring you? I'm so sorry! It's just that there hasn't been such excitement here in ages!"

"It's fine Professor Lowell." Stella waved away the apology, "But please tell me, why everyone is so excited?"

Perceval, who could not pull his eyes from the frenzied mob that had begun disassembling the Teleportascope, asked sheepishly, "What was your question? I seem to have forgotten, please forgive me."

Soon everyone in the lab was frantically pulling, tugging and twisting parts of the device. Amidst the creaking and clanging sounds of that spectacle, she asked her question again. "What is everyone so excited about?"

"Excited?" Perceval's voice squeaked, "Who is excited? Not I!" His eyes were glued to the chaos of men tearing at the scope, twisting screws and wrenching bolts from the casing. His face was beaded with sweat, Perceval seemed poised to bolt and join in the operation, though his sense of etiquette prevented him from leaving his guest.

"Professor, if you'd like to join them…" Stella asked.

"Uh mmm, I, uh, really? You wouldn't mind? I'd just be a moment." The professor was already rushing forward as he spoke. "If you would, please excuse me." And then he was gone, running straight into the fray. Rescuing discarded pieces of the telescope, he replaced them back onto the casing, all the while shouting for someone to bring him his tools.

Stella tried to follow Perceval's movements, but he was often lost in the shifting crowd. The scope was covered in a mad tangle of limbs and bodies, with a head peeking out now and then to shout an order that went unheeded. Ladders had lashed to the scope with lengths of rope and the men climbing them zealously disassembled the upper casings.

An old man crawled from beneath the crowd, making his way through the frenzy of bodies. His clothing, a velvet suit with matching cape, was torn and soiled with grease. Stella rushed to help him to his feet. "Those fools!" He shouted, straightening his dirty garments. His face was red with fury. "Don't they realize the focal length of the lens must be precisely adjusted towards the base of the Teleportascope and not at its tip? They will not listen, they never listen!" His hands went to the top of his head. "And where is my cap? Who has taken my cap? I must find my cap!"

Stella knew that his hat must be by the telescope, probably crushed beneath the feet of the mob, but she pretended to search anyway. "Sir?" she asked after going through the pretence for a few moments, "what are they doing to that scope?"

The man glared irately at Stella "You do not know? You are the one who has delivered the lens, and you do not know what we seek to do with it?"

"The lens? I didn't come to deliver the lens", Stella corrected, "I'm here because I need help and directions."

"Directions? And where would you go? There is but one way to leave this place and that is through the Teleportascope. There is no escape while going out into the stars; our researches have proven the futility of that. We have learned that the only chance of escape is to travel inwards. Going in, we have discovered, is the only way out."

"Are you sure? I would think the end of the universe was somewhere out there." Stella pointed out the skylight.

"Young lady", the man asked, "Do you do not know who I am??" Stella shook her head, she really couldn't guess, but it sounded like he was certain of his own important. "I am Galileo Galilei, discover of the moons of Jupiter and the phases of Venus. And you dare ask me how I am sure?"

Stella wished this vain nasty man would go back to work, but he showed no inclination to rejoin his fellows and was content to advise them from the sidelines. "Ah yes," noted Galileo, "I see they are finally following the advice I had given them." Stella was sure that this was not true, but that he was only saying this because he thought it might impress her.

Whatever the cause, it did appear that the task was drawing to a close as from the top of the Teleportascope, on scaffolding the men had constructed from their ladders, Abu Warif proudly proclaimed. "We have succeeded! The lens functions perfectly!"

A cheer came up from the crowd. Abu Warif looked down into the large lens that capped the scope. "I can see the depths! Freedom is ours!"

At that, all the men in the laboratory shouted in one loud cry, "The only way out is in!"

"Prepare for departure!" Aristotle shouted. "Hurry! We do not know how long the portal will remain open. The final lens is very fragile. All must pass through quickly if we wish to escape."

Stella couldn't remember the last time she had seen such hubbub, as the men dispersed from the scope and ran back to their stations. Galileo scooted in a flurry of velvet to his desk. Soon everywhere, the inhabitants of the lab were feverishly packing tools, books and papers. The greatest commotion was centered about the workplace of Jacques Vaucason. One by one, birds fluttered from the clutter of equipment and took to the air, flying wildly above the heads of the frenetic scientists.

"The birds!" Stella cheered, "Jacques is releasing the birds!"

It was immediately apparent that Jacques would need help if he were going to release all the birds. Stella rushed to his aid, weaving through the ruckus of men who frantically raced around the laboratory. At one point she found herself facing Svenn, who bounded down a crowded walkway, bowling over anyone who stood in his path. Ducking under a desk, she narrowly dodged being trampled by the Viking's heavy leather boots. As the danger passed, Stella continued down the aisle and between the tall bookshelves she could see bird after bird launched to the sky. Using these as a target, she quickly found her way to the Frenchman's cubicle.

"Can I help?" Stella asked, noticing that only a few of the many shelves of birds had been emptied.

Both the clockmaker and the girl were startled by shouts. "Hurry! There is not much time! Leave that which you cannot carry!"

Jacques looked up nervously to the top of the telescope where already a line had formed and one by one the inhabitants of the laboratory were disappearing. "I do not wish to be left behind, but I cannot bear to leave my birds trapped in their coops."

"I'll help you. What should I do?" Stella asked.

The Frenchman looked worriedly to the telescope where the rush to escape was underway. "Yes, yes, you can help. Take one of the birds and find the key under its wing. Give it four turns, no more, no less, and throw it up high. It will then be free to fly."

In example, Jacques reached up to the shelves and quickly pulled down a brightly colored bird. Lifting its wing, he turned the key and threw it. As it shot away, a squawking voice repeated, over and over, "*Polly, want a cracker? Polly, want a cracker?*"

Following the clockmaker's example Stella took a bird, a lark she guessed, and did the same. It took off like a rocket to join the flock of mechanical birds that circled near around the Teleportascope.

"How will they be able to stay aloft if we only wind them four times?" Stella asked, careful not to slow down in her labors.

"Keep winding!" The Frenchman responded tersely.

"I am, but how can they stay up with only four turns?"

The Frenchman gave the girl an impatient glare and then reached back into the shelf and pulled out another bird which Stella thought was a finch, and as he hastily turned the key he answered. "It is perhaps my most ingenious invention," throwing the bird and reaching for the next, a sparrow, "These mechanical birds will be wound by the rush of air under their wings. They only need these first four turns," he deftly turned the small key, "and they will remain aloft indefinitely. If they remain in flight they will not wind down. The rushing of air across their wings keeps them wound." Stella was impressed with Jacques' ingenuity but dared not pause in the launching of the birds to mention it.

"Hurry, hurry! We must escape before the Teleportascope ceases functioning!" Abu Warif shouted over the noise of packing and the cacophony of clashing birdsong.

Stella looked over to see that a line of the men had formed at the base of the scope, some with arms full of packages and books, while others carried nothing at all. Ptolemy had climbed the ladder and stood atop the giant lens of the Teleportascope, a bundle of papyrus scrolls tucked under his arm. "After all this time, we escape! I'll see you all in the worlds within!" He shouted as he jumped and disappeared into the scope.

Another man hurriedly took his place atop the ladder. "My friends; I stand at the threshold of a new world! The way to freedom begins with but one step!" And with that he too leapt into the lens and vanished.

Abu Warif issued another warning, "Hurry, the portal will not hold open indefinitely. We must all escape this prison while there is still time."

As Jacques Vaucason worked desperately on winding the birds, he admitted anxiously. "I do not wish to be left behind, but I cannot leave without knowing all my birds are freed."

Stella, trying to match his speed, wound and threw bird after bird into the air but it was quickly becoming apparent that this job would take much more time than Jacques had, judging by how fast the line was moving up the ladder and into the lens. After flinging a chirping canary into the air, Stella stopped and turned to the Frenchman.

"Please continue! There is little time! You must help me!" He implored. "I cannot miss my chance to leave this dreadful place. Do not stop winding."

. "Mr. Vaucason?" Stella squeaked, as her stopping caused the clockmaker anguish which clearly showed on his face.

"Please child, not now. Continue winding!" He threw a hooting owl to the ceiling.

Stella did not move. "Mr. Vaucason?"

The distressed Frenchman pulled a white dove from the shelves and holding its downy form in his trembling hands questioned the girl. "What is so important that you would risk my being stranded here?"

Stella spoke quickly, knowing she had only a moment of the Frenchman's attention. "You should go," she suggested, "I'll stay and make sure all the birds are set free."

It took the clockmaker only a second to understand the girl's offer. "You would do that?" His eyes softened with tears. "It is my responsibility… These are my creatures…But if you would promise..." He looked to the Teleportascope desperately, as another man jumped through its wide lens.

"I promise! I'll stay here until all the birds are freed. You have my word." She reached out her hand. The Frenchman took it and they shook, sealing the deal.

"Thank you very much! Now, with little time left, I need to gather my tools." He moved to his desk sorting through the dense clutter and began to extract tiny instruments, placing them in a soft leather case. "Where we are going, these may prove invaluable!"

As the clockmaker packed, Stella glimpsed Perceval in the disorderly line of men stretching from the foot of the ladder. She caught his eye, and he stopped jostling long enough to return her glance, before looking anxiously to the top of the scope where another scientist had just vanished into the lens.

Though concerned that whatever she might say to Perceval, would interrupt the joyful mood of his departure, Stella was even more worried about what she would do when he and the rest of the scientists had all gone. She hadn't found out anything about how to get out of the universe, or even how to get out of the lab. She couldn't go through the Teleportascope, because that would take her in, and she needed to go out. And even though everyone in the lab believed there was no end to the universe, Stella still had to try to find the Celestial Clockwork. They said the only way out was in, but if she went in with them and time stopped, no one would be going anywhere. And then, there was the more terrifying thought, that if she stayed here and couldn't find a way out, she would be alone maybe forever.

"Stella? Are you there?" Stella broke from her worried thoughts to find Professor Lowell snapping his fingers in her face. "Are you okay?"

"Uh, I'm here! I'm fine. I'm just, I'm just…."

"Just what?"

"I'm just trying to figure out what I'm supposed to do when you all leave."

A booming voice echoed through the Astrophelarium. It was Giordy, shouting from the top of the Teleportascope. "I sever my bonds to this prison!" He declared dramatically. Jumping from the ladder he executed a perfect jackknife, diving headfirst into the lens and with a silent splash was gone.

Svenn the Viking climbed the ladder, its rungs creaking as the giant lumbered upwards. Reaching the top he dipped one toe into the lens and asked timidly. "Is it cold in there?"

The watching crowd laughed and someone shouted, "Don't be a baby! Jump!" Svenn blushed, held his nose and jumped into the lens feet first; his long red braids the last to disappear. The line of men at the base of the telescope was shortening rapidly.

"Are you leaving too?" Stella asked, desperately wanting to hear that Perceval might stay.

"I am. I can't stay here any longer. I must go with the others" He stated regretfully. "We need to continue our journeys. The lens made from your tear has opened the gate for which we had been searching. Now we will go inwards and seek our destinies there."

"What will I do when you're gone?" Stella asked.

Perceval stroked his chin with his hand slowly. "You can always come with us. We'd greatly appreciate your company. Why, without your fortuitous appearance, we'd have been stuck here for who knows how long. Yes!" He exclaimed. "You must come on our journey with us!"

Stella took the Compyxx out from beneath her coat. It pointed up toward the skylight and the ladder, not to the device through which the men were exiting. Managing a slight smile, she whispered. "My mother is expecting a baby and she'll need my help taking care of it. I need to get home as soon as possible. But I can't go home until I find a way out of the universe; there's something very important I have to do there. To be honest, if I can't find a way to do that, I don't think anywhere will be safe."

There was rousing cheer as another man jumped into the scope, and Stella thinking perhaps she had already revealed too much, changed the subject. "Why do you need to go inwards?"

"That is not easy to explain, but I will try..." Perceval looked to the Teleportascope where the line of men had grown very short. "Stars which we once studied with wonder and awe, no longer hold promise for us, and we have come to the conclusion that we need to journey inward if we wish to discover the true mysteries of life. If space is endless, then our science is susceptible to infinite searching. There will be no meaningful end to our studies, no final understanding. By going inward we hope to find the ultimate reality, the hidden firmament on which all else rests. There we can end our studies having gained knowledge of an absolute sort."

Abu Warif, now the only person who had not yet departed, stood alone at the top of the ladder and shouted. "Lowell!! Are you coming with us or not?"

"Yes! Yes! I am! Please be patient! I'll be just a moment!" Perceval answered.

Abu Warif sniffed testily. "I can wait no longer. The others are already journeying inwards and if you do not come quickly, you may not be able to follow our trail. Inner space is vast." He surveyed the deserted laboratory one last time. "I bid farewell to this prison. I am a bird in God's garden, and I do not belong to this dusty world!" And with that, he leapt and disappeared into the lens.

Seeing that indeed he was the last, Perceval leapt from his seat. "I'm sorry Stella, but I have to run. I'll lose the others if I lag too far behind. You will be okay here alone won't you, for a short while?" He asked with genuine concern, "I'm sure you'll find a way out quickly, yes I'm sure of it. You are a very bright and special girl!" He sprinted towards the telescope and asked once more as he climbed the ladder. "Are you sure you won't come with us?"

Stella silently shook her head.

"Good luck then, Stella! I will think of you often! Remember, the only way out is through!" And with that he pinched his nose, stepped into the lens and was gone.

Stella raced up the Teleportascope's ladder. Reaching the top, she looked into the wide lens to catch a glimpse of a minuscule Professor Lowell chasing after a long line of men, and watched as with each step, this caravan of scientists diminished until they receded out of sight.

From the ladder the deserted laboratory appeared ominously inhospitable. After all the commotion that had been the norm in the laboratory, for it to be so still gave Stella the creeps. The only motion was of Jacques' birds sailing through the air, and to Stella's eyes they more resembled bats than birds. Looking out the skylight to the distant ladder, she despaired. "I doubt I'll ever find a way to reach that. What if I was stuck here forever, alone with no means of escape? Maybe," the thought rose to mind on a wave of panic, "I'd better follow the scientists." Frightened of her prospects she resolved to take the plunge.

As Stella stepped to the lens of the Teleportascope, on its glassy surface a reflected spark glistened and her attention was drawn upwards to a star far beyond the ladder. It hung there brilliant and undiminished, a pure light defiant against the surrounding darkness, and the girl marveled at how the star could maintain its light against the crush of so much dark space. But it did, and had been doing so for millions of years. If this star could stay bright under such circumstances, Stella thought maybe she could too.

For a few long moments she sat quietly contemplating just how close she had come to giving up. She looked out across the laboratory and what had moments before appeared threatening, was now only a clutter filled room.

Shaking her head at how she had let her imagination get the best of her, Stella climbed down the ladder, determined to find a way back up to Sol's lighthouse. Reaching the floor she went first to Perceval's desk. There were so many books on so many subjects that although Stella wasn't certain what she was looking for, she had to believe that in one of them there would be a clue as to how to escape. So she read until her eyelids were heavy and then she read some more.

When Stella awoke, she was lying in the nest of books on which she had fallen asleep. Sometime during the night she had taken off her parka to blanket her body, and for a pillow used a nearby bag of scrolls which had rustled with every turn of her head. She rolled over to take a book from the heap where she had slept and at random opened it to an article titled, *Talking with the Planets, by Nikola Tesla*. Stella scanned the pages to see it was about Mars and the chances of communicating with the red planet by radio. Stella laughed. She had talked to Mars. He was mean, no fun at all and there was no good reason anyone should want to talk with him.

She read on, but there was nothing about celestial clockworks or the end of the universe or how to reach an out of reach ladder, so she dropped the book and picked up another, and after that another, and then another.

Upon finishing all the books on Perceval's desk, Stella realized she was no closer to finding a solution than when she started. Taking a break, she wandered to where she had met the Viking and poked through the pile of lenses he had left behind. She found the least cracked one and holding it to her eye, looked out across the lab. It magnified her sight in a funny fish eyed way, and through the lozenge of glass she followed the colorful flash of a mechanical bird as it skimmed the cavernous lab's ceiling. Stella asked herself, "*A finch?*"

The bird reminded Stella of the promise she had made. "Before I do anything else," she thought, "I should wind the rest. A promise is a promise." Going to the cabinets where Jacques Vaucason stored his birds, she began to work her way down the rows. Taking the nearest, a mechanical seagull, she lifted its wing and turned the key four times, then threw the bird up to join the others in the air. One by one Stella made her way across the shelf and when that was empty she moved to the next. With all the tall cases and the amount of birds left in them, she wondered how long it would take to wind every one and if perhaps she should instead use the time to find a way out of the lab. Reminding herself she had no idea how to accomplish that, freeing the birds seemed the right thing to do as with each bird that took flight in song, a warm feeling coursed through her body. Seeing the birds free to soar, gave Stella hope that she could be freed too. "And," she told herself, "I could probably use the winding practice."

After hours of winding and throwing, Stella reached the end of her chore. The flock above was dense with hundreds of the windup birds swooping through the air. Falling back into Jacques' chair, she found the small button in the desk's carvings and pressed it. The three hands appeared and poured a steaming cup of tea and Stella taking it, sat back. Now that she had fulfilled her promise to Jacques Vaucason, it was time to find a way out. Stella needed to think, to concentrate, and a hot cup of tea seemed just the thing to aid that endeavor.

But the noise! No wonder the scientists had complained. Stella had always loved the sound of birds chirping, but the deafening racket from above was maddening. Even clamping her hands down on her ears did little to lessen the piercing shrieks. Begrudgingly setting aside her drink, she went to the apparatus that controlled the skylight and turned the crank. In a great rush the flock of mechanical birds whooshed through the open skylight. "If only escape were as simple for me," Stella lamented as the cacophonous song faded away.

Back at the desk she retrieved her tea, happy to find it still warm. Determined to think of some way to reach the ladder, she sat back down and tried to clear her mind. But then Stella experienced the strangest feeling, for even though she had watched all the scientists leave through the scope and every one of the birds fly out the skylight, she had the undeniable sensation that she was being watched. The uncanny feeling that she was not alone was overwhelming, but as she surveyed the Astrophelarium for some sign of life, there was none.

Only minutes before, Stella fretted about being alone, but now the thought that she might not be alone, that someone was watching her, was unsettling. To ease her nerves, she fidgeted with one of the small mechanisms Jacques had left behind, and with trembling fingers attempted to wind it. There was already tension on the spring, but Stella gave the key one more turn and as she did, there was a loud pop. With a snap the key turned freely in her hand and tiny gears fell out and rolled across the desktop, spinning like so many tiny tops.

A muffled voice chastised the girl, "Well; now you've done it. I certainly will be wary when asking you to wind me!"

13 A CLOCKWORK WATCHER

Right away Stella knew exactly where the voice had come from. Rushing over to the large standing cabinet, she loosened the lock and swung open the door. Out fell the clockwork watcher landing in a heap on the floor and from beneath the assortment of telescopes and microscopes, magnifying glasses and monocles, tubes and binoculars, shutters and lenses, a wooden mouth swung open to speak. "Well, hello!"

Stella hesitated for a moment, wondering just what type of conversation she should engage in with such a strange machine. "Hello to you too," she ventured.

The clockwork man's eyes, or the appendages that acted as eyes for him, fanned out stiffly from his head and in that instant he resembled nothing less than a peacock, a wonderful multitude of eyes, all aware, all seeing. But just as quickly, the eyes dissembled and fell back into a mess of tubes and lenses.

"Would you mind," he asked from the floor in a voice that sounded like a scratchy old phonograph, "winding me?" A copper tipped finger pointed to a stubby protrusion rising from his chest. "But please be careful!"

Reaching for the knob whose cleverly carved design made it easy to grasp, the girl began to wind. "Careful! Not too much!" the mechanical man squeaked.

"What's your name?" Stella asked, as she carefully turned the key.

"A name? I don't believe I have one," answered the cluttered heap. "What might be yours?"

"I am Stella Ray. But even if you are a robot, you should have a name too."

"I may not have a name, Stella Ray, but I am most certainly not a robot. If you had learned anything at all from my maker, Jacques Vaucason, you would remember that I am an automaton!" He said the word proudly, as if the distinction between robot and automaton was of some great importance.

The automaton's wooden hand lightly touched Stella's flesh. "Thank you for winding me, but that's quite enough!" As he shambled up from the floor with limbs clacking, the gears and the cogs within his casing whirred audibly. The eyes on his head rose on their cables to survey the empty laboratory. "I see the scientists have finally found a way to escape. It's about time. They've been looking for a way inwards for longer than I remember." His eyes turned towards Stella and began to snake around on their cables, bobbing and weaving as they studied her. "But, if I may ask, why are you still here?"

Looking at the odd character before her, its incredibly strange face covered with so many eyes and the little mouth that opened and shut like a puppet's, Stella realized that he wasn't one of the human scientists from which she had promised to keep her secret. This clockwork man was not a, *someone,* really it was more of a, *something,* she surmised, because it was built, not born. So she could tell him, or it, about her mission and not break her promise.

"I have been sent here by the Sun to find a way out of the universe!" Stella announced, and then waited a second to see if the clockwork man was at all impressed. He wasn't, she noticed glumly. His glass eyes only stared at her with ridicule as if what she had said was so far from belief, so preposterous, that even here in this laboratory full of the most absurd devices and ideas imaginable, her statement was unbelievable.

"Is that so?" The shuddering mass of metal and wood queried. "And what do you propose to do when you find your way out?"

"Save the universe." Stella answered, with all the certainty she could muster.

Which obviously wasn't enough, for the automaton responded snidely, "Oh you will, will you? Save the whole universe?"

Stella was not in the mood for mockery, especially from someone's windup toy. "When I find the way out, the Sun wants me to wind the Celestial Clockwork and defeat the forces of darkness," she stated proudly.

The mechanical man's eyes snapped suddenly to attention, "*The Celestial Clockwork*? I should very much like to see such a place. I, if you have not noticed, am clockwork also." His bellows puffed air excitedly through his voice box, amplifying his words. "Perhaps I should accompany you on your journey." From the forest of eyes, a number of devices gestured toward the broken duck that lay on the table. "I think that I have more skill with clockwork than you have demonstrated. So how do you intend to get to this *Celestial Clockwork*?"

"I'm not sure yet." Stella admitted. "Old Sol told me that there might be a map here in the Astrophelarium that showed the way, but I haven't been able to find one."

"If I were not confined to this laboratory I suppose I could see the way to go."

Stella wondered if it were possible that this clockwork watcher could see to the end of the universe, but then had another idea. "If we got up to that ladder, do you think that you'd be able to see Earth?"

"You came down from that ladder?" A few of his devices looked up towards the line in the sky. "Yes, it is a ladder isn't it? Incredible! A ladder from the sky! My goodness, it goes very high doesn't it?" There was the soft buzz as the devices recalibrated for a better look. "It ends", the clockwork man said in astonishment, "in a blaze of light! How could you have climbed down from there?"

"I told you, the Sun sent me here. But now I'm stranded because someone messed up. But I'd rather not talk about that now." She abruptly changed the subject, "What are the chances of you seeing Earth?" she asked, desperate for some news of her family.

As the optical devices receded back on their cables, Stella got the distinct impression the clockwork man was pausing to think. "That would be possible if I were properly wound and had achieved a high enough elevation."

Though wondering if he was exaggerating, just to convince her to bring him along, Stella decided that it could not hurt to believe him. If she knew that her family was all right, she'd be able to go on with her mission. "I'm sure if we can find a way up to that ladder, from up there…" Stella pointed through the window to the distant ladder. "…You'll be able to see everything."

"See? Yes, that's what I do!" The mechanical man quivered with excitement, eager to see anything he could; even now his eyes darted on their stalks, studying this, staring at that.

"I can't even imagine what it's like to see with so many eyes. It must be amazing."

The forest of devices abruptly stilled as he admitted, "It can be very confusing. I often wonder what it would be like to not have so many eyes, seeing would be so simple then. I'm certain that less can be more. Even with just two of my eyes open…" With a quick flip of shutters, all but two of his devices closed and that duo of glass lenses aligned themselves with Stella's orbs of flesh and blood… "I cannot perceive more simply."

Stella thought she understood what the clockwork man was talking about. "I guess it would be like me closing one of my eyes. I'd still be thinking like there are two eyes, but one is just closed. I guess my brain can only think in a two eyed way."

"Exactly!" The clockwork man seemed very happy that Stella understood what he had been trying to explain.

"But you were built to see, right?" Stella asked.

"I always see, but I was made to watch. Jacques called me a clock work watcher."

Stella whispered tentatively, "*C…W…W…*"

"See what?" The mechanical man asked confusedly, searching about the room. "What would you like me to see?

"*C. W. W.*" Stella said aloud. "It's the initials of what you are. *A Clock Work Watcher.*" Stella answered, "It could also be your name, *CWW*. It's what I'll call you, *SEE…*" Before she could say anything more, the clockwork man's eyes were flailing about searching. "*DUB DUB*" Stella continued, surprised that this time she didn't say, *double-ewe,* but used *dub,* instead. It was how her mother would pronounce the three double-ewes that always came before a web address. She would always start, when naming some website she had found, *dub-dub-dub.*

"I'll just call you '*DubDub'*. How's that? Then I won't have to say '*see*' anymore, and you won't be confused. Okay?"

"DubDub? The clockwork man said, his voice sounding like an old fashioned record skipping. "I like that. Yes, please call me DubDub."

"Well now at least you have a real name. The next thing we need to do is find a way up to the ladder."

"Are you sure you have to go up? Perhaps there is another way to the end of the universe." DubDub asked.

"Where will we go after we climb that ladder?"

"I'm not sure," Stella admitted, "this is the only clue I have." Hoping DubDub would recognize what it showed; she took the map from her pocket and held it up for him to see.

"It looks very much to me like a map of some island." The clockwork man clattered to a nearby bookcase and pulled a dusty volume from its shelf, the word, *Atlas,* in very fancy lettering on its cover. Walking back to the desk, he lay the book down. "If I may?" DubDub asked taking the map from the girl's hand and flattening it out beside the book. A number of his eyes quickly stretched on their stalks over the map, while others uncoiled like robotic snakes to stare down at the book.

"This should only take a moment." And with those words the mechanical man began to flip rapidly through the pages of the book. On every page was a large colored map, and DubDub's eyes would scan the image, sometimes very closely as if something of importance might be there, but more often with just a cursory glance before the next page was flipped. In no time at all, he had reached the last page. "Just as I supposed." he declared, slamming the back cover closed.

"What was that?" Stella asked.

"This is an atlas of Earth." He tapped the atlas with a metal tipped finger. "And your map matches none of the islands depicted within. If your island is not on Earth, I'd surmise that it is somewhere out there." His eyes looked up to the skylight.

"Okay," Stella said, thinking that bit of information was no help at all, "but how can I get back up? That's really what I want to know." Though she was glad the automaton was here and she was not trapped in the laboratory alone, she wished he would concentrate on getting to the ladder. "Do you have any ideas?"

As if he had not heard the request, DubDub responded, "I will continue looking for where your island might be. Perhaps one of the astronomers had glimpsed it and recorded the sighting." He began to gather books and with four or five opened in front of him, his rickety mechanical arms busily turned pages. Ocular devices shifted about his head and Stella saw what looked like a monocle floating on a thin stalk being pulled back, to be replaced with a magnifying glass and then a microscope as each of the books simultaneously underwent DubDub's intense scrutiny.

As DubDub looked for an answer to his problem, Stella continued to search the Astrophelarium for anything that might help with hers. As she wandered down the aisles she noticed that wherever she went, some of DubDub's eyes followed her. It was a bit disturbing being watched so intently, but the automaton was made to be a watcher and Stella supposed that was just what he was doing.

Deciding to test just how well DubDub was tracking her Stella stepped behind a high bookcase and then keeping low between the desks, crawled away from where she had last been seen. This was something she was very good at, having many times eluded her brothers as they mischievously pursued her around Dome C. Stella stopped crawling when she found a desk far from where she had started, and slid beneath it keeping very still so as not to be discovered by DubDub.

"Stella?" DubDub asked while slamming shut the heavy book he had been reading. He raced to the bookcase the girl had vanished behind, and seeing her gone squealed anxiously. "Stella Ray, where are you?" When the girl did not answer the nervous clattering of wooden limbs filled the Astrophelarium. A desperate wheeze groaned from his bellows, as DubDub pleaded in stark terror, "Please don't leave me alone, Stella! I'll run down and…and…"

Feeling suddenly horrible for the trick she had played, Stella jumped from her hiding place. "Don't worry! Here I am!"

"Please!" DubDub gasped, "Do not frighten me like that! You have no idea what would happen to me if there were no one around to wind me."

Curious about what had frightened him so, Stella asked, "What is it like to wind down?"

DubDub repeated the question with a tone of hysterical incredulity. "What is it like to wind down? Do you really want to know?" DubDub asked gravely. "Do you?"

A voice inside her head warned, *don't say yes!!* but her curiosity demanded to know. "Sure, what's it like?"

Passing around the desks and gliding down the aisle as if his eyes were leading him on, the mechanical man moved toward Stella. She found herself backing against a desk as the mass of eyes swarmed before her like a cloud of bees.

"You'd like to know, what is it like to wind down?" DubDub's wooden jaw spat. "It's like being thrust into the deepest darkest grave, beyond all hope of even the faintest hint of light. Picture yourself at the bottom of that hole as it's filled with heavy suffocating tar. Imagine being entombed in that darkness, unable to move, unable to breathe, but still capable of understanding that you are going to be there forever, trapped with only horror and terror as your companions. That is what it feels like to wind down."

DubDub walked back to Jacques desk to continue his studies. No longer did his eyes track the girl, but stayed purposefully focused on the pages before them, making it painfully obvious that he was peeved at having been forced to relive his anguish. Stella tried to shake the dreadful impression her encounter with the mechanical man had left. "Words," she shuddered, "They were only words." But she knew that was not quite true, for DubDub had spoken from painful experience. What he said left no question as to why he was so frightened of winding down.

It was Pythagoras' desk that Stella had backed against, and thinking it best to steer clear of DubDub for a bit, she rustled through the philosopher's papers. A flash of green glinted from beneath a piles of ancient scrolls. Pushing them away, Stella uncovered a square of thin jade the size of a large pizza box lying on the desk. Looking down into the emerald tablet, she saw her face reflected with a pale green tinge. Framing her reflection were the words, *As above, so below,* that had been carved on the glossy surface.

Stella gripped the edges of the emerald tablet with the tips of her fingers and pulled. It felt like a bit of suction had held the plate to the desk, but as she lifted, it came up with a soft, *pop.* Thinking maybe something so interesting might lighten his foul mood; she carried the plate to the desk where the automaton sat brooding. The tablet wasn't heavy but felt awkward to hold, like a pane of glass might feel.

"Do you know what this is?" She asked as she neared Jacques' desk. "It's really weird." DubDub would not take any of his eyes away from his many books, which now covered the desk. "Can I put it on your desk?" Stella asked in her most courteous voice. DubDub offered no response, so Stella ignoring her companion's icy demeanor, looked for another place to lay her load. Finding every desk covered with equipment and paraphernalia Stella had no option but to place the unwieldy tablet on the floor. As she did it made a small whooshing sound as if suction were locking it to the ground.

With the toe of her sneaker Stella gave the green tablet a push and was surprised to find it wouldn't budge. Wondering of the plate were somehow stuck, she grabbed the front of the plate with the tips of her fingers and lifted. It came up with a soft, *phhhsssst*, just like the sound a can of soda would make when its tab was pulled. Lifting the edge to see where that sound had come from, Stella took one peek and dropped the square back to the floor. "DubDub? You need to see this," she squealed. Then, just to make sure that what she had seen was real and not some figment of her imagination, she lifted the square again. What lay underneath had not changed. "DubDub!! Come here, I need you!"

Still the mechanical man couldn't spare the time to look at what she had found. "I hear you Stella, but I'm very busy," the automaton said with more than a bit of testiness in his voice, "and can't spare the time."

Even if she were the cause of his being upset, Stella had taken enough of DubDub's rudeness. Stomping over to the desk she grabbed a handful of the mechanical stalks and jerked their eyes around until they faced her. She glared into the glass orbs. "I need you to look at something, now!"

"There's no need to be so rough." DubDub protested as Stella led him by the stalks to the jade square.

In response, Stella held the handful of eyes down to the tablet. "What is this?" she demanded.

"Why, I have no idea. I've never seen it before. Now if you please, might you unhand my eyes, it's quite uncomfortable."

"In a minute", Stella insisted. With her free hand she dug her fingers under the edge of the tablet and though it took a bit of effort to lift with just one hand, the soft pop let her know she had succeeded. Grasping the eyes on the stalks tightly, she shoved them under the uplifted plate. "What do you see?"

"I see… I see…" The mechanical man gasped, "I see this room, only upside down!"

Letting go of the stalks which quickly retreated to the front of DubDub's face, Stella let the plate down slowly. The two sat on the floor staring at the emerald tablet in mute disbelief; the only sound being the excited pumping of the bellows in the mechanical man's chest. "Okay", the girl said after a moment's pause, "Now calm down and tell me exactly what you saw."

DubDub moved to the desk where he had been studying. "This desk was there, but it was hanging from the ceiling. And the ceiling, in that place beneath the tablet, was lower than the floor. Everything in this room was in that room, but as a mirror image."

"That's what I saw too!" Stella agreed. "How bizarre! Should we look again?" Before the mechanical man could answer, she lifted the slab and flipped it back, like a hatch hinged to the floor. They went cautiously to the hole in the floor and with her hands gripping its rim, Stella peered through. A few of DubDub's eyes snaked past her to share the view.

What they saw was indeed an exact duplicate of the Astrophelarium, only upside down. The desk at which DubDub had been reading was a precise replica of its counterpart above, complete with duplicate papers and books hanging over the desktop edges.

Moving an eye to the edge of the hole so she could see both rooms at once, Stella shifted her head up and down, looking first at the room she was in, and then looking down at the duplicate room. "*As above, so below,*" she pronounced, recalling the words inscribed on the tablet.

"This is quite amazing." DubDub commented from above. "Though I have seen much, this is the strangest thing I have ever seen."

"I wonder what would happen if…" Stella asked, as she reached for a nearby book. She dropped it through the hole, and it fell through the reverse Astrophelarium until it hit the ceiling. It bounced slightly and then sat there, just as if it had been dropped onto a floor.

Both Stella and DubDub stared at the book as if aware something was going to happen, which it did. The book fell from the ceiling down towards the hole from which it was dropped and as it flew past Stella she snatched it from the air.

"What does that mean?" DubDub asked, curiously examining the volume in the girl's hands.

"I'm not sure," Stella answered, "but I have another idea." Racing to the Teleportascope, she untied a length of rope from its side and ran back to the hole. "Let's see what this does." She dropped the rope down the hole until it hung straight down like a thin pole rising from the mirror Astrophelarium's floor. DubDub and the girl waited again, only this time nothing happened.

"Now that's interesting", Stella said, pulling the rope out of the hole. She sat upright on the floor stroking her chin just the way her father would when he was trying to solve some problem. "Okay, I have an idea." Like a hinged lid, Stella flipped the jade tablet back over the hole.

"Why are you doing that?" DubDub asked.

"*Watch!*" Stella slid her fingers around the edges of the emerald tablet and when she thought she had a good grip, lifted up. The tablet came away with the soft sound of a vacuum being broken. Where it had been, nothing remained but the bare wooden floor.

"Where did the hole go?" DubDub asked, chasing Stella as she carried the emerald tablet through the Astrophelarium. "And where are you going?"

Stella was going to the center of the laboratory to find a place under the open window, though she didn't feel like she needed to explain to DubDub at the moment; being still a bit annoyed at the way he had ignored her. When near the Teleportascope she spent a few moments trying to find the exact spot to place the tablet. The feeling of suction pulled the plate from her fingers as she set it down.

"Okay, I think that should be it." Stella said confidently. She gripped the tablet, carefully lifted an edge and flipped the jade square back. Where there had been a worn wooden floor, there was now a perfectly square hole into the mirror world. Looking into the hole she exclaimed. "I think I got it! Now we need a longer rope!"

Stella and DubDub ran through the lab gathering all the rope they could find. When they had a small pile Stella began to tie the pieces together. Though DubDub tried to help, his wooden fingers weren't made to tie knots. No matter, for soon where there had been many bits there was now one long rope.

"Let's see how this works." Stella dropped an end of the rope into the hole and began to feed its length down. Passing through the upside down laboratory, it made its way toward the open skylight. Stella let more of the rope out and watched as it fell into the open air past the window and inched towards the ladder far below.

"Can you see how close I am, DubDub? Am I getting nearer to the ladder?"

Mechanical eyes slid to the opening and softly whirred as they focused. "You're almost there, Stella. Just a little to the left. There! You're right next to the ladder." A pair of binoculars extended from DubDub's head and found their way to a place in front of Stella's eyes.

Clearly seeing that the rope was mere inches from the ladder Stella announced proudly, "I think we've found our way out of here." Taking the end of the rope she tied it, carefully, with a very good knot, to the base of the Teleportascope, and then leaned back with all her weight until she was confident it would hold. "That should do", she said walking back to the rim of the hole where DubDub stood waiting to see the rest of her plan.

Taking the rope in her hands, Stella whispered, "I can do this," then slid into the hole. She didn't look down as she climbed, not wanting to see the black pit of endless space framed by the mirror skylight below, instead she focused her attention upwards toward the hole from where DubDub watched.

It was a strange climb through the upside down world, first past the desks and workbenches where in defiance of gravity, books and tools clung unnaturally to their surfaces, then into the open air between the floor and the ceiling of the Astrophelarium. Moving downward past the elaborate chandeliers that sprouted like a garden of flowers on taut chain stems, she looked up at the desks and workbenches that hung over her head like so many boxy stalactites.

Moving past the frame of the skylight and out into the open space below, Stella felt even more discombobulated. Just a short while ago she had been on the ladder looking down at the skylight, and now she was climbing down to it from above. The floor of the mirror laboratory was now high above and she could see the exact spot where the scientists had held out Socrates' robe. But suddenly, something in the scene seemed not right; and clinging to the rope Stella stopped, trying to figure out just what it was.

"What are you waiting for?" DubDub shouted from above.

He watched from the hole which was next to the Teleportascope base, right inside the circle of letters that spelled out the motto of the laboratory. The golden text stating, *Wisdom begins in wonder,* was reversed, as if viewed in a mirror.

"Pull me up!" Stella yelled. The grinding sound of DubDub's labor echoed through the hole as he pulled the rope. Stella began to rise through the air. Hanging just below the opening in the floor she shouted, "Stop here!"

DubDub peeked through the hole. "What are you doing now?"

"We can't escape this way. There's something wrong with this place! Watch, I'll show you." Stella held tight to the rope and in a quick flip had her feet on the upside down floor. Taking a second to make sure her theory was correct, she cautiously let go and stood straight upside down. DubDub gaped in surprise.

Stella picked up a book from a desk and taking it to the hole she held it out for DubDub to read. "I've no idea what, *REGNESSEM YRRATS EHT,* means! What kind of title is that?"

"Now go to the same desk on your side and get the same book." Stella suggested.

DubDub retrieved the twin volume and read the words on its cover. "*THE STARRY MESSENGER*!" he exclaimed, "Why, Galileo wrote this book!" He raced back to the hole where Stella fanned open the pages of her book for him to see. "All the words are reversed!" he squawked. His eyes darted from the book to fan out in all directions and scrutinize the surroundings. "Everything in this place is backwards!"

Stella quickly told DubDub, if they escaped into this mirror world, they would be living in a backwards world. If Stella ever did get home the spots on Sirius' back would be reversed and the dimple on her mother's left cheek would be on the right. Even the planets would orbit in the direction opposite of what they had always done. "I don't think I could bear living that way," she stated, studying the rope that stood straight up through the hole like some snake charmer's trick.

"We have to climb up from our world; we can't go down on to that." Stella jerked a thumb over her shoulder towards the ladder that stretched into the sky below.

"So what are we going to do?" DubDub asked with his head of tentacles framed in the hole.

It was a bit unnerving see him peeking through as if he were hanging upside down, so Stella looked past him to the ladder far below her feet. "I need to find a way *down* to that ladder, which is *up* for you." She said, confused by her own words. "Let me see what I can find to help us. I'll be right back."

Walking around the room Stella found pieces of rope in the same places they had been in the upper room, but backwards. After carrying them to the hole she tied them together, experiencing a strange sense of déjà vu as she repeated the actions. Dropping this rope through the hole, she was not at all surprised that it settled into a position exactly mirroring the first rope, stopping right near the ladder.

"Very interesting!" DubDub wheezed as a number of his mechanical eyes followed the stiff rope up into the air. "Now all we have to do is climb up!" He touched the knotted rope, which promptly collapsed and fell back through the hole. Stella snatched it as it dropped.

"Why did that happen?"

"I'm not sure," Stella stroked her chin, trying to sort out the problem they were presented with now, "but I think you'll have to come to this side if you want to climb *down* with me."

Tentatively, DubDub climbed down the first rope into the mirror world and with Stella's help lifted his feet until they rested on the upside down floor. Reluctantly releasing the rope the mechanical man grabbed the girl's outstretched hands and with a loud creak, pulled his body erect.

Once they were together, Stella touched the rope DubDub had climbed. It collapsed in a pile on the floor. "It appears, things behave according to which world they're part of, until something from the other side touches them", Stella explained. "Then they go back to remembering their original…" What was the word her father would use? "…Polarity!"

"So when we get to our ladder, the one that's going to take us out of here, we can't touch it until we're both ready to get off the rope, otherwise," Stella worked out the last piece to the puzzle, "otherwise, the rope might collapse and drop us both to the floor."

"Okay," DubDub said, "but before we go, would you mind making sure I'm fully wound?"

Stella turned the key on his chest until the tension tightened. "That's fine, thank you. Now I'm ready to try," the automaton said with all the confidence he could muster.

Gripping the rope, Stella went first, sliding through the hole while making certain to avoid touching its edge. When she had gone a few feet, she called for DubDub to follow. As he made his way down into the open space beyond the hole, Stella warned, "Be careful not to touch anything until we reach the ladder!" Soon they had descended past the lab and down through the skylight where the vault beneath their feet glowed with the light of twinkling stars. "We'll be there soon. I hope my plan works!"

There was no reply, and when Stella looked up she saw the clockwork man gazing into space in rapt ecstasy. "DubDub?" she asked softly, with a pang of guilt for disturbing the mechanical man's moment of bliss.

The sky was filled with so many twinkling lights, as to be uncountable, and Stella marveled at how each of the lights was a star, and each star was a being, and how around those stars might be planets and on some of those planets were beings. And each and every of those, the stars, the planets and the beings, held within their own vivid light.

"There's so much of it, and all so beautiful! Nothing in the workshop could have prepared me for this." DubDub exclaimed, his eyes circling his head, observing every sector of the sky. "All I've known was what I could see through the skylight. I never imagined that outside could be so big! It goes on and on!"

Hearing the thrill in his voice, Stella knew that taking him along was the right thing to do, if only for this one happy moment. "Yes, it is beautiful," she responded dreamily, as the sheer splendor of the universe worked its enchantment. "But we need to go." Remembering her mission was all it took to shatter the spell.

"Just a few more minutes!" the mechanical man begged.

"DubDub," Stella was gentle but firm as, in the same voice she would use when asking the twins to do something they didn't want to do, she explained to the clockwork man. "If we waste time, there's a good chance that soon there'll be no Stars at all."

"No stars at all?" DubDub squealed from above as his eyes turned from the bespangled sky and twisted toward Stella.

"That's right. If I don't wind the clockwork soon, Moros will be free to extinguish their lights. If you want to stay here and look at the stars..." Stella continued her climb down.... "That's fine with me; but I have a job to do."

DubDub shuddered in horror. "Stay here alone? No! I wouldn't like that at all!" The mechanical man came clambering down the rope. "Well, what are you waiting for, Stella Ray! There's not a moment to lose. Let's get going!"

When they were near the ladder, Stella slid far enough down the rope so DubDub could grab the very bottom of the ladder, because, and she was beginning to have difficulty with all these flips in logic, he was on top. "Okay," she said, "What I think will happen is that once we touch the ladder, the rope won't hold us anymore. So we'll have to grab the ladder at exactly the same time, understand?" The mechanical man nodded. "*And*," she emphasized, "When we touch the ladder, our bodies are going to think that down is up and up is down, so hold on real tight because we're going to flip over. Grab on with both hands!"

"Ready?" She asked the clockwork man hanging on the rope above, who, if her plan worked out, would soon be holding onto the ladder below. If it didn't work, it would be a long fall down.

"I suppose so." DubDub whimpered as he struggled to muster his courage, much as Stella was doing.

"On the count of three, grab the rungs and hold tight." Stella took a deep breath, shouted "*One! Two! Three!*" and lunged for the ladder. As her fingers touched its rungs the rope went slack and there was just a split second to get a tighter grip before gravity flipped. What had been *up* was now *down,* and Stella held on for dear life as her body swung and slammed into the ladder. She struggled briefly until her feet found a rung, and then she was standing safely on the ladder.

DubDub had no such luck. Though his wooden fingers were clenched tightly to the last rung on the ladder, his flip had left the rest of his body dangling below and his legs kicking wildly to find a foothold. Locking one arm around the ladder, Stella grabbed the joint of his wrist with her free hand and pulled with all her strength. "I have you, DubDub! I won't let you fall!" With the girl's help, the automaton climbed to where both his wooden feet were firmly on the ladder.

Now once again on Loony's ladder, Stella huffed to catch her breath, while from below, DubDub's bellows wheezed even louder. Looking at its endless length disappearing into the starry sky above, she wondered how they would ever have the strength to make the climb. She tried to think of something encouraging but nothing came to mind, so without another thought she began the ascent. From below came the whirring of DubDub's gears as he laboriously followed along.

After what felt like hours of strenuous climbing, DubDub's spring needed to be wound, so Stella hung from the rungs and turned the dial that protruded from the his chest. "My friends should've helped us by now." she said, obviously upset that they hadn't.

"Perhaps something came up that needed their attention? I'm sure they'd help if they could." DubDub's voice strengthened with every turn of the dial, "Just as you have helped me."

Stella marveled at the amazing machine below her. Though he was constructed of only wood and metal, he was doing his best to make her feel better. She could see that he would be a very good friend, quite unlike the type of friend Loony was turning out to be.

"I suppose you're right," Stella responded, "But I can't see what would be more important to them than getting me on my way. They said it was crucial I hurried, though so far they've done nothing to help me along." She looked down into the swarm of eyes below, devices of all different sizes and shapes. What a strange friend to have! A few of the eyes looked up to her, but most of the others could not stop scanning the vast array of glittering stars. "Well let's keep moving. I think this climb might take a while." But as Stella reached for the next rung, a terrified cry stopped her cold.

"*Look*!" shrieked DubDub. Stella followed his gaze to a dark stain, much like she had seen through her father's telescope, blooming in the starry sky. Like a sinister amoeba grimly determined to feed, it pulsed malevolently and moved toward a cluster of glittering stars.

"No!" Stella shouted, "Not again!"

"Not again? What is that thing?" DubDub squealed excitedly, "What's happening?"

As if she could somehow stop the inevitable, Stella lunged up the ladder and shouted to the stars as if they might hear. "Escape! He's coming for you!"

The stars offered no response, but only hung complacent in their places, their jeweled indifference oblivious to the deadly peril that approached. Tendrils oozed from the throbbing blotch to encircle the cluster of stars.

"Someone has to help them." Stella cried desperately to the heavens above. "Astraea! Please! Help them!"

From below DubDub gasped in disbelief. "The darkness! It's swallowing those stars!"

As the deadly amoeba tightened its circle, the luminaries seemed unaware of the fate that awaited them. Then, as a famished mouth might devour a handful of crumbs, the maw snapped shut. The ensnared stars fell together in a brief burst; their captive light raging against the dark, but their resistance was brutally crushed. The trap closed and the Stars were no more. Savoring its feast, the malignant splotch heaved in a shuddering belch. It hung defiantly in space for a moment, a proud and profane tumor staining the night, and then slowly began to move. The girl and the automaton watched helplessly as the horror crept on, a streak of murk growing behind it as it did. "Can you see where it's heading?" Stella asked.

In response, his instruments shifted to follow the dark line across the sky. "Oh No!" DubDub blurted before falling dead silent. Thinking what an inopportune time it was for him to wind down, Stella reached for his key. As she did his hand shot out to clutch her wrist.

"What is it?" Stella's heart rose in her throat as she pulled herself free of the automaton's grasp. "Tell me!"

"That thing that swallowed the stars!" DubDub howled, "Its trajectory is aimed right for Earth!"

"For Earth?" Fighting back panic, Stella sputtered, "How long until it reaches Earth?"

"At the speed it's traveling I would calculate," the gears in the mechanical man's head loudly grinded, "that it will impact Earth in only a matter of days. And then it will be on a direct course for the Sun."

Stella hung limply from the ladder.

"You need to do something," DubDub pleaded. "There must be some way to warn them."

"I don't know how get back to Earth." Stella anguished. "And even if I could warn them, that wouldn't save them. The only way to stop the darkness from destroying Earth is to defeat Moros, and to do that we have to find our way out of the universe."

"Well then," the mechanical man asked, "what are we waiting for?"

Then, both girl and machine resumed their climb. If Stella slowed, the automaton would come up quickly behind and spur her on to greater heights. Only pausing when DubDub needed to be wound, they climbed until Stella's arms and legs felt like they were made of lead.

"I'm not sure how much longer I can climb like this," she moaned.

"Don't give up! One rung at a time will do it!" DubDub offered, doing his best to spur the girl on.

As hard as she tried to heed the advice, concentrating only on the next rung and nothing else, it was hopeless. "I can't go on." Stella whimpered, ashamed at her lack of willpower.

"Just try!" The mechanical voice encouraged from below.

She tried, she really did. She lunged for the next rung with the last of her strength but her hand fell back in limp defeat. "I can't go any further," she sobbed. "I really can't!" She hung to the rungs of the endless ladder, a thin thread floating in the void, and cried, "Old Sol! Astraea! Why won't help me? How did you think I could do this alone?"

The hurt voice that came from below was barely a whisper, "You're not alone. I'm with you."

Looking down, a multitude of eyes met the Stella's glance, glittering glass orbs catching the starlight. It was true, Stella realized; she was not alone. Even though she was far from the Earth, the distance did not mean that her family and friends weren't with her. She felt the small globe of the Earth at her chest and pulled from beneath her jacket, the Compyxx that was supposed to lead her home. The needle pointed up.

"You're right, DubDub", Stella said, trying to manage a smile. "But I just can't see how I can continue climbing."

"See?" The mechanical man gushed. "Why, that's my job. It's what I was made for. Just rest a moment and let me, *see,* what I can find."

Stella held tightly to the ladder, wrapping her elbows around its rungs to give her fingers a break. There was a flurry of activity as the array of ocular devices on DubDub's head scrutinized the surroundings.

"I see something."

"What is it? What do you see?"

"Birds!" He shouted happily. "I can see Jacques Vaucanson's birds!"

Stella wasn't sure why DubDub was so excited but it sounded as if he had some sort of plan in mind, if she considered the mechanical man had a mind at all.

"Stella?" DubDub asked urgently, "Can you whistle?"

"Yes, of course. Can't you?"

"My lips are made of wood, so no, I can't. But could you whistle for me, just a bit?"

Too tired to wonder if perhaps the climb had so unwound the mechanical man that he was malfunctioning, Stella managed to whistle, not any tune but only random bursts of sound.

"That's good, perhaps a little louder?"

Stella blew through her pursed lips as hard as she could.

"Yes! Yes! They hear us! Can you whistle in a higher pitch?"

Stella pursed her lips tighter until the whistle became higher, and began to modulate its pitch with slight movements of her tongue.

"That's perfect!" DubDub exclaimed, "They're coming!" He took a hand off the ladder and pointed to where Stella could see gliding through space, the dense flock of mechanical birds.

"Keep whistling!"

And Stella did, trying to copy the sound of a bird, doing her best to lure the flock closer.

"They're getting nearer!" DubDub shouted as the thick flock of birds flew in wide circles about them. "Don't stop whistling!"

Within the flock Stella could see birds that she had wound and set free. There were the falcon and the dove, the pelican and the finch and dozens of others, turning and turning in tightening circles around the ladder.

"Now what?" Stella asked, taking a momentary break from whistling, "Why did we call them?"

"Hold on." DubDub shouted; his voice all but lost in the onslaught of birdsongs and flapping wings. "I think they're near enough that I can communicate with them. After all, we have the same father."

Stella thought that was very strange, but when she thought about it, she could see how DubDub might consider Jacques Vaucason his father. And being that the clever Frenchman also made the birds, they were in a way, DubDub's family. From the mechanical man's mouth came an astonishing rush of sound. Snapping clicks and grinding whirs, high buzzes and low hums filled the air as if the door to some busy factory had been opened. And what was even more amazing was that the birds seemed to understand this metallic cacophony. They had ceased circling and now hovered around the stranded pair.

"What are you saying?" Stella shouted, interrupting DubDub's mechanical soliloquy.

"I'm asking for a favor." He responded in English, before turning his attention back to the birds to continue speaking in the strange machine language. Even though Stella knew that he could not smile, as his lips were made of a rigid wood, she was sure she caught a grin on DubDub's face. "They've agreed." He announced, "Get ready!"

Before Stella could even ask what it was she should get ready for, the birds swooped in. Hundreds of tiny claws clutched her parka and in an instant lifted her from the ladder. Up flew the mechanical birds with their human cargo. Looking down, she saw the remainder of the flock seize hold of DubDub, gripping his frame wherever they could. And then he was carried up too, floating with the help of hundreds of flapping wings.

In no time the mechanical man was next to Stella, "They'll bring us as high as they can," he shouted, "Which I think will be far enough."

And it was. Because after they had flown a while higher and higher into space, Stella could see the beacon of Old Sol's lighthouse, brilliantly alight in the darkness of space. Following DubDub's instructions, the birds deposited the two companions on the ladder a short distance from the lighthouse; a climb Stella was sure would be no problem.

14 THE GOLDEN ROAD

"Did you find a map?" Astraea asked as soon as the girl climbed into the room.

"Do you mind if I catch my breath first?" Stella snapped testily. She wasn't going to pretend that she wasn't upset at having been left trapped in the lab.

Before Astraea could offer any consolation, DubDub clambered into the lighthouse. The woman's lovely jaw slackened at the sight of the shambling contraption. "What is that?"

Stella couldn't let her off the hook that easily, "Why didn't you check to make sure the ladder was long enough to reach the laboratory?"

Astraea was taken aback. "We did! I myself double-checked to make sure the ladder was aimed perfectly. It should have brought you right into the lab!"

"Well it didn't!" Stella retorted crossly. "I almost fell when I reached the ladder's end! And when I was in the lab I almost couldn't find my way back up. I'm lucky I made it back at all." She moved to stand beside the mechanical man. "If it wasn't for DubDub here, I'd still be hanging on the ladder."

Flustered, Astraea managed an apology. "I'm sorry, but I promise you, the ladder did reach the lab. I don't know what could have happened. The only other person in the room while you were gone was…" Her eyes widened in realization…"Loony!"

When the moon man heard his name the blue pools of his eyes shot daggers at the Star woman. "Don't dare accuse me! It isn't my fault you didn't make sure the ladder was all the way down!"

As the two extraterrestrials fought, DubDub sidled up to Stella. "Who is that?" He asked breathlessly, his eyes glued to the luminous form of Astraea.

"She," Stella whispered in response while observing the stare down between Loony and Astraea, "is a Star!"

"A Star?" DubDub straightened himself and rushed nervously towards Astraea. Extending a mechanical hand timidly and obviously intimidated by meeting a real Star, he gushed. "Hello, I have come to assist Stella on her journey. She has given me the name DubDub."

Astraea, turning away from Loony, politely took the automaton's hand. "Thank you for your help, DubDub. I'm glad to meet anyone who is an ally in our struggle against the darkness."

Convinced he had won the showdown with the Star woman Loony slipped away. Stella watched as he continued to snoop around the lighthouse, only then realizing what was missing. "Where's Old Sol?"

The look on Astraea's face told Stella that something was awfully wrong. "Old Sol had to leave. There was something that needed his attention."

"What's wrong? What happened?" Stella blurted but even as she spoke, understood why the Sun was not there. "He went to stop Moros, didn't he? Old Sol has gone to protect the Earth from attack."

The round head of the moon popped up from the cranny he was investigating. "Earth is under attack? How do you know that?"

DubDub reported his observations. "I saw a blot of darkness devour two stars and then watched as that same shadow moved toward the planetary system of Sol."

Loony began to race around the room, wailing uncontrollably. "What are we going to do? We have to help Earth! You have no idea how horrible Moros can be!"

Astraea glided gracefully across the room. Putting her hands on the moon man's shoulders, she stopped his panicky outburst. "Calm yourself, Moon of Earth. She will be safe. Old Sol has gone to make sure that no harm comes to her."

Stella, remembering the blemishes that had formed on Sol's surface as a result of that encounter, could not be so sure. "Can Old Sol really stop Moros? I saw what happened the last time Moros attacked him."

Astraea's answer to these doubts came with a light in her eyes so pure; that Stella knew whatever the Star woman said would be true. Something so fine and so brilliant would be incapable of deception. "As we struggle against the darkness, each of us has a part to play. Old Sol will do his, and keep Earth safe. We are all emissaries of light, and as long as we hold true to that bond we will not fail."

Blinding light suddenly flooded the room. Shielding her eyes, Stella spied rocketing towards the lighthouse, nothing less than the sun she had known from Earth's sky. The fiery ball had entered the room and what had been an incandescent ball of blazing nuclear fury, was now the boisterous and buoyant form of Old Sol. He beamed a warm smile at the startled girl. "Why Stella, you've returned! I had hoped to make it back before your return."

Stella felt distress turn to relief as she stood bathed in the rays of the Sun. Loony's demeanor too, lightened as the Sol's glow illuminated the gray sphere of his head, giving it a warm golden hue. Immediately the moon questioned Sol. "Is Earth okay? Is she alright?"

"She is fine, Loony." the Sun patted the moon's head with his fiery hand, "For now. But it is important that Stella accomplish her mission. Moros has turned his attention to Earth and though I am capable of holding him off for now, if the darkness and his powers increase, he will make his move. I fear for the humans of Earth if that happens."

The concern for the inhabitants of Earth was obvious on the Sun's face. But Stella remembered he had trapped those men in the Astrophelarium. "If you care so much about humans," She asked, in not the nicest of tones, "why did you leave all those men trapped down there? How could you put them there against their will? That's almost as bad as what Moros is trying to do!"

As the brilliance of the Sun wilted under the girl's accusations, Stella could see that her vehement missives had hit their target.

The Sun frowned, "the men in the Astrophelarium? Trapped? Why, I never realized. I was certain I had done them a favor. They weren't happy to be there?"

"They felt trapped," Stella replied, with a hinted tinge of spite in her voice. "They told me there was no way out of the universe, so the only escape was to go inward. They made a device, a Teleportascope, and left to travel deeper into the universe. When they left the Astrophelarium, I was alone until I discovered DubDub."

"All the scientists have gone? And they traveled inward? Why, you humans are so resourceful!" Sol said with obvious admiration, "I am always surprised at your cleverness! But I am sorry if they weren't happy there," Old Sol added apologetically, "I was sure I was doing the right thing by sending them there. I can't believe I had so misjudged their desires. Humans are so strange I fear I will never understand them."

Seeing how regretful Sol was, Stella could forgive him the ill effects of his good intentions, but there was still the ladder and the fact that she had been sent to the Astrophelarium on a wild goose chase. "Well, anyway, my trip down to the Astrophelarium was all for nothing." Stella stated, "There was no map to the end of the universe. All the scientists were certain the universe was endless."

"Endless, eh?" Old Sol raised a skeptical eyebrow, "Well, they are certainly entitled to their opinion, but all things eventually come to an end."

"You found nothing that might aid us in finding the Celestial Clockwork?" Astraea interjected. "The human scientists could offer you no help at all?"

"Nothing." Stella answered.

With a loud creak DubDub moved forward. "Perhaps they should see the strange map you showed me."

"It's just an old map that has nothing to do with the universe. It's worthless." Stella responded.

"Worthless! Why, I would seriously doubt that! I find everything I cast my rays upon to have worth." the Sun said with a jolly smile, "Now, if it's okay with you, would you mind showing us this map?"

Finding it impossible to stay angry at the Sun, Stella retrieved the map from where it had been stowed inside her parka, unfolded the square and held out the parchment. "Professor Lowell, who gave this to me, said it was the oldest map in the Astrophelarium. But it doesn't look anything like a galaxy should look."

"Nor like any island I could find in the laboratory's books!" DubDub added, clattering to Stella's side.

Astraea peered over Old Sol's shoulder as he studied the map. The two Stars exchanged surprised glances. "Both Sol and I know this place well," Astraea pronounced. "It is the homeland of the Stars; *Empyriania*."

"Homeland of the Stars?" Stella questioned.

Old Sol traced around the sparsely illustrated area at the outer most part of the island. "Here," he said in a matter of fact manner, "is where all Stars of the Milky Way galaxy reside. It is where they meet to take part in the great dance."

Stella looked to where printed along the map's border were the words "The Milky Way." Then she thought of the penciled letters on the back that spelled out "Empyriania." It boggled her mind to think that the mysterious map from the Astrophelarium could represent both the Milky Way galaxy and an island that was the home of the Stars at the same time.

"And what is this in the middle?" DubDub asked, curious about the dense and phantasmagoric shapes that filled the center of the map.

"Those are the Nebula Mountains. What lies there is a mystery even to the Stars of Empyriania. Legend tells, it is an area of great danger", Astraea answered gravely.

"Well then, what's this?" Stella poked a finger at the blue circle that lay at the center of the mountains, marked with the bright red, *X*.

"What lies within those mountains is a mystery to me," Said Astraea.

"And also to me," Old Sol sighed regretfully. "The gloomy peaks and valleys of those regions are shunned by all who dance on the plains of Empyriania."

Acting on a hunch, Stella took the Compyxx from beneath her jacket, opened it and hung it over the map by its chain. The little arrow pointed to the blue circle with the red *X,* in the center. Slowly she moved the Compyxx around the map, circling the center. Its arrow remained pointed at the red *X*.

"It looks like I'm supposed to go through those mountains and to the red *X*." Stella said. "Maybe it's the way that leads out of the universe."

Old Sol thought for a moment. "The only Star who might know is Heo, though he has never spoken of what lies in those hills."

"Who is Heo?" Stella asked.

Before Old Sol could answer, DubDub interjected. "Heo is the oldest of the Stars in the Milky Way galaxy, according to Star charts in the Astrophelarium."

"Precisely!" Old Sol beamed at the mechanical man. "What a wonderful device you are! And to think, humans constructed you! Humans from my solar system!"

"It is said," Astraea offered, "that Heo knows secrets from eons long passed,"

"Well, "Stella responded, "If Heo knows these secrets, it's about time he starts talking. When he finds out that the universe is being threatened, he'll tell me what I need to know, right?" Astraea smiled at the girl's resolve. "How do I get to this *Empyriania* anyway?" Stella asked.

"You'll have to walk. It's quite a ways, but I'll be waiting for you when you arrive." Old Sol answered.

"You'll be waiting?" Stella wasn't looking forward to another long journey. "If I have to walk, how are you getting there?"

Old Sol turned toward the girl. "By now you should have noticed that we're different from you, Stella. We're Stars. We might always be up in the sky twinkling for humans to see, but at the same time we are also at our home, engaged in the great dance of light that is the universe. So we're not really going anywhere because we are already there."

Stella rolled her eyes thinking how naïve she was, to have expected an answer that made any sense at all. "Already there? She repeated skeptically.

"I'm still in the sky of Earth and the planets are still orbiting me, but I'm here too with you, right?"

Stella nodded. "I guess so."

"But, I am also in Empyriania." With a laugh Sol disappeared, leaving a shimmering glow that rapidly dissolved into the air.

Stella reached out and waved her hand through the empty space. Turning to Astraea, she asked, "Where'd he go?"

"He's gone to the homeland of the Stars. We Stars are like that. We can be in our places in the sky, while at the same time here with you or on the plains of Empyriania." The Star woman nodded to where Old Sol had been. "Just watch."

The air in front of Stella began to shimmer and glow as glittering sparkles hung in the air. They flared brightly. Stella blinked and by the time she opened her eyes, Old Sol was back where he had been before, but his happy demeanor was gone.

Astraea rushed quickly to his side, "What's wrong, Sol?"

"There is something very amiss in our land, Astraea. We're needed there immediately."

"You're leaving now?" Stella asked anxiously.

"We'll meet you in Empyriania. By the time you get there, we will have whatever the problem is under control." Astraea predicted in an attempt to ease the girl's concern.

Stella looked to the Sun for the same certainty but he responded only with a grimace of unease. "Okay," she said, putting an end to the awkward moment, "Which way do I go?"

Old Sol lifted a lighthouse window, pushed out the stardust flap beneath and opened a doorway to space. Like a magician would before executing a trick, he flexed his fingers. Putting his hands together he quickly yanked them apart. What appeared between them was like a piece of taffy, only it glowed like lava. As if unrolling a bolt of fabric, with a quick flick he sent a long sheet of light flying from the tube. It flew through the doorway and out into space, settling into a thin carpet that stretched beyond sight. "You go that way," Old Sol pointed down the golden road of unlimited distance. "When you reach the path's end, just turn around and come back in."

More nonsense, Stella thought, but too tired to question Sol's statement, she groaned reluctantly. "Okay, I guess then I should start out."

"*WE* should start out, you mean," DubDub corrected "You're not going anywhere without me; I need you to keep me wound! I'm going with you."

Stella managed a smile. She was very glad DubDub had volunteered to come along.

"And me too!" Loony insisted, "I'm not going to be left behind and miss all the fun!"

Stella cringed. If Loony came, she imagined it would be a full time job keeping him in line.

Old Sol spoke gently, "Now Loony, you know you can't join Stella on her journey. Why, I've taken great liberties just to be able to have you here in my home. I'm sorry, but it's impossible. It would be totally inappropriate for you to go to Empyriania."

The angry scowl on Loony's face showed just what he thought of that.

"Please, Loony. Don't be so grim. There's plenty for you to do here."

"Like what?" Loony asked.

Old Sol squished up his face as he pondered just how to answer. "At the moment I'm not exactly sure. But I'm certain that your part in our mission will prove of the utmost importance."

Before Loony could say any more, Sol turned away. "A human and a mechanical man in Empyriania!" he exclaimed to Stella and DubDub. "I wonder how you'll be welcomed. Many there are leery of anything not as bright and brilliant as they are themselves. Stars are a proud lot, and some have been blinded by that pride. So blinded," he lamented, "that many are not aware of what has been transpiring in their very midst." Ushering Stella and DubDub onto the golden carpet Old Sol urged. "But hurry along! I'm sure you'll cross that bridge when you come to it!"

Astraea came to the threshold and took the girl's hand. "We'll see you soon." She promised. "Just stay on the path and you'll be safe." With those words she faded away and Stella's hand was empty but for a shimmering mist of light.

"Good luck Stella!" Old Sol shouted, and in a wink he was gone too. Now there was only Loony who glared at the duo in the doorway.

"I suppose," she said as sincerely as she could sound, "That Sol has a much more important mission for you. Whatever it is, I'm sure it will be a lot more fun than just walking on this stupid carpet." The scowling moon man said nothing. "*Ooooh-kaaay then,*" Stella declared, starting down the carpet with DubDub clattering close behind. "I guess we should be going. We'll see you when we get back."

They had only been walking a short while when DubDub suddenly whispered. "We're being followed."

Stella saw that some of her companion's eyes were stealthily peeking back. "By whom?" she whispered, afraid to look for herself, fearing they were being pursued by a horrible darkness.

"It's Loony!"

Swinging around to see a round-headed figure approaching, Stella was the first to speak. "Why are you here? You know Old Sol said you couldn't come with us."

"Well," the moon man answered, his beady eyes darting from Stella to DubDub and back as he searched for which one might believe his story. "I was afraid. There was something back there, something dark and scary. It came right after you left. I waited to see if it would go away, but it just got bigger and darker. And then…"

"Then what?" Stella asked, not sure if she should believe the story.

"It talked to me!" Loony replied, suitably aghast.

Buying into the tale, DubDub asked fretfully, "*Wha... wha… what did it say?*"

"It whispered, 'I'm coming for you!' That's when I ran!" Loony said convincingly.

Stella deliberated on whether the imp was telling the truth. "You know what Old Sol said. You're not supposed to go further than his lighthouse."

Loony shot Stella a cold hard stare. "I can't go back there; he'll be waiting for me!" He turned to DubDub to continue his plea. "I have to go with you. When we meet Sol in Empyriania he'll tell you, *it is okay*. Besides, I'm all ready here and nothing bad has happened," he insisted. "Right?"

"I guess so," DubDub responded before guiltily looking to Stella to see if he had said the right thing.

Words Stella wasn't sure she wanted to say fell from her mouth. "Okay, we'll see what Old Sol says."

"Yippee!" Loony shouted, running off down the carpet. "I'm going to Empyriania!"

DubDub chased after. "Come back! We should all stay together."

Loony paid no mind and was soon far ahead. Stella, wondering just what she had agreed to, followed after her friends. When she reached DubDub, his eyes were hanging limply like a wet mop about his shoulders. "Before we continue," he whined weakly, having overexerted himself in his efforts to corral the moon man, "perhaps you can wind me; just a bit?" Stella pulled the dial from DubDub's chest and gave it a few quick turns. "Thank you very much!" the automaton said as he lively stepped forward. "I'm ready for anything now!"

"Come on!" The wayward moon hollered from the distance. "I can't wait to see what all the fuss is about in Empyriania."

"Just don't get too far ahead!" she yelled, knowing that just like her brothers, Loony would pay no heed.

Though Stella had still not recovered from the climb, with the soft path beneath their feet, the trek proved painless. Behind, the lighthouse was aglow in the distance, while ahead the golden carpet stretched like an incandescent ribbon through the deep purple of interstellar space. "Look at that!" DubDub suddenly exclaimed, pointing out from the walkway to a small red orb that passed slowly overhead. "It's Mars…!"

"And there's Venus!" Stella gushed. "And Saturn!" She reached for the ringed planet just beyond her reach, which could have easily fit into the palm of her hand. A tiny planet, barely the size of a ping-pong ball zipped quickly by, already out of reach. "There goes Mercury!"

"And way back there, I can see Pluto!" DubDub pointed to a tiny ball swinging in a wide orbit out from behind the lighthouse. Stella had to shield her eyes to see the cold planet through the glare of the sun. "But why are all the planets so small?"

"I guess we've entered a whole new level." Stella answered giddily as she watched Jupiter float by like a helium filled balloon. The floating planets brought back memories of the mobile her father had hung above her crib, and she could see in her mind's eye, chubby baby fingers reaching for the small dangling balls. And now as the planets themselves hung in the space around Stella, all she could think of was her family. "But where is Earth?"

"And here comes Neptune!" Loony shouted. The watery planet no bigger than a baseball, intersected the space above the carpet just a short distance ahead.

Stella strained her eyes, desperately searching for her home planet. "But where's Earth!"

DubDub came to her side to help in the search for the bright blue ball. "There she is!" He shouted, a binocular like device shot from his head pointing to just the left of the lighthouse, "See?"

"Where is Terra? Where?" Loony appeared from nowhere to grab the stalk from DubDub's head. The moon man pulled the device down towards his eyes. "Where is she? I can't see her!"

As DubDub squeaked in pain, Stella pried the moon man's hand from the stalk. "Let go Loony! Let him go!"

Stella tried to calm the quivering automaton down as he retreated from the malicious moon man. "It's okay… It's okay…now where did you see Earth."

DubDub pointed to the lighthouse, brilliant against the dark of space. Stella squinted, eager for a glimpse of Earth. She heard a soft whir as something brushed her face, and lifting her hand touched a set of goggles that extended from one of DubDub's stalks. They settled onto her nose lightly, the device shielding her eyes from the glare and magnifying her vision, so that now she could see moving towards Old Sol's lighthouse, a small blue ball. "Is that Earth?"

From DubDub's head, a complicated looking instrument extended, making a soft buzz as its lenses refocused. "Why yes it is, I can see mountains through the clouds. I do believe they are the Himalayas."

"You can see mountains?" Stella asked in amazement. Even with the aid of the goggles, she couldn't make out anything on the small ball. "What else can you see?"

"Let me look!" pleaded Loony as he tugged on Stella's sleeve. "Come on! Let me see!" Gently, without disturbing DubDub, Stella guided the goggles from her face and down to Loony's beady eyes.

"Hmmmm…" was all he had to say.

As the Earth passed by, DubDub focused intently. "Just a moment please." Another stalk tipped with a small telescope, shifted away from his head and joined the first device. "This is fascinating! I can see a building nestled in a valley of the mountain range."

Stella could barely contain her excitement. "You can see buildings?"

"I can't see anything!" Loony complained, pushing away the goggles. "These things don't work at all." He stalked off down the carpet, much to Stella's relief. She pulled the goggles back over her eyes and looked to the Earth.

"Why yes of course. I can almost make out the face of a monk who has just left the temple."

Stella barely heard his words. "Please DubDub! Look at the North Pole! Hurry, please, before the Earth is totally hidden!"

Instantly the instruments that were studying the mountain ranges recalibrated their position. "I see the Arctic, now if I can just find the pole." DubDub wheezed anxiously, "Yes, there it is. The North pole."

"Can you see my house? It's right at the pole and shaped like a dome. *Can you see it?*" Stella was all but screaming as the Earth drifted closer to the lighthouse.

The pair of instruments that scrutinized the globe whirred as they fine-tuned their focus. "Yes, I see a dome."

"*Look for my parents!!!* Look for the kitchen window! Can you see anything?"

"I can see the window!"

At DubDub's words Stella's heart leapt. If only she knew her family was all right, it wouldn't bother her so much to go further from home. "Can you see my mother or father?"

"No, I'm sorry, there's no one in the room." Stella could hear the strain in DubDub's voice as he struggled to see even better. "*Wait! There*, I see someone walking towards the window. Yes, I see her face!" The automaton was silent for a moment and then whispered sadly. "The Earth is gone. I can see no more."

"Who did you see? What did she look like? Was she okay?"

"The woman I saw", DubDub, overcome with exertion, panted, "she had your eyes!"

That could only be Stella's mother DubDub had seen in the kitchen! Verena Maldek had not done anything bad to her family, yet. There was still hope, Stella thought slightly relieved.

"What're you doing?" Loony asked suddenly back at his companion's side.

"He was just checking on something." Stella replied, for some reason not sure that she should tell the moon man what DubDub had seen on Earth.

"Well, you should quit playing around. We have places to go, things to do!" the moon man cracked a toothy grin, "And Old Sol and Astraea are probably waiting, so come on!" Loony grabbed Stella's wrist and pulled, "Let's go!"

At an ever-increasing speed Stella was towed down the golden carpet, further and further from her Solar System. DubDub clattered behind; valiantly attempting to keep up and when he began to fall behind, Stella grabbed his hand and pulled him along. As Loony's speed increased the surrounding stars became streaks of blurry light. Traveling at such a dizzying speed, Stella lost all track of where they were and where they were going. Her head was spinning, her wrist ached and her arm felt like it was being ripped from its socket as she held onto DubDub. Unable to take any more, she cried out "Stop!" and dug her heels deep into the carpet.

It was not a moment too soon. Mere steps ahead, the carpet ended and the abyss of deep space waited beyond. Stella scowled at Loony who only smirked and shrugged his shoulders at his hazardous hastiness, "Well, it looks like this is the end of the road, time to go back!"

"Be quiet!" Stella snapped, making her annoyance at Loony's foolhardiness known. Refusing to even look at the imp, she scanned the space past the carpet's end for a way to progress. There was none, only the mystifying starless depths beyond the galaxy lay ahead. "We have to go on, there's too much at stake!" She pulled out the Compyxx, and the arrow that had before pointed down the golden carpet, now pointed back. "This never works!" she growled, tempted to throw the bauble into the void, but instead shoved it back under her parka.

An eye of glinting glass extended on its cable and snaked around the girl's head. "Don't you remember what Old Sol said? He said go as far as you can and then turn around." A glint in DubDub's eye formed a beacon as the reflection of Old Sol's lighthouse flared.

As she spun around to look toward it, she saw that the flash in DubDub's eye was not just that of Sol, but of a multitude of Stars. How she knew the congregation of light was the Milky Way and that it had appeared where only seconds before was deep space, she would never know; so taken in was she by the wonderful expanse of galaxy displayed before her at this moment, that mystery was the last thing on her mind. "If only I had a camera," she whispered to no one in particular, "I could make my father the happiest man on Earth. Imagine, having a picture from outside the galaxy."

"We're not technically outside of the galaxy, Stella. We are standing at the end of one of its spiral arms." DubDub offered gesturing down. Old Sol's carpet, straight without curves, was no longer beneath their feet. Instead they stood on a path that curved around the Milky Way's central bubble, just one that wreathed the galaxy in tightening spirals.

The Milky Way from this perspective looked nothing like astrophysicists had supposed it to look. Sure it was shaped like an egg cooked sunny side up, flat at the ends and bulging high in the middle where a yolk would be. Its appearance roughly matched the sketches and pictures that had been created to help visualize what the Milky Way galaxy might look like, but those images paled before the spectacular reality.

What Stella saw as she stood at the edge of her galaxy, was a glowing island adrift in the ocean of intergalactic space. Densely speckled with glittering stars, Stella knew that this island was Empyriania, the home of the Stars. But there was something more, as she was certain, she had seen this place before. On a hunch, she took out the parchment she had gotten in the Astrophelarium, and compared the topographies drawn on the map to those of the galaxy before her.

DubDub's eyes split into two sets. One composed of microscopes and magnifying glasses hovered before the map on their flexible stalks; the other set, telescopes and binoculars stared into the galaxy beyond. "They are very much alike," he whispered.

"So where are *we* on this map?" Stella asked.

The automaton spent a moment studying the map and the territory. "I would calculate that we are here." He said pinpointing a spot on the map with the tip of a thin wooden finger. Where he indicated, was at the very end of one of the spiral jetties that extended from the main body of the island.

Stella visually followed the spiral arm around the central island until it reached the mainland. Then she looked out to the landscape before them.

The path they were on curved behind the Milky Way and disappeared. "If we walk this way, will it bring us in?" she asked.

A long stalk rose from the mechanical man's head and its periscope like appendage surveyed the island. "Yes, I believe it will."

The three travelers began to make their way around the island. Loony would dash ahead leaving Stella and DubDub together to enjoy the view of their galaxy. They hadn't been hiking too long when Loony came racing back. "There's something on the path up ahead!" he announced with an excess of drama.

Stella, straining her eyes to see, could just make out a figure blocking the pathway far ahead. DubDub stepped forward and looked ahead. "It's very much the same type being as Astraea and Old Sol." He said after studying the shape for a moment. "But it doesn't seem to be moving."

"Can I see?" Stella requested. A pair of binoculars snaked from DubDub's head and floated on their stalk in front of Stella. The light cast by the snoozing Star was dim and bluish gray; unlike the brilliant gold of Old Sol's or the crystalline silver of Astraea's. He was bearded, but where Sol's beard had a warm yellow glow and bristled with energy, this Star's had a dim blue luminescence and drooped languidly. His whole body was thickly covered in gray stardust that had settled on his head and shoulders in deep patches. "It looks like a statue."

"My turn! My turn!" Loony pushed the girl from the binoculars and looked through. "I bet he's made of frozen stardust. It looks like we'll just have to climb over him." As if there was nothing left to discuss, the impish moon man moved away from the binoculars. Stella could see how much he relished the idea, and imagined the moon man gleefully scrambling up the figure's shoulders, and then pushing up with his rocky foot on the nose of the frozen man.

The galaxy ahead glowed with light, while all around, space was starless and bible black. The sphinx like man appeared to be the guardian between the vast ocean of deep space, and the warm island of light. "It must be very lonely out here." Stella observed.

"I think it will be safe for us to continue. He shouldn't be of any harm." DubDub offered. "Perhaps he might even be of help."

"I doubt it," Loony countered with complete confidence that he was right. "We'll definitely have to climb over him." The travelers continued on, two wondering just what waited for them on this lonely pathway, while the third raced eagerly ahead in hopes of some excitement.

Nearing the figure, Stella approached cautiously, wary of disturbing this being that must have been sleeping here for eons. The giant's cheeks were covered with thin wisps of dull bluish light that drooped to his knees. He snored loudly and with each exhalation a whistling song came from his pursed lips, blowing the wisps high into the air. It was a very lovely tune, Stella thought, even if it was constantly interrupted by blubbering inhalations. His hands clasped a cane of blue light, whose round handle was very near the size of Loony's head and almost at the same height. Stella had to suppress a giggle as she pictured this giant mistaking her companion for his cane and gripping Loony's head tightly in his hands

He was a man, Stella was certain, just as Astraea was a woman, but somehow also a Star. Though how these two states of being could coexist was baffling to Stella, she thought that perhaps she should stop straining her brain and just accept it for now. There were other things to think of at the moment. When she finished her mission and got back to Earth she could solve all of those riddles with her father's help. So deciding to take the journey one step at a time, Stella walked up to the giant slumbering form, reaching high to gingerly tap its knee and shouted. "Excuse me? I don't want to disturb you…"

A loud sputtering snore answered the query, and a spray of stardust filled the air. The Star stirred slightly before returning to his sleep. Stella looked back to her friends for some assistance. Loony only shrugged his shoulders and turned away, while the stalks on DubDub's head shifted nervously. It was painfully obvious they would be no help at all.

Turning back to the sleeping figure, Stella shouted as loudly but as politely as possible. "Sir? Please, if we could just have a moment of your time?" She poked his knee again but to no effect. Looking back again she saw that Loony had raised his fist, and was motioning in a punching gesture. Though trusting the moon man's advice gave Stella a bad feeling, they did need to wake the sleeping giant if they were going to get past. So she balled her fist up and swung. At the blow, the Star man's beard exploded in a flurry of glowing tendrils as a cloud of stardust covered Stella.

"What? Who?" The Star man sputtered, shaking himself awake. His hand reached up in a blossom of dust and wiped the thick cakes of stardust from around his eyes. Searching for the disturbance of his sleep, his head bobbed about sleepily.

"Down here!" Stella shouted.

The Star man looked down at the girl from the corners of his heavy lidded eyes. "Who are you?"

"I'm Stella Ray, a friend of Old Sol and Astraea. They're expecting me to meet them in Empyriania. We were told this path would lead us there. Does it?" As if the words were not worthy of his attention, the Star lifted his head and stared out into space, whistling softly while punctuating his ditty with the occasional stifled yawn.

"Hello?" She shouted trying to regain the Star's attention.

"Indeed it does," the Star finally grumbled, seemingly bothered by the effort of speaking those few words. Stella got the firm impression that the Star did not see the need to speak with her further.

"Who are you? Do you know Old Sol or Astraea?" she asked, trying to keep the conversation going.

"My name is Palomar, though I am not sure why you need to know this. And as for my association with other luminaries, they are in my distant past. I am as you may have noticed, far removed from the plains of Empyriania. "He gestured with his cane to the Milky Way galaxy, and the deep gray stardust that had accumulated on his clothing fell off in thick clumps.

Stella had heard of Palomar. She remembered he was a Star that lay beyond the bounds of the galaxy, but was still considered part of the Milky Way. Astronomers on Earth had always been baffled by Palomar's mysterious condition; with none sure of what it was doing so far away. Stella couldn't let the chance to solve the mystery go by.

"How did you get out here?" Stella asked, perhaps too enthusiastically for the drowsy Star.

"If you must know," He said warily, as Stella nodded her head enthusiastically, "I had begun to fade and I have chosen this farthest reach of our galaxy to spend the rest of my life contemplating of the riddle of the universe. Now please, stop wasting my time."

Loony snorted, "You weren't contemplating anything! You were sleeping!" Palomar's eyes widened to the size of dinner plates at the moon man's impertinence.

"You're fading out? You don't look that old!" Stella exclaimed, horrified by the Star's statement. Now that some of the Stardust had been shaken off, she could see that this Star was no older than Old Sol. She hated to think that her friend might also be dimming.

"I am not so old, true, but my time is up. I'd accepted that long ago," Palomar said quietly, "Everything has its time, and when that allotment has been exhausted, it is only right to fade with some…" he raised his eyebrows and huffed, "*DIG! NIT! TY!*" and banged his cane three times against the pathway to emphasize the word.

"*Allotment*?" DubDub squeaked. "Are you saying that even a Star has a set amount of time to exist?"

After letting out an impatient whistle, Palomar answered. "Time is not inexhaustible, it is a valuable commodity. When one's time is used, there is no more to be had. Therefore time should not be wasted, as you are wasting mine. Now leave me alone!" The blue giant waved his cane dismissively.

"We don't mean to waste your time; we just have to get past you to continue our journey…" Stella tried to look past the giant, "if you don't mind."

"I only hope that you have not traveled far, for I do not intend to have my meditations interrupted by your intrusion. My search for the answer to the riddle of the universe," he answered arrogantly, "is of much more importance than your need to pass me. Therefore, you must accept your fate. Turn back from here and await your fading as I await mine. It is not such a bad thing at all, to fade away into this grand and empty void." He raised his hand and gestured into the starless abyss of outer space.

"I wouldn't take him seriously." Loony said, "He's just a burnt out star. I'll find a way past him." Walking to the edge of the road, he knelt down and holding onto the edge of the road stuck his head out of sight beneath it.

Stella wanted to tell him to be careful, but she didn't want to annoy Palomar further by taking the time to chastise the moon man. "It's urgent that we get to Empyriania soon. Everything depends on that. You have to let us past." She pleaded.

Unmoved, the Star continued his tale. "Soon, I will fade. See how dim my light has become?" Moving his hand through the air left only the thinnest trail of vapor in its path. "It's my time to go, that's all there is. Why, I was so bright once," the star paused, an introspective smile on his lips. "Now go back to from where you have come and await your fate. It will be best for you all."

"But isn't that just surrendering to the darkness?" Stella asked anxiously.

"Ahhh!" The fading star shifted, and plumes of dust bloomed from his body. "You have so much to learn! Fading away is not letting the darkness win. A well lived life such as mine can never really die. The light of it just lives in the past, but it's still there for anyone who cares to look. Knowing that has brought me closer to solving the riddle."

"But, but, that's the past!" Stella sputtered," Moros wants to kill everything now. He wants to make it so there will be no future!"

"You call the darkness Moros? Why I wouldn't have thought it would even have a name. I have seen it passing amongst the stars, so hurried, so fearful." Palomar chuckled softly. "I would not worry. I'm sure he too will have only the time allotted him and no more. All things must pass."

Stella couldn't believe Palomar could be so casual about something so important. "But not everyone is ready to pass! I'm not! I can't believe you're so willing to die!" She fumed.

"Die?? Why not at all. I am not succumbing; I am only fading as all must. But that will not be a victory for the darkness, for to fade away is a part of life. I am choosing to await my end with dignity. The darkness has no sway over my choice"

Time was short, Stella reminded herself. If this Star wanted to stay here and fade that was fine, but she needed to keep moving. "Moros wants nothing at all. No choices, no life, no light. That's why we have to stop him, and why we need to get," she craned her neck to see around Palomar's massive body and saw there was no way around if he refused to move, "to Empyriania. Please, can't you let us past?"

"Yeah!" Loony interjected, though Stella wished he would shut up. "Stop playing games and let us past!!"

"Games?" The caked dust around Palomar's lips cracked, as for the first time in eons he smiled. "For all my studies of the universe I have only discovered that it behaves as a child playing with dice, with every moment ruled by chance. I left the great dance, hoping to find the secret of the universe, and what did I find?" He laughed. "Only a game!"

Stella couldn't help but notice how the Star's demeanor had changed. He had been dour and reserved, but now he seemed delighted at the prospect of a game. His voice now light and bubbling sounded more like Old Sol's or Astraea's. Much of the powdery stardust had been shaken from his body, and now she could see that his light wasn't as dim as she first thought. It was in fact, quite bright. "If you wish to pass", Palomar stated with newfound enthusiasm, "You'll need to play a game with me, and win."

"A game? Me first, me first!" The moon man pushed DubDub rudely aside and jumped in front of Stella.

"Now, what sort of game should we play?" The Star's eyes twinkled with a mischievous new light. "I know," he grinned, "You must answer a riddle."

Loony turned to Stella with a look of uncertainty. "Is a riddle like a game?"

Stella nodded. Loony grinned toothily and he turned back to wait for the riddle. Palomar caressed the top of his cane as he formulated his first question and then sang in a sonorous voice.

"I am the beginning of eternity
and the end of time and space
I am the beginning of every end,
and the end of every place."

The blue giant paused, letting the words fade into the vacuum of space and then solemnly inquired, "*What am I*?"

Stella began to blurt out the answer but before the breath left her throat Palomar pounded with his cane. "Do not speak! You will all have your chance. But for now it is this one's turn." Palomar's cane pointed towards Loony's face. The moon man looked anxiously to Stella for some help, but she remained silent, not wanting to cheat. Nothing good ever came from cheating.

After a few moments had passed with Loony fidgeting and Palomar sitting still, the Star spoke. "Do you not know the answer?"

"Uh, em, uh…" The moon man sputtered. "I guess not."

Stella couldn't hold her tongue any longer. "E" she shouted, "The answer is the letter, *E*!"

Without acknowledging the girl's answer, Palomar lifted his cane to push Loony back. "You may not pass." The Star pointed his cane toward DubDub and immediately the mechanical man's wooden arms and legs began to rattle nervously. "Answer this riddle correctly and I will allow you to pass. Otherwise you will not be allowed to enter Empyriania." Palomar stated.

"I am neither big nor small,

Liquid, gas or solid

But I can be broken without being dropped.

What am I?"

The mechanical man's jaw chattered and the joints of his wooden limbs squeaked as he fretfully pondered the riddle. Stella wished she could help him, but knew Polaris wouldn't allow it. Furthermore, this time she could be of no assistance, having no idea what the answer to the riddle might be.

"Do you have an answer?" Palomar boomed, very pleased with the unsettling effect he was having on the automaton.

"I honestly have no idea as to what the answer might be," DubDub wheezed before collapsing into a heap of nervous exhaustion. Stella quickly went to his aid, winding him until he jerked erect and shambled away humiliated.

Two had failed and one was left. With the look of impending victory on his face, Palomar shifted his cane in Stella's direction. Certain she would fail he smugly addressed her. "They will not be allowed to pass. If you cannot answer this next riddle, you must all return from whence you came."

"Hey! Wait a second!" Loony pushed past Stella to confront the Star. "Before you talk so tough and tell us what we can and can't do, what's the answer to that last riddle? And…" The globe of the moon man reddened visibly," It better have an answer. You better not be tricking us."

Stella couldn't believe the nerve of Loony to do what he was doing. He was less than a quarter of the size of the giant Palomar, who if he cared to, could crush the moon man like a bug. But Loony paying no mind to the danger, glared at the Star and demanded, "So what is the answer? Come on, tell me!"

"*SILENCE!*" Palomar bellowed, pounding his cane on the floor. The path they stood on shuddered with the impact.

Stunned for but a second, Loony took a few steps forward and thrust a rocky finger up towards Palomar's face. "I won't be quiet until you give me an answer! I think you're trying to cheat us!" Stella was afraid that Palomar might swing his massive cane, batting the pest straight into space.

"*SILENCE!*" The Star roared again, only now Stella saw the grin hidden beneath his wispy beard. Realizing just what sort of trick was being played; she rushed up to her friend and pulled him back out of reach of the Star man's cane.

"Loony," she counseled, "He's playing with you. He's just trying to make you angry and upset. Don't you get it? *Silence,* is the answer!"

The moon man looked up to the girl with questioning eyes. "The answer?"

"Think about it. Not made of anything and can be broken without being dropped. That's silence. Silence is the answer to his riddle." Stella waited to see if Loony was going to get angrier after finding out he had been played with, or if getting the answer would calm him down. It was the latter, and as he shrugged away from Stella's grip, the color of his head phased from red to a dark cloudy gray.

With Loony out of the way, Stella waited to hear the riddle she would need to solve. Placing both hands atop his cane Palomar asked in a singsong voice, "What has only one voice, but has first four, then two, and lastly three legs?"

Stella's jaw dropped. She knew this riddle! She had heard it before, in different words, but was sure of the answer. "The answer to your riddle," she announced," is a man…"

"Wrong..." Palomar started to say but Stella cut him off before the word was fully formed.

"Or in this realm, a Star!" She quickly added. "An old Star or man walks on three legs, with the third leg being a cane, just like yours." She pointed to the luminous blue stick that had not once left the Palomar's grasp. "During their lives they walk on two legs, like I am now. And babies," she continued, trying to sound confident that this was the right answer, for she had never seen a Star baby, "crawl on both their hands and knees, as if they had four legs."

"You are correct in your answer of Stars, and as for your answer of humans, I have only met one and that is you, and therefore I have no idea if you have ever actually been a baby." Stella wondered if Palomar was trying to cheat her, until the giant blue luminary suddenly smiled. "But as I cannot disqualify you for my lack of knowledge, you will be allowed to pass into Empyriania."

Stella breathed a sigh of relief as Palomar pivoted sideways to make a narrow passage on the pathway. Stella hurried through and once past, turned to watch DubDub move towards the thin sliver of road. Palomar's cane swung out, abruptly stopping his progress.

"Where are you going?" The blue giant boomed.

"With my friend?" DubDub responded timidly, with some stalks looking up to the Star and others stretching over his outstretched cane and imploring Stella for help.

"Did you answer my riddle correctly?"

DubDub creaked softly, "no."

"Then you cannot pass."

As DubDub stepped back, his eyes never left Stella's. "You have to let me go with her. I can't be left here alone," he pleaded as a handful of eyes darted back towards Loony, "with him! What if I need to be wound?"

Stella wished there was something she could do, but there seemed little chance Palomar would allow DubDub to go with her. Sliding back past the Star, she gave the knob on her friend's chest a turn, hoping it would be enough until they met again. As she did she spoke with phony casualness, "Maybe it's better if you both wait here. Old Sol said the Stars that live in Empyriania could be very picky about who they allow in their realm. I'll go first and get permission to bring you along."

"I didn't know there were so many rules up here. It's almost as bad as being with the Planets." The moon man complained angrily.

Stella wished Loony would not always be such a brat. Dealing with him was like babysitting her brothers, always having to think of a way to trick them into behaving. "I didn't mean you couldn't come with me, Loony." She said, hoping the moon man believed her. "I meant that DubDub wouldn't be allowed, and that maybe you should stay here with him." Seeing Loony's look of disbelief, Stella decided she would need to lay it on thicker. "To make sure he behaves…"

A devilish smile formed on the moon man's crooked lips as his eyes shifted towards the automaton. "Yeah, that's right," he said slyly. "He does need to be watched. I'm not sure he can really be trusted."

Stella felt bad leaving DubDub with Loony under such conditions. She knew the truth was that the mechanical man should watch the moon man so he didn't get into any mischief, but if she said that, Loony would have insisted on accompanying her. As Stella passed by Palomar once again, she looked once last time to check if Loony was behaving and DubDub was okay.

"Hurry along little human!" Palomar commanded. "If your mission is as urgent as you say, you have little time to waste."

15 THE SONG OF THE STARS

Once past Palomar, Stella could get a better look at her goal. What was the Milky Way galaxy to her father, an island called Empyriania to the Stars, and Starland to Loony and the planets, was now to Stella, all three and one in the same. The galaxy was a glowing cloud of stardust shaped like an enormous Mexican sombrero, its center an enormous bulge and it's flat brim ending in long streaming swirls of light. The path on which she stood was one of these, a tendril of bright stardust leading into the abode of the Stars. Stella hoped that it would not be as long a walk to reach it as it looked, though she had come to recognize that scale and magnitude behaved quite differently here than the way they behaved back on Earth. Checking the Compyxx, its little silver dart pointed down the path and with every step Stella took, the arrow changed its orientation slightly, always showing the way around the sombrero. As she walked, the whole of the galaxy swirled before her.

Closer to the shimmering wall, Stella could make out lights glowing in the mists. Placing her hand in the dense bank of fog, it was so warm and pleasant that she slowly continued into the bath of light, the luminous cloud tickling her nose as it breached the mist. For a moment Stella was uncertain of direction as the brilliance engulfed her, but with just another step the veil was pierced and she entered the domain of the Stars.

A vibrant landscape tinted with the colors of flame, brilliant reds, oranges and yellows greeted Stella's eyes. Rolling plains and soft meadows stretched to the horizon, resplendent like wheat fields on a warm summer day. From the sky fell soft sprays of shimmering sparkles as if someone had thrown handfuls of gold dust in the air. The way the light which seemed to come from everywhere, danced kaleidoscopically across every surface, was as if a thousand suns were being reflected through a thousand jewels. Everywhere in this sublime setting splendid creatures frolicked, dancing with a delight surpassing description. Clothed in garments covered with jewels that cast an ever-changing spectrum of colors, they moved gracefully in their play. Their radiance made Stella feel unworthy to be in such magnificent company.

The air was filled with music so lovely and serene that it had at first gone unnoticed. Music so perfect it was like the wind in the willows, always there but seldom noticed. As the beautiful creatures danced, they sang to each other and their voices filled the air with sounds so wonderful, that what filled Stella's ears could only be rivaled in beauty by what lay before her eyes. It was like the singing in a choir where everyone joined together to form some perfect union. She recalled the word for what she heard and saw. *Harmony*. As if it was impossible for anything less than perfection to occur.

There were thousands of these beings, but none seemed capable of making an erring step and all moved in perfect accord through a vast variety of elaborate arabesques. Some in the multitude were older and some were younger, but each face glowed with the radiance of a serene peace that was ageless and uniquely beautiful. As this grand pageant passed before her, each Star always seemed to be in the right place, as if every movement was preordained, fitting perfectly into a grand scheme. It all looked like a perfect painting, a beautiful work of art, and enraptured by her surroundings, all thoughts of darkness fled Stella's mind.

The moment did not last. Stella was suddenly ripped from her blissful reverie by a searing pain. A Star stood over her, his hand tight around her forearm. "What are you doing here?" The Star snarled as Stella tried to free herself from his claw like grip. His fingers only dug deeper, burning like points of frozen lead. "You are a human, are you not? You are one of the vermin that infest the system of Sol?" The Star's face was incandescent with rage, a rage Stella had not seen before in an astral being, not in Astraea, not in Sol, not even in Palomar. An anger so chilling that it froze Stella's heart. "What are you doing here? This is no place for your type!"

Stella's eyes ran wet with anguish as she squealed. "I'm...I'm..."

Pulling the girl into the air, he held her face to his livid gaze. "I, Antares, will not allow such filth in Empyriania!" In his eyes Stella saw not the glittering diamonds of light she had grown to expect in starry eyes, but darkness devoid of all warmth.

"Antares", the name echoed through Stella's head as pieces of the puzzle fell together. The monster at the end of the solar system had been Scorpius, and the two shadowy fish that followed Charon's boat had been Pisces, both constellations of the Zodiac! Confronting Stella in this place so full of light was Antares, a Star of Scorpius, one of the twelve constellations of the Zodiac. Suddenly it all made chilling sense. The Zodiac was working for Moros!

"I see you understand my secret," Antares hissed as he jerked his hand, "but your realization comes too late." Stella felt as if her shoulder was about to be wrenched from its socket when suddenly the pain was eased as her free arm was lifted.

An enormous fiery Star larger and brighter than Antares, with no trace of malice about him, held her up gently. He pulled her closer to his light, as he firmly stated, "Thank you for greeting Old Sol's guest, Antares, but I will help her from here."

"She does not need your assistance, Polaris. I have the situation firmly in hand." Antares sneered with animosity as he jerked the girl back towards him. With both arms being pulled, Stella felt like the rope in a game of tug of war.

Polaris countered, "I have promised Sol that I would make his friend, our guest, comfortable while she awaits him. It would be inconsiderate of you to ask me to break my word. Please …" Stella could hear in Polaris' voice that this was a request he would not allow to go unanswered. "…Release her to me."

Polaris rose up tall over Antares, towering above the malevolent Star. Antares' grip held stubbornly for a second and then let go. The Star skulked away and when he was far beyond Polaris' reach, shouted with all the vehemence of a curse, "Do not be so confident in your power, Polaris! The strongest light casts the deepest shadows!"

Polaris lifted Stella gently up onto his shoulder. "Pay no mind to Antares. His lack of manners is eclipsed only by his disdain for trespassers." Relieved to be out of Antares' clutches, Stella rubbed her arm through the insulation of the parka as she nestled against Polaris' warm billowing hair. From this new vantage point she could see further across the glowing hills and dales of Starland.

"It's so wonderful!" Stella whispered.

"Yes it is! We citizens of Empyriania take great pride in the serenity our land." Polaris' voice was so in tune with the rest of the wondrous music that filled the air that it took her a moment to realize she was being spoken to. She shifted on the broad shoulder to see Polaris' face, and for a moment thought it might be Old Sol, as this being had many of the same features as her jolly friend. But in a moment she saw there was a different demeanor upon the face beside her, for while Sol smiled easily and always seemed on the verge of laughter, this Star possessed a countenance of a more reserved nature. "I am Polaris and I am at your service," he said in a dignified though genial tone.

Stella wanted so badly to watch the dance that was proceeding all around her, but decided she needed to be polite and talk to this Star that had rescued her. "My name is Stella Ray." She said trying to somehow make her voice fit within the melodic sounds around her and realizing that she was failing dreadfully. "I'm a friend of Astraea and Old Sol's. I'm supposed to meet them here."

"Astraea? She is a bit of an, how should I say, aberration. But she is not the first of our young stars who have sought to forge their own way. Given a little time, she'll understand more fully her place in the dance. Old Sol was like that. When he and I were young, I noticed many of the same…" Polaris hesitated, as if speaking of these things caused him discomfort, "…peculiarities. But Sol is a friend of mine and when he asked me to watch for a stranger entering Empyriania, I could not refuse his request."

The sonorous voice spoke on, and though Stella heard him plainly and clearly, his voice merged with all the others that filled the air. Like an orchestra, where every instrument sounded its own strain of expression but merged effortlessly into a grander common theme, the voices of the Stars made a beautiful music.

"Sol warned me your appearance would be… How should I say this without appearing rude?" Polaris paused, "…different. But I was not quite prepared as to just how different."

"I'm a human," Stella said, a bit perturbed. "There's nothing shocking about my appearance."

Polaris sounded shocked. "A human? What might that be? You're not a planet?" Quickly taking Stella from his shoulder, he placed her on the ground and bent for a closer inspection. "Surely you must at least be a moon?" He asked quizzically.

The hasty way Polaris had set her to the ground, reminded Stella of what someone on Earth might do with a puppy, they just found out had fleas. "I'm a human being", Stella declared once more trying not to get upset or angry. "I've come from Earth!" The Star only seemed more bewildered. "From Terra," Stella tried again.

"Terra? That is one of Sol's planets, is it not?" Polaris thought for a moment and then rejoined. "Please! You can't expect me to believe that. You say you are not a planet or even a moon, but something that lives on the surface of one of Sol's planets? Preposterous!" And the star lifted its head and laughed, which sounded like the piping of a flute playing a lovely tune. "Surely you jest! I'm sure you will come to your senses soon. But now I must take my place in the dance! I will keep a watchful eye that no one accosts you further!" The Star laughed again, and with that gracefully reentered the dance that flowed continually around Stella.

Stella didn't mind being left alone at all. She couldn't imagine a nicer place to rest. She thought that if there were even just a painting or picture of this at a museum back home, the line to see it would be stretch for miles; it was that wonderful. And if such enchanting music were ever played back on earth, she doubted if anyone would ever want to listen to another boy band or pop singer ever again.

It was all so perfectly comfortable that Stella took off her parka, and finding a soft clump of warm stardust, sat down to watch the dance. Until Old Sol arrived, she promised herself, she would take a rest and enjoy the ever changing patterns of light and color.

And that was how Astraea found Stella, sitting alone amongst the flowing dance. "Stella?" She asked softly, breaking the girl from her rapture. "Are you alright?"

"It's all so beautiful," Stella sighed dreamily.

Astraea smiled a luminous smile and Stella thought that amongst all the resplendent Stars, she was the most beautiful by far. "Yes, though appearances can be deceiving even here in Empyriania."

Stella remembered her encounter with Antares, and though she wanted to believe that here in this beautiful place, the dark powers of Moros could not reach, she could not shake the feeling that it was not true. "Has something happened here?" She asked.

"Where energy resides, there is only eternal delight." Astraea reached to push a dark lock of hair from her young friend's face. "Or so it was, before Moros' sway set in. There is intrigue among the Stars and hidden secrets have come to light. It is time for the charade to end and the player's masks removed." Astraea no longer spoke to Stella alone but sang out loud, and as she did, a new strain was introduced into the majestic music of the Stars.

Standing with her hand on Stella's shoulder, Astraea addressed her fellow Stars with perfect clarity. At first her voice was scarcely noticeable, subtly blending among the blissful harmonies, but soon it soared clear and bold to weave a new theme in the brilliant tapestry of song. "Children of light! We are in danger! An adversary has arisen from the shadowy voids of space, an enemy who craves to destroy all Stars. This dark villain seeks to end our great dance and extinguish all life and light!"

To quell the disruption of their sublime joy, the Stars of Empyriania raised their voices like the choir of a magnificent cathedral, but Astraea resolutely sang on. Some voices drawn by the strength of her conviction, approached Astraea's melody, joined for a moment and then spun away like moths before a flame. But those voices went away less intent on conveying unfettered joy, and more willing to consider a concealed threat. At the realization of their plight, a number of Stars stopped singing and paused to concentrate on the words of Astraea's song.

"This menace is here and now among you! Darkness threatens Empyriania, and those who love the light must rally now to its defense!" As the somber warnings permeated the landscape, the masses of Stars that gamboled on the plains of Empyriania began to respond to Astraea's call, and slowly, tentatively, their resounding chorus took up the newfound theme.

Just as it seemed Astraea's melody would hold sway, a turbulent undercurrent swelled within the sea of music as a number of stars sang a rebuttal to Astraea. These voices rose rapidly, weaving doubt of her warnings. "She lies! She is the one who brings the danger with her! Why should we trouble ourselves with the deceptions of this wandering Star?" They wailed mocking Astraea, challenging her every note and twisting her every word. The clash quickly escalated into a whirl of counterpoint, accusation, rebuttal and threat, until the message within Astraea's song became hard to discern within the clamorous din.

"Moros... the Zodiac... Treachery... Constellatory marks!" Astraea sang with all her strength, struggling to maintain her tune. Some in the assembly of Stars struggled to maintain their bond to her song and resist the disorder, but others fell off, misled by the hidden chorus that had turned the harmonious orchestrations into a nightmare of cacophony. Soon all Astraea's allies were hushed, overwhelmed by the discordant horror that had invaded their land.

Alone again in her song, Astraea was assailed by waves of harsh dissonance. Emboldened by their success, small groups of Stars moved forward, to scream their slanders, no longer concerned with secrecy. "Liar! Fraud!" They shrieked wildly, "It is she who will ruin this land!" Every eye turned on Astraea, weighing her to see if this might not be true and if indeed she were the source of the turmoil. In the face of such scrutiny and abandoned by all, a quiver of doubt marred Astraea's pure tone. Sensing that their victory over the valiant Star was near, the spiteful singers increased their attack, their voices rising in a murderous rage. Under the withering attack, Astraea faltered, the resolution in her song fading and her lone voice weakening.

Suddenly Astraea was no longer alone though no other Star sang. A voice had joined with hers, and each note of the Star's song was supported and echoed by this other voice, plaintive and plain. As Astraea sang to her fellow Stars for vigilance, the second voice sang as a witness to the threat that lie ahead. When Astraea sang of courage, the second voice urged faith. Astraea's song pleaded for strength and her echo cried for hope.

Stella could not see from where this other voice had sounded. Less polished and less skilled as it were, as it struggled to match every urgent note of Astraea's it brought with it a new strain of conviction. And so it was with great bewilderment that Stella realized this voice that sang so intently was none but her own. She blushed, ashamed that she might suppose to be part of such beautiful music. But when Astraea turned amidst the conflict to proudly acknowledge her ally with a smile, Stella forgot her shame and opened her mouth to allow the light to use her as its channel.

Now, two groups of Stars were apparent in the crowd. The larger stood stunned, having never witnessed such discord before. The other was not as numerous, but what they lacked in number, was made up for by the sheer ferocity of their attack. Banded in small packs, the savage Stars pummeled the gentler Stars with incessant obscenities. If there had been any hope of resistance to the vulgar rabble, it failed as the malevolent Stars surged forward to converge upon Stella and Astraea. Though there were many more bright Stars, far outnumbering the rebellious Stars, no aid came from them. Their radiant faces only gaped blankly at the confrontation that had so violently disrupted their idyllic existence.

The Stars leered at their prey. Their screeching choir subsided until where there had been deafening noise; there was now a sickly lull. Over the snickering chatter of the mob blared a crowing howling. "You are ours now, Astraea! And we will extract our price from you for your interference." Astraea unsheathed her sword to ward off the dismal oncomers, and its flaming blade cast its pure light upon the face of Antares, a twisted mask and tormented.

"You have forced us to reveal ourselves sooner than the plan dictated, but no matter." The scowling Star spat in a mockery of song, "We have you and the human and none in this docile herd will assist you." He waved his hand toward the Stars outside the mob who had moved further from the ferocious exhibition, and now watched timidly from a distance. "They are weak and trust in a false light."

"And we," he bellowed, "are the Stars of the Zodiac!" Antares' tirade inflamed the mob. The rancorous swell of bodies broke into a wild frenzy, shrieking, wailing and circling the trapped duo like a pack of ravenous wolves. As Stella looked out on the sea of slavering faces, she could not understand how these Stars once angelic, could have become such hideous creatures. If Moros could do this, she thought, he must be much more powerful than anyone had guessed.

At the center of all the mayhem, Astraea stood with sword outstretched. "I know who you are, Antares!" She spoke fearlessly with no doubt in her voice. "I know of what constellation you inhabit, and I am well aware of the wretched pact into which you have entered. I ask you now to refute your alliance with darkness and rejoin the community of Stars. Do that now or suffer the fate of all who align with Moros."

Antares, fueled by the mob's fury, snarled. "We are the Zodiac! We are the agents of fate! And soon, yours will be sealed!" The furious ringleader of the belligerent band shrieked a piercing laugh. His fellow horde followed suit, and the uncouth bellowing filled Empyriania with loathsome sounds. Stella wanted to run, to hide, but there was nowhere to go. Anywhere she turned there was a distorted screaming face.

Astraea addressed the threat calmly, her voice serene in the midst of the unnerving cacophony. "Your poisonous clamor has no place here, Antares. If you and yours cannot behave civilly, you will be asked to leave this felicitous place of light." She held her sword aloft with a fearlessness that made Stella's heart soar.

"We will not choose to bow to the will of the weak, Astraea. These feeble puppets of the light…" Antares flicked his head back towards the crowd of stars behind, "…have no dominion over the Zodiac." The words spat like venom from his sneering lips.

"We are not the puppets here, Antares," responded Astraea calmly. "We participate freely in the dance of the cosmos, and choose to live in service of that energy which is eternal delight. Those who deem to serve the darkness will only find death." The luminescent Star woman paused pointedly before asking "I do not see Shaula nearby, where might she be?"

The image of a Star map formed in Stella's mind and her focus went immediately to the Star just named, grouped with others that together formed the constellation of Scorpio. Stella remembered how Astraea had maimed that shadowy crustacean as it attacked her at the edge of the Solar System.

Antares' face contorted in rage at Astraea's insinuation, but then relaxed into a sly smile. "Shaula has gone to the darkness, as darkness is the fate of all! You have given her the greatest gift! Now we, the agents of Moros and servants of the darkness that is unconquerable, have been charged to deliver you and all light to your ultimate destiny, *Death!*"

Addressing all the listening Stars, the good and the bad, the beautiful and now the ugly, Astraea sang. "The darkness seeks to control the fate of all, while the light offers the freedom to choose one's own destiny. Moros seeks to enslave all within his tyrannical grip, but as long as there is light and life, all are still free to choose their own destinies." At that she let out a loud clear blast of song, and Stella, though she did not know the language of the Stars, knew immediately what she sang of, Astraea sang of freedom.

That beautiful hymn so enraged the traitorous Stars that they rose to attack, but Astraea parried each entree with a swift flash of her blazing sword. In fear and frustration of her skilled defense, they commenced a new assault.

To Stella's left seven of the Stars of the Zodiac converged, chanting a blasphemous hymn as they dove into a dance that jerked and writhed in hideous lurches. In apparent answer to their grotesque ritual, a turbid mist seethed about the participants, enveloping them as they twirled and contorted. In seconds they were lost in a plume of churning smog while invisible hands tortured it into abominable form. While an arm, an eye, a horse's leg, and an arrow strung upon a bow all tumbled within the noxious smoke, the chanting turned to dreadful shrieking as if to signal the pain of transformation.

As each sculpted element in this appalling jumble of smog and shadow solidified, it shifted amongst the others, searching for its place until they all fit together. The smoke settled to reveal the form of an enormous archer whose torso blended into the body of a stallion. Within the foul murk that was the substance of this freakish being, points of light glowed dimly. Stella recognized the constellation and whispered their names as these dark stars assumed their proper positions. They were Rukbat, Arkab, Alnasl and Nunki, the stars of Sagittarius, the Centaur Archer, one of the twelve constellations that comprised the deadly army of the Zodiac.

All around, other groups of traitor Stars had begun their diabolical metamorphosis. Some were in the frenzied throes of demonic dance while others were lost in infernal mists that were quickly congealing into monstrous tails and horns and claws. Tremendous forms shot up around Stella and Astraea, blotting out the bright sky of Empyriania. Within one shaft of stormy cloud, the shape of a woman, Virgo materialized. Her face with its dark eyes and diabolical sneer seemed strangely familiar to Stella, though from where seemed hardly consequential as the fearsome constellation loomed overhead.

Soon twelve mammoth monstrosities, Aquarius and Libra, Sagittarius and Pisces, Gemini and Capricorn, Taurus and, Aries, Leo, Cancer, Virgo and the wounded Scorpio, stood in a seething wall of storm clouds, dwarfing the duo they surrounded. Astraea pulled Stella closer to shelter her from the noxious fumes that choked the air.

Scorpio stepped from the murk and even without its deadly stinger, the awful arachnid made Stella's blood run cold. "Yes," the nightmare of shadow and smoke hissed, "Shaula is gone. But that which can no longer sting, may bite." With its chattering claws snapping viciously, the scorpion skittered menacingly forward.

Before the creature could touch its prey, the sound of a forceful voice stopped it dead. All in the starry realm turned to the sound, as like a herald of coming good, Old Sol appeared in a blaze of brilliance from the mists that skirted Empyriania. Marching fearlessly toward the darkness, the Sun called the tune for a dance of a different kind. With a tongue of unquenchable flame he sang a call to action, asking those brave enough to stand with him and set aright the disorder that had upset their land of light.

Far back in the cowed crowd Polaris' face hardened with resolve. Unable to constrain his fury at the desecration of his land, his voice burst out in tandem with the Sun of Earth's. Striding toward the Zodiac, Polaris' voice strengthened with resolve and as it did, a number of bright Stars jarred from their complacency, joined him in taking up Sol's song. Rallying to confront the dark, this small fearless troop marched forward, each step in synchronization, and Stella's heart gladdened at the beauty of this new dance.

The coven of the Zodiac watched these developments with haughty indifference, as from behind marched Old Sol, and from ahead strode Polaris and his followers. Counting only six bright Stars besides Polaris, Stella watched with trepidation as they approached the Zodiac. Though her heart swelled with pride and admiration for the blue Star's courage, her head could not understand how he with his small handful of allies, could stand up to the monstrous creatures.

As they neared, Polaris and his small brave band suddenly joined hands and began to spin in a playful dance. A glittering mist began to coalesce and soon the whole band of valiant Stars was obscured in a swirling cloud of light. The cloud billowed upwards in a plume of white mist, and Polaris with his allies, were borne aloft, transformed into dazzling specks of light ascending within a white tornado as tall as any of the monsters of the Zodiac. The towering pillar of luminous twirling mists held a moment, until a massive clawed paw swung from within, tearing it asunder.

As the mists dispersed, an enormous bear, with its coat a lustrous white, stood confronting the turbid phantasms of the Zodiac. The newly formed beast lifted its head to roar and from its jaws issued a sound like the blast of trumpets. Stella could see deep within its chest, Polaris pulsing brightly and around him the other brave Stars all comprising the skeletal framework of the constellation, Ursa Minor. In harmony with the bear's roar, Old Sol's voice boomed out so boldly that all of the bright Stars of Empyriania hearkened to its sound. Spurred on by this new song, the whole of the crowd that had once cowered now raised their voices in unison answering the call.

Stella, through a gap between the shadowy Gemini twins, watched as everywhere on the fields of Empyriania, Stars joined hands and danced. Billowing clouds cloaked them as they swiftly rose to form luminous columns too numerous to count and stretching beyond sight. The white tornadoes, dazzling as snow on a clear winter day, reached the sky and within the shifting mists luminous Stars blazed in constellatory formations.

All around constellations sprung to life as Old Sol sang on, and Stella witnessed the transformations his song inspired. One spinning column of wind and light became an enormous ivory dragon that slithered forward to take its place next to the bear. From its mouth came blasts of flaming gold as it reared up on its back legs and brandished its diamond like claws. "Look Astraea! It's Draco!" Stella cheered. "And here comes Orion!"

Beyond the dragon appeared a man whose hair was like the whitest wool. At his waist was a belt of three incandescent jewels, and upon his shoulder was readied a heavy club. This hunter marched across the landscape to where the bear and dragon stood against the darkness. The gleaming coiled body of the serpent Hydra, its long tongue flickering and Hercules with muscles flexing, both moved to take their positions in the growing ring of fire.

From a shimmering whirlwind of light, Aquila the eagle, flew into the air on ivory wings and swiftly took his position with the other bright constellations. Close behind was Andromeda swinging silver chains. Alongside her loped Lupus, the giant white wolf. Stella's heart leapt as she saw a horse gamboling while beating its long powerful wings, and was certain the tide had turned when a larger bear, Ursa Major, rose and lumbered to the growing group that stood in opposition to the Zodiac. Gone were the fearful Stars who had been uncertain of the way to ward off evil from their land, and in their place stood towers of unwavering brilliance who showed no reservation in their eagerness for action. Shimmering with strength, these brightly embodied creatures surrounded the Zodiac who in turn encircled Astraea and Stella.

The Zodiac turned outward, readying for a fight. Stella who stood barely to the Gemini twins' shin, shifted to see between their legs what was going on outside the dark circle. A pale lovely lady had stepped forward and was casually flicking shafts of light into the eyes of the Zodiac creatures with the mirror she held to her face. Five Stars in the shape of the letter W blazed within her body. "Shall we dance?" Cassiopeia asked, with a coquettish smile.

With those words, the ground beneath Stella's feet shook as the armies of light and shadow rushed forward to clash in battle. The circle of darkness that had surrounded Astraea and Stella broke as the defenders of light rushed in.

Draco raced into the fray and targeted Cancer with a fiery blast from his jaws. The crab skittered clear of the flames, and as the dragon moved to pursue his carapaced foe, Leo leapt from behind. In a flash his claws were deep in Draco's back, piercing the snow white scales with ebony talons. As the mighty dragon thrashed to shake the maned beast, Leo sunk his teeth into the long muscular neck, and Cancer seeing an opening, skittered in and plunged a razor-sharp claw into the Dragon's chest. The Stars that had formed the constellation plunged to the ground as the Dragon collapsed into a cloud of white mist. Only one of those defenders of light remained aloft, the ill-fated Star that Cancer had plucked from the Draco's chest. "*Rastaban! Not Rastaban!*" Astraea cried as the body of the brilliant Star writhed in anguish in the grip of the wicked Crab's claw. Leo roared in triumph as Cancer held his grisly prize aloft and with a snap of his claw crushed the light from the Star. Hurling the dimming body to the ground, the Crab turned back to the raging battle.

Like white lightning Hydra struck, and in an instant held the two Gemini twins ensnared in his coils. As the diabolical twins clawed wildly, the snake responded by throttling his captives more forcefully. The twins shrieked in agony and just as it seemed they would burst from the pressure; an arrow flew and cleanly pierced the serpent's skull. Hydra went limp and Gemini jumped free, trampling the bright Stars as they fell from the vanishing coils. Sagittarius laughed wickedly as he pulled another arrow to his bow.

Taurus broke ranks with the tight circle of the Zodiac and charged headlong in attack. Hercules nimbly grabbed the bull by the horns and struggled to wrestle it down. Two spotless canines ran to assist the strongman, the smaller nipping at the bull's feet and the larger leaping for its throat. The muscles of both beast and man bulged as they fought for control. Hercules strained at the horns until a loud crack indicated he had broken the bull's neck. Taurus collapsed and four Stars fell in a spray of black sludge. Their jaws slathering, the dogs pursued the rebel Stars and quickly snatched them up squelching their ghastly light.

Caught in the midst of this thundering clash of giants, Astraea did her best to protect her young human charge, jerking Stella here and there to avoid being crushed. A hoof fell nearby with a crash and Astraea jumped to thrust her sword deep into the centaur's thigh. Enraged, Sagittarius lashed back striking the Star woman fully with the back of his hand and sending her flying. Dodging the titans who fought all about her, Stella darted through the battlefield to help her friend. Ursa Major stumbled past as the grappling twins of Gemini beset him. One of the twins had wrapped his arms around the bear's neck and clawed at its eyes, while the other was clenched to a leg, hoping to bring the great bear down.

As this trio of combatants lurched and staggered before her, Stella could see past to where Astraea had impacted the ground. The Star woman lifted herself and looked anxiously about for her ward, and Stella waved wildly to attract her attention. When the Star woman's eyes found what they sought, they widened in alarm. Turning to see what so dismayed her luminous friend, Stella met a wall of shadow.

"Leave her be, Virgo!" Astraea demanded as a massive hand lifted the girl from the ground. As Stella was carried through the havoc of battle, Astraea desperately chased after but quickly fell behind, unable to keep pace with the giantess's steps.

"Did you think we had forgotten you?" Virgo sneered, lifting the struggling girl to leer at her with cold sinister eyes. The face of the constellation was now clearly visible, and Stella noted with horror its resemblance to Verena Maldek. "You are the champion of the light. Moros will be pleased when I deliver you to him." Stella couldn't say a thing as the air was squeezed from her lungs, but could only silently question what madness possessed these once beautiful Constellations and the Stars that composed them.

All around darkness and light clashed. Stella caught a glimpse of the glittering constellation Orion, fighting with the goat-headed fish-tailed

Capricorn. The blows of the hunter's ivory club glanced off the beast's ebony horns as the chimera's finned tail swung wide and connected with its opponent's knees. As Orion staggered, the goat's horns pierced the hunter's chest, and it was only when Canis Major and Canis Minor with teeth flashing like diamonds, jumped into the skirmish, that he was saved. The dogs' jaws took hold of Capricorn's tail and pulled him back to allow the hunter to regain his footing. As the dogs dug deep into the scaly flesh, the Orion's club came down on Capricorn's head, shattering his horns and laying the beast low. There was a slur of dark smoke as the goatfish's body vaporized revealing within, dozens of traitorous Stars that plunged to the ground.

One of these fallen Stars of Capricorn shouted to his cohorts, "Scheddi! Marakk! Nashira! Dorsum! Quickly, join with me! We must regroup!" But as he did, Orion still clutching his wound, struck with his club, crushing the retreating Star completely beneath its weight. The other Stars panicked and ran off, pursued by Lupus who snatched them up and swallowed them down.

Stella's captor sidestepped Ursa Minor who was frantically swatting its clumsy paws at a pair of fish that swam through the air in rapid circles. The fish butted the fair beast with their dark heads, pounding him with a choreographed combination of blows. The frustrated bear roared and tore at the air with its claws, determined to catch one of the Pisces. A silver streak shot through the battlefield as Lupus rushed to aid the bear. In an enormous leap, the wolf, vaulting over the equine back of Sagittarius, flew through the air and when he had landed, one of the fish lay crushed within his slathering jaws. Spurred by the success, Ursa Minor reared up to snatch his other attacker from midair with his clawed paws, promptly cracking its back. From the fish's severed halves, dark stars poured, their former glory now merely falling ashes.

Not far past the bear stood a woman clad in brilliant white veils and swinging a large silver chain. Confronting her was a dark ram, its heavy hooves stamping at the ground. Waiting for an opportunity to attack, Aries tested the lady's stance and then streaking black smoke charged. He was not quick enough, for in a flash Andromeda flipped through the air and came down directly upon his back. Quickly wrapping her silver chains around Aries' neck, she rode the rampaging beast, steering it with sharp pulls on the chains. She aimed the ram at its fellow Zodiac and just as it was about to strike, leapt acrobatically to safety, her silver gown billowing as the dark constellations scattered before the spiral obsidian horns.

"Moros cannot be stopped!" Virgo howled, "Even if we the Zodiac are defeated, the clockwork will still wind down and all time will cease! No one will deny that destiny! Clear a way for me! I must deliver this prize to our master!" At her command, the remaining Zodiac began battling to clear a path to the wall of mist that encapsulated Empyriania.

As Virgo raced for the border, her captive screamed for help. The leaden fist tightened, forcing the air from Stella's lungs, and unable to draw a breath she felt her consciousness slipping away. The puzzling sound of rustling wings inexplicably filled her ears and Stella wondered as she was engulfed by darkness, if they were those of an angel, there to carry her away when she succumbed.

16 THE SORROW OF THE STARS

Stella awoke with the concerned faces of Astraea and Old Sol hovering over her like two morning suns. "How did I get here?" she asked anxiously, propping herself up to search around. She was in one of a long line of beds full of wounded stars, some whose light seemed very dim.

"It's alright. The battle has ended and you are safe. Perhaps a bit bruised, but you'll be okay. You just need to rest a little while longer." Old Sol gently helped the girl back into the warmth of the cushions. "If you lie still, I'll tell of what transpired this sad day, when Star fought Star on the fields of Empyriania. What can you remember?"

"I remember Verena carrying me off…" Stella started, but the memory of what happened refused to clarify in her mind.

"Verena?" Astraea looked from Stella to Old Sol with a questioning glance.

"Do you mean Virgo, Stella? Such awful traitors to the light are the Stars of that constellation." Old Sol shook his head sadly, the fiery locks of his beard crackling.

Stella was confused. She remembered the dark eyes of Verena Maldek leering as she was crushed in the massive manicured hand. And the voice! It was the same as that of the woman scientist who had arrived at dome C. But it was Virgo also, the mistress of the Zodiac and ally of Moros. "Right," she agreed. " Virgo. I remember her grabbing me… and then I woke up here."

"I failed you," Astraea replied with remorse. "Amid the confusion of battle I allowed you to be captured."

"The blame is not yours, Astraea," Old Sol consoled. "The fault lies with Moros and the Zodiac."

"How did I escape from Virgo?" Stella asked.

Not wishing to disturb the recuperating Stars, the three friends bent their heads together to confer, "With the aid of the good Stars of Empyriania," Astraea whispered. "They rose to the defense of the light."

"But only when Old Sol appeared," Stella remembered. She knew there were eighty-eight constellations, only twelve of which were the Zodiac, and wondered how so few of the Zodiac could have terrorized so many. Was it really the fact that they had been taken by surprise, or perhaps she considered, they had not been as diligent as they liked to believe? Having seen how blissfully and carefree they had danced, she could only think it was the latter.

Old Sol broke in on her thoughts, "When I heard your cry I rushed from my vigil of guarding Earth." He shook his head regretfully. "I was certain Moros' next move would be to attack Earth and eliminate the threat of humans against his plan. I thought he would not want the bright Stars of Empyriania to know his plans, for fear of their interference. But now it seems he has the power to challenge even the heavens."

"You heard my cry?" Stella asked.

"Why, of course. I've been paying special attention to you." Old Sol smiled and Stella smiled back; happy to hear he was watching over her. "When I arrived in Empyriania I saw the confusion that had been sown throughout our land. Sad to say, some here are still mistrustful of Astraea, as she is a wandering star. But it took only the briefest of songs for me to explain why you were being attacked. Once that was clear, all of Empyriania endeavored to free you. But before they could break the circle of the Zodiac, you were snatched by Virgo."

Stella blushed, "She came out of nowhere, I didn't even see her until her hand was around me!"

"There was much confusion on all sides," Sol offered. "The Zodiac fought with savage abandon to assist their cohort's escape. It was only when Pegasus took flight…"

"The flying horse?" Stella exclaimed. "I thought I heard wings!"

Old Sol explained, "It was those of Pegasus that you heard. That brave constellation saved you."

Astraea continued the tale. "As Virgo raced off, Pegasus flew over the battle and down upon her. The equine constellation fought valiantly, pummeling the traitor with his hooves. When that dark disciple of Moros saw that she would not be able to hold you, she threw you to your death. Luckily, Old Sol was there to catch you before you hit the ground." Astraea looked to the Sun who managed a humble smile.

Stella looked around cautiously and whispered. "So where is the Zodiac now? Where did they go?"

Old Sol chuckled. "There's no need to worry, Stella. The Zodiac left with Moros."

"Moros was here?" Stella sat up to scan the crowded landscape and though there were no sign of Moros or the Zodiac, somehow the fields and meadows looked less bright than when she first arrived. Whether that was from the running down of the clockwork or the increasing power of Moros, Stella could not tell.

Astraea put a comforting hand on the girl's shoulder. "When the Zodiac saw that they could not withstand our assault, they tightened their ranks. Suddenly from within their hellish circle a greater evil arose. Moros had come to claim his army."

Old Sol was livid at the recollection, flashes of red darted across his golden cheeks. "Moros dared to come here, dared to breach Empyriania's very walls. He must be very confident of his powers if he would risk that. Perhaps he will take a moment to allow his forces to heal, but then… I do not know for how much longer we can withstand his assault." Old Sol gestured to the rows of beds. "With each point of light he extinguishes, the universe comes that much closer to falling into darkness."

"And when a Star falls by choice or treachery," Astraea added, "it upsets the balance of the universe even further. For so many to fall so suddenly, it will certainly weaken the clockwork. It is a vicious cycle, for as the clockwork weakens, the dark powers grow stronger."

Stella could tell from the urgent tones of their voices that the situation was becoming increasingly dire. "What happened when Moros appeared?"

"It was a horrible scene," Astraea answered. "Upon the arrival of their profane savior, the constellations of the Zodiac rushed to merge with their master. Joining that lifeless void, they formed a sinister cyclone that tore at the very fiber of Empyriania. Some of the casualties you see are Stars of constellations unlucky enough to be near that horrific pit."

Astraea pointed to Stars that lay in anguish on their beds. Their faces, which had once been bright and lovely, now were blighted with a gloomy pallor. Other Stars still bright, hovered attentively around those beds trying to comfort their fallen comrades with song. Noticing Stella's attention shift to a nearby bed, she whispered sadly, "That is Rastaban of the constellation Draco. He will not be alight for much longer."

There were a number of Stars clustered around the wounded Star's bed. The song they sang as they tended their comrade, brought to mind the image of an autumn leaf floating on the surface of a stream. The tune quickly overtook Stella, taking her along on its ride, with all its currents and eddies, twists and turns. When the voices rose she could see as if in a dream, the river joining the ocean and the leaf drifting out to sea.

As the song faded, Stella broke from her reverie to see Astraea and Old Sol waking from the same solemn dream. Rastaban gave a short sharp gasp, and his light went out. Stella slipped from her bed and walked towards the bier. Looking into the face of the dead star, now cold as a diamond, she realized she recognized the features. She had seen Rastaban dancing and singing gaily when she had first come to this land, oblivious of the impending danger. She reached to gently touch the porcelain skin of this broken vessel, and from the depths of her being a wail of grief rose at the dying of his light.

"Where is Moros? Where are the Stars of the Zodiac?" Stella cried, certain if they were anywhere nearby, the burning rage she felt within would alone be enough to banish them.

Gently Astraea led the girl away, as those that had nursed Rastaban now attended to an empty shell. "After gathering his brood, Moros vanished. Only the vile echo of his voice was left in our midst."

"His voice? What did he say?" Stella asked.

Astraea looked to Old Sol who nodded his head as if to grant her permission to speak. "What the adversary shouted was, *Tell the human that in the end I will be waiting for her! It is a destiny she cannot escape!*"

The end, Stella somehow knew, would come when she reached the Celestial Clockwork. "Could Moros follow me outside the universe?"

"I am not certain. I can only guess of what affronts Moros is capable." Sol said candidly, "And since the Stars of the Zodiac have rebelled against the light, they are no longer bound by ordinary laws, but only by the perverse whims of Moros." He added gravely "They will be able to for a time, go where they like. They may attempt to follow you to the Celestial Clockwork, or," he paused, "perhaps even to Earth."

"Earth?" Stella sputtered. "If Moros or the Zodiac do anything to my family, I'll…I'll..."

Old Sol cut short the girl's threat. "The only way to stop Moros from achieving his aims is to fully wind the clockwork. If you truly wish for your family to be safe, there is really only one path to take. And while you do, I will do my best to protect Terra." There was a gleam in Sol's eye as he spoke the Earth's name. The deep affection he held for his daughter planet was unquestionable. "She," he continued, suddenly becoming very frank, "has been under attack for quite some time. She has resisted the assaults valiantly, but they have taken their toll. Terra has become quite ill."

"The other Planets blamed humans for that", Stella blurted. "Saturn and Uranus said humans were killing Terra. That's not true, is it?"

Old Sol answered decidedly, "The humans who live on Terra's surface are just part of the normal evolution of the planet, and how could that do her harm? Your mother planet has been through many changes, and has, I am proud to say, thrived through them all. The ailments afflicting Terra are due solely to the attacks of Moros. That is why I have her safely hidden, so I can better protect her."

"You've been protecting the Earth?" That was good news, Stella thought.

"As best I can," Sol answered.

"Then my family is safe?"

Old Sol became a bit flustered, "To be honest, there is a slight problem."

"What do you mean a *slight* problem?" Stella asked sharply.

"Well, your family is in the Arctic…."

"And?" Stella snapped.

"And even with my Terrascope I can't see what happens in the Arctic. During the long nights there, it is entirely out of my sight. It is only through Loony as he orbits above the Arctic continent, that I can obtain news of that land."

"Loony!" Stella exclaimed, "Are you sure you can trust him? He followed me here against your wishes."

"I am aware of that," Sol responded with glum resignation, "Just as I am aware of his passing through phases. It seems as if he is destined to misbehave."

"Are Loony and DubDub still with Palomar?" Stella asked, remembering where she left her friends.

"Word has been sent to Palomar to allow them to enter Empyriania, though I'm sure he has derived quite a bit of amusement from their company, he has so few passersby." Old Sol paused to help Stella from her bed. "But not all Stars agree with their admittance. Even your being here does not sit well, as many believe you share the responsibility with Moros for causing the gloaming. There is still much confusion as to why the Stars of the Zodiac have turned against the light. I have tried to explain that you are our only hope to set things aright, but some, blinded by their own light, have refused to accept that."

Astraea whispered urgently. "It has still not been decided if you will be allowed to travel through Empyriania."

"It will be up to you to open their eyes to the truth. But now," Sol said, "I must leave you and focus on keeping Terra safe."

"You're leaving? But you just got here. I… I don't want you to go!" Stella immediately felt embarrassed as to how childish she sounded. She was acting just like Tim or Pace would if they didn't get what they wanted.

Old Sol bent to take the girl's hands in his. "In another time, one where our tasks were not so pressing, I would stay to show you all the sights of this lovely land. But Terra needs me and the universe needs you."

Stella knew that Old Sol was right. She didn't quite understand, but she felt that Old Sol, by protecting the Earth, was somehow protecting her too. As much as she didn't like to, she knew she had to let him go. "Okay," she said, reluctantly releasing the Sun's soft warm hands. "But when will I see you again?"

In Old Sol's eyes, Stella saw sadness she had not known possible in those bright blazing eyes. "I am not sure, Stella. For you, daughter of Terra will travel, to where of I may only dream. And to those places, it saddens me to say, I cannot accompany you." Stella could see in his starry eyes, just how badly he wanted to go with her. "As I do not have the gift of autonomy, this is the only galaxy I will ever know." He stretched his arms out as if to encompass the fields of Empyriania. "Such is my fate as a Star, to be bound to my preordained place, but it is a fate I do not resent. Though we all may at times envy another's part in the dance, it is only by dutifully performing our role that the clockwork functions."

Astraea continued, "If Old Sol were to abandon his post, many would perish. Therefore he must sacrifice his liberty for those that depend on him. It is through such sacrifice that the inmost light glows most brightly."

Old Sol nodded in confirmation of Astraea's words. "My place is here where for ages upon ages I have held off the darkness. My lot is to light the worlds that orbit me and keep them safe."

"And mine," Astraea said, "Is to go with you to where no star has gone before, and keep you safe."

Stella hated to, but she needed to ask. "I still don't understand why Old Sol needs to stay here, yet Astraea can come with me."

Astraea moved forward, her austere beauty eclipsing the Earth's Sun. "Old Sol and I are Stars of very different sorts. I," She whispered, as if revealing a shameful secret, "was born a wandering Star. With no planets to anchor me, my role is to wander with no place in the heavens to call my own. Even here in Empyriania I feel like a stranger." Astraea's eyes fell downwards, and it was impossible not to hear the pain in her voice. "It seems that I alone have the ability to make this journey with you. No other Star, if they were to obey their true nature, would be able to leave their place and help you on your mission."

Suddenly it was as if a light greater than even the brightest to be found in Empyriania, descended from a realm beyond all space, all time, and mercifully transformed Astraea's anguish to pride. "For as far back as I can remember I have aimlessly wandered this galaxy. It was only when Moros appeared, did I realize that I too have a purpose." Pulling her sword swiftly from its sheath, she cried aloud, "And that purpose is to fight the darkness." With a rapid flourish, her blade cut through the air in a dazzling display of swordsmanship, ending with the flaming blade held aloft. Some of the Stars rolled in their bed to see what the commotion was, and Stella moved back from the brandished blade just to be safe.

"Uh, yes…" Old Sol muttered with a forced casualness to Stella. "As Astraea has displayed so dramatically, only she of all the Stars, is capable of accompanying you on your journey. That is her part to play in the dance, one now of the utmost importance." Turning to Astraea, he was met with her sword inches from his face. "If you wouldn't mind," he asked, gingerly pushing the blade away with a light touch of his finger, "please put away your weapon. I think you have fully convinced our young friend of your prowess."

In a graceful and deft motion Astraea had her sword sheathed. "I will protect you, Stella Ray, no matter what the cost. This I vow upon my inmost light!" Stella felt instantly better. If Old Sol could not travel with her, she could think of no one she would rather have along than the courageous Star woman.

"It is impossible to know what you will encounter when you leave this land," Old Sol said to Stella, "or as to which path you will take home when your mission is accomplished. Therefore I must admit it is possible we will not see each other again in these forms. But when you do return to Earth and look to me and no longer see this face," his eyes twinkled with glitters of gold, "please remember that of all of the humans on Earth, I hold you most dear."

Stella rushed forward and hugged the Sun, her tiny arms around his broad waist. The blazing Star stroked her head, leaving strands of hair, sun kissed and blonde. "But until you return home, I can give you something that might remind you of me. Would you like that?" Stella nodded; glad for anything that might remind her of home. "Open your mouth." Old Sol said, moving his face close to the girl's. "Wider." Stella looked down her nose, feeling like she was at the dentist, trying to see the dentist's tools as they moved towards her mouth. She could see his open mouth and the tongues of flames therein. "A little wider!"

The Sun puckered his lips slightly and blew gently, the way one might if they were trying to spin a pinwheel. Stella caught a glimpse of something blindingly bright floating toward her face. She could not make out just what it was as it entered her mouth, fluttered down her throat, and rested in her chest with delightful warmth. "Now, wherever you go a small piece of me will be with you."

"Can I tell you secret?" Stella asked. Old Sol bent to hear. "I'm afraid." She whispered into the mass of fiery tendrils that covered the Sun's ear. "I'm not sure I can do what you expect of me."

Old Sol stood up tall and straight, but not before whispering back. "You'll do exactly what you need to do, Stella. Of that I have no doubt." Smiling broadly he marched off, quickly disappearing over a hill. As the glowing orb set, Sol's rays lit the sky with the most spectacular sunset Stella had ever seen.

The loss Stella felt as her friend departed was echoed by a haunting sound that suddenly wafted across the fields. "Come," Astraea said solemnly, reaching for her hand, "I will show you where Stars go when they die." Together they walked to Rastaban's bed, where a heartbreaking scene was underway. The Stars had just finished wrapping the body of their companion in sheets of radiant starlight, thin as silk and light as air. Lifting the weight onto their shoulders, a procession formed and the air was filled with a song of such sadness that if it were not for the firm grasp of Astraea's hand, Stella did not know how she would bear such grief.

With every step synchronized to their song of mourning, the Stars marched somberly through the fields of Empyriania. More Stars joined the procession, until behind the body, flowed a vast river of light. Astraea led Stella smoothly into the following, where they were quickly caught up in the solemn parade, and arriving at the shimmering veil that surrounded Empyriania, they found themselves unexpectedly at the front of the crowd.

The bearers carried the body forward and a Star addressed the crowd. "Rastaban," he intoned in a grave voice, "was a bright and true Star. Now we that remain must in his honor, take up his radiance to fortify the light that guides us all. It is a sad day for our land to lose so much light, and for what?" The speaker stared condemningly down at Stella before continuing. "Let us send our companion back to the source of all illumination, where he will dance forever in eternal light." Approaching the veil of light, the bearers lifted from their shoulders, the body of the dead Star Rastaban. It floated toward the bright mists and as it touched there burst into glorious flame. The whole of Empyriania let out a heaving mournful sigh. Stella thought she saw as this flash of fire passed through the veil, the flames sprout luminous wings and soar like an eagle to the spaces beyond.

As the flames flew out of sight, two shapes appeared in the depths of the mists, one small and round headed, the other tall, thin and rickety. "Loony!! DubDub!" Stella shouted and dropping Astraea's hand ran towards the two approaching figures.

DubDub was terribly upset, while Loony seemed in a peculiarly gleeful mood. Trailing behind the automaton at one moment and then slipping in front of him at another, the moon caused the mechanical man to come to a lurching halt to avoid collision. When DubDub reached the girl he could barely express his relief. "Stella, I'm so glad to see you! I'm in desperate need of being wound. I've asked Loony to do it, but he refused to help. Only once, after I begged did he wind my key, but it was with a mere half turn, done only to tease me." As the automaton implored her with a bouquet of drooping eyes, Stella could only imagine what he had gone through out there alone with the mischievous moon man.

Finding the knob on her friend's chest, Stella turned it and as she did she could feel the spring within tighten, tension storing energy in a metal coil. "Thank you!!" the mechanical man purred. "That feels so much better!" The lethargic bobbing of his eyes ceased and they sprang to life to examine the marvelous landscape. The congregation that had gathered to send their extinguished comrade off presented a dazzling sight for the new arrivals.

"So this is Empyriania? My God, it's full of stars!" DubDub exclaimed. The top of his head resembled a nest of writhing snakes as each optical device shifted on its flexing stalk to view a dazzling Star strolling by here, a gathering of Stars singing there or some constellation of luminaries performing a stately dance through the nearby fields. "Why this is simply magnificent!"

Stella stood next to her friend of wood and metal, beaming. Hearing his joyful reaction to the sights of Empyriania, reminded Stella how she had felt when first viewing this starry realm. After the horrible battle, she had almost forgotten just how wonderful this place was, but now her spirit was lifted once again by the delight emanating from the mechanical marvel at her side.

The enchantment though, did not last. Loony, noticing how peaceful his companions were as they gazed out on the glittering hills, was not keen to allow it to continue. In an irate outburst, he ran towards a cluster of Stars screaming. "Why did you leave me out there for so long? I missed all the excitement!"

From behind a nearby hill the sounds of a choir rose. No, Stella realized, there were two choirs, and as one sang out her spirit was buoyed on its lovely song, but when the other rejoined her heart sank. "Listen," Astraea whispered, as if Stella could do anything else, "Your fate is being determined." Following the sound to a deep dell surrounded by soft hills, Astraea herded the three companions before her. DubDub and Stella went along willingly, but it took a firm hand on Loony's shoulder for the Star woman to hold him in check. Nestled within the depths of the amphitheatre was the source of the choirs, a large group of Stars that glowed like a swarm of fireflies on a spring night.

As Stella walked down the slope there was an eruption from further within the crowd, "I see that Sol has decided not to join you, Astraea. Is he ashamed to be seen with the humans who infest his system?"

Astraea laughed off the vulgar outburst, responding lightheartedly. "Old Sol is proud of all his planets, but Terra most of all! The humans in his system are a blessing, not a curse."

The mocking voice sung out again, "But humans are so... *UGLY*!" Snickering titters erupted throughout the crowd.

A Star approached Stella's small group, glowing with embarrassment. "I must apologize to you for such rude remarks. I too, once believed that darkness could never find its way here. But now I see that we were blinded to that danger by our own pride." The Star walked alongside Stella, shielding her from the harsh glares that shot from some in the crowd. "My name is Proxima. Sol is a close friend of mine. His word carries great weight for me and many others in Empyriania. Since the mutiny of the Zodiac, many now believe in the danger he has warned us of, but others have expressed doubt as to the severity of the threat. This council has been convened to decide whether you will be allowed to pass through our land. I for one, believe that much rests on your doing so."

"Belief does not make it true." A nearby Star huffed loudly. "It is obvious this human has brought the blight to our land, and it is Sol's pandering to his troublesome Terra which is the cause of the turmoil which has transpired."

Though neither Stella nor Astraea answered the taunt, Loony broke from their meager ranks. "No one talks about Terra like that!"

"Loony! No!" Stella cried, catching him by the shoulders as he flailed with stony clenched fists. "Don't let them bait you!"

"Whose side are you on? Didn't you hear what he said about Terra?"

"I heard, Loony. But we can't forget why we're here. We're here to save the Earth and everything else. Fighting with these Stars will only delay us from doing that. So please Loony, just stay with us." Stella could hardly believe it but the moon man did follow her, all the while muttering under his breath and shooting threatening glances at the Stars nearby.

When they had reached the center of the meadow, Stella and her friends climbed a small hillock. All around, starry eyes examined these creatures so alien to their dazzling world of radiance, and although she had never been on trial and had only seen courtrooms on TV, Stella had no doubt that it was she who was being judged. A ripple ran through the throng. As it approached, a song from within the crowd grew louder, stark in its grimness and unnerving in its unexplainable seductiveness. Stella shuddered.

"Brace yourselves;" Astraea whispered, "Algol approaches. He will be our inquisitor." Through the crush of the crowd moved two Stars, one whose face was sapphire blue, the other ruby red. They pirouetted about each other and though these two Stars danced as graceful as any other in Empyriania, there was something vaguely disturbing in the way they approached, almost as if they were preparing to engage in a knife fight.

"So," the red Algol stated, with an air of pomposity that made Stella cringe, "these are the intruders who seek permission to pass through our land."

With a dismissive wave of his hand, Blue Algol introduced the quartet to the growing crowd. "Stella Ray, a human from Terra, one of Sol's more insignificant planets; Loony, is a satellite of the aforementioned ball of dirt, and last and least, DubDub, a mechanical contrivance built by humans. I suppose some of you are familiar with their escort, Astraea." His words dripped with disdain. "She is here in Sol's stead, as he has conveniently found it inconvenient to be here at this crucial time."

Before Loony could bark out some angry retort, Astraea clamped her hand over his rocky mouth. She did not speak to the Algol twins, but endeavored to soothe the concerns of the surrounding throng of Stars. "Yes, just these three and I, a small party barely noticeable against the grandeur of Empyriania. If you would grant your consent, we will pass quickly through these lands to spaces beyond."

Red Algol arched a skeptical eyebrow. "And just where is this exit? I know of no portal through which one may pass beyond this galaxy. On what evidence do you base such claims?"

Stella could think of none, but could only hope that there was such an exit. "There has to be a way out. I need to get to the Celestial Clockwork," she answered feebly though; she knew her reply would be inadequate to convince this dubious Star. "You've never heard of the *Celestial Clockwork?*"

Looking down his nose at the inquiring girl, red Algol hissed through tightly closed jaws. "Of course I have heard of the clockwork. But what does it matter? It is only a myth!"

From the crowd came a sonorous retort, "*To the open heart not all myths are untrue.*"

Stella scanned the crowd, searching for its source and quickly found him, a radiant luminary tinged with turquoise flame. The crowd parted respectfully as he hobbled slowly forward. Astraea whispered in Stella's ear. "That is Heo, oldest of our Stars."

Blue Algol snorted towards the aged Star, "We are in no need of your assistance, Heo. These creatures will be judged by all in Empyriania."

"Yes, yes, of course." The ancient Star purred, "I would not dare to interfere in the pursuit of justice." He smiled broadly, a carefree smile that only those who had lived through much could muster. "I merely propose to offer myself as a witness."

"A witness?" Algol scoffed, "In what regard?"

"In regard to humans. Of all the Stars in Empyriania, I believe that I am the only one alight that remembers when a human passed through our land." Heo took Stella's hand, steadying himself as he sat down on the small hillock of stardust. "Perhaps it would shed some light on the situation if I tell that tale."

Both Blue and Red Algol opened their mouths to object but Astraea spoke first, firmly declaring, "It is every Star's right to bear witness."

The surrounding crowd of Stars, every one, nodded in agreement. Heo fidgeted getting comfortable on the low mound, and then with a twinkle in his eye and a smile toward Stella, began to sing. "The story I wish to tell happened long ago, before most of the Stars now alight had been born. Though it was here in these very fields that my tale transpired any other Star to witness it has long passed. Now I alone, live to tell the tale. I was the youngest of the Stars and after arriving in Empyriania under the usual mystifying circumstances, was uncertain of the part I was to play in the great dance." Heo glanced sympathetically at Astraea before continuing in his pleasant singsong voice.

"I had been dancing as best I could and concentrating on performing my part as naturally as possible. The elder Stars were very helpful, confident that I would soon learn my place in the dance, but it struck me as strange to have no memories of where I had been before finding myself upon these pleasant pastures. But there I was, and any thoughts of what had come before, were soon lost amidst the joy of the dance." A hum of agreement rose from the crowd as Stella was aware just how easy it was to get lost in the mesmerizing splendor of the dance.

"Then suddenly, just as I felt that I understood my role, an inexplicable hint of twilight fell over the land. I of course had no idea what it meant, but the elder Stars were quite vexed by this occurrence. We continued to dance, though none could help being distracted as we nervously watched the sky for any further darkening."

The Stars listened intently, riveted by the mere suggestion that the light of their land could fade. Even Loony stopped fidgeting and sat transfixed by the old Star's every word. "And it did come, dimming the landscape until fear reigned supreme in each Star's breast. Horror replaced ecstasy as Empyriania became a haven for shadows. All we could do was to wait for darkness to envelope us completely. Our songs and dance all but ended as we lingered in dusk."

"Young and naïve, I wandered from cluster to cluster of my fellow Stars, searching for someone to tell me the end was not inevitable. I found no one who could offer me solace. So I sat alone contemplating our demise when suddenly, from the mists that gird Empyriania came a jaunty whistled tune. It had been so long since any display of cheerfulness was to be found in our land that I raced excitedly to the veil, to learn from which brave Star it came." Heo paused and his audience anxiously waited for his tale to resume.

"To my surprise, the source of the tune was no Star at all, but a human. I watched as this man strode confidently into our midst and in an offhanded manner asked how he might find the *Nebula Mountains.* To my surprise none of the Stars of Empyriania would assist him, viewing this dim faced intruder as not worthy of their attention."

"Hello! My name is Kairos! I am on a quest to roll back the darkness," he shouted to our company, *will none tell me the way to the portal that leads out of this galaxy? It is there I hope to find the Celestial Clockwork whose running down is the cause of this darkness. I have been charged to wind it to set our worlds aright. Now, please, if you will, point me in the right direction. Time is of the essence."*

"I remember well and carry the shame with me to this day, how the Elder Stars ridiculed the human. It was one particular Star, Jura, now long extinguished, who seemed most angry with the human. Even though he had been one of the first to surrender to despair, he still found the strength to vent his bitter rage. *Does no one notice that this human has come in the wake of the darkness?* he argued. *Might it not be that he is its cause?"*

"Never have I been so ashamed to be a Star. To accuse a guest in our land with no basis in fact…" Heo stared at the binary Stars named Algol… "Struck me as the blackest of deeds."

"Others joined in, some on the side of Jura, some advocating that the human be allowed to continue on his journey. It struck me then as to how these Stars who moments before had wallowed in despair, now relished arguing amongst themselves." Heo shook his fiery head in disgust.

Stella couldn't wait, "What happened? Did Kairos find his way?" she blurted, anxious to know if the journey was possible.

"The debate among the Stars became very intense, with some accusing others of not remaining faithful to the Light, while others questioned if perhaps the human was not telling the truth. As the argument intensified the human used the opportunity to slip away, and when the Stars could finally be bothered to notice him again, he had long since gone."

"How did he know which way to go?" Stella asked breathlessly.

"One Star, who could not stand to let the only chance to stop the darkness go unaided, pointed the human in the direction to the Nebula Mountains."

"Which Star was that?" Blue Algol inquired angrily, "Who would believe a human over his fellow Stars? Which Star would help a human escape Empyriania's judgment?"

"Which Star?" Heo asked, pulling himself tall to address the twin Algols. "Why it was I. Now if you would allow me, I'll finish my story."

"After Kairos disappeared within the Nebula Mountains, things only got worse. I remember how the darkness doubled and it seemed that the end would come very soon. Resigning themselves to extinction, none of the once bright Stars of Empyriania could sustain a glimmer of hope. So mired in the depths of despair, we readied ourselves for an ignoble end."

From the surrounding Stars came not a sound as they waited in uneasy anticipation. "But then a miracle happened. Without warning a torrent of light flooded from the Nebula Mountains and swept away the dusk that had beset us. I remember vividly, that grand golden dawn washing over me and the shadows fleeing as Empyriania was reborn."

The crowd, long caught up in Heo's harrowing tale, flared happily at its outcome. Small groups broke out in merry dance and choruses of triumph filled the air as the citizens of Empyriania celebrated their long forgotten redemption. The tale had given Stella hope as well, for to know that the darkness had been banished once before was reason to rejoice. She smiled broadly at DubDub, whose gears whirred in excitement, and then Loony, who was doing a peculiar jig, pointed elbows and knees flying everywhere. Only when Stella turned to Heo, did her joy falter, for she saw that he had not quite finished his song. Amidst the euphoria of celebration, she alone listened to his story's final words.

"I knew immediately, it was the intrepid human Kairos who had released that flood of light, but I never saw him again. He never returned to Empyriania." The words tore at Stella's heart.

"I know only this," Heo finished, "that at the beginning of my life I met a human, one whose bravery redeemed the universe, and now here at the end of my life I meet another, equally brave by all appearances. It is how it should be, the two ends meeting. I will take that as a sign that the circle goes on unbroken and the radiance of life will continue."

Without any warning the twin Demon Stars butted between Stella and Heo. Red Algol angrily confronted the ancient Star. "If you are finished with your fable Heo, let us continue with the business at hand. We have spent enough time listening to your myths."

Blue Algol continued, "Perhaps you are too old to see the logic in our argument. It is simple, she appeared and the darkness followed her."

The ancient Star responded sagely, "It is by hope not logic, and faith rather than reason by which the universe is redeemed."

"If you believe this girl has brought such horror, then why delay in being rid of her?" Heo asked.

"Very true! We will all be safer when she is gone!" The Algols responded, each grasping an arm of the girl and marching her towards the veil.

Jostled and shaken, Stella barely noticed the dazzling blur that moved to block their path. From the crowd situated nearby, came a hushed gasp as Astraea's hand suggestively grasped the hilt of her sword. "But she will not go back; our goal lies ahead. Release the girl."

Blue Algol complied, his eyes unable to leave the hilt of the Star woman's sword. "And if we were to allow you to make your way to the Nebula Mountains, then what? Where would you go from there?"

In a flamboyant mockery of concern Red Algol continued, "If this human is free to roam unchecked, she could hide within the mountains, safe from reprisal and resume her plot of dragging us into darkness. Stars of Empyriania, before we give consent for passage through our lands, I ask just this, where will they go when they reach the Nebula Mountains?"

Stella took the map of Empyriania from her pocket. "The man who gave me this..." she said as she held it up for all to see, "...said this was a map of the Milky Way galaxy. We'll use it to find our way out."

When the nearest Stars saw the map, they began to trill excitedly, their excitement spreading until the whole crowd was buzzing about the scandalous map.

"How did a human get a map of our land?" One Star warbled to another.

"It's impossible, no human could possibly know what Empyriania looks like, but it was there, I saw it, all drawn out!" Another cooed.

While the Stars were engaged in their excited speculation and gossip, Stella studied the map and the island depicted on it. At the middle of the island were drawn tumultuous mountain regions. Stella looked from the map and out toward the mountains that lie in the distance. The thick black clouds topping the mountainous landscape made those faraway peaks look anything but hospitable. "Are those the Nebula Mountains?" she asked Heo.

Staring off to the faraway peaks, the friendly Star answered, a hint of anxiety shading his speech. "Yes they are."

"What's in them?"

"No one really knows." Heo answered warily. "We stay on the plains where we can participate in the great dance. Any Star, and there have been few in recent memory, who has attempted to learn the secrets of those peaks, has been turned back. The smog is too dense for our light to penetrate and the passages through have proven themselves impassable."

"Well," Stella responded," someone has been in those mountains because they're drawn right here."

Astraea peered over Stella's shoulder. "I see no sign of where we are to go after we enter those mountains. We could spend an eternity searching them for some way out."

Glimpsing something, Stella pointed. "Look here." Some of the Stars nearby took her invitation as their own and huddled around for a better view. Astraea stayed close in the crush as the girl placed her fingertip near a small blue circle that sat squarely at the center of the parchment. Stella squinted to read the tiny text scrawled next to it. "It's labeled, *Meta Incognito.*"

A Star within earshot overheard those words and began to warble excitedly, "*The Inland Ocean* is on the human's map!" The dot did not seem to be any ocean to Stella, but its mention was cause for excitement amongst the Stars. Waves of rumors spread through the crowd as they discussed the possibilities of finding the ocean. DubDub's head whipped from side to side trying to catch all that was being said, but to hear all of the Stars' gossip was proving impossible.

Loony, on the other hand, was having the time of his life. As one Star passed a rumor to the next, he would intercept it and with wicked glee pass it on to the next Star with some, to Loony's twisted humor, hysterical change. That Star, unaware of the deception, would pass the altered version on. The false rumor of what was on Stella's map proliferated rapidly, resulting in some unwitting Stars singing out with unfettered enthusiasm, the moon man's fraud, "*Mega Burrito! Mega Burrito!*" The ball headed lunatic rolled on the floor in fits of laughter.

Over the din of this constantly changing chorale, Astraea conferred with Stella. "I would trust the legend of the vast inland sea," she suggested. "If Heo says the human made his way out of this galaxy, then perhaps he did so by crossing the inland ocean."

"Then that's where we're going." Stella said uncertainly, wondering how the dot could symbolize an ocean, and where that ocean could lead, if the Nebula Mountains were surrounded by the plains of Empyriania. "The clockwork is outside the universe, outside of what anyone knows. If whatever is in those mountains is beyond the knowledge of the Stars, then that's where we want to be. It sounds like crossing this ocean," she looked at the small blue dot on the map and corrected herself, "or whatever it is… might lead out of the galaxy."

Red Algol slunk towards Stella and with just a few words brought her spirit down. "Do you realize how dangerous those mountains are?"

His blue counterpart shook his head with dramatic woe. "It is a mystery as to what inhabits those loathsome peaks. Rumor tells that what lives in those turbulent terrains are little better than wild beasts."

"But that is only rumor," Astraea countered, annoyed at the pleasure the Algols took in frightening Stella. "No one knows for certain what waits in those heights, although we've all lingered near their foothills once."

Stella noticed the uncomfortable reaction her words evoked not only from the Algols, but all the nearby Stars. "Once?" She asked. "You've all been there once? And why are the Stars so bothered by that?"

Heo sighed softly. "It is the sad fact that even we Stars have shameful secrets."

"What secrets?" Stella asked anxiously.

Astraea answered the question in obvious defiance of the Stars around her. "It is the shame of all who shine on these plains, that we are foundlings, orphans left at the border of the Nebula Mountains." She turned to address her fellow Stars, "The mystery of our origin has tormented us far too long. I will go with Stella and discover what secrets those mountains contain."

Together Red and Blue Algol hissed, "Not all knowledge illuminates. What you find in those mountains, Astraea, might not be to your liking. Though diamonds are found in mines, they are not meant to wallow in the dirt for all time." Clucking irritably the twin Stars twirled away. "But if that is what it will take to rid the human from our land, so be it. It has become clear to me that it would be better if she were gone, whichever way she goes."

As Stella and her small troop made their way through Empyriania, it was as if a fine gray dust had rained down and dampened the brilliance that once invigorated the land. Even the sky had lost its vibrancy, its colors fading to pallor. Amidst the dreariness they marched staunchly onward the Nebula Mountains. The songs from the Stars they encountered were laden with despair, perhaps hinged on the deaths that had occurred in this land of light, or possibly because the Stars were dismayed to watch the travelers pass, knowing their destination was the mysterious mountains from which none had ever returned. Whatever it was, the songs of the Stars now matched their surroundings, diminished and dull.

"So this is the woeful fruit that the seed of betrayal has borne," sighed Astraea. "Once there had been little concern among these bright and pleasant hills, and now…" She nodded to a Star dancing slowly and somberly, his face stricken with dismay. "I fear it is hopeless that the damage can be undone, so deeply has our world been wounded."

The defection of their fellow Stars, to Moros' pact of death and darkness had affected all the inhabitants of Empyriania, perhaps Astraea most of all. Her beauty was still wondrous to behold but nevertheless, her brightness like every other Star's since the battle with the Zodiac, had dimmed. Into what had once been unshakable confidence, the seed of doubt had been sown and under her breath Stella cursed Moros for what he had done to her friend.

Stella took Astraea's hand. "There is hope, there's always hope, there has to be hope," she whispered softly, her words a promise to all lost in shadow. Then, with only hope to guide her, she led her friends into the dark and stormy mountains.

17 THE STARLIT MIRE

The meadows of Empyriania ended where the Nebula Mountains jutted up through the gentle rolling hills. Obscured by clouds of dank smog, the mountain's towering heights flared forebodingly as lightning blasted the craggy peaks. Stella and her friends, after searching the range for some means of access, tentatively approached a gash ripped in a steep wall. Slipping through the crack, the quartet was welcomed by a wave of choking ash. When it passed, they found themselves at the mouth of a deep valley bordered by immense hills whose tortuous topographies confounded their sight.

Once on Earth, Stella had lain on the beach and watched the clouds for hours discovering animals and objects in the puffy miasma. And just like those clouds, she saw in every protrusion of this Nebula landscape, forms that mimicked any number of things. Wherever she laid her eyes, the amorphous blob would take on the form of some malformed visage, sculptural fantasy, or phantom object, all blending into each other in a mind-bending array of warped, melted and misshapen representations. A large outcropping close by, assumed the distorted shape of a kitten reaching for some treat suspended invisibly in the sky. The kitten's body, in an indescribable twist of topology, formed the basis of Abraham Lincoln's forehead. The feline's tail snaked along the mountainside to end in a messy configuration that resembled nothing less than an enormous pile of spaghetti and meatballs. To complete this surreal vision, each and every of the meatballs bore the face of a smirking monkey.

Stella wished her father were with her to see all of this, remembering how excited he was when the first photos of these nebulas had been transmitted from the heart of the galaxy. And now here she was, walking among those very formations. Looking away from the bizarre exhibitions, Stella turned back to the now familiar strangeness of her friends' faces, the multi-eyed DubDub, the warm conflagration of Astraea, and the grimacing moonscape of Loony.

"I guess now you want us to hike through this mess?" Loony asked, dipping the tip of his shoe into the muck they were about to venture through. It came back covered in sludge.

As Stella gestured to the mountains, they flared dully and a thunderous boom rocked the ground beneath her feet. "The inland sea is somewhere in there, and beyond the sea is the end of the universe, so yes, I guess we'll have to get through these hills."

"And past whatever lives in them, right?" The moon man turned to aim his words at Astraea. "I have a feeling there's something about these mountains the Stars don't want us to know. Something they're ashamed of."

Stella wondered how Astraea could take the moon man's needling so lightly; he was an expert at being an annoyance. Pretending to be unaware of his taunts, there was resignation in her voice as she asked, "What does the map show, Stella? Check it while I scout ahead for any danger." In a flash Astraea was trudging forward, the splattering mud soiling her diaphanous gown.

"Oh, right, the map." Stella had been so engrossed by the phantasmagoria about her that she had forgotten to look at the map. Pulling the parchment from her pocket, she looked for where they should be headed.

From over the girl's shoulder, a mechanical finger poked at a nebula peak on the map that looked exactly like a melted tuba. "I see that formation there." DubDub pointed into a thick maelstrom of black dust.

"I can't see anything." Stella stated, shielding her eyes from a volley of ash that blew into her face.

"Wait," DubDub recommended, "until that cloud passes."

Stella tried to keep her eyes on the spot, squinting against the grime that assaulted her vision. After a moment the smoke cleared and sure enough the shape on the map matched the shape in the mountains.

"And it seems," DubDub pointed to a number of cracks drawn next to the tuba, "that there are passes, through which we can proceed."

Stella scrutinized the map. It did show there were four ways that lead inwards from the tuba, but all were so wildly convoluted, she was unable to follow them very far. She concentrated on the pass to the right and traced it inward through the maze of canyons and crevices. It soon split into three more passages and each of those into others, until it was impossible to keep track of any one path. Pointing to the right most of the passes, she tried to sound as confident as she could, "I guess we could go this way."

"I'd rather not slog through this muck just on your guess." Loony retorted, the roar of thunder punctuating his disdain. "Why don't you see where the toy that Venus gave you points?"

"Which toy?" Stella asked, confused. "You mean the Compyxx? It's not a toy!"

"That's what you think!" Loony snorted. Though she knew it was probably due to a phase he was in, Stella wished the moon man didn't take such pleasure in being so snotty. Loony was only a half moon now, and Stella didn't like to think about how Loony would behave when he was a new moon, and completely dark. Something she remembered hearing, (was it from that song her mother had played so often?) suddenly came to mind almost as a warning. *There is no dark side of the moon, as a matter of fact its all dark.* Casting a skeptical look towards the impudent imp, Stella only could hope he would behave with there being so much at stake.

Talking out the Compyxx, she waited for its arrow to point the way. When it settled, it pointed not to any of the available routes but directly towards a high sheer cliff, one Stella knew immediately they would be unable to scale.

"So which way do we go?" Loony asked, sidling nearer to catch a glimpse at where the Compyxx pointed. Stella snapped its lid shut. She was not going give the lunatic the satisfaction of knowing that she had no idea.

"That way?" He jabbed a crooked finger off to the left. "Or that way?" pointing to the right. "Or do we just keep walking straight through that mountain?" He laughed sarcastically, pointing to the large bubbling mass the Compyxx had indicated.

A gust whistled eerily through the valley and as the shrill sound subsided a spectral voice was left in its wake. "Stella? Stella?" it implored faintly. The voice was hollow and frightening. Stella hunted fearfully for its source, only half relaxing when she found it. The voice came from DubDub, who had collapsed in a heap on the ground. "Do you think you could wind me," he pleaded weakly, "I'm almost run down again."

Chuckling at DubDub's plight, Loony strolled casually away to study a muddy bubble that only vaguely resembled a two-headed pig, swimming in the canyon floor. Disgusted with the moon's lack of compassion Stella hastily wound the automaton, turning the knob in quick hurried jerks.

"Uhhh," DubDub moaned.

"Am I hurting you?" Stella asked, surprised to find the machine might feel pain.

"Not... too much..."DubDub answered reluctantly. "I so appreciate your taking the time to do this."

Stella continued now intent on not letting her anger at Loony cause any discomfort for DubDub. As she finished winding, Astraea returned. Her dress was no longer brilliant, but drab and muddy and her face was smeared with grimy soot.

"The clouds are very thick in these valleys and I could not see beyond them." Astraea confessed. "But I think it is safe to proceed. Which path have you chosen?"

Stella really wished it wasn't her decision to make, and looked to DubDub for assistance. "Have you seen anything that would give you some idea of which way to go?" She asked with just a hint of desperation.

DubDub shook his head slowly and answered pitifully, "How could I presume to choose, when I am unable to sustain myself?"

Stella's glance shifted to Loony. She didn't ask his advice, knowing he would have them wandering endlessly, if just for a joke. So it was up to her. Quickly, she numbered the crevices ahead, one to four, from left to right. Then, turning to mechanical man, she asked as casually as she could, "DubDub, did I wind you enough?"

Mechanical eyes widened, surprised by his young friend's concern at such a crucial time. "Uh, yes you did, Stella. I am now fully wound."

"How many turns did it take to wind you?" At the question, Astraea looked at the girl curiously, wondering what she was up to.

"Uh…" the puzzled automaton answered, "It took three turns to wind me fully."

Ignoring her friends' bewilderment, Stella looked out to the four passages that lay before her. She silently counted, stopping at the third and narrowest of the four. "We go that way!"

As they marched, silent giants with bizarre visages observed the passing pilgrims from high above, but as for the most part the muck was only ankle deep, it didn't take long to cross the valley. "What is this goo anyway?" Loony complained. Stella didn't venture a guess, but whatever it was it didn't glitter and sparkle like the rest of Empyriania, and had already coated her jacket and boots with unpleasant muddy patches. Astraea helped DubDub along, as his stiff limbs proved incapable of navigating the slippery terrain. It was all quite a mess.

Reaching the passage, Stella scrutinized her pick. It was a desolate ravine with only a slit of sky visible above, though thick clouds of ash partially obscured even that. "Let's get going," she suggested and in single file they moved slowly through the narrow canyon. As they slid into the mountain pass, staccato crashes of thunder accompanied the high whistling of winds, and lightning flared in eldritch bursts. Stella thought it all a bit spooky. "I wonder when the last time someone passed through here was," she whispered.

"Hello! Anyone there?" Loony shouted, his gravely voice echoing down the crevice.

"Hush up! " Stella chided. "We don't want to attract the attention of whatever might be hiding in these mountains."

"You wondered who was around here, not me." Loony sulked. "I don't understand why you're always ruining my fun!" In a huff he turned to find DubDub blocking his way. Shoving the automaton, a brief scuffle ensued leaving both collapsed in a noisy heap. Loony let loose a string of invectives as he fought to disentangle himself from the clattering mess.

"Loony!" Stella hissed, "Stop it now! Someone will hear!" The moon man righted himself by putting a hand on DubDub's head and shoving it roughly into the mud. Rankled by his misconduct, Stella issued a harsh reprimand, "Loony! If you don't behave, I'm going to tell Old Sol what you've done!"

Stella had never seen Loony look so dark and gloomy. Where was the silvery glow of the imp she had first met who seemed so happy to help Old Sol? Now, little light reflected from his head and there was smoldering fire in his eyes as he furiously shook his fist. "Yeah, I always knew you were a rat. If you tell on me… I'll… I'll…" Exhausted by his outburst, Loony slunk into the muck and began to sob uncontrollably, "You're not my friend! None of you are my friends!"

Loony faded from Stella's sight as a squall of blinding dust blew through the ravine. As she shielded her eyes, a hand took her by the shoulder to guide her. "We should continue." Astraea suggested. Together they pulled DubDub from the mud and made their way through the blustering smog. A ball headed figure straggled through the haze a few feet behind, leaving Stella unsure if that sight made her glad or uneasy.

They made their way slowly through the ravine. With winds howling wildly all about and visibility next to nothing, Stella tightened her hood around her face and reached back for DubDub's hand. Guiding him along, with every step the wind forced them back, but together they pushed on through the gale. Coming to a three way split and with no clue which way to proceed, Stella managed a peek at the Compyxx. It pointed left.

"Which way now?" Loony grumbled impatiently.

The left-handed path was very narrow and looked very uninviting with many overhangs under which they would have to crawl. The right was wider but turned sharply back, not at all in the direction they had been heading. The middle seemed the most hospitable, and least difficult. Stella debated a moment whether she should trust the Compyxx, but remembering just how many times it had mislead her, turned to the middle path. "This way," she reluctantly answered.

In a matter of moments they had reached a dead end. Loony snarled something nasty before turning to retrace his steps. The others followed, equally unhappy. As they neared the fork, Stella shouted to Loony, "Go right!" but to no avail as he had already made his choice and was stomping down the path to the left. Stella, deciding it hardly mattered which way they went, followed. This corridor went on interminably, but with no obstructions to stop the travelers' progress they proceeded on. A slight slope downward unexpectedly became a steep decline and the quartet slid into a deep basin. Knee deep in the muck and with a maelstrom of ash swirling thickly overhead, they waded against the winds to an outcropping that resembled a sleeping dragon. There they crouched shielded from the winds in a nook formed by its coiling tail.

Once ensconced in the tight cubby, Stella noticed their party was missing a member. "Where is Loony?"

A mechanical eye snaked over the muddy dragon's tail and rose like a periscope into the sooty air. "I see him. He is not far behind," the clockwork watcher reported.

The three welcomed the momentary reprieve as they conferred on their next step. "I thought we were in this canyon." Stella pointed to a tiny scratch on the map but there was no sign of the basin or the slumbering dragon where they had found their meager shelter. She traced her way through the passes on the map. Soon her mud caked finger was lost among the confusing twists and turns. "It's like a maze in these mountains", she whispered worriedly. "I don't think we're anywhere near the inland ocean."

Amidst the flicker of lightning, Loony appeared and proceeded to cram himself into the already overcrowded nook. "So you're saying we're lost?" Stella couldn't be sure if his rocky lips had formed a grimace or a grin. Probably the latter she imagined, as he would be more satisfied knowing she had blundered.

Staring straight into Loony's beady blue eyes, Stella fibbed. "I said, I think we're very near the inland ocean."

Realizing the young girl's dilemma in dealing with the moon man, Astraea joined in her charade. "Yes, I think we are not too far from our goal."

Loony, confused by the show of bravura, crumpled his brow as he mulled over why his companions were so jubilant, when he was certain they were hopelessly lost.

"Yes," confirmed DubDub. "I have seen a peak that stands nearby." Stella felt proud of her mechanical friend who even though the grimy had him wheezing horribly, joined in on the ruse. "If we continue on, we will be there shortly."

"Yes, we must continue!" Stella slid from the shelter into the mud and slogged onward through the howling rain of ash. "Come on! We're almost there!"

Now they wandered blindly with no idea of where they were heading, stopping only briefly wherever they might find shelter. The Compyxx, when Stella could muster up enough courage to check it, would more than likely point off a high cliff or up an insurmountable mountain. If it was pointing to a way out, it was one reachable only by a bird. But still she forged onward, DubDub and Astraea following loyally and Loony grumpily behind. It quickly became that Stella hoped for the blasts of thunder, just for relief from the moon's constant complaints.

Through the smog DubDub might now and again catch a glance of a particularly distinct peak, and then they would check the map for some idea of their location, only to find they were nowhere near where they had supposed. It only served to further confound them when a passage on the map that appeared to connect with another, abruptly dead-ended leaving them no choice but to back track. Stella could only wonder if over the eons the landscape had changed, for the map though expertly drawn, was proving useless in guiding them through the labyrinthine mountains.

Added to all that, the uneasy feeling they were being drawn into a trap grew with each step. So unnerved by this premonition was Stella, that she gasped aloud when confronted by the face of a witch looming gigantically overhead, as if floating in the smog. The phantasm was terrifying, as the contours of the bubbling nebula blob resembled to a disquieting degree the face of Verena Maldek.

Shuddering at the sight, Stella tried not to think of what was going on back at the dome. Heartsick and wanting more than anything to see her family, she fumbled though the pockets of her parka for anything that would remind her of home and a time when unending darkness was just a thing of bad dreams. Her fingers brushed past the keys of her house in Florida, rubber bands she had found on sidewalks, and a small bit of shell she had found long ago. Just touching the shell brought back memories of warm days at the beach; memories that made her feel much, much better. She wondered if Moros ever did end time, would those memories still be there or would they be snuffed out too, as if they had never even existed. Finished fishing for memories, she pulled her hand from the pocket and as she did a piece of paper, carefully folded, fluttered to the ground.

DubDub, who had been walking behind the young girl diligently observing all he could, bent and plucked the paper from the muck. "I see you've dropped something, Stella." The automaton attempted to clean the sheet, but a thunderclap so jarred him, his wooden fingers flew open and the paper fluttered into the mud.

"Oh, thanks," Stella said, retrieving the paper. Not wishing to litter she stuffed it, in a clump, back into her pocket.

"What was that?" Astraea asked sounding overly interested in the illegible scribbles, Stella thought.

"Just something one of the men in the Astrophelarium drew for me. He said it was my horoscope, but I have no idea how to read it."

"May I see?" the Star woman asked.

Stella pulled the crumpled wad from her pocket and tried to smooth it quickly with her sleeve before handing it to Astraea. The Star woman's eyes widened as she viewed the thin parchment. "Who gave this to you?"

"His name was Doctor Dee. He said this was a chart of my future, and of some futures I might want to avoid. I'm really not sure what he meant by that, but he was a very nice man."

"If I am not mistaken," Astraea said, "this might well be the guidance we need. May I see the map?" Stella took out the map of Empyriania and handed it over. "DubDub! May I have your assistance?" Eager to offer any help he could to the luminous lady, the mechanical man clattered over. 'Please, if you will turn around?" Presenting his back, a few of DubDub's eyes drifted over his shoulders to watch.

Astraea took the map of Empyriania and flattened it on the flat wooden surface. Then she took the horoscope and smoothed it out on top of the map. The geography of Empyriania was faint but visible through the thin parchment. "I believe if I align these properly…" Astraea said, matching the corners of the horoscope with the corners of the map.

Suddenly the images on the two papers merged to form one. The outer circle of the horoscope fit perfectly against the outline of the island's perimeter, and the inner ring where Doctor Dee had drawn arcane signs and symbols, fell on the hills and meadows of Starland marking certain areas with significances beyond Stella's comprehension. But it was the correspondences at the center of the overlapped images that drew the attention of all, for the lines that crisscrossed Doctor Dee's chart and which fell within the area of the mountains on the map, were no longer only random and indecipherable marks.

Now they showed themselves to be paths through the Nebula Mountains, different colored lines that followed exactly the valleys and canyons sketched on the map. Some of these brightly colored trails ended abruptly in the confusing mountain maze, but a few found their way by circuitous routes to the blue circle at the island's center. Then Stella found it, a yellow line that traced a direct route through this land so dark and savage. Her broad smile was matched in brightness only by Astraea's gleaming grin.

"What's going on?" Loony bound over to the woman and the girl. "What are you smiling about? "

"These paths will lead us through the mountain passes." Astraea surmised, running her finger across the various routes. "This one will lead us to the inland sea." She traced the warm yellow line.

"We just have to find where we are on the map now, so we can get to that trail." Stella stated. "DubDub, can you help?"

Other eyes joined those that dangled from the back of DubDub's head, to carefully study the overlay of the chart and the map. Stella could hear the gears spinning and bellows pumping as the optical devices flitted back and forth, taking note of every detail. As the smog parted momentarily, one eye darted to a pineapple shaped peak nearby while another scanned the map to find its representation there. "This and this is a match. And that outcropping is very distinct, but where is it on the map. Oh yes, there it is. Now where is this?" DubDub asked, investigating every clue.

After several minutes of frenetic ocular acrobatics, the clockwork watcher ceased his exertions and stated confidently, "We are located precisely here." He placed a wooden fingertip on the map, right atop the facsimile of Verena Maldek's face. In the adjacent valley sat the Lincoln with the kitten forehead and the yellow line running around under the ancient president's nose. It became painfully obvious to Stella that they had been going in circles since first entering these dank mountains. Though she should have been happy that a way had been found, she wasn't. All she could think of was that if she hadn't taken all those reckless chances, they wouldn't have wasted so much time in pointless wandering.

She slunk back against the wall of the crevice, the grimy mud leaving a long splotch on her bright red parka, and turned away too embarrassed to face her friends. "What's wrong?" Astraea asked, rushing to the girl's side.

"Everyone was depending on me to find a way, but I just couldn't admit I had no idea…" Stella confessed, "…So I guessed, and my guesses led us nowhere."

Astraea saw how ashamed the girl was, although could not honestly see why. "True it has been a rather strenuous trip, but your choices have led us to where we are now, and I believe that," she stated emphatically," this is exactly where we should be. We are no longer lost! You must trust the benevolence of the light to always lead us forward and try not to question the route. Maybe we can't see things from light's perspective, maybe we can't understand its plans, but that doesn't mean it's not shining through everything we do. Try looking at it this way." She poked two holes into the mud on the wall, one above and one below and then scratched a squiggly line, looping and spiraling every which way, connecting both. "It seems a confusing path, don't you think, from here to there?"

Stella nodded, imagining that it was probably very much like the route they just had taken. "Now look from here." Astraea moved her face close to the wall and closed an eye. Stella copied her friend's actions and as she did the squiggly lines squeezed together. The closer to the wall she got, the thinner the whole mess grew, until with her cheek almost touching the muddy wall, the squiggles were a straight solid line, connecting the two dots.

"How you perceive things is a matter of perspective," Astraea stated, "and as time goes by you'll find yourself seeing things in different ways. Maybe then you'll understand how what might have seemed a mistake, was actually the perfect choice. Why the way I see it, if we hadn't walked so far, I doubt we would have ever discovered the way those two papers fit together, and without that we would never have found our way through these mountains. Your guess was exactly what was needed. "Stella wondered if she was being teased, though she knew the Star woman was not one to joke.

"Though fate might fool with us at the moment," Astraea clasped Stella's hand and started to walk, "in good time all destinies meet in the light."

It was only a short march to where the kitten sat on Lincoln's head. From there, surprisingly, the joined maps indicated the same passage Stella had chosen. When they reached the fork in the ravine it pointed them left. It was a short passage and not as difficult as Stella had imagined. Beyond only a few overhangs, it opened up into a wide canyon dotted with monumental dinosaurs, distorted as if they were sculpted of melted wax. Continuing to follow the map, they turned into another gully then up a hillside, then down through a deep ravine. As they hiked its many twists and turns, the smog slowly dissipated and it was with great relief that the travelers turned a corner of the ravine to see a wide clearing, all but free of the choking dust.

As they stepped into the valley, the light haze that blanketed the landscape was blown away by a stiff wind, and suddenly the rainbow sky that sheltered the starry realm of Empyriania was visible above. The thunder however, continued to rumble low and ominously.

"The sky is clear; the storm is gone, so where is all that noise coming from?" Stella asked.

"Look to the walls of the canyon," Astraea suggested.

Stella scanned the towering walls of the craggy canyon and with each resounding thud came a corresponding flash from within the nebulous cliffs. After a number of booms, she realized that what she was hearing was not thunder, but explosions from deep within the walls. It was as if the cliffs themselves were alive with energy.

The phenomena seemed of little interest to Astraea as she chirped enthusiastically. "The map shows that once we cross this plateau, the inland ocean will be not far away. This way! "A ferocious roar echoed through the valley.

"What was that?" DubDub asked nervously, his devices stiffly attentive.

Another roar shook the canyon. "It's only the cliffs," Stella responded, "and whatever's in them."

"It's not the cliffs! "DubDub shrieked in horror. "Look!"

Atop the crest of the valley, a dark shape moved stealthily from peak to peak. It stopped for a moment on a low outcropping to roar once more and then leaped across to a more advantageous cliff. In the moment of flight, its dark outline hung silhouetted against the rainbow sky. Its slender tail, its massive paws and its thick mane gave name to the stalking shadow's identity.

"Leo!" the travelers gasped as one. The fearsome lion was searching diligently and methodically, every craggy peak

"I think perhaps that this is not the route we wish to take." DubDub suggested. " Perhaps we should find another way." There was no argument from any of the group as they took the suggestion and in unison moved back into the narrow ravine from which they had come.

Astraea stopped them before they stepped around the corner of the sheltering crack. "Do you hear that?"

They all froze in their retreat, for from within the narrow chasm came the coarse clomping of hooves. A gleaming glass eye telescoped from DubDub's head and snaked around the corner. The sound of gears clenching screeched from his wooden chest came as he gasped, "Look!"

A set of binoculars swung forward and Stella peered into them to see ambling through the canyon, a monstrous shadowy ram. Stella handed the binoculars to Astraea, but Loony snatched them away. "It's Aries!" he squealed and as if the binoculars had become some venomous serpent, thrust them into the still outstretched hand of Astraea. "They're hunting us!"

As the clopping from the canyon grew louder, Stella looked for a place to hide. With no other option, she herded her friends to a muddy hollow shaped remarkably like a giant teacup. The foursome vaulted the mug's grimy lip and crammed into its hollow, but even tightly squashed together it was painfully obvious there was not enough cover.

"Maybe I can defeat them both," Astraea offered, with uncharacteristic uncertainty.

"Maybe we should surrender," Loony replied and moved to show himself. Stella quickly clapped a hand over the moon man's mouth. As she struggled with the imp she felt something pulling her from below. Tumbling backwards with Loony still tight in her grip, she saw that small dirty hands were reaching through cracks in the mud and dragging Astraea and DubDub after her.

"*Teide*! Bind them tightly! Do not allow them to move!" A harsh voice ordered. Two short whistling bursts answered the command. Stella, prone on the floor, felt her hands and feet being tightly tied.

"Astraea?" Stella shouted into the dingy fog that enveloped her.

"Quiet!" A sharp jab to her ribs knocked the air out of the Stella. "*Calar*! Gag this one!" Another whistle acknowledged the command as a grimy rag was stuffed into the girl's mouth. "And tie this one's hands and feet." There was the rattle of wood as DubDub's limbs were bound. As her eyes adjusted to the dismal light, Stella made out three heaps nearby, and a crowd of gnomish figures skittering about them.

"To the nursery!" the voice squeaked, and the random whistles resolved into a rhythmic work song. Strong small hands grasped Stella's parka and passed her along, jostling and squeezing her bound body through an endless succession of tight tunnels. Stella couldn't be sure how many beings carried them, but the peeping voices of which there had been few at the outset, were now many and piping their tune conspiratorially.

From ahead came loud rattling which caused Stella to worry that the rough handling might damage DubDub's machinery. The muffled mutterings of Loony ensured that he was alive, and if his deadened squeals of discomfort meant anything, angry. There was no clue of Astraea's presence, but Stella imagined the Star woman was silently chagrined at allowing her charges to be captured.

As she was being carried downward, Stella glimpsed in the thick muck overhead, a fleeting parade of weird figures presented as if to convey some message. Flashing in the dim light, these sagging globs of mud appeared to trace an untold history, one of unacknowledged labors and unrecognized efforts on which the entirety of the galaxy, it avowed, was sustained. It was just mud Stella reminded herself, sloppy mire from which no meaning could come, and looked away from the arcane tableau to see Astraea disappear around a sharp turn, floating on a sea of grubby hands. Following, Stella was carried into a large chamber awash in slop.

The whistling stopped when a squeaking voice ordered, "Lock her in with the rest!" Stella was thrown unceremoniously down and hit the floor with a splash. Her bound hands and feet offering no chance to cushion the fall, she rolled onward until she found herself face to face with Astraea.

"Are you okay?" The Star woman asked as her fingers nimbly undid the girl's bonds.

When freed, Stella helped untie the others. "I'm fine but what's happened?"

"We've been captured by these… things!" Astraea answered, stricken with revulsion. They were prisoners indeed, sealed in a small dreary cell dug into a muddy nebulous wall. From the other side of the cell's rough bars, studying the captive foursome like animals at the zoo, peered hundreds of large saucer eyes. Behind those eyes were the dirtiest creatures Stella had ever seen, either on Earth or in her travels through the space.

DubDub's devices were calibrating, measuring, observing. After a few moments of activity they receded noisily into his head, forming a helmet that resembled some enormous insect's eye. When the devices came fully to rest, he pronounced with total certainty. "Brown dwarves,"

Stella, Astraea and Loony looked inquisitively towards their clockwork friend as he continued. "I read about them when Stella and I were trapped in the Astrophelarium. They are brown dwarves, or in more general terms, Stars that have failed to ignite."

Astraea walked quickly to the bars of the cell to more closely inspect the muddy mob. She walked back to DubDub, rankled at his suggestion. "You are mistaken, DubDub. Those filthy creatures are no kin to Stars."

DubDub further scrutinized the filthy horde beyond the bars. "I am certain, there can be no doubt. They are brown dwarves, Stars fated to never alight."

A gleeful shout came from the corner of the cell. "Ha! That's priceless!" Loony snickered. "Those things are Astraea's brothers and sisters!"

"Be quiet Loony!" Astraea snarled angrily. "DubDub, perhaps you have erred in your observations, for there can be no way such repulsive creatures are related to beings of light."

Loony's mocking laughter filled the room. "It looks like our illuminated one can't deal with such dull relatives."

"I'm sorry if it offends you, Astraea. But it is a fact, not a theory. These creatures," DubDub gestured towards what congregated outside the cell, "are the nearest things to Stars in our universe. You are more akin to them than to

Stella or to me. They have much more in common with Stars than they do with even a moon such as Loony."

The moon man let out a loud hoot. "Perhaps our Star *princess* has a dark side too. It's called her family."

In a flash, Astraea was across the cell and had Loony off the ground, his throat gripped tightly in her hand. "Do not toy with me, moon!"

Loony's gray face quickly turned a ghastly shade of blue. Stella tried desperately to pull the Star woman's hand from Loony's throat, but the grip was so strong she couldn't pry the fingers free. She'd never imagined Astraea capable of such uncontrollable rage.

"Let him go! You're hurting him!" Stella begged Astraea. The crowd of brown dwarves began to hoot and whistle as they watched the confrontation. Stella couldn't be bothered to tell if these sounds were of amusement or concern, but only shouted over the din, "Stop it Astraea! Let him go!"

Abruptly, the look of rage left Astraea's face. Dropping Loony, gasping for breath to the floor, she reddened with shame. "That was wrong of me. I should not allow myself to be goaded by Loony." Without facing her antagonist, she pronounced out loud. "I am sorry, Moon of Earth. I should not permit myself to fall so easily into your traps."

Loony jumped to his feet, pointed his crooked finger up into the Star woman's face and began to hurl invectives. "My traps! HA! You know nothing about *my traps*! But you'll be sorry you did that, I can tell you that! You'll be sorry!"

Astraea, listless and despondent, did not respond but walked to the far side of the cell and slid down to the floor with her head in her hands.

"Loony, please!" Stella pleaded, hoping the unpredictable moon would listen to reason. "We're stuck in this together. It won't help if we fight amongst ourselves. We need to find a way out of here, and get to the Celestial Clockwork before things get worse."

How could it get any worse Stella asked herself, after first being imprisoned and now having Astraea and Loony literally at each other's throats? Everything that could go wrong had gone wrong.

Through gritted teeth the moon man hissed. "She thinks she's better than them." He gestured to the dingy dwarves. "Just like the Planets thought they were better than me. Well, they'll see who's important." He glared at the downcast Star woman. "You'll all see." Finished with his tirade, he stomped to an empty corner of the cell and sat face to the wall.

In all the turmoil Stella had not noticed that DubDub had run down. She saw him now collapsed in a crumpled heap on the muddy floor. Winding him, he revived instantly. "What has happened?" he asked, noticing how upset his cellmates were.

Deciding there was no reason for him to know of their dire predicament, she only answered "We'll talk about it in the morning." Then going to an empty corner she squatted in the mud and pulled her hood over her head. She fell asleep with the incessant whistling of the dwarves in her ears.

When Stella awoke from dreams of home, it was to the whirring and clicking of DubDub's devices. She rolled over and shifted her hood to see her mechanical friend at the bars of the cell with his telescopes, periscopes and binoculars, peering out through the spaces between the bars. Rubbing the sleep from her eyes, she sat up and found Astraea at her side. "He's been there the whole time you slept. I've kept him wound but he won't leave that spot. Something happening with the dwarves has him fixated."

When Stella went to the bars, she saw what it was that so held DubDub's attention. The scene was reminiscent of industrious ants laboring in an anthill, as hundreds of the dwarves scurried about in a chaotic frenzy. It took more than a few moments for her to realize they were working together for some common purpose, and that two muddy mounds in the center of the cavern were the focus of their activity. Wrestling armfuls of murky matter swarms of dwarves climbed to the top of the mounds. Once there, they dropped their loads and vigorously stamped them down.

Now empty handed the dwarves made their way back down the mounds and toward tunnels dug in the cavern walls. For every dwarf that disappeared into those dark burrows, another would appear carrying a load of heavy nebula mud. So laden, they would stagger with difficulty back to the center of the cave, and climb again to the top of one of the growing mounds. It was dirty grueling work and made the dwarves' lives seem that much more wretched.

"Fascinating!" exclaimed DubDub. "Watch carefully, Stella. You are probably the first human to be in such a nursery."

Stella wondered what DubDub was talking about. She knew all about nurseries, having spent a lot of time helping her mother with the twins'. Nurseries are clean, bright and white, not dark, murky and filled with grungy dwarves crawling everywhere like so many bugs. "A nursery? This filthy place?" she scoffed.

"Yes Stella! A nursery!" DubDub watched in rapt fascination the proceedings. When Stella looked to Astraea for an explanation, she only shrugged her muddied shoulders.

Loony was still curled sullenly, silent in the corner of the cell. Stella hoped he'd stay there a while, maybe until they figured out a way to escape. At the moment however, surrounded by a multitude of captors, that seemed out of the question. As she dwelled on their predicament, Stella watched the endless procession of dwarves who never tired in their endless toil, and whose greatest treasure was only more mud.

Even though the dwarves all looked very much alike, caked as they were with the muddy stuff they mined, Stella tried to keep track of just one, to see how he progressed. It was the smallest of the workers, but always came from the dark tunnels bearing the largest load. Once it had almost made it up the mound's steep embankment, only to fall and crash headlong to the ground. It immediately jumped up, gathered its load and resumed its climb undaunted. The persistence of this creature was impressive, though Stella had no idea what it was trying to accomplish.

Struggling with its oversized load, the littlest dwarf pulled itself up to the top. Dropping the weight of its mined booty upon the mound's peak, it raised its foot and stomped it down. *KABOOOM!!!* With a thundering bang the mound convulsed and the little dwarf was flung into the air. Landing in a splatter, nearby dwarves rushed to him and when the little dwarf was pulled from the mud, a wide smile beamed on his repugnant face. The other dwarves around him were smiling, and if Stella could believe her eyes, congratulating him.

"Wonderful!" DubDub exclaimed, "They have achieved the correct density to trigger ignition!"

KABOOM! The mound roared again and Stella covered her ears. From within the depths of the shuddering mound a dull light glowed. The dwarves began to jump wildly about, doing hand flips and cartwheels, grunting, whistling and slapping each other's backs. As if he were a hero, some lifted the littlest dwarf on their shoulders and began to run in circles around the base of the shuddering mound.

At the other mound the dwarves redoubled their efforts. Every load of nebula stuff that was brought from the tunnels was rapidly heaped on the top of this second pile, of which all seemed eager to achieve the same ignition that had been sparked in the other.

Finally after arduous efforts, the second mound boomed but with nowhere near the intensity of the first. At that the dwarves ceased their labors and flooded from every tunnel to form a seething ring about the two shuddering mounds, responding to their pounding explosions with a squealing high-pitched chant that was more akin to the howling of an animal pack. Caught up in their crazed rite, the dwarves reveled in ecstatic furor, dancing wildly as the thundering drumbeat filled the massive cavern.

With every deafening boom, the glowing mound crushed in upon itself, its dazzling light flaring, fading, and then flaring again with ever brightening incandescence. The second mound sluggishly followed the lead of the first, collapsing tighter with its every thunderous boom, but without the brilliant intensity of the first and never igniting above a dull, tepid glow.

Driven wild by the rhythmic booms, the frenzy of raucous jubilation peaked. As their cavern was lit with ever-increasing light, the dwarves flailed and howled in frenetic celebration. The diminished piles now shrunk to a half their original size, stood like two upright pulsating eggs, one blazing white hot, the other smoldering with a feeble glow. The explosions contained within both had heightened to an almost unbearable volume. The dwarves' horrific chanting struggled to match the drumbeat as it increased in volume and tempo, to an incessant, unbearable booming.

Then suddenly with a final tremendous roar, the bright egg cracked. A blast of radiance filled the cavern as light poured from the cracking egg in blinding waves. Wincing, Stella covered her eyes. DubDub's instruments whirred and clicked, recalibrating to function in the new light, and then Stella felt something hover over her face as his voice said "Perhaps these might help."

DubDub's assistance came in the form of a pair of shaded lenses, which extended obligingly on a mechanical stalk. Feeling the goggles come to rest on her nose, Stella opened her eyes. Where there had been madness and frenzy, there was now only reverential awe. Where the glowing egg had been, there was just a brilliant haze in which all the dwarves bathed, whistling in a single warbling tone that reverberated pleasurably through the room. The light, nearly blinding, even with DubDub's shades, held aloft in its glowing midst a small figure. "A baby! There's a baby floating in that light!" Stella shouted, before realizing that the light was coming from the baby.

From out of the horde stepped the littlest dwarf who walked into the dazzling fountain of light, to gently pluck the infant from its lofty bower. As he gathered the baby into his thin arms, the luminance retreated into the infant's body as if the cover on a lantern had been closed. The light was still within, but had been tempered so its brilliance was less blinding. The little dwarf carried the glowing bundle into the crowd and was immediately surrounded by a joyous throng. On the muddied faces, Stella saw the same look she had seen when her friends and relatives had come to the hospital to see the new born twins, Tim and Pace.

From the second mound, abandoned and neglected after the birth of the luminous child, a blurting noise erupted and its dim light sputtered with the sound. The mob took noticeable offense at this rude intrusion on their celebration as the dull egg shaped mound blurted once again. Stella almost laughed out loud, as the dull mound was making what sounded just like farts. All the dwarves did their best to ignore the dull egg and its nasty eruptions, as every one of them was eager to focus their attention on the glowing newborn.

For a moment the dull egg was silent. Then suddenly, as if it had only been storing up the energy for its next offense, it blurted explosively and split with a poof. A brackish cloud of smoke welled from the collapsing mound and when the smoke had cleared, there crawling from the ruins of its shell, was the ugliest baby Stella had ever seen. It crept to the edge of the clamoring crowd, narrowly missing being trampled by its ebullient elders. The pathetic creature tried to attract the attention of its kin but none paid it any mind, all being enthralled by the brilliant light born into their midst.

"It's going to be crushed!" Stella cried. Even though there were so many of the brown dwarves that she was sure this one wouldn't be missed, she couldn't bear to see the innocent get stomped. "Hey! Watch out!" She yelled, trying to attract its attention. The newborn dwarf paid the shout no mind and maneuvered to the edge of the crowd, eagerly trying to become part of whatever it imagined might be going on.

As the cave was basked in the glow of the newborn Star, its warm light melted the tortured grimaces on the dwarves' faces, replacing them with countenances of sublime peace. Even though she was a prisoner, Stella had to smile too; so remarkable was the scene she was witnessing.

18 A MESSY HOMECOMING

It was without warning that a shroud of darkness intruded, squelching the jubilant mood. Moving through the cavern an inky shroud covered dwarf after dwarf, leaving their bright eyes blinking in confusion as they were thrust into gloom. The shadow passed over the Star baby, eclipsing its light until night ruled where lovely light had reigned. Stella looked for the source of the shadow, and high above, vague through the translucence of the nebula, glimpsed a dark shape stalking on four legs. As the cold edge of its shadow brushed the Star baby, it began to bawl in distress.

"It's Leo!" DubDub exclaimed with the entirety of his devices focused on the ceiling. "He is passing above, hunting for us."

"Does he know we're here? Can he see us?" Stella whispered breathlessly. The only sounds in the cavern were the whirring of DubDub's mechanisms and the heaving sobs of the baby.

"He senses something, but cannot see us." DubDub responded softly. "He's leaving." As the darkness relinquished its hold, sliding across the cavern like a pulled curtain, the little dwarf cradling the Star baby rushed out of the receding darkness and the infant let out one last gurgling sob as the shadow was stripped from its face.

"He heard that." DubDub stated, his terrified voice just the slightest squeak. The shadow shot back and the baby cried out loud. The little dwarf did its best to silence the sobs, somehow aware they were dangerous, perhaps even deadly, but the infant was inconsolable.

"Leo hears that! If we don't keep quiet, we will be discovered." DubDub whispered as the little dwarf rocked the baby, and rocked it roughly. The baby let out a bawl.

DubDub squealed in panic. "We have to stop that…"

A soft song aloft on the breath of Astraea calmed the automaton. Briefly pausing to caress Stella's ear it proceeded to slip effortlessly through the bars of the cell. It fluttered above the heads of the dwarves, who looked around in wonder for what could make such a beautiful sound, before landing on the shoulder of the sobbing Star baby. Even through the shadows Stella could see the smile on the newborn's face as it stopped crying to hear the song more clearly. All present were silent with only the gentle whispering of Astraea's song audible, but so lightly it could easily be the breeze.

"Leo's listening…" DubDub whispered with his voice so low Stella bent to hear. "He's going…" The darkness slid away. "He's gone." Stella's heart leapt at the words. There was a distant roar that echoed away to an eerie quiet. The room was still, the only exception was the brilliant baby, whose head bobbed in simple pleasure to Astraea's song until DubDub said. "Leo has past beyond my sight."

The song that had nestled on the baby's chest faded, and puzzled as to its whereabouts, tiny starry eyes searched the cavern. Astraea launched more bursts of song, which flew through the cavern in a wonderful aerial ballet. The dwarves closed their eyes, and followed the flight with bobbing motions of their heads. The baby giggled and gurgled along with the songs, its light intensifying with every laugh, and as it swayed enthusiastically the dwarf that held the baby struggled to maintain its hold.

The littlest dwarf looked for someone to help with his fidgeting burden but with all the other dwarves entranced by Astraea's songs, none offered assistance. As the baby began to slip from the littlest dwarf's hold, Stella impulsively reached through the bars to catch the falling bundle. Seeing the outstretched arms reaching from the cell where the music had come from, the littlest dwarf lugged the newborn across the cavern to the cell. Through the bars Stella took the radiant child from the worn out dwarf, who instantly collapsed to the floor.

Seeing the glowing face of the baby, Stella exclaimed, "It's a boy!" Eyes sprinkled with stardust twinkled, as tiny lips smiled in response.

"He's beautiful!" Astraea cooed from Stella's side.

Gingerly, Stella tried to maneuver the baby through the bars. Its legs slid through, and turning the baby sideways, the shoulders too. Its head, unfortunately, was just a tad too big. Not wanting to hurt the child, Stella gently slid him back through the bars, and did her best to cradle the newborn through them.

As Astraea's songs faded into faint whispers, the dwarves opened their eyes. Dismayed to see the luminous baby being held by their captives, they began to move towards the cell. Nervous of their intentions, Stella clutched the baby tighter. "Astraea? What are we going to do?" She asked, as the terrifying faces came nearer.

Without pausing to answer, Astraea sung out again and immediately the dwarves stopped their advance. The song was in the Star language, and though Stella couldn't understand the words, she could somehow follow the story it told.

Astraea's story began with Stars dancing along the brilliant plains of Empyriania. {Suddenly four, in a surprising turn in the dance, found themselves at the foothills of the Nebula Mountains. Knowing the legends and the dangers said to lie within those peaks, they were wary, but since their dance had brought them to this spot, they accepted it as right. As they waltzed away from the mountains the Stars noticed something on an outcropping, something bright, shining and unlike anything else in the dismal foreboding hills. Curious to see what it might be, but careful not to disturb whatever might be waiting in any of the dark cracks and crevices, one of the stars cautiously spun nearer.

"It's a baby!" the brave Star shouted to his companions and without breaking from his dance, swiftly pirouetted towards the outcropping, and plucked the child away. Within seconds he was away from the hazardous hills, carrying his prize.

The three who had waited behind broke out in happy applause. "A new Star! This is a happy day! The light of Empyriania has increased!" Singing a happy tune, the four with the baby, danced away.}

A loud sob interrupted the story. Not able to move from the bars without dropping the infant, Stella twisted her head back to see Loony, moaning in the corner. "They're orphans too! All the stars! Alone like me! Orphans like me!"

Stella spoke quietly, not wanting to upset the Star baby. "You're not an orphan, Loony. The Earth is your mother!"

"And I haven't seen her for so long. For all I know," he blubbered, "she could be dead."

"Earth is not dead!" Stella insisted, hating even hearing those words. "She just needs to stay hidden for a while, until we can get this whole mess straightened out."

"But I'm not even allowed to see her! All the other moons have brothers and sisters, but I'm alone. I'm an orphan!" Ramping up the histrionics and milking the situation for any sympathy he could get, Loony threw himself against the wall and sobbed.

Stella tried to ignore Loony and focus on Astraea's story. Now, the Star woman was singing of how as she wandered, she would often look off to the stormy Nebula Mountains and wonder why she too had been left on its borders, as all Stars had been. Astraea's voice was pained, as if somewhere deep inside she doubted that she was as perfect as she appeared. For if Stars were so lovely, so radiant, why had whoever had birthed them, cast them away?

Her song was now a lament whose every note quivered with anguish. Stella would never have imagined that Astraea, so perfect and beautiful, could ever harbor such a pain as she now revealed. As the emotion grew too strong for the Star woman to continue, the song stopped. And another song continued the story. Not a song perhaps, but a whistled chant, if even that. The whistles joined together roughly, but the story they told took place deep beneath the sculptured canyons and valleys, the fantastic chasms, and peaks of the Nebula Mountains.

The story told how in those caves, the dwarves' labored incessantly with not a word of complaint to hamper their toil. With no thought for themselves or their comfort, they worked for some higher goal. In whistling grunts, the tale progressed and Stella understood what lay in the heart of every dirty dwarf, as she now knew the secret shame that lay within each Star. Though they were dirty and destined to endless toil, they were not ashamed but pleased with the lot that had been cast for them. For while they did not move with the elegance of the Stars as they dug with their hands and crawled like moles through their mines, their every movement every scrape and scramble was as perfect as could be. For although they were not brilliant and bright, they knew precisely the part they played in the great dance.

Some are fated to brilliance; the dwarves' story stated matter-of-factly, while others are destined to the dull and dismal and it is only chance that dictates which. But it was the privilege and honor of the dull brown dwarves, to labor to bring forth the light. By that choice their inmost light blazed unseen while fueling the fire of the brightest of all.

The dwarves' story prompted Astraea to recall what she never had before, the circumstances of her birth, and absent of shame, her voice joined with those of her kin. She sang remembrances of awakening and of being gathered in thin grimy arms as dwarves gazed upon her, basking in her light and admiring the miracle she represented. In song she recounted newfound memories of the dwarves carrying her from the cavern and leaving her at the foot of the mountains. Sacrificing the fruit of their labors, they hid, guarding the baby as they waited for a bright Star to find her. Astraea's voice rose as she remembered being discovered, while the dwarves secretly watched as another of their creations was spirited away to the great dance. At this heartrending memory, Astraea's voice sadly blended with the dwarves in a culminating duet of the losers and the lost. It was only then, that the dwarves' realized Astraea herself was one of their Star babies who they had loved so much, grown and returned home.

Stella imagined how all the energy that seethed through these Nebula Mountains could form a Star. Indeed all Stars in the Milky Way were born in these nurseries, like diamonds in the deep dark earth. The thought made Stella remember that her mother Celeste was in the dark Arctic, waiting to give birth.

The singing stopped and the echoes in the cavern faded to still solemn silence, as a gleaming smile adorned Astraea's face. "I know where I am from," she whispered looking out of the bars of the cell, glowing with pride. "This is my family." Beams of radiant light bathed the dingy dwarves' faces, as the littlest of their brood undid the latch securing the cell. Astraea walked out into the horde of dwarves, approaching them not as unkempt captors, but as one would who has been away far too long and now had returned. In homecoming she walked joyfully through the crowd and bent to touch the cheek of each dwarf.

Stella still clutched the Star baby through the cell's bars. "DubDub?" she asked, "Can you go around these bars and take the baby?"

"I'll do it." Loony offered. He raced out the door and before Stella knew what had happened, the bright baby was in the moon's embrace.

With her arms freed, Stella rushed from the cell frightened at how Loony might treat the baby. Her fears proved unfounded, for when she reached him he was cooing and cuddling the infant gently. Fascinated by the funny imp who held him, the giggling baby glowed even brighter and Loony's warm silvery hue returned as his round head reflected the warm light. The moon man seemed not to notice Stella's presence as she waited for him to relinquish the child. "Okay," she finally said, "I'll take him now." The shadow returned to Loony's face as he possessively squeezed the baby.

"Loony, he doesn't belong to you." Stella held her arms out.

Shielding the baby, the moon man's voice dripped with resentment. "And he doesn't belong to you either! " Stella decided it would be best not to fight over the baby.

Astraea was deep within the crowd of brown dwarves, taking care to meet every one. After bending particularly low, Astraea stood, and Stella was delighted to see in her arms the newborn brown dwarf. Carrying the foul looking baby, the Star woman worked her way through the crowd towards her friends. "This", she said when reaching Loony, "Is the twin of him." She pointed to the infant Loony held.

Astraea reached for the Star child and Stella was relieved to see the moon relinquish his hold. In each arm Astraea cradled a child, beaming down proudly on both. The eyes of the babies met and with a squealing giggle from both, their tiny hands extended and their fingers locked.

"This is truly a joyous occasion. For though we Stars of Empyriania were in the dark as to our past, we now know our origins. Never again shall we fear these mountains, the place of our birth."

The grimy dwarves shared her joy. For, all the brilliant babies they had sent to the world outside, they had known the fate of none. And now here among them, stood evidence of the fruit of their labors, a beautiful radiant Star.

From the crowd came Gliese's voice. "We welcome you home, sister. Long have we been reluctant to show ourselves to the bright ones we might glimpse at the borders of our mountains. We only knew that it was our responsibility to deliver our babies into the open air, where their beauty was more apt to flourish."

Astraea smiled. "Though you are dim, my brother, you are not dark. Within you I see the grandeur of the inmost light that animates all who prize its gifts. I salute you for all your sacrifices in service to the one who calls the tune of the great dance." She executed a perfect curtsy, her head bowing low to the murky floor of nebula. As the Star woman stood, the crowds of dwarfs packed within the cavern all bent at the waist to bow in return.

From above came the bellow of an all too close roar. "Leo is returning to this vicinity." DubDub warned.

"What is that?" Gliese asked, staring at the cavern ceiling.

Terrified, Stella answered. "That's Leo, one of the Zodiac. He works for Moros. They're hunting us!" The dwarves, their bright eyes unblinking, seemed unmoved by her outburst. Pointing to the bright vulnerable baby she continued. "If Moros had his way he'd snuff out all the light in the universe and kill everything, humans, brown dwarves, Stars… even this baby!"

An angry grumble rose from the dingy dwarves as Gliese asked, "Who is this Moros who seeks to snuff out the light? Show him to us and we will put an end to his evil, even if it takes the last of our lives." The cavern rang with the noisy assent of the crowd.

"We're not sure he can be killed, but we are on a mission to thwart his plan. I need to make it to the end of the universe, where I can to wind the Celestial Clockwork." Pulling the map from her pocket, Stella showed the dwarf the blue circle that marked the inland ocean. "We need to get here," she poked the spot on the map, "as fast as we can."

Gliese whistled a long and low tune that riled the crowd about him. When the resulting murmurs had died down and every dwarf had been informed of the perils they faced, Gliese began to direct his army. "The new born Star is not safe here." A group of dwarves, maybe twenty or so, stepped from the crowd. "They will bring it to a safe spot outside the mountains, and stand guard until some bright Stars pass nearby to care for it."

One of the dwarves took the bright baby from Astraea, who sighed like her heart was being yanked from her chest. As the troop of dwarves disappeared into one of the tunnels, the light of the newborn Star brightly lit the muddy hole and then faded. "Perhaps someday", Astraea hoped, clutching the dingy dwarf baby tighter to her breast, "I may meet that child again on the Great Plains, and join in song with him."

Gliese continued with his plans. "We will guide you through the mountains and defend you as best we can. We must leave now before we are discovered." His hands reached for the dwarf to which had Astraea clung, "You must leave the child, to allow him take his place in our great work."

"But he is only a baby!" Astraea countered. "Who will care for him?"

Gliese took the baby dwarf from the Star's arms and placed it on the dirty floor. Without a pause it began to dig into the mud and form piles, as if knowing exactly what to do. For a second Stella thought she saw, through the caked dirt on the Gliese' face, the proud look of a father. The baby dug a pile of muddy nebula from the ground, stopping its excavations only to wipe its dirty face with a thin arm, smearing mud across its cheeks. Then with armfuls of mud it stood intrepidly on its toddler legs and marched off to deposit its load on a newly accumulated mound. As it tottered back to its pit, Stella and Astraea saw on its face, a smile happier than any ever seen on the bright planes of Empyriania.

"We do our work because it is what we love to do, just as song and dance is the delight of those who live on the plains. Now we must hurry, before the enemy learns where you are." Gliese led his guests forward as the sea of dwarves parted before them, and as the four passed through, they swiftly closed back in behind them.

"I think we might be safe with the dwarves traveling by our side." Astraea mentioned to her friends as they trudged toward a muddy tunnel.

Stella agreed, "I'm glad they're with us. I don't think Leo knows what he'd be getting into if he tangled with them."

"I would be very happy," DubDub remarked," If we never encountered Leo again, or any other of the Zodiac."

"Me too." Stella agreed, as they climbed up into a dank hole.

"Me three!" Astraea laughed from behind.

The absence of a snarky response froze Stella in her tracks, and each of dwarves that had been rushing behind in line, careened into the one ahead. "We have to go back! We've lost Loony!"

Stella pushed her way back through the crumpled crowd, all the while wondering why she should even care where the moon man had gone and if she might be better off without him, but she knew she couldn't just leave him behind. If she completed her mission and got back home, it just wouldn't be the same if the moon weren't in the sky.

Racing back to the cell, Stella found Loony inside, entertaining a dingy dwarf who sat cross-legged on the muddy floor before him. By the enraptured look on the dwarf's face, she could see that Loony must be spinning quite a tale. "Without me," the ball-headed imp bragged, proudly parading before his audience of one, "they would never have gotten this far. I've had to lead them all along, and if they're ever going to find the clockwork, it'll be me who'll have to show them the way. Why, I'll probably have to wind that clock, if they want the job done right."

When Stella stepped through the doorway of the cell, the little dwarf watched her entrance with bright eyes that peeked from a mud encrusted face. Loony however, remained absorbed in his self aggrandizement. "I'm not sure why I even brought that human along. You know what they say, don't you?" The dwarf's eyes widened in anticipation, of what threatened to be, a most important bit of information. "They say humans like her are the reason Earth is sick in the first place. Someone told me that everything might be a whole lot better if there were no humans at all. And, you know, I'm starting to think he might be right."

"And who told you that?" When Loony turned, Stella was standing behind him, hands on hips and foot angrily tapping in the splashing mud.

"Uhh, uhh, no one." He muttered nervously, his face turning an autumnal shade of red.

"Who told you such a horrible thing? Who have you been talking to? "

"I said no one, okay? Now leave me alone!" The moon man snapped nastily, "What do you want anyway? Can't you see I'm busy?"

"Well, we have to go; Gliese is leading us to the inland sea. Everyone is waiting for you."

The moon man scowled. "Maybe you should go without me; I don't think I want to help you anymore."

Stella didn't want to leave him, but there was nothing she could do. She left the cell, and then turned back for one last attempt. "Well, I guess I'll have to figure out something to tell Terra." She used the saddest voice she could. "I'm sure she's going to miss you terribly."

"Do you think so?" Loony asked.

"I sure do. Why, she'd be so heartbroken," Stella assured. "I was sure that when you came home from our mission, and were such a big hero, that she'd be the proudest Planet in the solar system, proud of her brave clever moon."

The moon man raised his cratered brows. "You really think so?"

"Thinking," Stella stated, "has nothing to do with it. It's just the way it is."

Loony turned toward the dwarf who had been industriously scraping mud from the floor while waiting for the exchange to be over, and huffed, "I have work to do. Catch you later." With that he marched out of the cell, leaving Stella chasing after him.

When Stella regained her friends, the tunnel resounded with the sound of feet slogging through thick viscous sludge. Their route was full of twists and turns with many confusing splits, but like ants navigating their tunnels, the dwarves marched on with unrelenting vigor and showed no doubt in their choice of direction. At times the tunnel angled so steeply that the travelers needed to crawl up the slippery nebulous slopes. In no time Stella's clothes were caked with mud, while grime covered the Star woman's gown, hiding her light under a grungy crust. As filthy as they were, it was DubDub who was taking the worst of it. The thick mud was clogging his pulleys and gears, and Stella worried just how much abuse his mechanisms could take. Slowing down her already lagging pace to allow DubDub to catch up, she asked. "How are you doing?"

"I'm coping, but I'll be glad when we're out of this muck."

"So will I", she agreed.

"Be quiet!" The voice of Gliese hissed from ahead, "We are nearing the surface and do not want to be detected by the enemy."

As the dinginess of the tunnel decreased and more light filtered in from above, Stella was reinvigorated by the prospect of an end to the climb. She risked a whisper of encouragement. "Almost there, DubDub, and then I'll give you a good winding."

Coming to a narrowing in the tunnel the climbers funneled into a single line. Stella tried not to be separated from her friends, but Loony was already far ahead climbing at the front of the pack. The dull clatter of DubDub's wooden limbs behind her was a comfort for the girl, signaling that she was not without friends in the increasingly claustrophobic tunnel.

Stella let out a yelp of pain as tiny hands tugged at her arms and wrists, pulling her roughly through a bottleneck in the tightly constricted tunnel. She felt herself being squeezed and then…*Plop*! Like a cork unplugged was released from the hole.

After flying through the air and landing in the mud, Stella realized she had reached the surface. At the narrow crevice she had popped through, quite a commotion was in progress, as two wooden arms were being yanked mercilessly from the ground by a distressed group of dwarves. Though they struggled mightily to pull DubDub through the opening, their only result was a series of pained cries. "Be careful!! You'll break him!" Stella shouted as she rushed to her friend's assistance. Pushing aside dwarves who were viciously wrenching one of DubDub's arms Stella looked into the crevice. It was painfully obvious that the mechanical man was stuck.

"I can't move!" A bouquet of desperate eyes stared up helplessly.

"Maybe if Astraea pushed?" Stella suggested.

A grunt came from the hole and the artificial eyes winced in pain. "I think she is!" DubDub whimpered.

Gliese appeared at Stella's shoulder, worried and jabbering. "What is the problem? We cannot stay here. Dark forces will corner us if we tarry!"

Loony, unable to offer any helpful suggestions but appearing more than pleased to put pressure on Stella, "I'm not waiting for him, let's just leave him behind."

"We can't leave him!" Stella blurted, annoyed the moon man would even suggest the idea. "Astraea is stuck behind him. We have to get them out."

"Have it your way then," Loony chortled, taking a seat on the muddy floor. "Just let me know when you're ready to give up."

Stella addressed the cluster of worried eyes in the hole. "Do you think if I pushed and Astraea pulled you could slide back down a bit?"

"Let me try. I think maybe, if you…" The mechanical man hesitated.

"If I what?" Stella asked in desperation, "What should I do DubDub, tell me? Hurry, we don't have much time."

"Well," he suggested timidly, "Perhaps if you stepped on my head."

Gingerly placing her foot into the crevice Stella found a spot where she wouldn't crush any of DubDub's instruments. "If you can hear me Astraea, pull now!" Feeling a shift beneath her foot, Stella responded by standing with all her weight on the wooden head.

"It's working!" Stella cheered as DubDub slid down the hole.

"I have him!" Astraea shouted from within.

That was fine, Stella thought, but what now? Even if Astraea could slide through, and she probably could, being much more limber than the awkward wooden man, DubDub was still stranded. Stella addressed the open hole, as if seeking counsel from some oracle. "Does anyone have any idea as to what to do?"

"Perhaps there's another way out?" A voice suggested.

"All other openings to the surface are far from here." Gliese intoned with little emotion.

Stella conveyed the message to her friends below. "It's too far; we need to get you out through this hole. Let's think of some other idea."

With brazen casualness Loony interrupted Stella's concentration. "Tear him apart." He quipped.

Stella fumed. "Loony! If you're not going to help, be quiet. I'm trying to think!"

"Maybe," The moon man responded, "If you weren't so quick to correct me you'd see I was trying to help."

"Tear DubDub apart? Are you kidding?" She felt like ripping Loony apart.

DubDub's shouted from the hole. "Maybe that is not such a bad idea."

"What are you talking about? We can't tear you apart!"

"Maybe you can. After all, I was built in parts. I don't see why you couldn't dismantle me and slide my pieces through the hole. Let me try something." DubDub said over a creaking noise rising from the hole. "Grab this." A hand extended from the hole. Stella took it and pulled, almost fainting as it came out absent the rest of a body.

"Oh my!" she cried, and holding the arm as if it were a live snake, laid it carefully on the ground.

"Now if Astraea could help me," a wheezing voice from the hole asked. There was another creaking noise and a leg poked from the hole. A horrified Stella took it gingerly by the ankle and stacked it next to the first appendage.

Another leg, another arm, and then the girl waited for what she knew would be the hardest part for her to bear. A horrible wrenching sound emitted from the hole and Astraea's voice called up. "Be careful with this." Grasping a coil, Stella pulled and from the hole burst DubDub's lifeless head, its mechanical eyes staring blankly into space and hanging limp on their stalks.

"Look at that!" Loony shrieked hysterically. "I've never seen anything so funny!"

Stella didn't want to drop the head in the mud, but she couldn't bear to hold the dead head any longer. "Take this Loony! And be careful with it." Stella wondered if she had done the right thing as the moon man took the head and laughed.

"This piece might be a tight fit." Astraea said from below. "You might have to twist it a bit to get it through."

A wooden box slid up through the crevice, and Stella grasped its edges with both hands pulling as Astraea pushed, shouldering the bulk of the weight. From inside the box came a sound that reminded Stella of her father's toolbox, all clanking metal and shifting tools. With the help of the dwarves, she dragged the box up onto the ground. Mere seconds after Astraea emerged and even while covered with mud, she rose to the surface like a vision of beauty in this dirty dingy land. "Now, let's reconstruct our friend, and we can be on our way," she suggested.

Gliese, who had been hovering impatiently, disagreed. "We have been here too long. It is not safe to stay another moment. We must keep moving if we are to elude your pursuer."

Before Stella could object, Gliese made a series of gestures and a number of dwarves quickly gathered up the parts of DubDub. Six or seven hauled away the body, while two or three took each of the arms and legs. Stella looked to see where Loony had gone with the head, and spotted him on a rough platform of nebula stuff, surrounded by a small audience of dingy dwarves who were enjoying the entertainment he was gleefully supplying.

"Alas, Poor DubDub!" Loony orated grimly, holding the lifeless head aloft. "I knew him well!" Then cackling wildly, he spun the head on his finger like a lopsided basketball.

"Stop that!" Stella, horrified to see the lifeless head spinning in the air, pushed through the crowd of amused dwarves. "Don't play with DubDub's head!" Blankly staring eyes twisted limply as she jumped on the platform and snatched the head away. "Loony! How could you!"

Loony snarled, "I'm really getting tired of you always stopping me just when I'm having fun. This whole trip has been all about you, and your problems."

Stella was exasperated. "It's not about me, Loony, it's about stopping Moros. You know that!"

Loony whispered under his breath, but Stella heard the words sharp and clear. "Sometimes I think he would be more fun."

As the moon man turned angrily away, landmarks seen from Earth, familiar craters and mountains passed before Stella's eyes. As his head spun, a side of him came into view that she had never seen before, something she had often presumed was there but had always been afraid to admit existed; the utter lightlessness of the dark side of the moon. Recoiling from the sight, Stella stumbled away. Only the firm hand of Astraea stopped her flight.

"Do you see that?" Stella fearfully asked the Star woman.

Putting her arm around Stella's shoulder Astraea addressed the moon. "Loony," she said, and as she spoke a soft light shone from her face and caressed the darkness of the moon's orb. "Loony, listen to me." The angry shadow on the moon's face retreated as Astraea spoke sensibly and simply, "Old Sol is counting on you. Earth is counting on you. We're all counting on you. Now please, Moon of Earth, come with us."

Silver light dappled the moon as he asked, "Why does Stella always stop me just when I'm having fun?" The little man's whining tone was exactly like that of Tim and Pace when they were asked to clean their room or put their dishes in the sink.

"We're not here to have fun. We have a job to do." Stella snapped back.

"But I want to have some fun!" Loony roared as his face rapidly turned dark.

"There is no time for this!" Gliese growled, with his patience at an end. His fellow dwarves, who waited with various parts of DubDub, balanced on their heads, whistled shrilly in agreement.

Sensing the dwarves were not going to wait any longer, Astraea tried to reason with the lunatic. "Okay Loony. So, now that you've had your fun, we really have to get going. We don't want to be trapped here by the Zodiac."

As if in response to her words, a roar echoed through the canyon. Gliese tugged at Stella's jacket. "We have to leave, now! Your enemy is near."

Astraea walked up to the platform and extended her hand. "Come along, Moon of Earth. We need to go." She bent and kissed the cheek of the moon and a scintillating crescent lit at the touch. Surprisingly to all who watched, Loony took the offered hand to quietly follow.

They trudged onward silently and stealthily, the dwarves leading them expertly through crevices and cracks, up high slopes and down steep declines, with all aware the slightest sound might alert Moros' minions to their passage. Loony however, was behaving less than cautiously. On more than one occasion Stella looked back to see him lagging behind, almost as if he wanted to be caught. When she would whisper to him to keep up, he would respond loudly, causing everyone grave concern, "I'm coming, don't rush me. I'm moving as fast as I can." Ever since seeing his dark side Stella had been very concerned about the moon man, and as he straggled behind muttering crazily, she could only hope he could keep his mischievousness in check.

After a strenuous climb up a particularly steep cliff, the dwarves dropped their loads. It was the first time they had stopped to rest. Astraea studied the pile of parts and wondered if she could ever reassemble DubDub. Taking advantage of the moment, Stella pulled the parchment from her pocket. Pointing to the sailboat shaped mountain sketched deep within the map's nebula range, she asked a particularly filthy dwarf who had been curiously watching the operation. "Are we near here?"

Stella took the dwarf's guttural grunt for a response as it leaned its ugly head nearer and looked inquisitively to where she pointed on the map. Extending a thin scraggly finger toward a hill, he nodded his head enthusiastically, affirming Stella's suspicion that they were not far from the inland sea. Checking the Compyxx, she was excited to find it pointed in the same direction and rushed to Astraea who was trying to adjust a linkage of gears and pulleys. "This dwarf," Stella said, "believes we're getting closer to the inland sea. My Compyxx says the same."

"I imagine we'll be seeing its shores shortly then," Astraea replied, studying the map. "Perhaps when we rebuild DubDub, he can see something we cannot."

Taking the head Stella tried to fit it to the body. Astraea bent to help with the reconnection, searching at the headless torso's neck for the correct belt to attach to a pulley protruding from the lifeless head. Looking into the casing that served as DubDub's body, Stella saw its innards were even more complicated than she would have thought. Crowded tightly and precisely into the wooden box, was an elaborately engineered arrangement. Expertly tooled parts joined together in the most amazing ways to form complex assemblages, leaving Stella to marvel at the ingenuity of Jacques Vaucason and how one man alone could accomplish such an astounding feat.

Studying a leather belt, Stella pulled it carefully onto an empty pulley. As it seemed to be a correct fit, she continued with the Star woman to join head to body. When Astraea was satisfied their work was done, she reached down to turn the knob on the clockwork man's chest, but as her fingers brushed the dial she stopped. "Perhaps you should do this, Stella. It might be good practice."

Stella reached down to DubDub's chest, pulled the dial out from its recess, and gave it a series of quick turns. With each, she felt the spring inside tightening. "Be careful not to over wind!" Astraea cautioned. Stella gave the dial half a turn, and feeling the resistance intensify, stopped. Immediately gears could be heard whirring and bellows wheezing.

The girl whispered into the side of the automaton's head "DubDub? Are you there? Do you think you can see the ocean?"

From the mechanical man's head, a periscope rose and scanned about. "No, I can't see the ocean; these cliffs are much too high for me to get a look at what might lay beyond. Perhaps a higher vantage will reveal something. If it's not a problem, could you reattach my legs?" Grabbing a leg, Stella copied Astraea's actions; first attaching the polished wooden ball at the end of the leg into the socket at DubDub's hip and then tightening down the screw that held it in place. There were three belts that ran from the body to the leg and as Astraea attached each to its pulley Stella did the same.

"Stella?" DubDub mentioned timidly. "That might not be correct. It doesn't feel quite right." Seeing her mistake, Stella slipped the faulty belt off and replaced it with another, spinning the pulley until the belt slid into its groove. "Yes, that's better!" the mechanical man exclaimed happily.

When both legs were attached, together the ladies lifted their mechanical friend and stood DubDub on his feet. Staggering for only a second, he quickly found his balance. "That's much better. Now my arms, please?" The girl and Star woman found the arms and hurried to attach them. "I think perhaps, that you should recheck the thumbs?" DubDub suggested.

Switching arms with Astraea, Stella went back to work and soon heard a reassuring click as gears slipped into place. The reassembled automaton tested the limbs while effusively thanking his friends.

"You're welcome, DubDub. Now, can you see anything?" Stella inquired anxiously. "Do you see the ocean?"

The mechanical man climbed on a nearby out cropping. "No, still nothing, just more mountains and…and…" A distinct tone of terror possessed his voice as he fell backwards, his wiry limbs flailing in the air as mechanical hands grasped for a hold in the empty air.

In a blur of light Astraea moved to effortlessly catch the automaton before he hit the ground. "What did you see?" she asked, placing him on the ground.

His jaw chattered as the petrified clock watcher sputtered. "Leo! Up ahead!" "He's seen us!"

Scanning the peaks for their leonine pursuer, Stella saw a dark shadow bounding along the side of the ravine, leaping from precipice to precipice. As the shape approached, her heart pounded with fear.

Loony snapped sarcastically. "I wonder what it's going to feel like being eaten by a lion."

Pulling her sword from its sheath, Astraea commanded, "Warn the dwarves!"

"Hurry! Hide! Leo's coming! We need to hide!" In a panic Stella rushed through the sprawling crowd of dwarves. They barely moved as she worked her way through the throng. Gliese met her with a scowl, unhappy with the volume of the warning. "Gliese, Leo is coming!" He looked towards the mountains, and every head in his troop turned with him. Whistling sharply he made a quick series of hand signals and with that, all the dwarfs instantly melted into the landscape leaving Stella and her friends alone in the canyon.

"I knew we couldn't trust them!" Loony shouted. "I knew it!"

"Be quiet Loony!" Stella cried, seeing there was nowhere to hide, "Astraea, what are we going to do?"

The Star woman gravely answered. "I will stand here and fight, there is no other choice." Bending to the girl she whispered. "If I fall, you must escape. You are our only hope."

Looking around at the steep cliffs all around, Stella knew there would be no escape. "You won't fall, you'll win. You have to!"

Astraea's eyes still glittered and shined, but Stella saw they no longer held the confidence once so evident. "I am afraid I cannot win this battle. The power of the darkness has grown with the failing of the clockwork, and I have weakened. Now, Leo is too strong for me to fight alone."

A roar filled the air and DubDub whimpered. "He's here!"

From a nearby pinnacle, Leo with the dull stars of his constellation darkly visible within its body looked down upon his prey. Drawing her sword and holding it aloft, Astraea moved forward to defend her friends. Stella reached out to take the wooden hand of DubDub, surprised at how comforting the cool piece of carved wood could be.

. "She can't beat Leo. She's doomed." Loony commented coolly.

Leo roared, though it was Moros' voice that sounded through the jaws. "You are correct, moon! All who cling to the dying light are doomed. Only fools believe they can escape the fate allotted them. Now put down your sword, Star, and there is still a chance I will kill you quickly."

Astraea rebuked the shadowy figure above. "Chance? I ask not for a chance from one so debauched such as you. Kill us? You have not that ability, ignorant creature of the abyss! We who choose light will live forever in its blaze! Now delay your destiny no longer and come meet my sword."

Leo jumped from his perch and landed deftly in the mud before the travelers. The beast moved like a shadow slowly circling the quartet; while in its opened jaws, dark teeth like ebony blades dismally reflected the light of Astraea's sword. Leo moved in, testing the Star woman's resolve, and then backed off laughing at the terror his feints instilled. "In payment for your insolence I will extinguish you slowly Star, but first you will watch as I slowly rip your friends apart!"

The beast's crouched to pounce, but before his paws left the floor, armies of the brown dwarves were covering its dark form. Like a gush of mud they seethed from every crevice, flooding from every crack to converge upon Leo who buckled beneath the weight of his attackers. With strenuous exertion the downed Lion rose from the floor, struggling to shake the tiny assailants from its broad back. Handfuls of dwarves were dislodged, looking like nothing more than gobs of slimy mud filling the air. Any unlucky enough to fall near the frenzied beast were viciously slashed by its razor sharp claws. But the onslaught continued as dwarves raced around Stella and her friends to take their place in the unrelenting attack. Clinging to the coal black mane and the whipping tail, climbing up the thick columns of legs, diving from above and jumping from below the dense horde swarmed until the beast was completely covered in a carpet of antic clay. Thrashing violently Leo strove to free himself, but his attackers held even more doggedly as hundreds of tiny hands tore at the frenzied beast's flesh. Stella, along with DubDub and Loony, fell back from the fray, overwhelmed by the violence of the dwarves' assault.

Then gleaming sword in hand, Astraea strode forward wading waist deep through the torrent of dwarves. The lion reared up with a fearsome roar, towering over the radiant woman. A razor tipped paw swung through the air and Astraea spun to nimbly dodge the attack. Completing the turn with a powerful thrust she drove her blade upwards into the throat of the lion, light piercing darkness as the sword sunk to its hilt. The tip of the blade revealed itself at the top of the beast's head; a luminous triangle nestled within the dark tangle of the mane.

For a moment Leo hung there impaled, his head suspended on Astraea's sword. The dwarves, feeling the lion's body go limp, halted their attack. Then like dust in the wind, Leo's body dissipated leaving the hundreds of dwarves that had encased the beast, hanging in the air. They held the shape of the lion for just an instant before collapsing, when from the air fell a shower of brown dwarves who hit the ground like so many mud patties.

There was a scramble of confusion as the dwarves extricated themselves from the resulting heap. As the dwarves scrambled away, strewn on the muddy ground were a handful of crumpled bodies.

Sheathing her flaming sword, Astraea walked towards the dying husks. "These are the members of Leo's constellation. No longer will they be held in the sway of darkness, unless Moros can control death itself." She stopped at one body, a charred and perverse remnant of the glorious Star it had once been. "This is all that remains of Regulus… he was one of the brightest stars of the heavens, and now his light is extinguished. Woe to those who cast their lot with Moros'!" She knelt in the mud beside the body, lifted its head into her hands and began to sob. "Regulus was my friend when we were young. I cannot bear that I have failed him and allowed him to be seduced by the powers of darkness."

The fallen Star stirred and gasping in pain, his eyes opened to narrow slits. "Astraea? Is that you?"

"I am here, Regulus"

"Forgive me, my sister. I believed the lies of the great deceiver, and obeying his commands, sought to disrupt the great dance." Regulus wheezed. "I wish only to somehow mend the damage I have done before I fade."

Wiping the sheen of black oil from the brow of the dying Star, Astraea asked gently. "Where is Moros? Is he near?"

The dying Star's body convulsed in terror at Moros' name, "He sees …everything!!" His hand like a blackened burned claw clutched Astraea's luminous arm for solace. "He, he…he, he is everywhere!" The words came with a choking effort, that Stella though she could hate this Star for his part in such evil schemes, instead felt pity.

Like two boiled eggs, the incinerated Star's eyes bulged, popping from charred lids. Muscles tore shriveled lips as a grimace of terror seized the scorched face. With a shuddering wheeze, Regulus spat out his final words. "He is here!" An icy wind blew though the canyon and Regulus' body disintegrated into ash escaping Astraea's arms and flying in a turbulent swirl to the air, where it joined a passing cloud of smog.

From above came a laugh of such malicious gloating that Stella quickly held her ears to block the poisonous sound. "Each and every Star's light will be snuffed! Then all that lives will know the endless embrace of death!" It was the voice of Moros, now with a sickening neighing twist. Whistles of alarm piped as the dwarves spotted on a peak high above, a stark silhouette.

"Aries!" DubDub wailed. Already dwarves were nimbly scaling the steep cliffs and making their way in droves towards the sinister goat. They moved swiftly, eager to drag this horned evil from its lofty peak.

The constellation looked down, scoffing. "Your allies fight bravely, human, but they cannot thwart destiny! The loss of Leo is of no consequence. He would have died anyway! Servants of the light, the time of your end is now!" As the first wave of dwarves reached its perch with a mocking "Bah!" the giant ram jumped away, and bounding from mountaintop to mountaintop leapt out of sight.

"Fear not," said Gliese, as the valley drained of dwarves. "We will track the goat and deal it the same fate as the lion. Our mountains will be purged of Moros' influence." The armies of dwarves disappeared over the ridge, hot in pursuit of the darkness that had defiled their domain. Gliese held back, though Stella could see that he was eager to join the pursuit. "Where you seek to go is beyond the ridge ahead. We will watch you as we track the goat and its allies. No one will stop you on your passage through these hills, this is our oath." The dirty dwarf turned to leave.

"Gliese! Please wait!" Astraea called out and going to him, knelt and put her arms around the dirty dwarf. "Thank you, my brother! Perhaps someday in happier times, I hope I may have the pleasure of a dance with you."

The leader of the dwarves scurried away, following the last of his troops and leaving the four travelers alone in the canyon. Stella studied her compatriots and tried not to think about how they looked; four dirty tired beings, alone in a cosmic wilderness, stalked by deadly foes, and unsure of where their next step would take them. If this was on whom the fate of the universe hung, if these were the best champions the universe could muster, then maybe the universe, Stella thought, wasn't worth all the trouble.

"I guess we should get going," Stella said warily eyeing the hilltops, "In case Aries comes back."

Astraea, dutifully but wearily began the march. DubDub rearranged the mess on his head, pushing devices back into place, and followed. Only Loony didn't move, but sat on a clump of nebula, arms folded, sulking and obstinate. "Come on!" Stella pleaded, "It's not safe to stay here!"

Pulling the Compyxx globe from within her parka and separating the two halves, Stella looked inside to see its arrow indicating the same low ridge where Gliese had pointed. Though she trusted the dwarf, she couldn't forget how the Compyxx had gotten them lost in the mountains and almost caught by Leo. She wondered if somehow Venus might have given her the Compyxx, only to thwart her efforts or worse, because she worked for Moros. Thinking maybe it would be best to leave the device here in the mud and be done with it; Stella lifted her hand to throw, only stopping when her finger felt the tiny gold nub protruding from the globe's Arctic pole.

She dropped her hand and inspected the ball whose wooden surface and metallic chain all meant one thing, home. "Even if I'm not getting back, there are still people there who need me." Stella thought, "I'm not going to let them down, even if Venus tricked me," she concluded, there was no doubt Moros was real. If he was trying to stop me, then that means I must be dangerous to him, and that must mean I still have a chance to defeat him."

"We're going that way." Stella said sticking the Compyxx back under her parka and walking off towards the ridge. Her three companions recognized the resolve in her voice, and that was reason enough for them to follow.

19 THE STARFISH POOL

Eager to see the great ocean of which the Stars had told her, Stella forged ahead with mud sloshing beneath her feet. "Come on, we're almost there! The ocean should be right over this hill." Astraea followed behind with DubDub clattering after. Loony continued his sullen strut, kicking up clods as he sauntered. Reaching the summit Stella suddenly paused.

"What do you see?" Astraea asked as Stella proceeded out of sight over the hill. "Is it the ocean? Is it…?" Her voice trailed off as she reached where her human friend had halted.

"What is it?" asked DubDub excitedly chasing after his friends, with his eyes fluttering behind like cans trailing a car painted, *just married.* "Can you see the sea? Is there a distant shore?" The eyes on the clock-watcher's head bulged, eager for new sights to record and as he reached the top of the ridge all his devices unfurled, searching the endless ranges of nebula that confronted him.

"Where is the ocean? Where are the crashing waves? Where are the endless depths? And where," the mud splattered automaton asked as he slogged down the muddy hill to where his friends stood in a small hollow, "is the place that I can wash this mess off me?"

"Look down." Stella sighed.

At his feet the mechanical man saw neatly cut into the nebula ground, a circular pool no wider than a few arm's lengths across. "What is this?" he asked, his eyes pointing down into the puddle. "Where is the vast sea we were to cross to the end of the universe?"

The filthy crew of travelers stood perplexed around the pool. The fluid within was the color of milky coffee. Stella fished out the map. The circle that marked the inland ocean was surrounded with a number of expertly sketched mountains. Astraea put a finger on one drawn near the circle. "This one here, that looks like a foot sticking up from the ground, it matches that peak."

"And here," Stella said jabbing into the parchment," this one that looks like a melting telephone, is right there."

"And that mountain," DubDub pointed to the sailboat mountain that rose behind the small clearing," matches this one." The three mountains that surrounded the small pool were also drawn on the map and surrounded the small circle with the wavy lines.

"This is it then." Stella said despondently. "This is the place the map has marked. But how could this be the way out of our galaxy?" she asked looking down into the pool. On her reflection's face was an expression of utter bewilderment.

"That map is wrong, and those dwarves tricked you. This is just a puddle. We're not going anywhere. I guess its time we quit." Loony offered. "Maybe Moros will still let us surrender."

Stella found it easy to ignore the moon man's negativity, as deep within the pool small minnow like shapes appeared darting about. Kneeling at the edge to get a better look she touched a finger carefully to the fluid. Ripples moved across the pond's surface, fracturing the mysterious creatures below into shimmering fragments. Loony edged next to her. "What are those things?" he asked down her neck.

Stella had never seen anything quite like them before. "They must be some kind of fish. Star fish, I guess you'd call them." She said spreading her elbows to reclaim some space.

"Starfish? I've never heard of Starfish." Loony pushed closer to see, upsetting the girl's balance.

"Loony! Stop pushing!" Stella shouted, flapping at the surface of the water. Before she knew what was happening, she was plunging headfirst into the starfish pool with barely a chance to catch a breath. Tumbling down she quickly lost all sense of which way was up. Though stunned, she realized immediately that if she didn't want to drown she would have to reach the surface quickly. Stella desperately searched for the hole through which she had fallen, but all around were only endless beige depths and the strange minnow like creatures. Alarmed at her dilemma, she whirled wildly about and immediately butted against a barrier that had not been there only seconds before.

The wall she faced stretched into the distance on all sides, and it sank soft and spongy beneath her touch. From outside the pool she hadn't noticed any walls, so it seemed only logical that this was the underside of the land above. She searched along this surface, moving hand over hand, anxious to find where she fallen through. Frustrated by her lack of success, she screamed, "Loony! You've really done it now! When I get back, you'd better watch out!"

As the words ballooned from her mouth Stella realized there was something very, very strange about this oceanic place. Holding her hand before her face warm breath swirled in her palm. She inhaled, tentatively at first and then deeply. "Yes!" she laughed giddily, "I'm breathing!"

Stella wasn't so surprised. Just as the spaces she had been traveling through were not filled with air, or at least not the kind of air that filled the atmosphere on Earth, she had somehow been able to breathe quite easily all along her journey. And now whatever she was swimming in, she could breathe that too. "And I guess that's all that really matters," thought Stella.

Thinking that if she could get far enough away, she might see the hole, she kicked off from the wall. Its spongy surface gave her feet a nice spring, and as she darted out into the ocean, she saw in the distance the minnow like "starfish" drifting peacefully through the endless depths. When she thought she had gone far enough, Stella turned to discover that what she faced was not a wall at all, but the broad side of a colossal creature larger than a whale. Quickly surveying the gargantuan body from its long gracefully flowing tail, to what could only be called a head, complete with a small round eye, it took Stella only a heartbeat to surmise that these gigantic creatures were the same *minnows,* she had seen from the pond's rim.

Looking around she suddenly realized that the other "starfish" swimming, were of equal magnitude and were slowly moving toward her, the small speck that had fallen into their ocean. Slowly the whales began to circle her, inspecting this most alien of visitors.

It brought to Stella's mind, how once in Florida her family had visited an aquarium where a friend of her father's had worked. Invited to play with the dolphins, Celeste and Stella slid into the cool water and were immediately surrounded by the friendly sea creatures. The dolphins seamlessly integrated the humans into their casual play, swimming around and under the mother and daughter with casual ease. Stella would never forget the dolphins' eyes as they moved past her, gazing in absolute unending contemplation and radiating pure and simple joy.

Now, these whales that drifted about the young girl in their midst, shared that same serenity but on a much grander scale. As they approached, each of the colossal whales emitted a pure tone. Stella felt a tickle in her ears, as if a tuning fork had been struck. The vibrant sound that filled the ocean hummed like a crystal glass whose rim had been stroked, and with their tranquil songs engulfing her, Stella understood that their vibrations composed the very substance in which she was suspended.

The lyrical leviathans of the deep held Stella in their gaze as they drifted past. She could see in those giant eyes, a reflection of her body stretched across those shiny pools. As one of these creatures contemplated her longer than the others, Stella felt certain it was the one she had found herself next to when first entering this strange ocean. Something within that massive whale tugged at her heart, and feeling inexplicably homesick, Stella swam towards its eye. Holding her position nearby, she could soon see more clearly what lay beyond its translucent membrane. Peering over the eye's rim was the fiery head of Astraea, and at her side was DubDub keenly watching her every movement. Stella waved from the vast ocean of the cosmos and her astonished friends waved back. Over their shoulders millions of glowing stars burned brightly within the whale and Stella knew instantly that the giant creature she swam alongside of was in fact the Milky Way, and somewhere amongst those millions of stars was her home planet.

It was a beautiful galaxy that lay within the body of the whale. Marvelously sculpted nebula floated like candy colored clouds, while pulses of warm light within foretold of stars to be born. There were novas here and there, raging so bright that one had to squint just to look at them. Stella sighed at all she could see from this whale's eye view, and wondered what lay within the eyes of all the other galactic whales that swam within this universal sea.

Remembering that the pool or "inland sea" would lead to the end of the universe, Stella pulled out the Compyxx and made a silent wish for it to show her the way. Opening the carved wooden lid, she saw the thin arrow within pointed into the coffee colored depths. Deciding to investigate, Stella gestured to her friends with one finger straight up to indicate she'd be gone only a minute, and then a full flat hand to let them know they should wait and not follow. Astraea nodded at the signals and the bobbing of DubDub's eyes mirrored that acknowledgment. With all the mechanical man's scopes fixed so intently on her, Stella imagined she could go rather far and he would still be able to see her, which made her feel much safer.

Swimming out into the ocean, it struck Stella that its color was one she had seen before. "It's, cosmic latte," she told herself, and smiled thinking of where she had first heard the term.

It was on Earth at the restaurant her family went to for breakfast every Sunday. While they waited to order, Stella's father scribbled equations on the paper tablecloth, writing numbers here and adding a string of symbols there. As he worked he consulted a printed readout of a long series of numbers. "Uh huh," he said, before he bent back to his figures erasing a digit and replacing it with a quick stroke of his pencil.

With her curiosity getting the better of her, Stella finally had to ask though she knew that her father would not give her his attention until he had worked out his problem. "What're you trying to figure out?"

While looking up only slightly, he murmured, "just a moment Stella, please," and returned to his equations. The waiter came with their drinks, and Stella sipped her orange juice waiting for her father to resurface from the depths of numbers and symbols in which he was submerged. "Uh huh, Uh huh." He muttered, and from the tone of his voice she knew he had almost reached a conclusion. With a quick flurry, he wrote out a line of numbers and with a flourish underlined it.

"What is it?" Stella asked eager to know to what solution he had come.

"Watch!" Perceval said before taking a large gulp of his coffee. Then he picked up a small container of cream and began to pour it into his cup while

stirring quickly with his spoon. He studied the cup's contents a moment, took another gulp, and poured in more of the creamer.

"Almost..." he said stirring again, then sipped and carefully poured just the smallest drop of the creamer into the paling coffee, stirred once more, checked the numbers on his paper, then sat back with a beaming grin of accomplishment.

Stella looked into the cup. "Okay?" she asked dumbfounded, "What am I looking at?"

Her father was so pleased with himself he bubbled with glee. "This," he said, pointing to the milky coffee in his cup, "is cosmic latte."

Stella wondered for a moment if perhaps her father hadn't gone over the edge this time, and looked over at her mother who was too busy trying to control Tim and Pace as they amused each other by shooting spitballs, Celeste did not notice her daughter's glance.

Stella turned back to her father. "Cosmic latte?" she repeated incredulously.

"Yes, Cosmic Latte!" Perceval beamed and picking up the paper covered with equations, he pointed to the string of underlined numbers and then to the light beige in his cup. "This is the numerical equivalent of the color of the coffee in my cup. The numbers are the average of all colors in the universe, which if blended together would have a shade precisely as this."

Then Stella understood and her grin grew as big as her father's. "Cosmic Latte!" she laughed.

Celeste, having gotten the boys under control, turned to the grinning duo of father and daughter and asked, "Now what has gotten into you?" But before they could answer, the waiter had come with their food, stacks of pancakes and heaps of eggs and mouthwatering strips of crisp bacon, and the family hungrily dug in.

All this, Stella remembered in an instant with the events in her mind moving much faster than those outside, and as she returned from those happy memories she found herself back in dire straights.

With so many others of the galactic whales floating about, Stella wanted to make sure she didn't lose the one from which she had come. Now far enough away to view the entire bulk of her galaxy, she took a good look and memorized the features that would allow her to recognize it, if it somehow drifted away. Stella found she was unable not to notice the strange resemblance between it and the island of Empyriania, both stretched and flattened with a bulge in its center. Although one was an island and the other a living creature, she felt deep in her heart that they were one and the same.

As she studied her galaxy an icy current chilled Stella's feet. Glancing down she caught a glimpse of something gliding swiftly below, something definitely not one of the peaceful galactic whales. It cut a sinister silhouette against the cream colored depths and although it was far away, Stella could see it was some sort of giant squid, pulsing as it propelled itself through the sea. While the whales gave off a warm glow, the grim squid exuded an icy malevolence with tentacles extending at rhythmic intervals to form a blasphemous dark star.

The squid trailed one of the whales, matching its speed, following its turns and deftly copying it's every move. It could be just a game these creatures were playing, but something in the aggressive behavior of the squid told Stella it was a deadly competition for the highest of stakes. Feeling that something terrible was about to happen and doubting these peaceful creatures were aware of the danger that was now in their midst, Stella swam to the creature that contained her home and friends, thinking of how she might aid the galactic whale that was being pursued by the menacing squid.

When Stella made it back to her galaxy, Astraea and DubDub were waiting in the eye but Loony, oddly was nowhere in sight. Perceiving Stella's fright the Star woman poked her hand through the eye's membrane. Stella swam forward to grip the hand and a sinewy arm glistening like ivory pulled her up with the greatest of ease. Only when her knuckles met the surface of the pool did the rescue halt. Easing off for just a second, Astraea tugged vigorously once again. Stella yelped in pain as her fist met the barrier of the eye. As the girl's hand jerked open, Astraea loosened her grip.

Stella pushed and shoved against the membrane. It flexed only slightly and after a few fitful moments she gave up, realizing the membrane would not budge. It was passable evidently, only one way. On the other side Astraea and DubDub hunched at the rim of the pool, conferring while looking forlornly toward their trapped friend. Then when both seemed to agree on a plan, Astraea leaned far over the pool's edge, put her face close to its surface and attempted to communicate. Before she could get a word out Stella shrieked, "Look Out!"

From behind Loony charged, and with a nasty shove pushed Astraea and DubDub over the pool's edge. They plunged through the eye, a trail of murky nebula mud pluming behind them as the grime that had covered them peeled from their bodies. In seconds they were fully cleansed. The clockwork man was his old spotless self, wood shiny and the optical devices covering his head crystal clear and the Star woman's gown had returned to its original resplendent state.

In the whale's eye, Loony was howling with laughter as he peeked over the eye's edge and then he was gone, leaving only the starry night sky. "I can't believe he did that!" Stella exclaimed. "I couldn't be sure, when I thought he pushed me, but he shoved you in on purpose!"

"He did not want to go any further with us," answered DubDub in a matter of fact manner. "He said he had enough and all you've done is picked on him, and talked about finding his way back to Earth."

Pick on him! Stella wanted to scream. She'd never picked on Loony; she had just been trying to keep him on the right track. "Well," she said, trying to not sound either hurt or annoyed but knowing she was a little of both, "we have other things to worry about." She paused for a moment then whispered dramatically, "There aren't just whales here! I saw something, and I don't think it's friendly."

DubDub's whole body stiffened in fright as his eyes extended in all directions giving his body the look of a pinwheel. "Saw something? Where?"

"Somewhere in this ocean. We should find our way out of it as fast as we can."

"This is an ocean?" was the mechanical man's curious but skeptical response. "I've read of them, but have never seen one." His eyes scanned the depths, "How can you be sure that this is an ocean?"

"Well, those are like whales," Stella pointed to one of the enormous galactic creatures that floated by. "And whales live in the ocean, no? So this must be some sort of ocean." Stella knew that this wasn't quite a logical argument and if her father were here he'd be a little upset to hear her make such a faulty supposition. He would frown a second and then easily point out the flaws. But he wasn't here Stella thought, and so far on this whole adventure there had been very little that had been logical.

"I suppose," observed Astraea who had been floating nearby, suspiciously silent while listening to her friend's discussion, "but oceans are something about which I know very little."

DubDub asked, "And if this were an ocean? In what way would that be of any help to our current predicament?"

"DubDub", Stella said gravely, "We need to leave here as quickly as possible. There was something about that squid I really didn't like."

It was only then that Stella noticed how suddenly ashen Astraea had become, the lambent gold of her cheeks having gone strangely pale. Though he prided himself on his ability to see, DubDub did not notice the troubles of the Star woman and couldn't help but open his wooden mouth one more time. "I'm still not sure that this is an ocean."

Stella ignored the remark to focus on her friend. "Astraea, are you okay?"

"I... I…I don't think so," the Star woman answered, her voice quivering as she spoke. "I have the distinct feeling that I shouldn't be here. If that pool was the gateway out of Empyriania, then I have left the galaxy to which I was destined to stay. I have gone beyond my limit. It is no wonder I feel so…weak."

Astraea's plight was worrying, but Stella struggled to hide her concern. "Well, maybe when we get out of this ocean you'll feel better," she said. "If this is an ocean, and I think it is…" She said this with a special emphasis, to let DubDub know that she really didn't care what he thought. "And if it is an ocean, then it must have a surface."

"And which way would that be?" The mechanical man asked searching around.

Looking around for some clue, all Stella could see was the pod of galactic whales swimming slowly through the cosmic latte. She flipped the lid of the Compyxx to see where the needle pointed. Noting the direction it indicated was away from where she had seen the shadowy squid, she quickly decided to follow its lead.

"This way!" she shouted and darted off, but promptly realized that only DubDub had followed. Seeing Astraea limply adrift in the depths she quickly went to her aid and taking her wrist, pulled the Star woman along.

Half the devices on DubDub's head were trained in the direction they headed, straining to see further. "I'm not sure this is the way out, I cannot see any surface." The other half pointed behind anxiously scanning the ocean for the malevolent presence. "But neither do I see anything behind, except for the whales."

"Well, we can't go back and we can't stand still," Stella shouted. "So we have to get out of this ocean, and when we do we'll be one step closer to the clockwork." The girl kicked harder, propelling herself and Astraea through the coffee colored ocean. "Now come on! We're not going to quit!"

So they swam, Stella with Astraea pulled along behind, and DubDub following at her side. All around were the peaceful galactic whales swimming in the vast expanse, and though Stella hoped to see once more, her home galaxy the Milky Way, it had swum out of sight. "I wonder where our galaxy has gone."

With only silence as a response Stella looked back to see how the Star woman was, and suddenly in the depths below, spotted the ghastly squid. Its long black tentacles contracted, then shot stiffly out, propelling the monster's bulbous body through the water, leaving behind a grim inky trail. Its grotesque appearance gave the girl a sick feeling in her stomach and at this distance she could see the creature's glowing demonic eyes. Stella had seen those eyes before, when Old Sol was attacked by…

"*MOROS*!" DubDub shrieked. "The squid; it's Moros!"

Stella's heart pounded as she took a quick count of seven tentacles and five short stumps. As if in answer to her unrealized thought, Astraea murmured distantly as if from a dream or nightmare. "Five of the zodiac had been destroyed, Capricorn, Pisces and Taurus at the battle in Empyriania and Leo and Aries by the brown dwarfs. Now there are only seven left of the twelve."

"That squid is the remainder of the Zodiac, possessed by Moros." Astraea continued as she gazed vacantly at the seven-pointed star that wheeled below. "Now that the constellations of the Zodiac have left their natural position in the universe, the chains of the law have been broken. They are no longer subject to that which once gave their lives form and meaning. It comes as no surprise that they should find themselves capable of even greater perversions. As for myself, my abrupt detachment from Empyriania has left me feeling less than well."

"Look!" The dread in DubDub's voice stopped Stella's heart. She watched as the giant squid turned and shot through the sea, now heading directly toward them. "It's heading our way!" DubDub frantically kicked his fabricated legs and Stella joined him as they swam with all they had. It took only seconds for the squid to close half the distance between itself and its prey.

Whatever the mechanical man saw through those of his lenses that pointed back at their pursuer was horrible enough to make him shriek, "It's almost on us! We don't have a chance of escape!"

Realizing the monster was too big and too fast to evade, Astraea pulled from Stella' grip and stopped to confront the darkness below. "That is not true DubDub," she stated boldly, though her voice had not the vigor it displayed in the past, "There is always a chance, while there is still light."

Stella raced back to her friend whose starry eyes sparked dully as a grim smile of resignation appeared on her lips. "Whatever happens, do not lose hope. Hope is the light that will lead you to the clockwork." As she slid her sword from its sheath, the blade still gleamed.

A bloodcurdling cry erupted from DubDub's wooden jaws, "It's here!"

Stella noted with horror, the enormity of this blasphemous creature larger than even the whale galaxies, as it ascended from the depths. Standing together with the fiery sword brandished before them, the trio braced themselves to be engulfed by the darkness. The squid was almost upon them when Astraea swung her weapon in a mighty arc to parry an attack. A tentacle went suddenly limp and plummeted motionlessly through the cosmic ocean, cut from the body by the sharp shining blade. As it sunk, the snakelike limb shed its skin in putrid clumps revealing within a clawed arachnid shape. The scorpion, rattling in violent death throes quickly disintegrated leaving a slurry ash. From that foul miasma the burnt out Stars of Scorpio slid lightless into the ocean's endless depths.

Though visibly weakened, the Star woman fought on, thrusting her sword to the hilt into another tentacle. As she yanked it out, a noxious trail of black ooze began to flow from the gaping wound. Stella and DubDub fell back as their champion battling fearlessly, forced the squid to retreat. Fending off each of the remaining tentacles Astraea worked inwards, aiming to strike a blow between the squid's infernal eyes. Stella watched the dazzling blaze move in the midst of the black forest of limbs, a single lightning swift blade battling a quintet of grappling serpents.

Then just as the light seemed ready to pierce a smoldering eye, a jet of ink squirted from the squid, blinding the Star woman in its shroud of darkness. For the first time the sword missed its mark and a tentacle struck its target. It fell hard across the back of the woman who under the weight of the blow crumpled. With their opponent stunned, the tentacles began to rain their rage down upon the woman, battering her senseless.

Coils of black constricted around Astraea and as consciousness was squeezed from her body, the grip on her fiery sword went slack. The weapon fell from her hand and plummeted silently into the endless depths. The squid held its prize out, briefly displaying to all who could see its trophy, captive and unconscious. Stella's own scream roared in her ears as the monstrous beast then wrapped four tentacles around each of the woman's limbs and one about her neck and began to pull…

From out of the depths of the ocean a blur whizzed and like a rocket a galactic whale shot towards the squid. It hit hard and with its impact the coils that held the Star woman loosened, and as Astraea dropped free the valiant whale dashed away, but tentacles lashed out, stopping its retreat. While the two giants wrestled Stella swam to her stunned friend and pulled her clear of the fray.

As the squid's tentacles wrapped around the galactic whale, the ocean was filled with the sound of a piercing screech so high it made Stella's eardrum throb. The tone of the squeal modulated as the whale fought to escape the monster's grasp. The snake-like tentacles only coiled tighter around the whale's body. The captured galaxy's howl of pain intensified as it bucked and writhed, trying to break free of its shadowy captor. Hearing the tortured shriek, other galactic whales raced towards their imperiled comrade like arrows flying to a target.

The first to reach the writhing combatants rammed the squid, smashing the black bulb of its body with massive force. Another rushed in to strike again and two of the tentacles dislodged from their catch. The squid lashed out at the attacking whales with its free tentacles, but the other three tightened, cutting deeply into their captive's body. Seeing the ensnared whale in such serious trouble, Stella's only comfort was that Astraea, who watched the skirmish through shocked glassy eyes, had been saved.

More whales rushed to rescue their comrade and preparing to mount a full on assault, tightened their circle around the squid. Some dashed inwards and feigned attack, hoping to distract their enemy while one fearless whale dared to rush in to pummel the squid with a powerful blow. As dark coils flailed out to thwart the attack, it seemed for a moment that the captured whale might break from its bonds. It was not to be, for in a flurry of limbs, the squid regained its hold on the captive and began to throttle it mercilessly. From within the entangled duo, black ink began to pour and a dark blossom bloomed about captive and captor, grimly shrouding their deadly struggle within. The circle of whales fell into disorder as the blackness spread, its malignant wafts reaching out like grim fingers of a death. An eerie squeal erupted from the poisonous cloud and then as quickly as it had flowered, the dark blossom faded revealing in it's midst, the crumpled husk of the doomed galactic whale, alone.

What had once been a magnificently vibrant being was now only a mangled shell. As the throttled creature drifted lifelessly away, Stella winced upon realizing she had just witnessed the death of a galaxy. In the horrific instance of violence that had just occurred, millions of stars and possibly billions of beings had been wiped from existence by a blasphemous agent of darkness.

Wherever the murderous squid had gone, Stella was not waiting to find out. "We have to get out of here, now!" she shouted to her friends. Gripping Astraea's hand, she kicked upwards, rushing from the ghastly scene. Her progress was abruptly stopped as the Star woman would not budge. Stella tugged in a silent gesture of departure, but felt in response only dead weight anchored to the devastation below. Past tightly gripped white knuckles, Stella saw Astraea's ashen face; the golden glow drained and in her wide starry eyes, the reflection of the dead universe.

"Moros!! He… he… killed them all," she gasped, choking out the words in a cadence bordering delirium. "So many lights! All snuffed!" Stricken by the loss, Astraea fell numbly silent.

The giant whales raced in a frenzy about the body of their brother, searching for the murderer who was nowhere in sight. If Astraea, a Star, had felt the pain of the loss so much more deeply than Stella, the anguish of the bereaved whales must be beyond comprehension.

Somewhere in the ocean, Moros' monster was waiting to strike again and Stella had a mission to complete if she were to end this madness, to stop all this death. "We need to get going!" Astraea's focus did not wander from the crumpled corpse of the galaxy.

"DubDub!" Stella shouted. The clockwork man stirred from his mournful contemplation of the body, his eyes shifting away from the senseless murder. "Help me! We need to get away from here now! That squid… Moros is near." At the mention of their enemy's name DubDub sprang to attention. "Take Astraea's hand and help me pull!"

Up through the ocean the girl and her clockwork companion swam, dragging behind them the limp body of their starry friend. Even with the weight, they made steady progress, propelled by their desperation to escape. Far below, the pod of whales circled their dead comrade, once again appearing as mere minnows. Stella had no idea how much further they would need to go to find safety, if anywhere in the universe was still safe from Moros. So frightened was she of facing the hideous squid again, that as she swam she found herself talking to Astraea, talking through the fear.

She pleaded with the semiconscious Star. "Please be okay! If anything ever happened to you, I don't know what I'd do. When this is all over, when I, I mean when we, because we're going to do this together, when we wind the clockwork, then we won't have to worry anymore about Moros or the darkness or anything. Then maybe there's a way you could visit me on Earth, maybe that can be our reward. I'll show you trees and water, real water, and maybe when we move back to Florida you can come there too, and we can swim together in the ocean and play on the beach. I know you'd love it Astraea, I just do. But you have to promise me that you won't leave me."

She wasn't sure, but she thought she heard the Star woman answer "yes" and although the response had been feeble and weak, that small word was a balm for her soul, but not unfortunately for her arm. Though keen to make distance from the devastation below, Stella felt that with every stroke her arm was being wrenched from its socket. It was as if the weight of Astraea had doubled, so laborious had the swimming become. "I'm sorry DubDub," she gasped finally with tears in her eyes from the pain, "I can't go much further. My arm feels like it's ready to fall off."

Whatever Stella had expected the mechanical man to say; only silence answered her complaint. Looking down, she first saw Astraea still dazed and unresponsive, but trailing behind the Star was a stiff and motionless form. "DubDub! Have I been pulling you too?"

The mechanical man did not answer. His eyes floated limply on their stalks. Only a few seemed capable of focusing, and those stared pleadingly at Stella. As she moved down towards the automaton she could hear a request emanating from his wooden head. "Wind me?" the voice from behind clenched jaws begged, "Please?"

Dropping Astraea's hand, Stella maneuvered around to where she could reach the knob on DubDub's chest. At its first turn, the automaton lurched alive with the stalks on his head stiffening and the wooden fingers of his clenched hand opening to release their grip on the Star woman's wrist.

The wooden jaws parted, "Thank you, Stella. Please, another few turns and I should be fine."

A figure drifting downwards caught Stella's attention before she could turn the knob again. Astraea was plummeting back into the depths, away and out of reach, her gown trailing ghostly behind. As Stella rushed to pursue her sinking friend, a cry whined from above. "Please don't leave me! Finish winding me!"

At their rapid rate of descent, the pod of whales below grew larger by the second and Stella was stunned by how quickly the distance they had made was erased. Closing in on her sinking friend, Stella with a desperate lunge seized the hem of her gown and stopped the Star's descent.

"Stella! Don't leave, finish winding me!" was the panicked cry of the mechanical man that paddled weakly above her. "I think I'm sinking!"

Getting a firm hold on the Astraea's hand Stella began the laborious swim upwards once again, all the while watching anxiously for any sign of the squid. The shape of the mechanical man grew larger as Stella made her way up, cutting an odd silhouette against the cream colored sea. His angular wooden limbs jerked spastically as he begged. "Stella! I'm getting weaker.... Please... come back and rewind me? Please!" Each panicked plea was more hysterical and shrill, and each grated more and more on Stella's frayed nerves.

"Be quiet!" Stella hissed. "If Moros hears you, we're in big trouble." She wished the mechanical man would be quiet…and patient. Couldn't he see, with all his many eyes that she was swimming as fast as she could? And why, Stella thought feeling angrier by the moment, couldn't he have noticed he was running down and ask to be wound then, so that she wouldn't have knocked herself out dragging not only Astraea, but also his rundown body up through the ocean. And why, her blood boiled at the thought, did he always pick the absolute worst times to run down?

"Stella, please! Hurry back and wind me!"

The frazzled girl could stand it no longer and her anger at the clockwork man exploded. "*Wind yourself!*" She screamed back.

"Wind…? Myself…?" The clockwork man reached to his chest and tentatively touched the knob. He turned it once and paused, surprised at his action and gauging what effect it might have had. Then with increased vigor he turned it again twice, three times, and when Stella had made her way back to him she saw what might pass for a smile on the wooden lips of the invigorated clockwork man.

"I did it! I did just what you said!" the automaton gushed to the approaching girl. As the realization of what he had accomplished sunk in, he exclaimed, "I can wind myself!"

A look of surprise was in each of his many eyes, and reflected in those glassy orbs Stella could see her own face gawking in astonishment. "You wound yourself?" she asked breathlessly.

"I'll never have to bother you again," DubDub said happily, "and I'm never going wind down again." All his eyes fanned out until his head looked like nothing less than a dandelion flower and his body a long brown stem, "It feels like a great weight has been lifted from me. Why, I feel free! Free as a bird."

Rushing to help DubDub jetted through the water, slid under Astraea's arm and took with eager verve and to Stella's great relief, the weight of the Star. Jostled, the Star woman moaned feebly and reached to her side for her sword.

"I'm sorry," Stella offered apologetically, "Your sword is lost in the depths. I couldn't catch it… but what's important is that you're okay."

Now as they swam, it was DubDub alone who carried Astraea. DubDub did not seem to mind the efforts at all, but pulled the dazed Star steadily along, all the while chatting breathlessly of his plans. Stella couldn't tell whether he spoke out of his own excitement or to try to cheer the crushed warrior. "I imagine, Astraea, that I can go any place I'd like now that I don't have to worry about having someone around to wind me. There are so many places I read about back in the Astrophelarium. Now I'll be able to explore them all! Isn't that wonderful, Astraea?" The star woman weakly moaned in response. "Why, I feel as if I'm brand new."

Stella was glad that some good had come from their time in this endless ocean, but the sickening feeling in her stomach would not leave, knowing that whatever had lived in the crumpled galaxy below was now dead. She scanned the ocean for any sign of the murderous squid. Fortunately, it was nowhere in sight, but a small pinpoint of light that flashed curiously in the distance caught Stella's attention. Getting the distinct feeling it had nothing to do with Moros; she decided not to say anything for fear of alarming her friends.

Stella was suddenly sure that the glint had grown larger; even though it was so small that it was hard to see exactly how much closer it had come. DubDub who with all his energies focused on carrying Astraea to safety, had still not noticed this anomaly that grew imperceptibly larger, in the way airplanes on Earth might, Stella thought. At first, a plane would be only the faintest spot on the horizon, easily dismissed as an illusion; but soon this indistinct phantom would gradually accumulate substance and form, until reaching the point where it was recognizable for what it was and all question as to its unreality no longer entertained. And just as this mysterious object slipped near to that point of recognition, Stella heard a distant cry. "Hello! Are you survivors?"

Stella connected the distant hail, to the small dot she had been watching; only now the dot was a small craft, maybe some sort of jet. "Hello!! Can you hear me?" the voice asked again, "Ahoy! Are you survivors of the cataclysm?"

Not wanting to attract the attention of the deadly squid, Stella was reluctant to answer. But if whatever was in the craft was looking for survivors, they must be looking to help. She decided to risk it and shouted. "Yes! Yes! We're here! Can you help us?"

"Please!!" was the sharp response, "Lower your voice! You're deafening me!" With the ship so far away, she couldn't understand how she could have deafened the inhabitant of the silver craft. "Now tell me, and keep your voice low, are you survivors?"

Survivors of what? Stella wanted to ask, but then the answer came to her. The voice wanted to know if they were survivors of the galaxy that had been crushed by the squid. In her lowest whisper the girl replied, "No, we are not *survivors*. We've come here from another galaxy, and are on an urgent mission to stop Moros, on whose orders that galactic whale was destroyed." She said this all in a soft whisper, and when she was done she noticed that DubDub was next to her still holding Astraea. The star woman was still pale and weak, but her eyes managed to open, revealing glassy orbs.

"Who are you talking to?" The mechanical man asked.

Stella nodded towards the glinting craft which was now even closer, though still very small. "That ship or whatever it is. It's still too far away for me to see clearly, but there is someone calling to us from it."

DubDub's eyes extended on their stalks, "To my eyes the craft does not look so distant. Why," with a whirring sound a telescope at the forefront of his devices was replaced by a magnifying glass, "it's right here."

Stella was confused, "Right here? It can't be. It looks so far away."

Without another word DubDub held out a wooden hand, and the craft which only a moment before had seemed so large and distant, hovered forward to land in his palm. "It's called being small", DubDub whispered as a magnifying glass slithered on its stalk, and both he and Stella began to inspect the small silver ship he held in his palm.

Stella had seen this type of craft before; on Earth they were called UFOs. Her father hated them. Every time some report of a person seeing one of these vessels would come up on the television, he would go nuts. "Simply impossible!" Perceval would exclaim. "No ship can travel so fast. It defies all the laws of physics!"

"You are not from my galaxy?" A voice from the tiny craft asked. "You are from a place beyond?"

"I am from Earth," Stella responded, "A planet in the system of Sol, located in the Milky Way galaxy."

"And you say you are here to fight the darkness, which you call *Moros*?"

"Yes, we are!" Stella said emphatically, "You can leave your ship if you like," She offered, interested to see what the inhabitant might look like. "We're able to breath here."

A small hatch the size of a bottle cap opened in the UFO's shiny surface. What crept out onto the wooden surface of DubDub's hand was stranger than anything Stella could have ever imagined. Desperate not to be rude, she struggled to not look startled. As far as she could tell, what crawled from the ship was some kind of spider, but with a human face.

"Then we are allies, I suppose," The spider stated, "if you intend to defeat the darkness that has destroyed my home."

Maybe a spider was not exactly what this being was. Upon closer inspection Stella could see that there were six legs that touched the ground while four arms gesticulated as he spoke. She also noticed that on the sides of his head were double sets of ears. "You're from the galaxy that was destroyed?" She asked in amazement.

"Yes I am. From the planet Haresis, a satellite of the Star, Hyle, in what was the galaxy we called Heimarmene." A tiny tear sparkled in the little being's third eye as he mentioned his home. One of his four hands rose and wiped it away, "I am known as Zeb Zibulon. I was a member of a group of scientists whose duty it was to study and decode the cipher of the stars. We watched the skies and studied their mysteries, devoted to understanding our place in the web of existence. I personally felt compelled to understand what lie beyond the bounds of our galaxy."

The tone of his voice filled with wonder and awe when he spoke of exploring space, reminded Stella so much of her father that she forgot immediately the being's strange appearance, and saw only a colleague. "It was in the course of those investigations that I came upon what would bring doom to my galaxy. Using devices of my own design, I peered ever outward, always searching, until I found a place at the furthest reaches of our galaxy through which I could glimpse beyond my galaxy. I named this place the Oculus Cetus. It was there that I first caught a glimpse of…"

The tiny Haresian hesitated and Stella waited only a second before coming to his aid. "The darkness?" She offered.

"Yes," he said inhaling wearily, "the darkness. At first, the empty void of space I saw through the Oculus Cetus fascinated me. It was so serene, peaceful and eternal. Only after endless hours studying the skies, did I begin to notice a blemish growing in the furthest reaches of space." Stella could not help but think of the event that had started her adventure. The little man's words brought back that horrible moment when Stella had first seen the foe of all light.

Zeb continued, "I felt no apprehension at this development, having no precedent as to the behavior of the spaces beyond my own. I calmly studied the phenomenon, waiting until I could form some hypothesis as to its nature. For years I watched the darkness slowly fill the void, thinking perhaps that this darkening was a natural cycle of the universe." Shaking his head in regret he continued, "Eventually it reached the farthest star of our galaxy, and then mercilessly and violently extinguished it. In that awful moment I realized that I had been seduced by the darkness. And as this unnatural shadow moved further into our universe, snuffing star after star, I realized it could not be stopped."

"When I realized the jeopardy to my own world, I desperately tried to warn my fellow Haresians of the danger. They only laughed, accusing me of irrational hysteria. Though I tried to convince them, they paid me no mind. I built this ship in which to escape, wondering if there were somewhere beyond my galaxy, where I might find a safe harbor from the darkness. When the end came, it was horrible."

Hearing this, the small group silently reflected on the loss of so much life. DubDub finally whispered, "How did you know where to go?"

"In my ship I raced for the only way I knew out of my dying galaxy, to the Oculus Cetus, the portal where I had glimpsed the spaces beyond. As the darkness devoured my galaxy, I escaped to find myself here." He waved his hands towards the tawny depths. "But where exactly am I?"

Stella wasn't sure she could explain but was willing to try. "I think this is the cosmic ocean where galaxies live. When I came here through a small pool at the center of our galaxy, the Milky Way, I wasn't sure where I was either. I thought I had fallen into some vast sea populated with strange whales. It was only when I saw my friends," she gestured to Astraea and DubDub, "in the eye of one of the whales, did I realize that it was my galaxy."

"Those creatures?" Zeb waved to the minnows below, "You'd have me believe they are galaxies?"

"Yes, they are." Stella responded firmly. "My friends followed me through the eye and we had just begun to swim up to the surface of this ocean…"

"If there is a surface…" DubDub cut in.

"When we were attacked by Moros, in the form of a giant squid," Stella continued. "It would have ended for us right there, only your galaxy sacrificed itself to save us." Zeb Zibulon saw his reflection in the young girl's eyes, and seeing the soft swell of tears at their rims, knew she was telling the truth. "When we escaped, we watched as it was crushed to death in the monster's tentacles."

Astraea stirred briefly from her stupor. "So many lives lost!" She whined. "The horror, the horror!"

Zeb's small eyes moved from face to face and saw the grief on each. "My galaxy was destroyed to save you three?"

Stella felt embarrassed and ashamed. "Maybe somehow your galaxy knew how important our mission was…" she offered lamely.

DubDub interjected, trying to say something to make Zeb's loss somehow more understandable. "Maybe it knew that if we fail in our mission everything is doomed to darkness…"

"Or perhaps," The little spider like being whispered sadly, "My galaxy rescued you simply because it saw you were in need."

A hush fell over the group as they all contemplated the loss of that brave galaxy. Mercifully, Zeb broke the silence. "Perhaps others from my galaxy have survived the cataclysm. It was a very large galaxy, and with so many inhabited planets, others may have escaped. "Stella did not think that was likely, but nodded her head in agreement anyway. Zeb continued, "I believe I understand the importance of your mission and I wish you luck in succeeding with your task. I would offer my help, but I cannot accompany you until I am certain that there are no other survivors. I can however, tell you that there is a surface to this ocean, for I have been there."

All three of the companions responded together. "You have?"

Their combined shout knocked the little spider back against his ship. Zeb's four little hands reached to his head and four tiny fingers were stuck into four diminutive ears. Straightening himself, he replied. "Why yes, but please, control yourself. Another shout like that and I'll be deaf."

Stella pointed in the direction they had been swimming and asked in the softest whisper she could manage, "Is this the way up?"

"Yes, of course, the surface is not far at all, but I'm not sure what you hope to find there. When I reached the surface I expected to find other survivors, but there were none. I returned below to search further, and almost immediately I came upon you three. But alas, you are not from my galaxy and if I find no others, I am the last of my kind."

Stella felt terrible for the little spider man, who would never be able to go home again. "Well, if you don't find anyone and you get lonely, you'd be welcome on my planet, Earth. I'd be happy to show you around. Those whales down there, there's one that's longer than the others. You're small enough so maybe you can find a way through its eye. If you look around in that galaxy enough, you'll find some planets orbiting a yellow sun named Sol. Go to the third planet, Earth. That's where, when I finish my mission, you'll find me." She said this as if it was a fact, wanting to believe she would get home so badly, that she would not allow herself to think otherwise.

"Okay", Zeb replied gratefully. "I'll do that. If no one from my galaxy has survived I'll meet you there."

Stella reached out her finger and the little spider touched it, and she shook his hand very gently. Zeb crawled back into his ship, waved from the closing hatch and prepared to leave. "Zeb, please, wait a minute."

A voice came from the ship. "What is it, Stella?"

When she answered it was with a lump in her throat, "Would you mind taking a note home for me," she gulped, knowing she might never get back to her home and this might be her one chance to say goodbye, "in case you get there before I do?"

The tiny ship settled once again onto DubDub's palm. "My ship is not very big. I won't be able to spare the room if I find many survivors," Zeb explained, but Stella understood he was only being brave like she was, and saying what he hoped to come true. "But until my ship is filled, I will carry your message and if I find your home, deliver it." The tiny hatch on the ship swung open.

Stella searched her pockets and pulled out a pencil and paper. Tearing off a small corner of the paper, she in the smallest print possible, wrote, "Be home soon. Love, Stella". Rolling the scrap into a tight wad, she carefully slid it through the hatch and into the empty space behind Zeb. When the note was in place, Zeb pushed a tiny button no larger then a pinhead and the hatch closed.

The ship hovered for a moment over DubDub's wooden palm before shooting off. "Till, we meet again Stella Ray, in a happier place!" Zeb Zibulon's voice rung out as his ship disappeared down into the deep blue. Stella waved goodbye, feeling like she had just thrown a message in a bottle into the vast ocean.

Taking Astraea by the arms, DubDub and Stella resumed their flight to the surface. No sooner had they taken their first strokes upward than a whir rose from below. Zeb Zibulon's ship darted back into view, and extending from its front was a tiny claw that held a gleaming sword. As the claw opened the sword floated down. Astraea reached and missed but Stella quickly snatched it as it drifted past. "I imagine you'll need that! Good luck on your journey!" Zeb's voice faded as the tiny UFO zoomed off once more into the vast sea.

They broke the surface silently, with nary the slightest ripple on the surface as they emerged. As the three heads bobbed in the vast ocean and surveyed their sterile surroundings, the evidence that they were beyond any realm known to Planet, Star or Galaxy was apparent in dramatic fashion. Below were the universal creamy depths, still and serene, but above spread a sky of the deepest sapphire blue, the purity of which had a peculiar and almost indescribable effect on Stella's eye. It was a crystalline color that seemed capable of pulling her in, further and further, until trapping her inextricably in its infinite depths.

"What an amazing blue," Stella noted in awe, her voice shattering the silence of millions of years.

"What an odd sky," DubDub's voice soundly strangely squishy as he spoke. "I've never seen anything quite like it. There is nothing in it, whatsoever. It is completely empty." His instruments strained as they scanned the empty blue.

In every direction the defining line of the far off horizon presented a stark contrast between the ocean below and the sky above leaving no doubt that this new territory was irrefutably different from any they had been in before. "The horizon," Stella mentioned, "Seems somehow not right."

DubDub's eyes shifted from the sky to where the blue and the beige met. Paddling slowly he spun. "There is no curvature. We are on a plane, perfectly flat." His eyes recalibrated, focusing. "I cannot see any end to this sea, it goes on forever."

Astraea floated listlessly in the vibratory sea, staring down into the beige depths. A glint of light still sparkled in her eyes, but the shattered look on her face remained. The beating she had sustained at the tentacles of the monster had wounded her deeply and the death of the galaxy lay heavy upon her as if she were responsible for all the deaths. "Astraea? Are you okay?" Stella asked.

"Yes, I think so," she answered bravely but it was obviously not true. Since she had left her galaxy, her brightness had greatly diminished.

Stella pulled out the Compyxx, and flipping the clasp with her lip, opened the wooden ball. Its arrow pointed out into the empty sea. "Where are we supposed to go? Zeb was right, there's nothing here," She searched the horizon, squinting, straining to see further. "I can't see anything!"

"See?" The machinery on DubDub's head stirred, devices whirring attentively. "That would be my job, wouldn't it?" DubDub's head went through a series of permutations. Different devices coupled with others, telescopes shifted to different lengths, lens adjusted in precise fittings, all forming a dense circle around his head.

Stella waited anxiously and quietly, not wanting to break the concentration of the watcher. Suddenly the lens shifted. "There!" DubDub announced, pointing in the exact direction the Compyxx pointed. "Can you see it? I don't know how Zeb could have missed it." From the back of his head, a telescope swung out on a thin wooden contrivance and placed itself to Stella's eye. She inhaled to calm down, to focus the way her father had taught to her when she looked through a telescope. Breathing out slowly she looked through the eyepiece and saw far away a small protuberance rising from the sea.

"It's an island!" Stella shouted, "Let's get to it! Come on! I bet it's not as far as it looks! Lets swim for it" Astraea splashed her arms in a spastic flailing movement.

"Astraea?" Stella asked. "Can't you swim?"

"I don't think so," she answered, "I'm a Star, Stella, what would I know about swimming?" Even battered and bruised Astraea managed to turn up a smile for her young friend.

"I can assist you!" DubDub swam to the Star and buoyed her up on his body. The automaton's wooden cabinet floated easily in the cosmic ocean as Astraea rode atop it. "Now, can we please get to the island?" The mechanical man wheezed, a hint of his old testiness back in his voice," If this is anything like water, it will definitely rust my gears. I'd like to minimize the damage as much as possible, so can we move along?"

As they swam Stella concentrated on getting the most out of each stroke. Carrying the weight of Astraea on his back, DubDub stayed at her side, paddling with a steady mechanical rhythm. They had not gone too far when suddenly, with irrepressible fear Astraea whispered, "It's below us."

Stella thought nothing could frighten Astraea, but it was obvious the Star was shaken to her core. "It'll be okay," she assured, "We're almost to the island. It won't be long until we're safe on land." And it was true; the island was getting closer by the second, and on it, a singular structure could be seen beyond a stretch of glistening beach, shimmering like a mirage. Stella focused on reaching that shelter and not on the dark shape that crisscrossed below in the cream colored sea, coming ever nearer the trio.

20 THE SHORES OF TIME

Though gripped by paralyzing fear, the trio managed to reach the island intact. Feeling her feet touch the sands Stella struggled to rush ashore, seeing that DubDub had already pulled himself and Astraea onto the shore. "Don't stop! Get to the building!" Stella shouted as she crawled onto the sand. "We're still not safe! Help Astraea!" She reached for the Star woman's arm and DubDub moved to help, and then suddenly stopped short.

"Moros!!" The mechanical man whispered breathlessly. Stella followed his horrified stare to what moments before had been a flat calm sea. Now the ocean was a churning chaos whose surface roiled with boiling intensity. The blue sky blackened as menacing storm clouds bloomed from the chaos, rising over the trio in the form of an enormous squid. As the leviathan lurched from the sea Stella shrieked, "Run!"

Racing before the oncoming tempest, there was a swish through the air as a dark tentacle swung dangerously close. Spurred on by the near miss, Stella put all her energy into a last desperate sprint pulling Astraea over a dune of glistening sand. DubDub helped with the burden, trailing a forest of eyes from the back of his head that stared in abject horror. Stella didn't care to know what it was he was seeing. The quick glimpse she had gotten as the squid rose from the sea, had been so ugly and bristling with malevolent energy that she looked away before the picture of it set in her mind and had not looked back since.

Over the dune they saw their goal. The sole structure on the island was a massive cube, many stories high and constructed of spotless mirror. Each of its perfectly square sides was covered with doors, some round, and some square, also mirrored and only barely perceptible against the surrounding wall.

Racing to the cube, Stella watched her reflection approach her, as they each grabbed at the first door handle they could reach. Locked! The haggard look on her reflection's face was terrifying as she jumped to the next and pulled on its handle. Locked! Astraea, who had somehow beat DubDub to the wall, was trying a door, hand in hand with her duplicate. This too would not yield. In the mirrored wall, Stella watched the shape of the abysmal squid rising huge behind the clattering figure of DubDub. "We're doomed!" she shouted as he reached the wall. "They're all locked!"

"Are you sure? DubDub squealed as he slammed into the wall. "Have you tried this one?" he asked, reeling back from the impact, his wooden hand clutched at the handle of a nearby door… that somehow swung back under the weight of his ricocheting body.

Stella's heart leapt as DubDub disappeared inside. Pushing Astraea through the opening she rushed in behind her. A giant tentacle following quickly after, groping wildly for something to fill its greedy grasp. Retreating, Stella and Astraea stumbled back, only to trip over a cowering DubDub. The tentacle, an undulating cable devoid of color, bulged at the door before lashing out in a blur. Its tip wrapped around the spindly leg of DubDub, and as quickly as it had entered the sanctuary it retreated, now with the rickety mechanical man in tow. Stella grabbed a wooden arm, pulling uselessly against the strength of the giant squid. In that desperate moment Astraea came to life. Her sword flashed from its scabbard and began to slash at the tentacle that quickly flung DubDub away, to blindly thrash at its attacker. The blade sunk deep into the black hide and from the wound spewed a dark cloud of noxious gas. Astraea moved to attack again but before she could strike, the wounded tentacle retreated, its wide girth jarring the sides of the doorframe as it slithered out. DubDub and Stella both rushed to slam the door. Like with the passing of a storm, there was an eerie calm and the trio sat uneasily in the sand, savoring the reprieve and doubting it would last for long.

Ahead was another mirrored cube nested comfortably inside the first, and their arrangement confronted Stella with infinite repetitions of herself and her friends, as a hall of mirrors might do. The cube ahead, though nearly indistinguishable amongst the endless reflections, had considerably fewer doors than the first, though they were still countless. "Come on, DubDub, we have to try to find a way out of here. Fast, before the Zodiac find a way in."

"I agree, but first I must wind myself before I run down," DubDub stated with a rather strange sense of pride. Grasping the knob on his chest he turned the key, once twice, three times until the spring tightened. "I don't think I've ever done so much on one winding before! That was quite strenuous, what with all that swimming and running! And that thrashing I took!" He rose up refreshed and an exhausted Stella wished it were that easy for her, to just be wound up and ready to go again.

As DubDub stood a flow of sand slid from gaps within the wooden frame and fell to the ground with a tinkling sound. Stella reached into the pile that had formed on the floor to take a handful, then letting it trickle out until there were only a few grains left. "DubDub? Can you lend me a magnifying glass?" The mechanical man said nothing, but from within his forest of devices a magnifying glass appeared and positioned itself at the girl's eye.

"Astraea, Look at this!" Stella called excitedly, hoping her Starry friend would answer. She did not. After the galactic whale was murdered and all those Stars, Planets and beings had been killed, Astraea had changed. Stella knew that sometimes when bad things, "tragic things" her mother would probably correct her, happened to people on Earth they would change. Maybe they would not be as happy, or maybe they seemed a little less interested in just being around other people. Stella hoped neither had happened to Astraea. "Look!" She continued, holding the grains to the magnifying glass. "This isn't sand!"

A few of DubDub's devices shifted, and something that looked like a microscope moved curiously towards the girl's outstretched palm while other eyes swung to examine the floor. "Why, you're right! This isn't sand at all! These are all tiny gears!"

Lethargically, Astraea lifted herself from the floor and moved to Stella's side. The two heads stared together into the lens hung suspended before them, where each tiny grain now largely magnified, was revealed as a perfectly formed gear. The Star's face warmed as she whispered, "Do you know what this means, Stella?" Scooping a handful of the tiny gears in her hand and dropping them in a tinkling cascade, she beamed. "If these are gears we must be near the Celestial Clockwork!"

As if the squid outside could hear their words, its angry assault began. A terrible shudder jolted the chamber as the monster attempted to breech the walls. "We're near the clockwork?" Stella took the Compyxx from beneath her coat and followed its arrow to a round door in the inner cube. Reaching the door she tugged its handle. "It's locked!" In disgust and dismay, she ripped the pendant from her neck and flung it across the floor to be rid of it.

"Maybe this one," DubDub suggested, trying a door that opened easily at his touch. "Go help Astraea." Stella barely blinked at the automaton's luck, but rushed to lead Astraea to the open door. She glanced back to see the outer wall collapsing, shards of mirror falling in a shower of fractured light, as the amalgamated darkness of the Zodiac rampaged through the breach. As soon as she was through the door DubDub slammed it shut.

Stella shouted over the sound of a tentacle slamming the door, "We don't have much time." The whole space came alive with movement, her desperation reflected from every angle, as she raced ahead to the next cube. The door she tried, as her luck would have it, was locked. Again the first door DubDub touched swung open. In this way they moved ahead through cube after cube, each with fewer doors than the last, and each with reflections that grew closer all around. While she and DubDub crossed the sand strewn spaces between cubes, Astraea stayed back to brace the door, holding it with her failing strength as it bulged and shook. The brave Star would only leave her post when she saw that DubDub had opened the next door.

With each new chamber they entered, the thundering of the clockwork's labored ticks resonated louder. As the cubes grew increasingly smaller, Stella couldn't understand how the clockwork, if it was the source of light for the whole universe, could fit in such ever-decreasing spaces. There was no time to ponder that mystery, for as DubDub flung another door open, Stella hurried to retrieve Astraea from her station. Inky smoke was seeping through the door the Star barricaded. Wondering just how long they could keep ahead of the darkness, Stella pulled her friend away from the door and hoped it would hold until they made it into the next cube.

With the number of doors diminishing significantly, Stella could almost count them as she pulled Astraea along, *19, 17, 13, 11, 9, 7…* By now she had stopped trying to find the unlocked door, as somehow none had opened for her. DubDub though, had no problem immediately making the correct choice from the array of circle and square portals presented him. A fleeting thought passed through Stella's mind, that perhaps he could see something she couldn't see. Whatever the reason, Stella had concentrated her efforts on helping Astraea from chamber to chamber. As they passed into the cube with five doors, the Star woman was incapable of continuing, and slumped against the door once it had shut. Immediately there was pounding and curses from the other side and the putrid black smoke leaked in plumes from the doorframe.

"DubDub! Did you find the next door?" Stella screamed ahead to where the automaton had stopped just short of the cube with only four doors.

"Yes, I will, I just need... It's just that…" The mechanical man fumbled frantically with the key on his chest, his wooden fingers shaking as he tried to take hold, "I'm running down. I need to wind myself."

"Well hurry!!!" Stella shrieked, before realizing that she was only making DubDub more nervous. Hoping she could wind him more quickly than his awkward hands would allow, Stella reluctantly left Astraea and ran to aid the rattled automaton. Only halfway to DubDub she was knocked from her feet as a massive explosion pulverized the door Astraea guarded. Shards of mirror rained down as the Star woman was thrown high into the air and landed with a sickening thud in a crumpled heap. As Stella rose to help her friend, the four other doors burst open with four deafening blasts, and noxious black gas began to seethe from their shattered frames.

"Which door?" Astraea asked weakly while struggling to stand.

As Stella tried to help the Star from the floor, within the five doorways storm clouds gathered. Thin tendrils of sinister mist began to snake across the floor towards the faltering duo. "Are you alright?"

"Which door?" The Star woman demanded, gasping for air.

"That one…" Stella pointed to the open circular portal from which DubDub now raced to assist his friends.

Astraea clutched at Stella's sleeve to push her away. "Then go! Leave me. I will hold them here."

Tears rolled down the girl's face as she saw how badly the Star was hurt. "Don't say that, Astraea. We can still make it together."

DubDub was next to them now, terror filling his eyes as forms began to fester in the dark clouds that billowed through the shattered doors. The menacing outlines of Gemini, Cancer, Libra, Aquarius, and Sagittarius resolved within the smoky mists.

"What about your future?" Stella pleaded through her tears. "You were going to teach the Stars about the brown dwarves! You were going to be my friend!"

"If I were to clutch my dreams too tightly, they would surely perish. When I pass from this place, I have faith you will carry my hopes with you." With a bruised hand Astraea moved a strand hair from the girl's wet face.

"Will I ever see you again?" Stella sobbed.

A duo of snickers mocked the girl from the shroud of shadow. "Yes, say your goodbyes," laughed a Gemini twin. "For your time is at an end," the other sneered. Gloating demonically, the dark constellations seemed in no hurry to attack while reveling in their triumph.

Astraea ignored the taunts. "I'm sure we will meet again, although in what forms I do not know. As long as the clockwork ticks the future is endless. All possibilities may occur in its time. Knowing that allows me to do what I must, though I cannot say I do so wholly without fear." Jeering and cursing, the Zodiac assembled behind a wall of crude shadow. "But it is the only way. Now help me up."

Astraea winced as her friends lifted her to her feet. DubDub's eyes never left the Zodiac as he retrieved the sword from where it had fallen and placed it in his friend's hand. With excruciating effort, the Star held it aloft and for a moment her sword shone brightly. The enemy's taunts were silenced as shafts of light pierced the clouds in which the quintet of monsters hid. Sadly, this audacious display was short lived as the weight of the blade proved too much, and the valiant champion dropped her sword.

The Zodiac hooted in wicked delight. "Yes", hissed Cancer, "Surrender! Let us embrace you. There will be no more pain, no more suffering. We will annihilate you and set you free…" Bobbing and weaving, the hideous crustacean darted towards the Star and thrust out a claw. Astraea stumbled forward to shield her friends and parried the attack with a feeble swipe of her sword. As the blade swung the crab's other claw plunged in to snip a swatch of the Star's gown. Cancer chortled as he flaunted the scrap of glistening fabric in his noxious claw and then skittered back into the smog with his prize.

The Zodiac jeered as the luminous scrap was swallowed in a cloak of darkness. The centaur archer, Sagittarius took the tattered ribbon of gown. "So pretty", he brayed, fondling the fabric and making it painfully obvious he was toying with Astraea. "I will hold this for Verena, until she returns from her mission on Earth."

Stella recoiled at the mention of Earth and shouted at the dark. "What do you know about Verena?"

While the other constellations cackled at the question, the Gemini twins traded taunting words. "What do we know about Verena? Why she's like a sister to us. But we usually call her Virgo." They sneered as they joined arms and whirled in a rambunctious jig.

"Verena Maldek is Virgo?" Stella sputtered.

Libra scoffed, her scales rattling as she shook with laughter, "Has it really taken you so long to reach that conclusion? Why, humans must be even more stupid than we had thought. Virgo is on Earth at the bidding of Moros, to deal with any problems that might arise there."

Sagittarius galloped forward, the sound of his hooves echoing ominously. "Moros did not know whether it was you or that pathetic creature you call a father who was the threat to his plans. But now he sees how his concerns were unfounded. None will escape the snare he has set, not Stars, not Planets and especially not humans."

Still twirling, the Gemini twins chanted a chorus, "He snuffs out stars! He crushes galaxies. None can stand against him! He snuffs out stars! He crushes galaxies. None can stand against him!"

"And he will be here shortly…" Aquarius belched, "to deal with you! It should be most entertaining!"

Stella looked to the door DubDub had opened. If she ran, she might escape the monstrosities of the Zodiac, but knew she couldn't leave. Propping Astraea up, she held tight with no intention of ever letting go. "I'm going to stay with you and fight," she whispered, "I won't lose you!"

"Being alight is not about what you have, Stella", Astraea looked into the young girl's face, "but what it is you are willing to leave behind." Turning to the automaton she commanded, "DubDub, see that Stella gets to the clockwork unharmed. I leave her fate in your care." Then facing the Zodiac she shouted defiantly, a blaze of light in every word. "Know that what I do now is of my choice and mine alone. This decision has not been forced upon me by the hand of chance."

As if Astraea had stumbled upon their private joke, the creatures of the Zodiac laughed loudly, mocking her bravado. "Yes!! The hand!! The hand of chance! The hand of fate! The hand of glorious death!"

Stella reached for Astraea's hand. Clasping it tightly she could sense deep within the luminous beauty, still strong beneath the wounds and the bruises. The Star whispered to her young human friend. "I choose to stay, but you must choose to go. Wind the clock before it halts. The fate of all that is alight rides on that."

Aquarius moved to circle behind the duo, but Astraea seeing that Stella's escape would be blocked, moved in a final burst of energy and with a swift stroke of her sword shattered the water bearer's jug, sending a flood of black oily liquid streaming across the floor.

"Now, Stella! Run!"

Feeling Astraea's hand leave her grasp, Stella pulled by DubDub, ran. As she did, the valiant Star lifted her sword and swung it in a wide arc to hold the dark forms at bay. An angry roar filled the room as the Zodiac watched the duo reach the open door. DubDub stepped over the threshold but there Stella stopped. As the Zodiac advanced on the Star woman, she shouted, "Come on Astraea! You can still make it!"

"Don't stop! Get to the clockwork!" Astraea urged as howling infernal shrieks of rage, the Zodiac converged upon her.

Tumbling together in a black storm, they hurtled towards their prey and in a heartbeat their congealed darkness loomed over the wounded woman in the form of a horrific hand, with each of the five dark constellations now a crooked finger. With a thunderous clap the ebony hand closed upon Astraea. As the fingers clamped shut, the light of the Star was gone, swallowed in the abominable fist

Stella stood paralyzed at the doorway, arms limp and legs numb. In her throat the breath had stopped as she stared blankly at the five-fingered nightmare that had taken her friend. She managed a sobbing shriek "Astraea!" as the fist lurched forward, determined to hammer her out of existence.

In answer to the call a light flashed from between the clenched fingers. The fist squeezed back with merciless aggression to snuff this spark, and for the smallest time its cabled muscles contained the flare. Then bright rays of light burst from every crevice, and although the dismal hand strained to maintain its hold, what blazed within proved too strong. Stella was jolted as the fist exploded, its fingers blasted open as radiant waves of light surged from where Astraea had been held. Ripped apart by the force, the hand's dark shards were annihilated, cast into oblivion upon the pulse of brilliance. The dumbfounded girl was buffeted by waves emitting from the white-hot point. Momentarily blinded by the light, when she could look back, no sign of the hand or the Zodiac remained.

"A nova!" DubDub whispered in awe from Stella's side, "Now I've seen it all!"

The waves of light ceased and all the energy that had comprised the Star named Astraea dissipated into space. For just a moment the panic of loss overwhelmed Stella, but then the pain she felt at her friend's demise fell from her heart and was gone. Gratitude filled the girl, as suddenly Astraea's selfless sacrifice made sense. "Thank you!" Stella whispered to the emptiness of space, hoping that somehow her absent friend might hear.

The cube ahead had just three doors from which to choose, two were square, one perfectly round. Sensing her goal was near, Stella sprinted across the chamber with DubDub at her side, certain one of these three would lead to a chamber with two doors, and one of those would open to the final chamber with the door, beyond which, the clockwork waited.

Before they could reach the cube, an icy bolt slammed Stella back, bringing her swiftly and painfully to her knees. Looking up she saw the crackling darkness of Moros above her as night surged from his fingers to freeze DubDub in a casing of black ice. Standing over his captives, he howled in a crow fit for the final dawn. "So your friend has succeeded in destroying the Zodiac." He curled his fingers, tightening the bonds around the girl's body. "If it were possible, I would thank her for ridding me of those creatures. They had long accomplished all I needed and were fast becoming a distraction. The Celestial Clock is ready to tick its last, and then the game will be over." Lifting a crackling hand to where his ear would be, he sneered. "Can you hear it waning?"

Stella listened. The labored ticking of the clockwork could be heard, slow and very low, but present. There was still time. "It hasn't stopped! You haven't won yet!" She shouted as she rolled across the floor.

"Listen to you. A grotesque abortion of matter, yet you prattle as if there is meaning in your stupid little life." Stella could feel the cold vacuum of Moros, pulling at her soul like a hellish magnet. "How do you humans stand it? Your lives are so desperate, so futile, and so…" the crackling void spat with disgust, "predictable."

"Matter suffers, matter dies," Moros sneered. "It seems to me, it would be better never to have been born. You humans make your choices and take your chances, but both bring only suffering in the end. If you'd only accept my way, all that would be over, there would be no more doubt, no more uncertainty. I would free you from those pains."

Standing before the three doors, the darkness offered. "Each of these doors contains a new future. You have only to step through one to find a new destiny. Stay here…" Moros' form crackled with malicious energy… "And I will kill you."

"Would you like to go home?"

Home! The word stopped Stella's heart. She wanted to go home more than anything. Astraea was gone and DubDub incapacitated, leaving Stella frightfully alone. Home was where she wanted to be, not here.

"I can help you get there; you only need to stop your pursuit of the goal set by those foolish agents of light. If you would just forget that futile mission, I will send you back to Earth where you can be with your family when time ends. Then you will be with them forever."

Stella stared hard at her enemy, wondering if what he promised to do was in his power. But more importantly she questioned how she could even entertain the thought of accepting his offer. She looked back to the frozen figure of DubDub, inert, immobile. She thought of Astraea, her light scattered, lost.

"Perhaps I can sweeten the pot. Your family from what I'm told," lifting a clawed hand to a nonexistent ear Moros chuckled," are suffering a bit of duress under an associate of mine. If you go home now, I will order Virgo away. She will not harm your family." As he tempted the girl, Moros smiled a seductive grin, not unlike a witch's when persuading a starving princess to take a bite from an irresistible apple. "And Astraea?" the void inquired, "She died to let you live. If I killed you now, for what was her sacrifice?"

Could that be true? Stella asked herself. Succumbing to the darkness of doubt she found herself questioning why she was even here at all. This was not the place for a mere human to be, so far from home, in the midst of a cosmic war. Who had ever hoped she could complete such an impossible mission? Suddenly, her reasons for winding the clock were no longer clear.

"There are three doors left, which will you pick? Will you take a chance or make a choice? Whichever, that which you truly desire will be revealed. I predict you will choose to go home to save your family."

Stella too frightened by the prospects, couldn't make a decision. She wanted to see her mother and father so badly, and couldn't believe they might be waiting on the other side of one of these doors. Moros passed his hands through the air and within his jagged claws, a pair of dice materialized. He held them out for Stella to see, their sharp angles glistening like black diamond. Grinding the dice in his hand, the two bits squealed like fingernails on a chalkboard. "If," Stella felt Moros' cold eyes penetrate her soul, "you are too weak to choose for yourself, then perhaps a game of chance is in order. You humans enjoy games, do you not?"

"*One.*" Moros purred, pointing to the square over his shoulder but not bothering to look back. The obsidian shard of his finger shifted to the circle. "*Two.*" And then once more back to a square. "*And door number three.*"

"I can tell you that two of these doors lead where your heart desires, to Earth and the Arctic waste you call home. The other leads to the next chamber, and the final gateway. It seems the odds are in your favor."

He shook the dice and their rattling echoed through the chamber. "Will you play this game with me?" With a flip of his hand the bonds fell from Stella, who raised herself up on her knees. She was hardly surprised at what he asked, wondering if perhaps she had been playing a game all along; *Cat and Mouse,* maybe, or *Hide and Seek*, or perhaps, with all the ups and downs, *Snakes and Ladders.*

"I'll let you in on a secret," pronounced the dark void; "neither chance nor choice matters, the future just, is. Any choice you have made hasn't changed anything, just as any risk you've taken, hasn't been chance at all. The outcome was all predetermined from the start. There can only be one future and it belongs to me. But shall we roll the dice anyway, just for fun?"

Stella wasn't sure what came over her or why she would ever agree with Moros about anything, but she nodded her head in agreement. Exploding with spiteful laughter, Moros threw the dice. Tumbling across the floor, they came to rest at Stella's feet, landing with a single glaring dot on top of each. Snake eyes!

"Door, number two!" Moros smiled wickedly. "I'll let you in on another secret; I knew that number would come up." Stepping aside, he cleared the way for Stella. "When I first met you I knew you did not really want to save this worthless universe, but would rather just be home. Now go! This game is over!"

At his command the angled door swung open and Stella found her feet stepping toward the threshold of the middle gate. Passing it, she dropped like a stone through the outer dark into an abyss of dismal night. Tumbling on, she looked for the slightest glimmer of light, but there was none. Darkness ruled.

Then was it really over? Had Moros extinguished the light of all the Stars? Were there no beacons to follow, no torches to bear? Speeding earthward, Stella's face flushed with shame as she realized that Moros had tricked her into playing his game. Tears streamed down her cheeks until the astral winds tore them free, setting the loosed droplets into flights of their own.

They came slowly at first, crystalline emblems emblazoned white sparsely peppering the dark sky. Then they came by the thousands; accompanying the girl on her flight to Earth. Each jewel revealed itself matchless, unique and inimitable. Flakes clung to the parka's glossy fabric; close enough for Stella to see their delicate lattice like structures, forming innumerable tiny ladders. And the descent became an ascent, upwards into the flurry of snow as night was lost in the blizzard and the dark of space became a whiteout.

Stella was awakened to find herself nestled in brightness so comfortable, she wished she could sleep longer. "Get up, there's work to do. You can sleep later, when there's all the time in the world," a voice in her ear insisted. Opening her eyes a crack, to find nothing but the soft and white substance, she rolled over luxuriating in the warmth.

"Get up!" Now the command squealed from a chorus of tiny voices. "You have more work to do!"

Pulling the parka's hood over her eyes Stella moaned, "Why can't anyone let me sleep?"

There was the pitter-patter of tiny feet as something, or some things, scurried across her chest and pulled the hood from her face. Squinting through the glare she saw tiny black dots, like stars in reverse, dotting the soft white cushion, and as she sat up the dark spots dispersed leaving tiny paw prints dotting the fresh snow. Knowing there were no mice in the Arctic, it took a moment for Stella to name the tiny stark white creatures. "Lemmings!" she gasped, her breath visible in the crisp winter air.

The first voice spoke out from behind her. "Yes, Lemmings. They've worked hard to keep you warm as you slept, so please," Stella struggled up in the deep snow to see who was addressing her, "don't tread on them." A pristine white fox stood nearby, almost invisible against the snow with its beady black eyes locked on the girl. Stella had seen one only once before, shortly after first arriving in the Arctic. Snow foxes were rare and very shy, so to see one playing in the snow around Base A, even at a distance, had been a treat. Now this fox was near enough to see its red tongue lolling between razor sharp teeth, and Stella fell back into the snow as it opened its mouth and spoke. "You must hurry. You've been asleep far too long."

"Where am I?" Stella asked. "How did I get here?"

"You are not too far from your home. Moros did not keep his word and dropped you here to freeze to death. But we found you and kept you warm while you recovered from your fall. But now you must hurry to your home, your family needs you. Virgo is holding them."

Stella bolted upright suddenly remembering it all; how Moros had tricked her into trading the entire universe, for the chance to be with her family, and how she had selfishly taken his poisonous bait. "How do I get to the base?" She asked as she began to struggle through the waist deep snow.

"Follow us, but you must hurry. Time is of the essence." The fox answered.

"Why would you help me?"

"Why are we helping?" The fox asked, and as it did a veritable army of lemmings grouped themselves around Stella. "We are the children of Earth, and we are here to aid you, our sibling, in your mission."

Stella looked across the swarm of black pinpoints that were the eyes of the lemmings, all gauging the girl's resolve. "It's too late. Moros fooled me into playing his game. And I was so close! But there's no chance of me winding the clockwork now. We're all doomed. I just want to be with my family when the end comes."

The fox's beady eyes took the measure of the girl and Stella felt as if the fox might somehow know that even though Moros had tempted her, she had come through the door by her own choice. Stella felt her face flush with shame in the cold arctic air. "Yes, I understand. Moros is the greatest of deceivers. There are few who would not be tempted by his false promises. However, your journey is not over or your work yet finished. Listen." The fox's ears perked up straight.

Stella turned her head to the gusts, where all she could hear was the howling of the wind across the arctic wastes. She pulled back the hood of her parka and concentrated, trying to hear what lay beyond the squall. Then she heard it, the booming tick of the clockwork rumbling inside her head. She waited breathlessly and then came the rejoinder, a tock that rose slowly to a crescendo.

The fox's ears fell. "Life and light have not been extinguished. While the clock yet ticks there is still hope."

"But how would I find my way back to the gate?" Stella asked, realizing just how far she had fallen.

"We can help you on the first leg of your journey back. We will bring you to your family, and from there others will show you the way. As you carry the hope of every being that loves light you will not fail." There was no doubt in the fox's voice.

All around her, tiny eyes silently pleading with Stella not to quit. "Okay," she responded to the cheering squeaks of the lemmings. "Which way do I go?"

The tribe of lemmings trotted before her as she ran, trampling the snow with the weight of their tiny bodies to make a path through the high snowdrifts. When she saw the Dome butting out from the deep snow, Stella wondered what waited inside and hoped her family was okay. Reaching the Dome's door, the lemmings and the fox pushed with her to open it.

"Hurry!" the fox barked as Stella raced inside to find her family. "There is little time left!"

Only a short distance down the hall, she heard the raucous roar of Tim and Pace playing. Following the sound, Stella raced towards the long corridor that connected the living areas and the observatory, and turning the final corner, stopped dead in her tracks. There at the door to the observatory, playing a game of S*mash'em up* with Tim and Pace was a widely grinning moon man.

"Loony!" Stella exclaimed, "What are you doing here?"

Lifting a toy car, the ball headed imp answered. "I told you I wanted to play, but you never let me." Loony smashed his car into one that Tim was wheeling across the floor. "I'm having so much fun; I don't know why I haven't visited Earth sooner." He hooted wildly, "And look, cookies!" In his rocky hand were a handful of Stella's mother's cookies. He crammed them between crooked lips and crumbs scattered across the floor as his cratered cheeks bulged with the sweets.

Though exactly what they meant she could not be sure, but the ridiculous words, *Food for the moon*, came to Stella's mind as she demanded, "Where's my mother?"

"Your mother? She locked herself in the kitchen." Loony replied casually, as if nothing were the matter. "I guess Verena's been too busy to dig her out."

Relieved Celeste was safe; Stella tried to reason with the imp. "Loony, you know you don't belong here. Your place is in the sky. I'm not sure what Old Sol will say when he finds out about what you're doing. Instead of playing around, maybe you should be worried about what's going to happen to you when you go back."

"I'm not going back." Loony had the widest craziest grin on his face that Stella had ever seen.

"What do you mean, you're not going back?" Of all the wacky things Stella had heard Loony say, and he was always saying such things, this was his nuttiest idea of all.

Within the rocky crags that held Loony's eyes, blazed an angry glow. "So I'm supposed to revolve around Earth forever? I'm supposed to stay up there to be picked on by those stupid Planets? I don't think so." Stella was taken aback by his seething anger. "There's a different time coming, if you haven't figured that out. Now I know that my destiny wasn't to be a slave to the Earth's pull. I'm fated for something different."

"How do you know you have a different fate?"

"Because I was told by someone who knows." snarled the rocky lips.

"And who was that, Loony?"

The moon man snickered, "Can't you guess?"

"This is no time for riddles, Loony! Who told you all those lies?"

As if on some invisible cue, Tim and Pace began to shout while slapping their cars rhythmically on the floor, "VEH-REEN-NAH! VEH-REEN-NAH! VEH-REEN-NAH!!"

Over the twin's irritating chant, Stella questioned the smirking moon man. "You've been talking to Verena? Loony! How could you do that? Don't you know she works for Moros? That's who we've been working to defeat!"

"Let's just say I've changed sides." The orb of the moon was dark, dismal and foreboding. "Now that it looks like Terra isn't going to make it, well I've got to look after myself."

"What do you mean by, Earth not making it? I knew there was something that I wasn't being told." Angrily Stella put her nose right against the Loony's, all the craters and cracks on his surface visible in sharp detail, and yelled at the top of her lungs. "What has happened to the Earth?"

As if invoked by the question, the doors to the laboratory flew open and there on the threshold stood Verena Maldek. "So, the brave hero has come home! Very good! Now we will no longer need to chase her across the universe." She snapped an order toward the darkened lab. "Professor Ray, come here immediately."

From the lab's shadowy depths stepped a being barely recognizable to Stella. Even in the gloomy darkness, she knew that what came from the lab was in fact her father, but something about him made her shudder. The ashen face that moved out from the shadows was drawn and hollow and the eyes dead. "Dad?" She questioned as the zombie took its place behind his enchantress.

"Yes, your father is probably still in there, somewhere," Verena cackled a hideous laugh so similar to that of Virgo's that Stella's skin crawled. "Escort this child into the laboratory, where I can question her more comfortably." The zombie lurched forward, arms outstretched to obey the command.

"Dad?" Stella pleaded as the husk of the man grasped her with hands withered to no more than claws. "Please don't." Stella dodged his grasp and tried to run, but three who stood behind her, shoved her squealing into her father's stiff open arms.

"Very good Loony! Excellent, Tim and Pace! You have done well! Moros will be pleased that you have chosen to serve him. Now bring this nuisance into the laboratory." Her dark eyes focused on Stella. "I will enjoy extracting retribution for your part in destroying my brethren. It was generous of Moros to send you to me."

Stella shrieked as her father carried her away, kicking and struggling to free herself from his clutches. "Dad, no! Don't do this to me; you don't understand what it means!" Cold breath chilled Stella's neck as Perceval's grip tightened in response.

"He cannot hear you to help, little troublemaker. What is left of him, is a slave to me. What will remain of you; will be much, much less."

"Not in my house!" The response to that threat sounded with such determination, that all turned to see its source. "You've worn out your welcome Verena. I think it's time you leave." At the end of the hall, a light flared in the darkness revealing silhouetted against the stark facility walls, a swollen bellied figure.

"So, it is the mother! This is much better, as now I will not have to waste my time ripping you out of your hole. You have wisely decided to bring yourself to me."

"I've come for my family."

"Alone?" Verena snickered.

"I'm not alone," Celeste declared. From behind the pregnant woman a brown streak shot, leaping over the trio of Tim and Pace and Loony, and in a quick bound was upon Verena Maldek. What happened next took only seconds, but to Stella it was an eternity, where past, present and future hung in the balance.

Sirius held Verena pinned to the floor as Celeste rushed past. Loony moved to block her progress, but with one quick push, she shoved the imp to the ground. "Perceval!" She stated calmly, her eyes boring deep into her husband's soul. "You're hurting our daughter. Let her go and remember who you are." At Celeste's request his dead eyes sparked and as his grip loosened, Stella fell free to the floor.

Celeste had grasped Tim and Pace by the wrists and was leading them into the lab. "Stella! Bring your father." Taking her father's hand, Stella pulled him along, his legs shuffling stiffly through the door of the lab.

Loony lunged for Celeste again, but even with both hands full, Stella's mother was more than a match for the frenzied moon. As he charged, she lifted a foot to meet him and with a swift kick booted him down the hall.

In seconds the entire Ray family was assembled across the threshold of the laboratory door. Celeste placed Tim and Pace near their father and said two words, in a voice not to be disobeyed and which rooted them to the floor. "Stay here!"

A dark haze began to emanate from the combatants in the hall. Stella shouted a warning to her mother. "Verena is transforming! We need to block the doors!" The figure of Verena, arms and legs flailing as she fought off the attacks of Stella's pet, was becoming engulfed in a shadowy seething cloud.

"Sirius, come here!" Celeste yelled over the commotion of growls and shrieks that came from the tangled pair. "Stella! Lock the doors!"

Sirius slipped through just as Stella swung the doors shut, but before they closed, Stella could see a large dark shape rising through the black smoke, only it was not Verena Maldek, but Virgo, the last surviving member of the Zodiac. Stella fastened the locks on the doors and spun to see the shocked look on her mother's face.

"What is that out there? What's happening to Verena?" Celeste asked.

Stella knew there was no time to explain. "We need to barricade these doors, now!"

Putting her shoulder to the door, Celeste shouted to her husband. "Perceval! Help us block the doors." Awakened from his nightmare and shedding the dreadful influence of Verena, Perceval nodded his head and began moving through the lab, bringing boxes and barrels to stack against the door. "Tim, Pace! Help your father!" The boys bolted upright at their mother's command, and in an instant were grabbing whatever they could find, and piling it in front of the observatory doors. As they braced the door, Celeste slid exhausted into a chair.

From outside the lab came an appeal. "Stella? Are you there? Can we talk?"

Stella climbed the barricade of boxes and barrels and hissed through a crack at the top of the door. "What do you want, Loony? Now that you've joined up with Moros, I have nothing to say to you." She peered through the thin crack and could just make out the moon man moving through the dark smoke filling the hall.

"There's no other choice. Moros controls our destinies. You can't beat him, so why try?" There was a brief pause. "I think you have only another couple seconds left before V breaks in there. She's not very happy you've locked her out." Stella heard something stir on the other side of the door, something that sounded very big. An exchange of murmurs penetrated the barricade. "She wants me to give you one last chance. Open the door now. If you don't, I think you're going to get her very angry. And believe me; you don't want to see *V* angry."

"Go away Loony. I don't want to know you anymore."

"You had your chance!" Loony shouted as he stomped off into the hall's smoky depths.

"Good! And stay away!" Stella retorted. The last she saw of the crazy moon man was his dropped trousers and tiny buttocks. As he disappeared the smoke swirled violently and a blast of turbid smog rocketed down the hall and slammed the door. The heavy blow jarred the barricade and sent Stella tumbling from the top of the heap. Even as she got to her feet, her mother was there next to her, and her father and brothers were already busy adding more support to the barricade. Sirius stood bravely guarding the door, ready to pounce on whatever might come through. Another crash walloped the door, shaking the laboratory.

"What's happening, Stella? Celeste asked.

"Virgo is here!" Stella wished she could have said the words with less fear, but the memory of being crushed in Virgo's hand like a rag doll forbade it. "I'm not sure how long we can hold her off. The Zodiac has grown too powerful."

Celeste reached a hand around her swollen belly to nervously stroke the baby that waited within, and trying to sound hopeful, whispered. "Maybe there's a way to call for help, maybe someone will come to help us…" Then straightening up, she put her other arm around her daughter. "And if no one comes to help, we'll just need to beat Verena or Virgo or whatever it is out there, ourselves, together. I won't let anything separate us again."

In her mother's eyes, Stella could see she believed what she said, and was confident that if there were a way for their family to survive the thing at the doorstep, her mother was the one who would find it. But Stella knew that there was only one way to stop the darkness's spread.

"Mom, you have to let me go. Moros lied to get me to come home. He promised if I did, you'd all be safe. But you're not. Only after the Celestial Clockwork is rewound will we be safe. If I don't find a way back up, everything will come to an end, there'll be no future for anyone. But I still have a one last chance, somehow I just know it."

The only way Stella knew of to get back to the clockwork, was the telescope in her room, and getting past Verena, Virgo or whatever monster Moros has summoned would not be easy. Searching the observatory for some way to escape, she stopped at her father's massive telescope. A loud crash jolted the room and the barricade began to collapse. Everyone in the observatory froze as a voice boomed. "There will be no future and there will be no past! *THAT IS YOUR FATE!* The darkness will devour you all." There was silence in the room as a look of terror covered Perceval's face and Tim and Pace began to cry.

Stella's knees were shaking, but she quickly collected herself. In her last moment of weakness she had fallen for Moros' trick, but now she refused to break. Rushing to the telescope, she looked through and there in the furthest reaches of the universe, she spied a tiny ring of light fading into the dark.

"Dad!" Stella jostled her father, trying to break the paralysis of fear that held him. "You need to focus the telescope on that nova." Perceval didn't move, but stood staring at the door, his mouth hung open in shock and awe. Racing over, Sirius took the sleeve of his jacket and pulled him towards the telescope controls.

"Perceval! Do what Stella says!" At the sound of his wife's voice, the astronomer began to adjust the controls. The giant scope swung upwards. Though the telescope was the most advanced in the world, even here in the clear still air of the Arctic, Stella knew it was not strong enough to view such a far off place as the end of the universe, but she had to try.

"This is totally ridiculous! I just can't aim this telescope without the proper calculations, and they would take hours to work out. Why without them, there's no precision, there's no…" argued the flustered Professor Ray, his identity returning as he worked his equipment… "Science!"

"Don't think about that dad! Just aim the scope as best you can." Stella spoke gently to her father, imagining how horrible it must have been for him to be under Verena's evil spell.

"Fools! You cannot succeed!" The pounding intensified, and the chairs, tables, and whatnot stacked at the door, shuddered and shifted with each deafening thud. A thick black haze began to seep through the blockade. "It is fated for all to fall into the darkness of Moros!"

The barricade shook as if it were about to collapse. Celeste flung the chair she where rested onto the quaking heap and rebuked the darkness. "Go away Verena! There is no place for you here!"

Tim and Pace, who had been running through the lab looking for anything else to put on the barricades, were now both tugging a heavy piece of electronic equipment towards the door. Perceval stopped adjusting the knobs on the telescope controls and hit the red button that locked the scope into place. "I'm locked on the nova. Now what?" he asked, glancing back to the confrontation at the door where Celeste stood bravely amid the dark fog that threatened to engulf her.

"Mom?" Stella cried out.

"Go Stella!" Celeste looked back over her shoulder. "Do what you need to do!"

Stella positioned herself at the eyepiece of the telescope, unsure if anything would happen. Where she wanted to go, was past the galaxies, much,

much further than from where Loony had first pulled her up. And Astraea or someone would need to be there to pull her up, except they were all… gone.

"Are you sure I have the scope positioned correctly?" Her father asked after a moment. Before Stella could answer, a loud whining pierced the air. "What is that?" Perceval exclaimed, pointing to the ceiling. Stella looked up to see a silvery blur zip through the lab and stop to hover right at her shoulder. A hatch in the tiny disc opened and a six-legged creature popped out.

"Zeb Zibulon!" Stella shouted.

"Yes Stella," the tiny spider answered. "I followed your instructions and found my way here to your home." He looked around the wreckage of the room, and the thick black smoke seething through the barricade. "But perhaps I have come at an inopportune time."

"It's Virgo, she works for Moros!" Stella replied anxiously eyeing the collapsing doorway, "I have to get back to from where I fell, right now. Do you know where that is?"

Zeb skittered back into his ship only to promptly reappear with a tiny tablet in his hands. "I believe these are the coordinates." Perceval's eyes bulged as the ship floated towards him and the spider on its hull offered him the note.

"Try those, dad, quick!" Grabbing a magnifying glass from his desk, Perceval read the miniscule numbers and entered them into the telescope's keyboard. The giant cylinder moved to its new position, a fraction of an inch from where it had been pointed.

Stella looked through the eyepiece, and saw emerging through a breach in the nebulous haze, a distant square of light. Her eyes widened in awe, as she gazed at the doorway so near the end of the universe, the doorway through which she had fallen. "Please! Please!" She whispered, to whom she wasn't sure. "Please help us!"

There was a black smoke surged through the buckled doors. terrible gut wrenching sound as the barricade collapsed and a torrent of Stella spun to see her mother standing defiant before the smashed doors, and her father moving next to her, and then Tim and Pace too. They were just four small figures standing against an immense darkness.

"Stella! Escape before…" A thunderous crash drowned out her mother's words.

"Mom? I..I.." What Stella wasn't sure of was, whether she could leave her mother here like this, or her father or the twins.

"Get going, you are our only hope!" Celeste urged her daughter on. "We'll hold Verena off, but hurry!" The barricade was blasted aside, and even over the sound of ripping metal, Stella heard the terror in her mother's voice.

Waves of fear rose up within Stella dark and deep, threatening to overwhelm her. "No, "she proclaimed, "I won't let it end like this. I won't!" Closing her eyes there was no more doubt, no more darkness. She knew where she was going. Behind the lids of her eyes was only light, pure and vibrant. She felt a gentle pull as her feet left the floor, and her body slid through the lens of the scope. Slipping through, she glanced back to see a wave of hideous darkness poised to engulf her family.

21 THE FINAL STEPS

Drawn up past the atmosphere of Earth and out of the solar system, Stella zipped like a silver dart through all the realms of space and into the strange void beyond, straight towards the target of the small square portal. With a familiar pop she was back in the chamber where she had fallen for Moros' deceits. The door closed behind her with an ominous thud.

Stricken, DubDub lay nearby on the floor. Stella tentatively approached his encased body and saw within the black ice's confines, the face of her friend, frozen in horror. Striking the casing in frustration, her hand glanced off its slick surface. She reached around to hug the coffin shaped prison and whispered, "I'm sorry I left you. I'm sorry I believed Moros' lies." Her cheek lay against the cold dark ice and her breath left a shallow puddle on its surface, glistening like mercury.

Seeing the thaw, Stella pulled her face from the ice and held her mouth open in a wide circle. Feeing within her chest a slight tickle, an exhalation of warmth flooded from her lungs and as the air passed her lips it glowed and swirled and thawed the frozen block. Wooden bits of DubDub's body were exposed as the black ice fell like drops of molten lead and as soon as it was free, Stella turned the knob to wind her friend. With the breath of light seeping into the mechanical man's casings, in seconds Stella could hear ice cracking as the gears within broke free from their bonds. DubDub lurched within his melting prison, the whirring of his accelerating gears signaling that he had not been conquered by Moros' attack.

"Which way did he go? Did you see?" Stella asked. The recovering automaton's eyes all pointed towards one door. "I've got to stop him. My family is in danger!" Stella jumped to her feet.

There was a distinct snap as DubDub's mouth cracked open, but only enough for him to mumble. "I'm coming with you! I won't let you face him alone."

In her friend's eyes Stella saw grim determination. "There isn't time to wait for you to thaw completely." Stella stated gently, the immediate peril of her family forefront in her mind. "But come once you can. I'm going to need all the help I can get."

Making sure to avoid the door through which she had fallen to Earth, Stella found another of the three ajar and checked to make sure Moros was not lurking within. The pristine mirrored walls reflected only themselves, with no sign or stain of darkness. Two doors, one square and one circular were at the base of the cube. The angular one was flung wide open. Stepping over its threshold Stella looked ahead, to where not a hundred feet away, was the final gate. It was sided by two tall columns, and from within, a rumbling tock reverberated. "It hasn't stopped ticking yet," Stella thought. "I still have time!"

Only steps from her goal, Moros materialized to block the way. "You are a persistent creature."

"No! Not now!" Stella cried. "Let me pass!"

"Let you pass? Of course not!" The darkness spat. "In moments the clockwork will tick for its final time. All I need do is hold you here while we wait for that magnificent event. You should've stayed on Earth, human. Your end would have been less… painful."

"You're a cheat! Verena was still there and she wasn't going anywhere." Stella spat back. She dashed left, and then darted right, but the shadow shifted to cutting her off from the gate.

Moros scoffed at the girl's attempts. "You seek validation in movement, as if the few feeble steps you take might imply that you are truly alive, and there is some goal towards which you could aspire, some truth to attain. But with each step only death is approached, for that is your only destiny. You are born to die and die you must. Your very being demands it."

"While we wait for my reign to begin, I ask you, what is the glory of the Stars, what is all their light, but vanity?" He crowed. "In time, they will fall into darkness, leaving nothing but a void. Then what will result from the labors of those suns? It will be as if they never even existed, just as your friend Astraea no longer exists."

"You're a liar!"

"I, a liar? What is the greatest lie but time? It tells you that you are alive, but in its grip you are merely dying." Moros bent his finger, and with that subtle gesture it became a hook of cold dark steel. "Have you thought about aging, child? The passing of time until your muscles fail and your bones weaken and the smile on your face becomes a harsh frown. Have you thought about these things at all?" Flicking his wrist abruptly he cast the hook deep into the girl's body, fishing for her very heart. "You cannot deny destiny, you cannot alter fate. Mine is to reign in darkness forever! And yours is to age and die!"

The hook began to pull… And Stella, feeling aches deep within her bones, was suddenly very, very tired. She noticed her hands were wrinkled and had lost their pink tone. And spots! There were spots on her hands like freckles, but darker, with none of the youthfulness freckles should have. Old! Stella thought. They made her hands look old.

"There's a mirror in here somewhere." As Moros looked on gloating, Stella's stiff fingers fumbled through her parka's cluttered pockets. As she flexed her hands, stabs of pain shot up her arms. In agony she grasped the mirror and pulled it from the pocket, needing both hands to hold it to her face, as even this smallest effort was excruciating.

The mirror before her was a mere blur, and a throbbing pain pulsed in her temple as she strained to focus. Struggling for a clear view, she dropped the mirror upon seeing what it reflected, a face not her own, a face old and wrinkled, a face like her grandmother's when Stella had seen her last.

When Moros laughed, even that was different, sounding dull and distant as if her ears were plugged. "Yes," he shouted, though Stella could barely make out the words. "Your fate is to fall to time, as it is the Stars, Planets and Galaxies! All age and decay and all die!! The only way to stop that horror, is to let the clockwork run down, and when it does, death itself will fall to Moros!"

With her body wracked with anguish, it took increased effort for Stella to stay erect. A shard of oblivion sliced the air, as the shifting abyss that was Moros, pointed toward the gate. "The clockwork has almost run down! Its rude mechanics will no longer sustain the charade of life! Soon there will be no past, no future! Soon, all will be a timeless, lightless and lifeless, now!"

The air around Stella darkened as if light itself was being extinguished in Moros' void. Cold numbed her limbs and icy chills ran through her veins. As her knees begin to buckle she knew then she did not have the strength to defeat Moros and doubted whether she had even the stamina to reach the gate, old age had weakened her so. Suddenly, the knowledge that she was dying, and would probably be dead even before the Celestial Clockwork stopped, was unquestionable. In her failing sight Stella could see death coming for her and knew it came to claim its final victory.

If time stopped and death held absolute and endless dominion, then all would have been for nothing. If time stopped Stella would never take her place in the long line of people who had come before her, who had given her life through their efforts. If time stopped, her mother's new baby would never be born. A curse croaked through Stella's dry, cracked lips. *"You're a monster!"*

There was the rattle of the clockwork, creaking and miserable and as the sound passed beyond hearing, from everywhere darkness flooded, filling in the space between the clockwork's ticks with a terrible nothingness. For a timeless moment the darkness held sway, then the clockwork sounded again, weary and worn, barely strong enough to send the gloom back to the void from which it had come. Deeper than ever this glimpse of the abyss had been, and Stella knew the clockwork was about to fail and its ability to sustain light was at an end.

Apocalypse raged as the reply came. "I am more than a monster! I am Moros! I am that which will destroy time itself!" The clattering from behind the final gate was intensifying, the sound of grinding, screeched through the air. "Do you hear that, vermin of Earth? *Time stops! Time ends! Now DIE!!!"*

Rage struck like lightning and every nerve in Stella's crippled body was seared in its transit. The flash set her mind ablaze, illuminating just one thought. If she were fated to fall, if this was where her journey ended, she would go to her death fighting. Rushing forward in a fury, a feeble and old Stella Ray flung her aged self at her enemy. Although the heart in her chest felt like it would burst from the exertion, with the last of her strength Stella raged on. With legs collapsing beneath her, she propelled her aging body onward. With wrinkled fingers poised to claw, she threw herself at the beast; cracked and broken teeth ready to tear at whatever substance it was composed. With aching arms outstretched, she fell upon Moros to capture him in a final wrathful embrace.

As Stella met the darkness nothing stopped her charge. An excruciating shriek pierced her ears as she slid through Moros and fell not to the ground, but through a monstrous black hole. The tortured scream that followed as she passed beyond the portal of her adversary's body confirmed she had hurt her foe badly, and managing to twist her aching neck to see behind, she saw his silhouette writhing in agony, and contained within that outline, was a view of the space from where she had leapt, a view of the past. The tormented figure jerked spasmodically and then crumpled in on itself, sealing the breach.

Below, if down was the direction she was indeed falling, the aged Stella spied a giant hoop, whose curved surfaces were covered with opalescent scales. As she passed through the circle the features of a snake presented themselves, the fanged mouth biting the tail. Beneath the reptilian circle stood a trio of tall mountains, and as Stella fell towards them, these towering edifices resolved into three statuesque women, their visages larger than those of Mount Rushmore. In these ladies' laps, six gargantuan hands worked with nimble fingers performing tasks with practiced ease. One pair measured a length of thread and held it out, while another cut it exactly at the prescribed place. The third set of hands held out a piece of cloth they had been weaving, took the thread, and wove it into the fabric. Then all six hands grasped ends of this wondrous web, and held it beneath the old woman to catch the falling crone in its fashioned warp and weft.

The impact of Stella's fall was softened as her aged body settled in the fabric's intricate weave. Each thread extended towards some destiny that lay far beyond the matrix in which she lay suspended, their fantastic colors shifting in ever changing patterns. Then as the six hands pulled its ends, the wondrous web went taut and Stella's aged body was propelled up in a rapid thrust. As if blessing her passing, enigmatic smiles curled on the lips of the faces of the titanic sisters as Stella shot past them.

Moving at a velocity that caused her joints to ache, Stella suddenly noticed an elderly woman flying alongside her. The old woman not only matched the speed of her flight, but also mimicked her movements, her face wincing with the aches and pains of old age. When with torturous effort Stella lifted her hand, her companion in flight did the same, and shouting to this duplicate, "Hello! Do I know you?" the other shouted back, at exactly the same time, "Hello! Do I know you?"

Suddenly the space around the doppelganger congealed into a vivid tableau even as they flew. Stella's twin now sat on a large cushioned couch surrounded by young children who played about her feet. This matron, who just moments ago was a reflection of the aching and aged body of Stella, now smiled happily as she watched the boisterous play of the youngsters. As they rocketed upwards, these toddlers, to Stella's astonishment, turned into babies, and those babies grew younger still. Soon they were only figures of soft mists and then gone completely.

The old woman continued to change, growing younger and shedding the ravages of age. The lines on her face were softening, her skin turning suppler, and color began replacing the gray in her hair. Holding her hand up, Stella examined it. Her skin also, was no longer that deathly shade of gray, and the aches that had wracked her body were no longer so severe. The woman was quickly reverting into middle age. It was like watching a flipbook, but flipped in reverse, with even the scenery changing. Stella noticed that her twin now stood with a young woman and this woman was growing younger too, quickly becoming a teenager, then a girl, then a toddler, and then a mere infant in the mirror Stella's arms.

The scene became a hospital room, and Stella was in bed holding the baby. There was someone else with her now; a man who smiled at the woman the way Perceval had smiled at Celeste, when they had brought Tim and Pace back from the hospital. The man and the woman cooed over the baby, laughing and smiling until the scene blurred again and when it solidified the couple was dressed for a wedding. The man wore a sharp tuxedo and she, the doppelganger, wore a beautiful white wedding dress, and even Stella, as she flew upwards watching this most peculiar scene, though she had always disliked dresses, thought that this one was not too bad and rather pretty.

The man who had been so happy in the hospital, shook hands with a man that looked very much like Stella's father, but much older. Then Stella's mother was next to the duplicate Stella, and helping her dress, fixing the long folds of the not so bad wedding gown and fussing over its veil. Celeste looked much the same as Stella remembered her, with only a hint of crow's feet at the corner of her eyes, and a tint of silver to her hair. A young girl with golden hair was standing nearby, beaming with pride at the bride and fidgeting with the bouquet of spring flowers she held. Two teenage boys, both wearing dark suits, suddenly appeared from behind the folds of the billowing wedding dress with mischievous grins on their faces, but before Stella could see what they were scheming the scene shuffled again, as if the next cards in the deck were being revealed.

Then there was Stella, no, it was still the mirror Stella, dressed in a cap and gown and standing at a podium accepting a diploma. It was a perfect summer day and Stella could feel the warm sun on her face. Brushing the tassel from her face she studied the girl across from her, a girl wearing a red parka who stared back with the same intensity. Suddenly Stella wasn't sure which of the two she was, or which eyes she was watching from, and then the two persons, the observer and the observed, the dreamer and the dream, joined as one.

When that happened, Stella no longer felt herself falling or rising and no longer felt old or tired or afraid. She didn't feel pulled by the future or pushed by the past. She felt like who she was, Stella, and that was good enough for anything that needed to be done. And realizing how this moment in time was just exactly what it should be, no matter how anyone might've tried to make it otherwise, there was a quiet pop and Stella found herself standing at the place where she had jumped into Moros. That terrible champion of death had vanished, almost as if he had never been there at all. Without another thought of the past Stella sprinted towards the final gate.

Two large pillars braced a towering door covered with engravings, with all manner of angled and jagged emblems interspersed amongst complex undulating curves. At the door's sides stood two gigantic entities and though they did not move, Stella was certain they were alive and watching. These beings were composed of segmented columns stacked upon each other, reminding Stella of the tottering, towering constructions her brothers would make with wooden toy blocks. On the topmost of these cylindrical blocks was carved a rudimentary face and upon that was perched a pointed rough-hewn cap. These were the Watchers who had been waiting and these were the guardians of the gate beyond which lay eternity.

As Stella approached the gate, the guardians swayed almost imperceptibly, with only the slightest bend in their stiff bodies. Pressing her palm against the door's surface she felt a labored tick, like the dull thud of a dying heartbeat, and as the tick subsided, the light about her faded with it. Stella stood in deepening gloom, praying for it to pass. Another tick thrummed and the light revived. Sensing that any tick might be the clockwork's last, Stella put both hands on the gate and pushed, lightly at first and then with more force. Nothing moved. With her shoulder against the massive door she heaved with all her might, but still it would not budge. The two imperious sentinels quivered slightly but with little regard to the small girl at their feet.

For a moment Stella thought of going back for DubDub, who had been so lucky with locked doors, but remembering how she had left him, knew he would already be at her side if he were able. Besides, she considered, there were no more choices to be made. There was just this final gate.

"Say the magic word." A soft voice advised and Stella spun around at the sound, but only her countless reflections were with her in the mirrored chamber. "Say the magic word." The voice whispered again.

"But I don't know any magic word!" Stella responded.

The voice spoke only once more, but with unquestionable conviction, "Stella, you know the word."

And then she did know the word and the word was "---------"

As she held the wondrous word in her thoughts, the tall sentinels bent. Slowly and solemnly they moved what were their ears to her, to take the word from her lips. As Stella uttered the word, the gate opened. But as soon as the breath had passed from her lips, she forgot what that word had been. She had felt its formation somewhere within, and the expelling of it across her tongue, but now could not recall its sound.

"Stella! You did it!" DubDub squealed as he ran to meet his friend, looking completely thawed and none the worse for wear.

"We did it!" Stella corrected and taking the automaton's wooden hand they strolled together through the final gate where, as if a veil had been pierced, what lay behind the stage that was the universe, stood revealed.

22 WITHIN THE CLOCKWORK

When Stella stepped through the final gate with DubDub, she found they were not outside the universe at all, but firmly ensconced within it. In going out, they had by some incomprehensible topological twist, arrived at the very heart of the universe. All around shone the absolute essence of every living being contained within the universe's bounds, and these were set like billions of shining jewels, arrayed to form a perfect sphere. The placement of each seemed so precise, that Stella had no doubt they were arranged so for some higher, sublime purpose. These essences were of the Stars, Planets, Humans, Galaxies, Moons and other beings impossible to identify, each obviously an integral part of the enormous mechanism that encompassed the duo.

Stella's attention settled, on a brilliant yellow gem nestled in the complex web of being, operating about her. Just as Old Sol had been a laughing friend, the Sun in Earth's sky, and a Star in the depths of the Milky Way galaxy, here he was gem whose glittering rays reached across the whole of the vast clockwork. On his gleaming facets every other gem in the clockwork was reflected and Stella saw that those gems also held Sol's reflection, upon which was visible, the likenesses of all in the clockwork. These reflections created an endless web and though it was a confounding sight, Stella could still see, behind the yellow jewel's shimmering veneer, the likeness of her friend, a warm happy Sun headed man.

From each and every of these jewel-like beings, countless shafts of light shot. These rays interconnected with others and as the myriad rays of these jeweled gears met, they all worked in concert with the rest to create the bonds that held the universe together. The whole arrangement of rays and jewels and inner essences formed an exquisite engine, designed to generate life.

But while Stella saw the perfection of its operation, she could also see here and there, rays that were failing, fading, like the worn down teeth on an overworked gear. Desperately these dimming beams strained for connection with the others and through their efforts maintained the contact that allowed the great machine to function. But Stella, as she moved toward a place at the center of the sphere where countless beams met in a dazzling conjunction, knew they could not sustain their pains indefinitely.

Weakly and feebly the clockwork ticked, and the rays of every being moved haltingly in accordance with it, staggered by the effort it took to stay in sync. Stella's heart beat with the clockwork's, and as it did rays of light emanated from her body, reaching out into the sphere surrounding her. Luminous shafts originating deep within her breast joined with uncountable others that crisscrossed the clockwork leaving Stella amazed at just how many beings with whom she was connected.

As she moved ahead, Stella followed one of these spikes of light out to where it meshed neatly with the rays of a radiant gem. She strained to see whose essence lay within and was surprised to recognize Doctor Dee. Following her link with him Stella traced a few of the rays that shot from within that kindly elder, and saw they met with those of other scientists from the lab. The rays of those men's inmost light, while dispersing themselves among millions of other beings, all had one ray that met a ray of her own, connecting Stella to all she had met in the Astrophelarium. Other rays from some of these men seemed to converge on a spot right behind Stella and she turned to see they met with the rays that emerged from DubDub's chest right where his spring was situated.

DubDub's complete attention was transfixed on the mechanism that surrounded him on all sides. Stella wondered what he was seeing, but there was no time to ask for the clockwork sounded again, as if to remind her of her duty. "Come on, DubDub! We have to wind the clockwork!"

Passing though the brilliant rays that ran through the globe connecting all to all, Stella continued on the path to the central place where she imagined the clockwork could be wound, still not certain exactly how that would be done. Within the haze of light ahead, she saw a place where every being's inmost light reached toward a spot dense with a profusion of rays. She did not know when, but at some point along the path the sound of the clockwork was not a "tick" at anymore, but a heartbeat. And there, where all beings found a familiar bond, where all differences were knit in commonality, at the point where each and every being converged in one and joined in communion, was the heart of the clockwork.

Pinioned on a million rays of light, the heart rested in a being of purest, crystalline energy, and the heart was a human heart, though transfigured beyond comprehension. It was quickly apparent that this heart was the central spoke, the axel around which the entire universe revolved. As Stella stepped onto the platform where this being central to all life in the universe stood, eyes human and blissful with joy, met her in greeting. "Hello." he said. "I'm so glad you've come. It's almost time."

"Time for what?"

"You don't know?" Though there was the slightest sense of puzzlement, there was no sign of distress. "You don't know why it is you are here?"

Stella replied with the only answer she knew, "I'm here to wind the clockwork."

"That's not quite it." The translucent man let out a weary sigh as in his chest, the ethereal heart beat and a shimmering pulse of energy blossomed out. All around the universe moved to the beat. "When I traveled here from Earth, I too believed that I would be called on only to wind the clockwork. I was surprised to find that I was fated to be the integral element in the clockwork itself, the one to anchor and balance all this activity. And now you are here as my replacement."

"Your replacement?" Stella gasped. "I'm supposed to replace you?"

"I've been here a very long time. I've watched most of the Stars I had once met; pass into the light beyond sight. I've run my course and fulfilled my destiny. Now it's time for the next to take their place. It is your heart that is needed, just as mine was. The beating of your heart will regulate the movements of the universe, keeping all operating in productive accord. It is quite an honor. Just imagine what it means to be the hub of the universe."

"Are you God?" Stella asked, awed by the possibility.

"Not in the slightest," he chuckled. "God, though perhaps I have felt that force more directly than most, resides in places that none of us yet recognize. I am an instrument of that power but still only a man, though I'm certain I have changed quite a bit since arriving here."

"Don't you miss your friends? Don't you miss your family?"

"I do." He declared decidedly. "I have since answering the call and leaving Earth. I missed them every step of the way, through the Solar System and Empyriania and the Universal Sea. But I did not shun my responsibility." The man's heart beat again and the universe lurched in rickety accord. Stella did not know quite what to say.

"There are few of those left, it is time for you to take your place." He stated with intense urgency. "The process is quite easy. You need only to step toward me and take my place, as I did for him who had come before me, those many, many years ago."

"I can't." Stella quivered. "I don't belong here. I belong with my family."

"You must take up this duty. It is your destiny. That is what has brought you here." On this the man was firm.

"Please?" Stella cried, "I can't do this. I want to go back to Earth. I want to go home."

"I wish there were some other way," was the sympathetic response. "But it is you who fate has brought here. The universe is depending on you. I assure you it is a painless transition. Now please, take my place. We can no longer wait, my time is up."

It was true. In the short time since they had met, the man had become even less substantial. The innumerable rays that joined him to the occupants of the universe seemed weaker, as if the strength of their bonds had lessened since Stella had first arrived, and now threatened to fail. All around rays were fading, faltering. "Come." He said, reaching out a barely tangible hand. "It is for the best."

Knowing that to refuse would mean the death of the universe, and resigning herself to the inevitable; Stella reached to accept his grasp. But before the two hands clasped, one of a child of Earth's and one of the being who had passed so far beyond the bounds of humanity, a voice stopped the pact from being sealed.

"Stella?" It asked meekly. "Would you like me to take your place?" DubDub with all his eyes focused on the girl, continued hesitantly, "If it's allowed… I know that I'm not human."

With cautious hope Stella made her appeal. "Could he?"

The heart beat again and all in attendance knew that its strength had come to an end. The vessel of that heart, whose face was now only the faintest outline of eyes, nose and lips, furrowed his brow.

"Fate has brought him here too." Stella stated determinedly.

"Why, yes it has!" was the astonished reply, and turning towards the automaton, Kairos commanded, "Now quickly, take my hand! The moment has come! The time of my leaving is nigh."

DubDub, formed of wood and steel and created by man, stepped forward to meet his destiny. Accepting the offered grasp he slid magically into the space where the fading man stood, taking his position as the nexus to which all who inhabited the galaxy were anchored. Merging together, the energy of the man traced over DubDub's wooden form in scintillating lines.

"My work is done," were Kairos' final words. As the transition was completed the last remnant of his being passed away and DubDub stood alone. Stella waited anxiously while all around there was only silence as the entire universe paused to see if this new center would hold.

"*AAAAAAAHHHHHHHHHH...*" DubDub heaved mightily.

"Is everything okay?" Stella asked. "Did it work?"

"*Urrrrrrrrrrr.*" DubDub groaned, in pleasure or in pain Stella could not tell, as within him a powerful whirring reverberated. At the sound, his wooden body went suddenly transparent and deep within his breast the spring glowed with immense cosmic energy, a coil of purest light. The aura of rays surrounding DubDub flared as the power flowed through every ray joined to him, rapidly reaching every gemlike being and then surging along every ray in the clockwork. Every man, every woman, every star, every planet and every galaxy seethed with revitalized life.

"Yes!" Stella cheered, "It did!"

The brilliant rays formed a linkage from the greatest to smallest being, and though some connections were impossible to trace, they were also impossible to deny. Everything was joined irrevocably; from the smallest human to the most enormous Galactic whale. Each played its part perfectly, equally and without fault, and any value that might be assigned to regard one part over another would be based on something other than truth. And at the center of it all was DubDub, who with his eyes extending in all directions resembled nothing less than an angelic peacock shimmering in a corona of light.

"DubDub? Are you okay?" Stella asked cautiously.

He responded slowly, weighing the question before answering. "Why, yes, I am. Actually, I've never felt better." His optical devices slowly shifted, taking in the entirety of his new found responsibility. Every jewel like being in the sphere was reflected in each of his many eyes. "I suppose now I must really take care to keep myself wound. So much depends on that." He turned the knob on his chest. "Why, just look around. There is so much to see! I could be here forever and never observe it all."

Stella, looking around at the sphere surrounding her, the system of the universe performing so perfectly, whispered, "It really is beautiful."

"Why, will you look at that!" DubDub laughed and Stella tried to remember if she had ever heard him do so before.

"What's so funny?"

"Look through my eyes, Stella! Quickly!" A telescopic device moved from DubDub's head and putting her eye to it, she could feel the raw power that was coursing through her friend's body. It tickled her face. "Sol's putting Loony back in his place!"

With the help of the device Stella could see beyond the dazzling, jeweled embodiments and witness the affairs of the renewed universe. DubDub first focused her augmented eye on the yellow jewel of the Sun, to watch the resplendent rays of Old Sol lift the moon from Earth. Though it was hard to see though all the shifting shimmering light, she could swear the sun had chastised the moon before returning him to his rightful place in the sky, his fiery hand swatting the moon man's buttocks briskly. Stella chuckled at the justice done.

Through the scope she saw the fruits of her labors. Old Sol rejuvenated, his strong rays meeting those of all the other Stars, who fawned over him like a hero. Her eye was drawn along a particularly strong ray that emanated from Sol, and at its end she saw… Earth! No, Terra, Stella corrected herself as she watched her home rejoin the Parliament of Planets. Basking in the loving rays from every being on Earth, Terra was just as beautiful as Venus, but in a different, more simple sort of way. As she made her way to her seat, the other Planets greeted her with awe and respect and

Stella could only imagine how they would have a much different opinion of humans from now on.

As her eye was drawn along one of the rays that reached toward Earth, Stella found at its end, her mother, ablaze. Seeing her so happily aglow, so brilliant in the luminous apparatus of the universe, Stella knew that the threat of Verena, or Virgo, was gone. Her family, she knew with certainty, along with the rest of the universe, was safe.

An incandescent orb moved from Celeste's body. One pure ray of light from that jewel maintained connection with its mother, but in mere moments other rays sprouted from the newborn. They reached across the clockwork to meet with Perceval, then the Sun's, and one bright shaft connected with Terra's. This new component of the universe took its place without pause, seamlessly integrating into the clockwork, fulfilling its own vital role. The baby's rays meshed with Tim, Pace and Sirius too, connecting the family by unbreakable luminous bonds. Stella felt a tug in her heart, as a ray seemingly the brightest of all, shot from her chest to span the universe and meet with her sibling's.

"Did you see that, DubDub? I think I have a new sister!" There was no response, and when Stella looked up to her friend she saw he was in a deep rapture, starkly staring, focusing on a point that lay beyond the sphere of the universe. "What're you looking at?" she asked.

"Goodness Gracious! I couldn't find the words to describe it!" DubDub admitted. "But it is wonderful." He fell silent, gazing beatifically towards the limitless light, but what he saw there Stella did not know.

With her friend so occupied, Stella was left alone with her thoughts, with one festering painfully. For though she had searched the clockwork for some sign of Astraea, there was none to be found. Astraea was gone. "Dead," Stella whimpered, the word she had not wanted to speak since seeing the stars fade in the sky.

But as she thought of her lost friend and her brilliant light, some flare of hope in Stella stirred. Maybe someday, she couldn't know when, she would see the Star woman again. There was always that chance, as it seemed now that there would be a lot of time for that chance to come. It would probably be on the other side, in a place most likely stranger than any she had seen on her journey, maybe even the place that DubDub was viewing now. And Astraea would be there; somehow Stella just knew it, waiting for her when she arrived.

As DubDub's spring uncoiled, and the gears within ticked off the time, Stella sat on the edge of the platform watching the universe's machinations and wondering what to do next. "I suppose I'm never getting home." She grumbled.

"Home?" DubDub responded, the word distracting him momentarily from his explorations. "Perhaps you should check the Compyxx," he suggested.

"Why? It's never pointed me anywhere. I think it was just a trick to get me here." She moaned. "Besides, I threw it away."

"Yes, I saw. But I saved it for you." And he had, for DubDub held the bauble dangling from his wooden hand. "Just as you saved me from Jacques' cabinet. Without you I would have been locked in there forever. You gave me a chance. Perhaps given another chance, the Compyxx will work properly," he suggested, in a tone suggesting he might know more than he was saying, "Now that the clockwork is at full strength. I see that everything has been restored to its proper place, except you. Maybe it was my destiny, not yours, to wind the clockwork. Your fate, it seems lies elsewhere. Maybe the Compyxx can tell where."

Reluctantly Stella reached for the bauble. As she did, it slid off its chain, a light whirr purring as each link passed through the small loop on which it hung. The tiny globe bounced twice before quickly rolling away. Stella moved to intercept it but the ball took an odd, unexpected turn, and before she could judge its new trajectory it was soaring off the platform's edge. Stella lunged to catch it. "I wish you good fortune, Stella Ray!" she heard shouted as she plunged after the Compyxx into the vast machinery of the Celestial Clockwork.

23 HOME FOR GOOD!

Suddenly finding herself at the base of her father's telescope, Stella immediately jumped to her feet. Running down the long hall that led to the dome's medical facility, hopes and fears battled in her head. Was everything okay or had something awful happened? True, Moros was gone and there was no sign of Verena Maldek, but maybe they had found some last opportunity to do damage. Maybe… Maybe... Each anxious step echoed through the hall, and each reverberating footfall was like a pounding hammer to Stella's heart.

Turning the corner to see her father standing at the medical ward's door, doubt deluged the girl. Why wasn't he inside with the new baby? Stella feared it could only mean bad news. For a dreadful moment she couldn't read her father's expression, but relief replaced dread as a wide smile broke on his face. Without a word he swung the door open and Stella ran through without breaking stride, straight to her mother who lay in the dazzling white sheets of her maternity bed, and in whose arms was a swaddled bundle. The baby! Stella came to a halt at the foot of the bed and stared into her mother's eyes. From the tired face of Celeste came a bright and beaming smile that left no doubt that everything was all right. Stella's adventure was over; successfully.

Celeste gently moved the cloth from the tiny face and carefully handed the blanketed bundle to Stella, whispering, "You have a baby sister." Taking the newborn gently in her arms Stella saw the sleeping face in its nest of brilliant white. It seemed already familiar. The baby stirred, tiny lips trembling and delicate eyelids fluttering. The small eyes opened and two glistening orbs of light looked upwards to study Stella's face. A smile of recognition came to the baby's diminutive mouth. "*Astraea*?" Stella whispered.

"What was that?" Stella's father was in the room, standing next to his daughters. "What did you say?"

"Astraea," Stella repeated, aware of only the two bright eyes locked to hers.

From the bed Stella heard Celeste speak as if from a dream. "Astraea? We were going to call the baby, Regina. But Astraea is such a lovely name"

At her side Stella heard the voice of her father. "*Astraea*! Why, doesn't that seem like the perfect name for our new daughter? Regina somehow didn't seem to fit her looks."

"*Astraea*." Celeste tested the name, feeling it roll tunefully off her lips. The newborn turned to the sound and cooed. Celeste sat up in her bed. "Why, she answered to it!"

The baby's mouth turned up in a small smile and bright eyes twinkled lovingly from the pale luminous face. "*Astraea!*" Stella exclaimed, hugging her new sister tightly.

The end

Made in the USA
Charleston, SC
29 November 2011